To request permissions, contact the publisher at
ScharaReevesPress@gmail.com

Paperback: 978-1-7362987-4-9

First paperback edition January 2023.

Edited by Alyson Montione
Proofread by ScribeCat (ScribeCat.ca)
Cover art by Jake Bartok

Schara Reeves Press

ScharaReevesPress.com

ACKNOWLEDGEMENTS

Editor:

Alyson Montione

Proofreader:

ScribeCat (ScribeCat.ca)

Cover Artist:

Jake Bartok

General Support:

Jesus Christ

Family

Friends

Schoharie Library Writing Club

Beta readers:

Rebecca Schmid

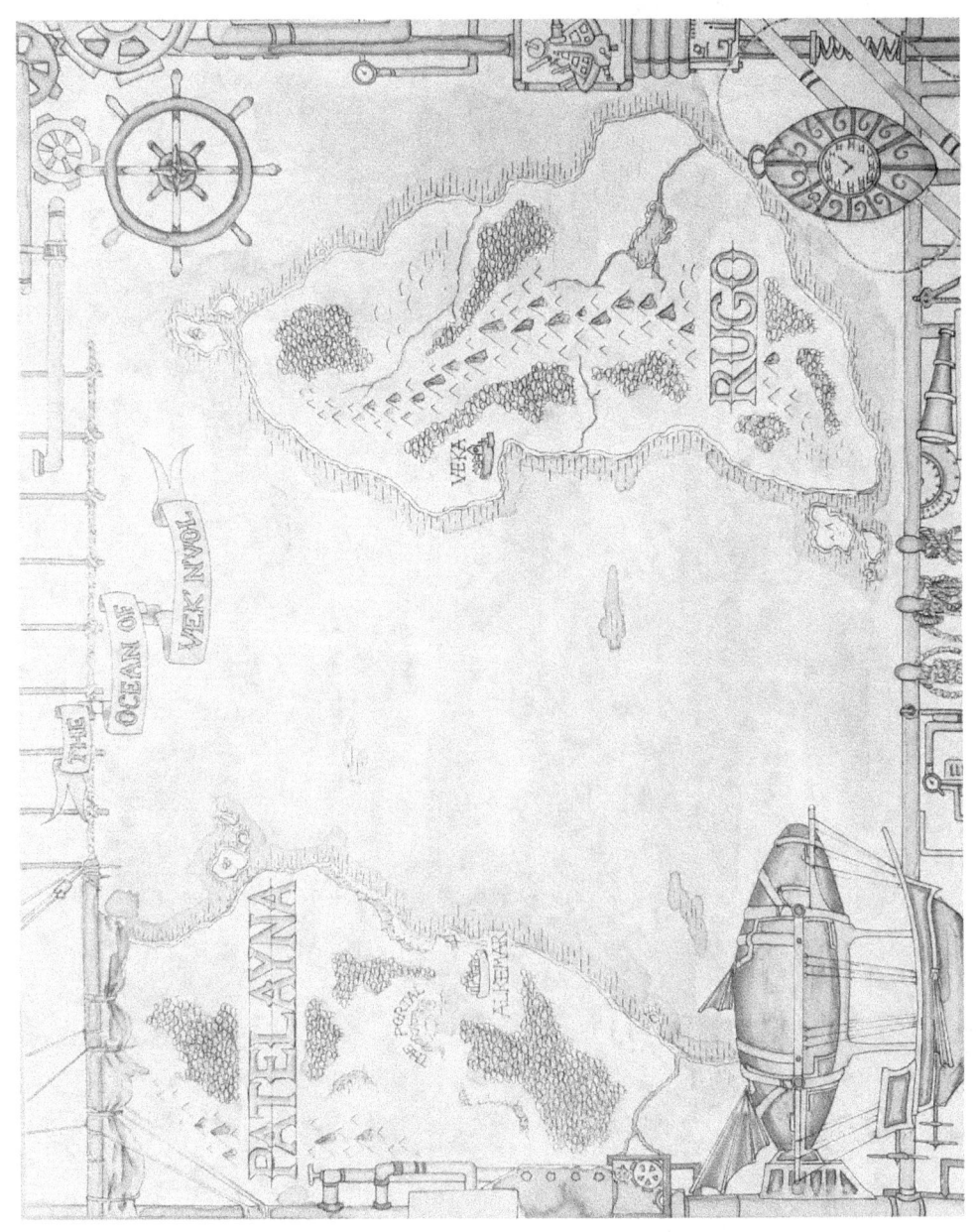

PRONUNCIATIONS

Alenor (AL•eh•nor)

Alkemar (AL•keh•mahr)

Atlys (AT•lis)

Baey (BAY)

Baeno (BAY•no)

Bafa (BAH•Fuh)

Bethynese (BETH•eh•neez)

Ckaknimaen (KAK•neh•mayn)

Darbeshay (DAR•beh•shay)

Eknemar (ECK•neh•mar)

Elsdar (ELZ•dar)

Emarian (eh•MAYR•ee•in)

Esmer (EZ•mer)

Estasia (es•TAY•zha)

Eugene Atarah (YOU•jeen ah•TAR•uh)

Glaedus Auroras (GLAY•dus ar•OR•us)

Greken (GREH•ken)

Grenedil (GREN•uh•dill)

Hytat (HY•tat)

Illan(il•OHN)

Jaythos (JAY•thohs)

Kaedna (KAYD•nuh)
Kaedovarna (KAY•doh•VAR•nuh)
Kassander Knyte (CAS•and•dur NIGHT)
Kayta (KAY•tuh)
Kearn (KEE•urn)
ky'Ki (key•KYE)
Kovo (KOH•voh)

Maeko Kuto (MAY•koh COO•Toh)
Merceri (MER•sur•ee)

Ovok (OH•vok)

Patelayna (pah•tuh•LAY•nuh)

Rugo (ROO•go)

Sefen Kalaesia (SEH•fehn Kel•AE•shee•uh)
Skayla (SKAY•luh)
Syvil (SIV•uhl)

Tanner Pardaya Armon (TAN•er par•DAY•uh ar•MOHN)

Thackeray (THAK•er•ay)

Thaesha (THAY•shuh)

Veka (VEHK•uh)

Vek' n'Vol (VEK noo•VOHL)

Vet de Lona (VET deh LOW•nuh)

Ques (CUE•ehs)

Quitts (CUE•ihts)

A Synopsis of To Take a World: The GhostMaker
Book II of A Daughter's Ransom

Baey and the warriors of the fortress Valdon were forced to flee from their home after a mysterious stranger showed up, exposing a spy in their midst and informing them that the formidable Skayla—a human with the ability to control minds—had already taken the last free city in the world of Baeno.

The stranger is revealed to be not only Skayla's younger brother, but also The GhostMaker, her former assassin. He helps young Baey and her friends flee from Skayla, befriending Baey and teaching her to defend herself. But trust from the others in the group is hard to gain.

After a former slave named Estasia joins their group, they decide to try and locate The Crafters, the ones who hid The Living Stone—the source of power for the world of Baeno—and created relics that could harness its power. In their search, they also join forces with a Drogan, the dragon-like beings from another world that Skayla has been using as weapons to defeat her enemies.

Finally, they are able to escape to Patelayna, a country across the ocean of Vek' n' Vol, and find one of The Crafters hiding in the capital city of Alkemar.

To my husband, Nick, who married this crazy lady and still puts up with her when she decides to cry over the emotional damage she causes her characters.

TO TAKE A WORLD:

THE LIVING STONE

A DAUGHTER'S RANSOM: BOOK IV

BY NIAMH SCHMID

THE LIVING STONE

My heart can weep no more for you,
I've mourned a thousand years
This weary road I've trod and seen,
The truth in all my fears.

I flew a thousand miles, my child,
For you I flew them all,
I let you go, I set you free,
Too late I watched you fall.

I found a chance to save your soul,
A stone of light and life,
I lost myself in death and war,
In blood and fear's delight.

The price of love, of my mistakes,
This death and world's collapse,
Are something I would gladly pay,
just to have you back.

THE LIVING STONE

PROLOGUE:

Twelve Years Ago
<u>**Skayla:**</u>

"You see now why I need it?" Ovok stood before me. I, alone, knew the secret of the Drogan's dual forms. I, alone, could be trusted to treat the information rationally.

But this newest piece of information? I wasn't sure how to take it. "I...we should tell Moira—my parents. They can help."

Ovok's face twisted in anguish, and I saw the conflict, the centuries of horrors and betrayal. "You know you can't trust your sister. You've told me what she's like. No. Skayla, think—no one is going to let me use The Living Stone. Not even for a noble cause."

He was right. And if we couldn't convince Moira, then she'd spin back time without us even knowing, meaning then there would be no hope for Ovok. "Ovok I...I understand, but the other options are...desperate."

"And I *am* desperate. My people are already controversial here. I can't stay here long. Please."

"I'm not—Ovok, I'm not strong enough. I can't do it. I'm..." Too afraid. I was too afraid of what people would think. That I would back down, even if I knew Ovok was right. He needed my help; he'd shown me how much he'd suffered, and yet I was too afraid.

Ovok put a fatherly hand on my arm, making me realize how much I missed my own father. The one that I'd been too afraid to talk to. The one I was afraid would see the way Moira and I had been going about keeping the world safe. "You are stronger than you realize. Maybe you need to give yourself one of those clever little pep talks you give others. After all, you're so persuasive."

CHAPTER I: How to Explain You're Not Dead to Your Mother...Sort Of...

<u>Sven:</u>

In her defense, there was nothing more shocking than her dead son showing up on her doorstep with a thief, a Drogan, the last Esmer, and a handful of very ragged looking strangers. In *my* defense, there was nothing more mind-blowing than seeing her here in front of me. Alive.

"Explain yourself *now*, before I make sure you're not a ghost by killing you," Mum said sternly, arms crossed as she glared at our whole group with her intense golden eyes.

We all stood in her parlor, having been quietly ushered into the presumed safety of the invisible house. The room was littered with gadgets and inventions, from the miniature steam engine that chugged above our heads, on tracks that disappeared into the other rooms of the house, to the clock that ticked away with its gears exposed for all to see. It was like something out of a vaguely familiar dream, and a part of me wished to be lost in it. Lost in that and my mother's eyes. Her loving, *living* eyes. In the moment of staring at the reality of my mother being alive, I completely forgot to answer her question.

I, at last, became aware of everyone looking at me, unsure whether my mother would make good on the threat of killing us if I didn't get it together and answer her.

"Sven?" Mum's voice again penetrated the silence.

"Mum. I…" I struggled to find my voice. "It…It's too long a story to explain. I was able to steal Moira's Timepiece from Skayla, but it's broken. The last Esmer The Creator told you and Da about is here, and I've brought her." I paused only the length of a breath so that I could point out Baey. "If we can get the Timepiece fixed, and Baey trained, we might have more of a chance at getting the upper hand on Skayla." And I was the GhostMaker. A killer. The murderer of my own friends. But I didn't say that out loud.

My mother's eyes flicked towards Baey, then the rest of the beaten-up group. "And who are the rest of these?"

"What remains of the Warriors of Valdon." I was unsure as to whether she would even know them—since they were formed after all of our disappearances—but the statement seemed to affect her.

"This is all that is left?" she asked, much of her previous bravado gone.

"Yes. But again, there is no time," I continued, thinking of all that had gone wrong already. Of barely healed wounds that still throbbed. "Can you fix the Timepiece?"

My mother's lips pressed tightly together, and she looked as if to reprimand me. I supposed that years ago I would have been ashamed for coming off as rude. Perhaps I still was—but there was so much at stake, so much more to lose. If she and I couldn't get past the shock of each other being alive, then we wouldn't be for much longer.

"Where is it?" Her voice was strained as she asked, searching me and the others for any sign of it. I pointed to Baey.

The girl came forward, wings close around her as she hesitantly took the burden she had been hiding. She looked at me for confirmation before handing it to my mother.

Mum keenly inspected the crack, tracing it with her finger as she held the work of art she had created. Then she took a small tool from a hidden pocket in her dress, using the metal pick to pry it open. We all watched quietly.

After a few minutes of inspecting the inner gears, Mum closed the Timepiece and looked back at me, her features taut. "Only The Living Stone can fix this."

My heart sank. The Living Stone was the source of, well, reality as we know it in our world, and what our Gifts from The Creator were made of. Mum and Da had hidden it after things started going south—it was why Skayla had gone after our parents.

"So, where can we find that, Mrs. Mara?" Baey's ignorant question was asked timidly.

My mother's smile was sad. "Please, call me Alenor. And unfortunately, we can't. I hid it where no one can find it, and Henry hid the key that helped lock it away. That way, if either of us were caught—" Her voice caught and she locked eyes with me. "We wouldn't be able to give the full location. And I...don't know where the key is. But he must have hidden it, with the way Skayla was looking for me."

I forced no reaction as the near unconscious question of why Da had not yet appeared was answered. I had assumed both my parents dead, and with Da not here next to her, why should I have thought any different? Why should I be surprised? But it felt like nothing more than another headstone in the already crowded graveyard of my mind. Da was dead, wasn't he. I wasn't going to force Mum to say it. But the thought echoed over and over in my head and fought to drown out even the relief of seeing my mother alive. It was now only a half victory…and another failure on my part.

Da was dead. I wished I had tears left to cry for him. I wished I had the strength left to even mourn. But all that came was the sharp, inconsolable ache. Just more pain.

"Well, this was thought out, clearly." Estasia's comment was finally enough to pull me out of my spiral. "Did anyone think what we would do if we couldn't fix it? I didn't realize that was the extent of our plan…."

Right. The watch. She was talking about fixing the watch. I struggled to stay focused on things that actually mattered right now. Things I could actually try and fix.

"Honestly, I'm surprised *we're* still alive at this point," Jaythos muttered.

A commotion built as the others chimed in, and I began feeling lost and confused.

"Why can't we see what Tanner can do?" I had never thought Baey's voice could have rung so clear as it somehow cut through the growing arguments. Then I realized she still had my ring. The girl was an even quicker learner than I'd thought.

The debating stopped, and everyone sort of stared at her. I could see the sudden doubt in the shade of her wings, and though I was very, very lost, I asked, "What do you mean, Baey?"

"Well. Tanner can see memories, right?" She looked to her friend, who nodded encouragement. "Um, so, yeah. Mrs—Alenor, is there anything of—Henry's?—that he could use to just see where he put the key?"

Perhaps if not for the horrors running amuck in my own head, I would have smiled. Everyone constantly tried to keep Baey out of things until they forgot she was quite good at helping with them. But the reminder of Da was enough to chase that thought away.

"I guess it's not that great an idea though...it would have to be something that was brought on the actual trip to hide it...." She trailed off, eyes looking down at her feet as her wings slowly crept closer around her.

"Wait—who can see memories?" Mum broke in now, looking perplexed.

Tanner raised his hand without shame.

"Hm. Interesting," she mused for only a second before announcing, "I think, actually, that I do have something." I caught the way her voice caught for a moment. Then she continued, "I will return. In the meantime, you can all sit down. Don't leave this room, though—I haven't dismantled all the booby traps." Her eyes flickered to me, and she repeated, "Please. Don't leave," before she vanished from the room.

I ached.

No one needed further encouragement, and soon everyone except me had found a seat. There was plenty of furniture around, but I didn't feel like sitting. It was all I could do to take in the dream before me. Mum was alive. She had been right in front of me...I could relate to her plea; I didn't want her to leave again. I wanted—no, I *needed*; I desperately needed—her to return, to fill the room with her presence. To chase away the shadows in my head. My mother was alive. She was here...the reality soured when I wondered: What would she do when she had found out what her son had become? When she was faced with the fact that not one, but *two* of her children had become murderers and heralds for the end of the world as we'd known it? Would she rather Da had showed up at her door than me? I wouldn't blame her.

I'd be lying if I didn't wish that myself.

"So, what happens when we have to go find it?" Estasia was the first to speak, doing little to scare away my wandering thoughts. "We make an awfully big target with all of us together. It wouldn't be smart to continue that way."

"I agree," Jaythos added darkly. "If this place is safe, there's no reason to send all of us out, again."

The thought of splitting up made my breath seize momentarily in panic, but I forced out of my head my stupid wish to argue. They were right. Staying together could be too much of a risk—and if we did plan on getting The Living Stone, we didn't want to attract Skayla's attention.

As if on cue, Mum returned to the room, eyes almost immediately on me again.

I looked away.

Still, her voice was a soothing presence. "Here is something you can try and use. Be careful…it is all I have." I looked back to find her handing a box to Tanner.

All she had left of Da.

The boy took the box gingerly and opened it, picking up an old pair of spectacles. Da's spectacles. Tanner's face turned to concentration as he focused on the object, and soon the overshadowed look spread

10

across his features. Then, all of a sudden, he gasped to life, looking shaken and momentarily lost.

"Are you alright?" I heard Baey whisper.

In reply, the boy looked right at me, saying, "I think I know where he hid the key."

Anyone who did not lean forward to hear better asked instead, "Where?"

"Rugo."

"Interesting. That is also where I hid The Living Stone," Mum said.

"Rugo?" I wasn't surprised that Maeko was the first to speak. "Where in Rugo?"

Handing the spectacles and their case back to the Crafter, Tanner answered, "I don't know—I mean, I know, I just can't explain it. I could lead you there, of course. But if you were to ask me to write it down, I think I'd get it out of order."

"O-out of order?" Syvil voiced my confusion for me.

"My hea—" He interrupted himself and added quickly, "The memory. It's all jumbled. I could lead you to it, but I don't know that I could just *tell* you where to go."

"Then we should leave for Rugo? Is it worth the risk of Skayla finding The Living Stone because of us?" Jaythos asked.

Mum and Da had hidden it for a reason…Da had died to keep it safe. Was I helping undo his last act? I felt like so much of this death was already for nothing.

"If things go on like this…" I could feel Mum's eyes on me as she spoke but dared not look directly into them. "Then Skayla will find The Living Stone eventually. She'll have the whole world. Getting it and fixing the watch is the best bet, I suppose." She sighed. "I can share my memories with Tanner so he will be able to locate The Living Stone after you get the key...but you must be careful. Please."

She was as scared as I was.

"Alright. So it's great we've established that we have to get The Living Stone and we should get it quickly. But we can't *all* go." Jaythos and I seemed to agree more and more these days. Hopefully that was a good sign.... If nothing else, the group seemed more on the same page than when I'd first met them all.

And then Sefen spoke. "Yes. We can't afford to get Baey killed if something happens."

I couldn't take it; I snapped, "She isn't a child to be coddled, Sefen—stop treating her like one."

"But she *is* a child, Sven! You can't keep pushing her into danger, expecting her to just figure her way out of it."

How could he talk about her like this when she was right in the room? She wasn't *dumb*. I opened my mouth to say something I would probably regret, but someone else was quicker.

"Children, *please*." Mum's voice somehow rang even without having to raise her voice, and we once more focused. "You cannot wake me up in the middle of the night, show up with the Timepiece and my eight-years-since-dead son, and expect to quarrel about what to do. The darkness under everyone's eyes is enough to tell me you are exhausted and have been on the run for too long. Sleep comes first—we can finish planning who will go and who will stay tomorrow. I've had this house to myself for a long while now, but I still have plenty of spare rooms for you all, with well-kept beds."

Estasia piped up, then. "Yes, that sounds like a fantastic idea."

"Excellent." Mum clapped her hands together. "I'll get some sheets, and then you can all lie down for some rest."

A commotion followed that resulted in everyone helping her get blankets and sheets for the beds, and soon we were all getting settled in our various rooms. I felt lost, hanging in the back and helping the others where I could.

I didn't want to sleep. Sleep had been hard to bear since Hytat....

"Sven?" It was Mum.

That was when I realized we were the only ones in the long hallway now. Everyone else had gone to bed.

"Yes, Mum?" I croaked, eyes riveted on the space behind her. I couldn't face her now. I couldn't watch her face when she knew what I'd done.

"Can I give you a hug now?" The question wrenched my gut, and I went rigid.

I stumbled for the words, shame and longing mixed together as I stuttered, "Mum...I...." What was I supposed to say? That I was The GhostMaker? That I'd killed all our friends—all my friends? That I'd murdered innocent people? That I'd helped Skayla take over the world? That unlike Da, I hadn't died to keep the world safe...that instead, I'd become the thing the world needed saving from?

"I just want to hold my son again." Her voice was thick with emotion.

I rubbed my face with one hand. "I've killed people, Mum. I don't...deserve it," I whispered.

"War makes murderers of us all, Sven. No one is ever clean of the violence." She again reached out for my arm.

13

I flinched. "No. Mum, you don't *understand*." My voice was hoarse from disuse and anger—anger at myself. "*I* was The GhostMaker. I was a fool. I thought...I thought I could defeat Skayla but instead...I'm sorry I couldn't bring you Da—"

Without warning, she grabbed my arm and pulled me into a fierce embrace, one somewhere between suffocating and life-giving. I could have choked, I was so desperate to give in—to hug her and keep her and make sure she was really here—that I could just melt away in her arms and for once escape the memories that would now never leave.

"Sven, don't you even dare. Don't you dare. I don't know what happened. But you're here now. Seeing you alive, it—it's more than I could have dreamed. I love you so much. Please. Just hug me back. Please," she whispered as she squeezed harder, her voice trembling with each word.

My resolve crumbled, and I found myself wrapping my arms around her, losing myself for a moment in my mother's embrace as I clung to the only real family I had left.

CHAPTER II: Parting Ways

<u>Baey:</u>

I swallowed my disappointment once more, forcing my wings to remain open and not curled around me as we stood before the lady's door. We had agreed upon the group that would be going: Tanner, Sefen, Jaythos, Syvil, and Maeko. Sven would be accompanying them just as far as the ship. It did not bother me that I was not going as much as the fact that Tanner was. I had calculated distances in my head over and over again, and I wouldn't be seeing him again for months, at least.

Months…if ever again.

So, I stood as close as possible to him as we said our brief goodbyes. It was early morning, and the sun was peeking through the beautiful glass windows, but it only made me wonder if anyone had been able to sleep at all in the fleeting hours allowed. I chanced a look at Sven, who was standing in the corner, still silent as he had been lately. He hadn't been right since Hytat. Since Skayla. It looked as if some bad dream was replaying before him over and over again, and more than anything, I wished I could help. Maybe I could. Maybe it was a good thing I was staying behind, after all.

Maybe...maybe it wasn't because I was useless. Sven just needed me more.

"Alright. Enough tears, we need to get moving," Jaythos said sarcastically, breaking through the hub of whispered conversation. To be honest, the only one anyone was saying goodbye to was me. Everyone from Valdon was going. Everyone I'd known growing up. Well, everyone *left* of who I'd known.

"Sven, are you ready?" Sefen asked.

Sven nodded, rubbing the silver ring around his finger as if it burned. I didn't need a relic around my neck to be able to feel Sven's pain. For that's all the ring's aching really had been; Sven's own agony.

"Then we'd best head out." Sefen's statement was said with eyes on me, as if I might burst into tears at any second. As if I couldn't handle being split from them. As if I hadn't had dozens of friends at Valdon leave and never return. I sighed, nodding all the same, as if they needed me to tell them I wasn't going to melt into a puddle. Sure, I was worried: What if they didn't come back? What if they *could* have used my help after all, and now they would fail because of it? But as I looked to Sven, I knew now I was needed more here. I wouldn't let this place be my new prison.

Everyone's eyes turned away, and Sven prepared to open the door. Alenor—who had been standing quietly near him—grabbed his arm then, whispering some inaudible request. I understood the worry hidden behind Alenor's composed demeanor, as I, too, found myself whispering, "Just come back. Promise," to Tanner.

"Of course, silly—I always come back," he replied, with an only half-sincere smile.

"Promise," I reiterated with force, staring at him.

Something in him changed, and with a very serious expression, he said, "I promise."

With that, they left.

"Well then, that was heartbreaking," Estasia muttered behind me.

"Yeah," I whispered back. "You get used to it, I suppose." I didn't really want to, though. I didn't want there to be a day where I'd seen this so much that I no longer worried if those I knew would come back. It would hurt more to be callous.

"So, do you want to stand around here and get really bored, or see if we can be of any help on this end?" Estasia brought me out of my little reverie.

My wings flicked in interest, and I turned to face her. "Help on this end?" I echoed, trying to process what she meant.

"I take that as a yes?"

This pulled a slight smile from me, but I was soon serious again. "Wait. But I can't be seen...you know—" I jabbed two thumbs behind me as I ruffled my wings for emphasis. Then they sagged. I was tired of having to hide, and yet nothing screamed "The Last Esmer" like wings.

The mischief remained. "We won't be above ground, theoretically. Don't worry."

"I still don't think this is wise…" Alenor shifted. "But I'll trust my son's judgment."

So apparently, I was the last to hear of this plan.

"Don't worry, I'm the one that's saved their necks the most. I'll keep her safe, ma'am." Estasia gave a small, weird bow. "But I have contacts in the city, and it's best not to dawdle. Sven said you have a discreet way into the sewers?"

My wings perked as the prospect of exploration seemed more and more likely.

"Yes. I have a way into the sewers. From here, actually." The woman's reply was even as it was guarded. I'd seen how she flinched at the mention of Sven.

"We'll be careful." I didn't know what in the world possessed me to reply, let alone think this woman I didn't even know would believe me— *me*, a sixteen-year-old who she'd known for a handful of hours. And yet I kept going. "Estasia is right; she saved Sven's life. She's the only reason we made it out of Hytat."

Alenor released a pent-up breath, giving a weak smile. I thought then of how much it reminded me of Sven's smile; the sincerity and depth in it was the same. The sadness, too.

"I promise this is to help. I might be able to secure allies…allies that can do much more than hide us forever," Estasia added when the woman didn't reply.

Alenor's gaze never wavered from me as she nodded. "Alright. Follow me." She seemed to force herself into movement, turning on her heel and motioning for us as she walked out of the vestibule and down the hall.

Sun filtered through the many glass windows, painting mosaics of light upon the brick and metal walls as we passed through the many rooms, each holding a new variety of strange and wonderful things. The first one was some sort of observatory, with an arched glass roof that reached up into the morning sky, capturing the warmth of the sun. We had to weave around several telescopes, a desk with star charts, and a large orrery that spun and took up the entire middle of the room. In fact, at one point, I was nearly smacked dead in the face by a planet and was forced to take to the air to jump over it.

The second room proved just as exciting, though much smaller, with the entire thing littered top to bottom with moving gears that clicked in a synchronized rhythm from their places in the walls. There was a fireplace that seemed to be feeding itself, and a giant bellows by it that was near a hook that moved in a circular motion—one that matched the clicking of the gears—making me realize that it was meant to pump the bellows when Alenor was working.

It was extraordinary the way the seemingly small house we'd seen from outside could fit all of these rooms, and yet I had little time to gawk before we again landed in a hallway. There, on the opposite wall, stood a large door with great big gears fixed inside of its metal frame. Instead of a knob, there was a funny-looking keyhole, and the whole door appeared to move as if it was alive—just like the gears in the other room, and the orrery in the first one.

Alenor took out a key to match the twisted keyhole, crossing the hallway and fixing the key inside the door. The gears turned and there was a clicking as the door pushed backward by about an inch. "This will bring you into the sewers."

"Thank you." Estasia's reply was brisk, as if it took physical effort to say the words. "Hopefully, we will return with good news and a few more allies."

Alenor did not immediately move. She stared at us, looking as if she was plotting out the possible outcomes. Again, I saw the family resemblance. She had the golden eyes—the same color Sven had once had. The color they'd been before his sister had changed him. But Alenor also had the same face marked with worry and kindness. But then there was something more...a keenness. Her face was narrower, and I realized suddenly she looked like another of her children: Skayla. Only, she didn't look crazy and didn't want to kill us.

"Which part of the sewers does this let out into?" I hadn't realized just how quickly I'd made all those observations until Estasia had asked the question.

Hm. Observing. I was getting better at this.

That's when it clicked that I was also going to have to go into the sewers again. Ugh.

"Southwestern section, tunnel system nine—keep Baey out of sight until my son returns. If anyone sees her wings, we will be made for sure." The warning was severe. I hated always having to hide my wings but did not disagree.

"I will. Don't worry," Estasia replied with firmness, looking at me through the corner of her eye as she did.

Only seeming partly satisfied, Alenor gave one push on the door to open it, revealing a dark, breezy tunnel that led steeply downwards. A couple lanterns lit the way. I shrunk back, not relishing another tunnel. Ugh.

"Tug on the rope when you return, and I'll open the door." Alenor pointed to a rope just inside the tunnel.

I bit back the desire to ask what it did, and instead followed Estasia—who had grabbed a lantern—as she plunged without hesitation into the dark. However, I was not so eager, lingering outside and scuffing the floor with my wings.

"You coming?" Estasia turned around and peered at me, looking amused.

It didn't help. Or maybe it did, because the embarrassment somehow moved my feet forward one step.

"Sure," I said, voice trembling even as my wings cocooned tightly around me. This reminded me of the tunnel at Valdon, and I tried to reason that this tunnel was much bigger. However, it was still dark, and underground, and I couldn't fly if something happened...and....

"Darlin'? Are you alright?" It was Alenor who broke the silence. Honestly, it took me a moment to realize it had been her, and not Sven suddenly returned or something. All the same, I couldn't help but think of him and all he had faced. I remembered Hytat—the haunted look always in his eye. Surely, I could manage a little tunnel.

"Yes," I replied with determination. "I'm fine. Thank you." Determined, I forced myself into the tunnel. Just when I thought I could do this...the door slammed shut behind us.

I let out an instinctive yelp, jumping in the air and promptly smacking my head again on the ceiling—which made me cry out again.

"Baey, calm down. It's fine, calm down." I vaguely heard Estasia, but my breathing was beginning to grow more and more rapid. As I fluttered to the ground, all I could think of was the door closed firmly behind us. We were trapped! The door was shut, what if we were lost?

Smack!

I gasped in shock at the albeit gentle slap across the face.

"Don't make me regret bringing you." Her whispered words were sharp as she grasped me by the shoulders, giving me a firm shake.

The words struck deep, and between them and the slap, I was able to collect myself. "Sorry," I murmured, glad it was at least dark enough

21

down here that she'd probably not catch the way my wings darkened in embarrassment.

Estasia breathed in relief. "You're fine—if you don't do it again." The last bit was added firmly, even if I caught a wisp of amusement behind it.

"Alright," I managed.

Appearing satisfied for now, Estasia let go of me. "Alright. So are you ready, now?"

I nodded. Don't think of the dark, or the tunnel, or the lack of sun, or the tunnel, or the....

"Great. Then let's go." With that, she turned and we started off again—with me constantly reminding myself not to jump at every sound as I followed her.

The tunnel was full of shadows, only causing me to fight my fears of the closed space further, but I decided the best way to counteract the stupid panic was to think of something else, so I forced myself to observe *anything* going on around us. I counted the lanterns that lined the walls. I wondered if Alenor went down here every day to light them, which led me to noticing the subtle piping along the walls. Eventually, the tunnel stopped short at a small door, much simpler than the one Alenor had led us through. However, this one had a knob.

Without a word, Estasia turned it, and I was met with the putrid smell of rot and ruin.

Here goes nothing.

Sven:

"Isn't this fun?" Skayla's mad laugh echoed in the chamber as I felt trapped in my own mind. She'd been making me do her every bidding for hours, now, every moment eroding my will away as I became her living puppet. My fists clenched and I went to move forward—to grab hold of her and make her stop. But she put up a finger. *"Nuh-uh, stay there. Don't you move."*

I halted, blood running cold. I couldn't do it. All I heard was her voice in my head—her voice screaming at me to be quiet—to listen, to follow. I didn't want to, and yet I was. I WAS. I had to stop, and yet weeks of this had slowly chipped away my resolve.

"We really need to get a handle on this, don't we?" Had she said it or was it her screaming in my head? I couldn't tell anymore.

"Are you done playing with your food?" This voice was definitely real. Kovo. He sounded exasperated.

I snarled like some feral animal, but Skayla clicked her fingers and my face was wiped clean of all emotion—against my will.

"You know...I'm not sure." Her smile was wicked. I could feel the cold grasp of it even in my head.

"Skayla." It took all my willpower and more to break through—to even vocalize a single word. *"Stop. You. Have. To. Stop."*

"No. I don't think I will." She swiveled around to face Kovo. *"What do you think? If he's going to be my little assassin, he needs a good getup, right?"* The laugh was cold enough to kill me. *"Maybe a mask? Just like those silly masquerade balls you used to love so much. Nothing screams dangerous like a nightmare's mask."*

23

Images flashed through my mind—plans she had for me. The things I was about to do. No. No, Skayla, please no.

There was a reason I'd been staying away from my ring. Memories were bad enough without the longing and emptiness the stupid thing gave me. I wasn't worthy of it anymore. I wasn't even *good* at it. After Hytat, it was clear I had not even a speck of my true ability remaining. The power that even Skayla and Moira had not known of was now quite lost in my wreck of a head.

Quickly, we wove our way through the busy streets, past the grand houses and ruined ones alike. We would be leaving through the gate instead of the sewers, the supplies we were carrying being the main reason. It would be more practical for me to hide them with the ring, as they might get ruined or dropped in the sewers. That being said, it still took concentration to hide them from prying eyes.

Everyone stayed close behind me, having been given instructions just like the ones in Hytat. Eventually, we got to the gates, where any incomers were being questioned before being allowed in. Of course, there were not many incomers—and even fewer outgoers. This was, after all, one of the first places that had been taken by Skayla.

A shadow passed over our heads, and I didn't have to look up to know what it was: a Drogan.

Stop it! I forced myself to focus.

Just as we had planned, we passed by the guards one at a time, my illusions holding up with more ease than before.

We still said not a word until the forest line, where we stopped for a moment of respite.

"We have a long day's journey ahead of us. Best not waste it on the first hour." I broke the silence, looking back at the city and noting the distant form of a Drogan sitting poised on one of its high towers. To one side of the city, one could still see the ruins of the old palace and Inner City.

"Yes. Better to not waste time," Maeko replied simply. He'd lost the edge to his tone when addressing me, but honestly, I wished he hadn't. He had every right to hate me after what I'd done to Sera. After what I'd done to everybody. Skayla was right...it had been a mercy to be without my memories, after all. But I didn't deserve such kindness.

It was no surprise when no one broke the silence as we made our way back to the boat.

I found myself spinning the ring on my finger nervously, trying not to think of Skayla. Trying not to think of anything, really. Having the ring on made it so much worse. I'd been a fool for staying behind and trying to reason with her. A fool for letting her get into my head.

And then there was Mum. Alive. Breathing. Alone.

Focus.

I scanned the skies in an attempt to distract myself, searching for any Drogans that might be passing overhead. We were purposefully staying off the road—as we had when coming in—and theoretically, Skayla still had no idea we were here, but still I searched.

The daylight waned, and I was glad when sunset began to approach. While two Drogans flew and cried in the distance, I saw nothing pass over our heads, and I allowed myself a very small amount of ease. Darkness would be a welcome blanket. At least, until I realized how tired it proved me to be. I glanced at everyone else and knew they felt the same. Poor Tanner looked about ready to fall down and hibernate for a month. Hopefully, they could rest on the ship. We'd only had an hour or two of sleep in the last few days. Carrying the supplies didn't help. They did, after all, need as much rest as possible for the journey ahead. I would not be able to hide them in Rugo...another thing I dreaded about splitting up.

Another hour or two passed before we found ourselves stumbling onto the small beach.

The two moons illuminated the waters of the inlet and gave a ghostly beauty to the place. It only made me more tense, of course.

"Look at the sky," Tanner said wistfully. Expecting a Drogan, my head snapped up. But then what I saw made me freeze for another reason.

Darting out between the gathering clouds were tendrils of blue and violet light, streaking wherever allowed and revealing millions of stars clearer behind it. Faint as it was, it was beautiful. I had not seen the colors since before Skayla's turn.

"The Glaedus Auroras," Jaythos murmured, even his normal droning tone turned to a reverent whisper.

Yes. That was its name. I remembered now. "We must continue." I broke the awed quiet and began moving to where we hid the rowboat, dropping my burden of supplies on the cold, wet sand. I heard the others follow closely behind.

After undoing the rowboat, we promptly pulled it into the shallows and loaded the supplies.

"Don't get lost," I murmured. The words echoed over and over in my mind even after I'd said them. *Don't get lost*...not like Moira, not like Da, not like everyone I'd ever known. Lost. Because of me.

"Ship, Skinny?" Maeko broke in, reminding me that I was the only one that could see through the illusion at the moment. Instead of answering, I simply lifted the disguise so that they could see it. Baey had been the one to use the ring for some sort of disguise on the way to Patelayna—or so I'd been told—and so the illusion had been a very simple one. No one off the ship could see it. But since I wouldn't be coming with the others, I settled for creating a wider radius for the ship's cloak. After all, Skayla knew we had stolen a ship, and by now, there were probably hordes of Drogans searching the skies.

"Be careful, Skinny."

I hid my mystified expression as I faced the Rugonian man. I could have laughed. Yeah. Be careful. I'd messed up plenty of times to warrant that. And it had cost Sera's life.

Realizing I had yet to reply, I managed a curt nod and a wince as I said, "You ought to be careful, as well." I didn't know if I could live with myself if they didn't return. This had to work.

Maeko put a hand on my shoulder, and with a surprised gasp, I flinched away before I could think better of it.

Somehow, I managed to say, "I'm fine. Sorry."

The way Maeko just stared at me didn't help, hand slowly recoiling as if he'd almost wanted to try and reach out again.

"We should go," Sefen said before he turned to the rowboat, getting in position to push it into deeper waters. Maeko joined without another word to me, and together they pushed the boat out onto the water.

"Well. Uh. Goodbye, Sven." Tanner was the only one still on the beach. He looked anguished and was blatantly ignoring the motion made by Maeko to get in the boat.

"Take care, Tanner," I whispered. In all honesty, I didn't know the boy very well. He'd been quiet, and perhaps too late did I see the loneliness. "Baey will miss you."

He rolled his eyes, at last turning around to get in the boat. The last thing he said was, "Yeah. Won't be the same without her."

Those were the last words that passed between me and the group, and I watched in silence as they rowed safely to the boat.

Reluctantly, I turned away and made my way back into the thick trees of the forest. It would be a long night of travel, and sleep sounded more terrifying than ever. The nightmares were no longer simply shadows, and now I knew *exactly* who I was when I awoke. Or rather, *what* I was.

So instead, I wandered in the night, the hours passing by slowly as I made my way, hoping the exhaustion would not be fully realized until I was safely back. But would I even be able to rest when I did return? Time was short, and I could not stand being useless. Estasia had seemed to have some sort of plan, and I—

"Hey, you! What are you doing?" The shout pierced the night sky.

I was an idiot.

I had somehow lost track of where I was and wandered out into the road. My stupid, useless head! And worse? I hadn't thought of disguising my presence to watchful eyes.

Of course, I had no time to reprimand myself, as I was at this moment standing in front of what appeared to be one of Alkemar's patrols. Several had the violet flecks in their eyes.

Great.

I pulled out my sword instantly, fighting the strong force that told me to kill them and leave no witnesses. It was as if I was fighting Skayla's voice in my head all over again, except this time, it was mine. It was the stupid kill switch that had been rammed into my head for the last eight years. With great effort, I controlled myself, instead using my ring to make me disappear. FOOL! They would tell Skayla I was here—who else could disappear out of thin air right now, besides me?

"It's the phantom!" one of the men screeched in terror, the rest beginning to follow suit in panic.

Phantom? Confusion stirred as I ran along the outskirts of their group, hidden from their sight but still not planning to stick around.

"No, you imbecile, there isn't any phantom! Besides, you all keep telling me it's a woman—not some man with a sword—this is some sort of trick!"

I had...no idea what they were talking about. Lady? I stopped in my tracks, turning around and keeping in the shadows as my ring hid me, hoping perhaps I would catch a little bit more of the conversation.

"Spread out and search! He couldn't have gone far."

Oh yes, he was right on that account, at least. As I watched them frantically search the area, I again rebuked myself. How could I be such a fool? Right. How, indeed. We'd seen just how many mistakes I could make. Just how many lives they'd cost, too. Somehow, even with my memories back, I seemed just as likely not to think. Only now, I had no excuse.

Eventually, the patrol regrouped, and again the murmurings of some phantom lady began rippling through the troupe.

"Would you all stop it with your silly superstitions? We're not even at the portal site! Now move out, we need to get back and report this to Lord Atlys and the rest."

Atlys? He was alive? More importantly...they were reporting *to* him? Never in my wildest dreams would I have thought that man would have turned coward to Skayla's hand.

But there was something else that caught my attention. Portal site.

"Garn and Caspian, head to Alkemar and let the nobles know. The rest of us will report back to the site and make sure whoever that was hasn't made for it," the captain barked.

Convenient.

I crept along with them, listening in for any more tidbits of conversation I could grab. It was funny how, while much quieter, those with the violet mark of Skayla still contributed to the conversation. Their movements were sharp, precise, and unnatural, but their personalities remained. They had given up fighting long ago, and as such, Skayla's influence was more a guide—a barrier—than a stifling grip choking the life out of them.

All the same, the whispers were still scarce, and I was left to follow them through the dark as I wondered if they would send a message to Skayla. I chillingly recalled hearing her voice all too often in my head— orders I had no option but to carry out. I had been stubborn. I'd aimlessly pulled against my puppet strings and never even tried to relay anything back to her unless forced. But the holds she had on people's minds varied, and my chest tightened as I wondered if she was already on her way. It depended on if they really understood what they'd seen.

By the whisperings, it seemed not. And yet, I knew it wouldn't be long until rumor of The GhostMaker's escape would make it to Patelayna. And then what?

I lost track of time as I followed in the shadows, concentration gone amid the lack of sleep. Which meant limiting my illusionary disguise and keeping more to my natural ability to blend into the background.

Slowly, things started to seem familiar. The path the soldiers were following...the thinning trees.... We suddenly came to the edge of the trees, and I hung back as the patrol continued on beyond the tree line, weighing my options as I oriented myself.

That's when I at last realized where I had found myself.

The portal site. The place the Drogans had first appeared, all those years ago. I looked out at the rising sun and noticed smoke coming from the ravine. Just on the other side of the ravine was a hill, and peeking up from it was indeed what appeared to be campfire smoke. Quite a bit, actually. What was going on? I didn't recall this at all. Skayla had never brought me here...nor mentioned it in my presence. Granted, she'd always been careful to keep me in the dark in regards to her plans, MindHold or not. But still. What else had I missed?

The patrol now having disappeared down the path along the ravine, I slowly crept forward into the light, getting a grip of my weariness enough to cast a simple illusion around me. It was not my greatest work—a mere mirage—but it was enough to shield me as I made it to the crest and peered over. What I saw below brought even more puzzlement.

The place was swarming with Bethynese soldiers, tents pitched and soldiers milling about in organized fashion. And then there were the Drogans, perched on the giant boulders that riddled the bottom. It all seemed to be centered around one area, where a littering of strange-looking contraptions stood, hooked up to seemingly nothing. But I knew what had once laid where the machines now were. It was the place where once had stood a sizzling blue doorway of energy. The place that had once torn the rift between our world and some unknown place, allowing the Drogans in and beginning the mystery of all this madness.

What was Skayla doing?

CHAPTER III: Friends, Enemies, and Wondering Where They Are

Estasia:

I figured the best way to approach Baey's claustrophobia was to face it head on. Not that Baey seemed to agree, stifling another yelp when the door made a loud clang as it closed behind her.

"You're fine," I reminded her firmly. She'd learn. She already had so much under her belt. Besides, now that those buffoons from Valdon were gone, I'd have the freedom to teach her.

"I know." Her reply was timid. Yeah, she would definitely need some help in the confidence department.

But for now, I would get her used to this confined space, so I led her on through the muck and mire of what had once been my home. I supposed it was the one thing in Baeno that *hadn't* changed. It was odd how I found fondness and memories in such a place, but I did. Fondness and an old loneliness I had long buried.

We walked on, the stench as aromatic as the sweetest of perfumes to me. Nostalgia was better than the sickly fakeness of other aromas, at least. But suddenly I hated the silence.

"So...what are we doing down here?" Baey's whisper echoed about the curved stone walls.

I was glad she had the sense to whisper. We were not alone down here, and I wouldn't be surprised if there were still thieves who roamed the lower sections of the city. If I hadn't been taken as a slave, I knew

33

that I, at least, would still be down here. Well, technically, I *was* down here.

Turning down another diverting tunnel, I motioned for her to come next to me so we could talk quietly. When she had obeyed, I explained, "We are going to the palace."

Her eyes went wide.

"My network," was all I was willing to say on the subject. After a couple years of being at the fortress, my network had really started to grow, and as slaves were often shifted around with Skayla's armies or some other need, it had spread out so that I had connections in Hytat, Veldyr, Eknemar, and Alkemar.

"So, we're going to see if we can get more help?" Baey asked hopefully.

"More or less, yes." Gethnor had said Illan had contacted him only a week before we'd shown up to Hytat, claiming that he was on the cusp of finding some *real* help. I needed to know what that meant.

I stopped under one of the many lights that poked through sewer outlets. After looking up and judging the distance, I turned back at Baey. "Now. Time for your first test. Before we get started...do you remember the way back?" I had been watching her, and with a highly educated guess, was fairly sure I knew the answer.

Hesitantly pleased with herself, Baey nodded, slowly reciting the way back.

What a clever little Birdy. "Excellent. If something happens, you need to go back—but don't enter Alenor's house unless you are *sure* you haven't been followed. Understood?"

I received an emphatic nod in response.

34

"Good. Now, fly up there and lift the lid to peek. Tell me what you see." I pointed up to the cap.

"Alright." She didn't need to be asked twice, obviously very ready to spread her wings. As she spread them, I noticed they were a dark grey and black, blending so well with the surrounding area that I could hardly see them. Huh. So, they were useful beyond mood alerts. Good to know. I'd have to keep that in mind.

Baey carefully flew up to the manhole cover for the sewer, trying and failing to make it budge. "It's locked. Looks like there's a keyhole" she reported as she came back down. "Sorry...."

As I had expected. "Alright. I'll have a look..." I trailed off as I looked for the spot where sewer workers had kept the ladder. It did not take my eyes long to settle on the small section of the wall that looked ever so slightly different.

Perfect. I handed Baey the lantern and then went over and gave a good shove against the section, which rewarded me with a groan as it slid to the side. Behind it was a small closet with some maintenance supplies...and a ladder.

"Why didn't you just use the ladder to begin with?" Baey asked, not bothering to hide her bafflement as she watched me take it out.

I shrugged. "Maybe I just wanted you to do the work yourself." With that, I set the ladder under the manhole cover, letting out its two metal base spikes in the appropriate holes in the ground. It was very clear that much of this was not currently used—but clearly some maintenance on the sewers was taking place, as this place wasn't *filled* with garbage. That being said, it definitely wasn't cleaned weekly anymore....

The spikes fitted into place, I gave one good tug to make sure the ladder would stand firm, and when convinced, I prepared to climb.

"If I decide it's safe, I am going to go out. Douse the lantern and stay here and guard. If you hear anyone, take the ladder and hide in the closet until they pass. Listen for any possible news if they are gossiping." I pointed to the small enclosure I'd opened.

She nodded, but I saw the way her wings dipped in disappointment.

I gave her a glare. "If you ever expect to do anything, you have to be a good sentry first. If you can't watch someone else's back, how do you expect to watch your own?"

"Sorry." Baey's wings turned a deep scarlet, betraying their presence for a moment before returning to the black and grey background.

"No apologies. Just show me you can do it," was the last thing I said before I began climbing.

The ladder only wiggled a little as I made it to the top, and just as Baey had done, I put my eyes to the keyhole. She was right; it was hard to see anything. But it did look like some sort of cellar....

Carefully, I took one step down on the ladder, and looked down at Baey, signaling that I was going out.

The ladder reached all the way up to the metal lid, and taking the two picks I kept in my hair, I picked the lock and heard the satisfying click. Quickly, I put my shoulders to the lid to help in forcing it up. I only lifted enough, however, for the thing to make noise. When I still heard nothing from above, I lifted further, and was able to see now into the room.

No one was there.

Wasting no time, I shifted the top and then managed to slide it on the ground next to the opening I was in. That done, I heaved myself out of the sewers and sat down on the cold stone floor of the cellar. After quickly retrieving my lock picks, I looked down at a worried Baey, gave a quick shrug, and then pushed the manhole cover back in place, leaving her behind.

Now to get to work.

There was no time to dawdle, and with no desire to get caught, I quickly located the first places to hide if anyone should come down. There were plenty of old building supplies down here—planks and whatnot—and the cellar went back for quite a ways. The new palace had already been under construction before Skayla had destroyed the new one, and she'd had it finished shortly after. I could only think of what a waste it was to keep the extra supplies down here—it looked like this place hadn't been touched in years. There wasn't even any lanterns in the place, only the light from the door filtering through. Well, and the light from Baey's lantern down below, until she'd extinguished it.

A little to my left were the wooden stairs that led up to a door, and I knew that was my next move. I would find Illan in the kitchen, probably. Slaves were switched in jobs often, especially if they were troublesome. Illan had been known for that, but of course, some of it had been a ploy to get him transferred here; Illan had been sent here to be separated from his brother, Lytho.

That being said, Illan was a good cook, and the plan had been for him to be on his best behavior after being transferred so that he could be found easily by either me or another of our group. Hopefully, he'd held to that.... The more trouble you were, the more someone wanted to make your life miserable. Hence why I was sent to the Kovian Fortress.

I slipped out of the cellar and heard footsteps way down the hall. Moving slow enough to keep my feet from echoing, I managed to cross to the door on the other side before anyone came down the hall. With calculated slowness, I opened the door and hid inside, carefully closing the door. Inside was a cleaning closet—which I had gathered from the ill-kept finish of the door and the staining near the bottom.

With an ear to the door, I waited for the group of people to pass by, identifying them as soldiers. No royals lived here anymore. Patelayna had not been like Bethyn, and as such the royals were all killed or put in a MindHold. Even the nobility was, for the most part, dead or in the concentration camps, working themselves to death. From what I had gathered, any nobles left were all groveling at Skayla's feet. So no, no king lived here. No, this place was now a garrison like the Kovian Fortress, saved for the soldiers and kept up for any surprise visit from Skayla.

The footsteps died away, and I waited another minute before cautiously opening the door. After taking a cleaning smock from the closet, I continued my task.

The rest of the journey through the palace was the same, with frequent dodges into nearby steam rooms and corridors full of noisy pipes in order to avoid any extra attention. The action was refreshing, to be honest. This was not running and hiding, this was *doing* something, and doing it *my* way.

I made it to the kitchen and quickly managed to get inside, instantly lost in the bustle of cooks and servers. With Skayla's soldiers here, there was always *someone* to feed.

My eyes darted about the room until I spotted Illan—studiously scrubbing at a pot and looking very displeased, as usual.

I made my way to him, weaving in and out of the mass of exhausted slaves and keeping my head down. Finally, I made it to him. He looked ragged and very spent. Spent and lonely. Two things perhaps I wouldn't have cared about a month ago. But somehow, since meeting Baey and Sven, it bothered me now. But it had been Illan's choice, and all of us had agreed to the risks. Still.

Putting a hand on his shoulder, I whispered, *"Kedor ben tathey keva?"* in his ear.

The touch of my hand caused his body to go rigid, but at the words, he relaxed. Without turning around, he murmured, *"Gyt tov."*

"The next step is in motion," I whispered, pretending to simply go alongside him and help with the cleaning. He'd know what that meant. "Stop staring at me, you're going to draw attention." I didn't care that he was shocked to see me all the way here. He knew better.

The reprimand worked, and he nodded. "My apologies," he murmured, returning to his task. "How? It's impossible to...." He stopped short, knowing better than to finish his sentence and give more opportunity at betraying our conversation as well as position.

Of course, I knew what he was asking. How was it possible to get someone out of a MindHold? We'd long known that Sven—though we'd known him only as The GhostMaker—was not willingly under Skayla, nor firmly under a MindHold as the rest, and we had hoped to somehow manage to get him out of her grasp. "Eyes," I hissed. "The less you know the better." I knew rumors would spark hope, but I was not about to fill

39

someone else's head with too much information. Skayla didn't need more ammo.

Illan's eyes narrowed, but he managed to bite his tongue, instead asking, "So, why are you here?" I was thankful for the loud kitchen hiding our conversation.

"Allies."

"I'll get you a list."

"Are you still the only contact here?"

"We'll speak tonight."

Illan was almost more distrusting than I, so I trusted his judgment on letting anyone else in on our little underground network. And then the way he'd said we'd speak tonight...seemed like there was something more.

"Meet me at nightfall in the cellar."

His nod was barely noticeable, but it was enough. Without another word, I left, leaving Illan behind me.

Now to wait for nightfall.

Baey:

I tried not to panic when the lid closed, leaving me alone down there. I even more so tried not to panic as I turned the valve to doused the lantern. But resolve outweighed the fear, and I refused to let Estasia down. Well, as long as the dark space and the putrid stench didn't drive me crazy, first....

Don't pace, that will draw attention...don't move, you don't want to get lost...stop getting distracted, someone will catch you unawares. Ugh, and get out of your head, silly.

The frantic thoughts came to a halt, and forcing a deep breath, I cleared my head.

No apologies. Just show me you can do it. I repeated Estasia's words over and over.

I committed my focus to listening and watching, determined to do just that: Show everyone I could do it.

And that's when I heard it...voices and the sound of footsteps. Armored footsteps.

My instinct was to fly as far away as I could and hide, but I knew better. I couldn't act like a frightened child, not *now*. Oh, what would Estasia do? I took a deep breath, observing the area quickly and springing into action. As swiftly as I could, I undid the ladder from its hold and managed to get it into the closet. The footsteps grew closer, and now I heard voices echoing off the sewer walls. How did I get this door to close?! I searched for some button, but nothing could be found. I pushed, pulled...everything I could think of, but nothing worked.

The voices grew closer.

My throat felt dry and swollen, and I knew that even if I closed the door now it would be heard by the oncoming soldiers. So, in a last ditch effort, I stepped quickly inside the opening and spread my wings so that they covered the full length of the opening.

Come on, control yourself, just hide. You can do this. Estasia trusted you—don't go getting caught. I forced myself not to murmur the words aloud, instead closing my eyes and forcing my wings to stay spread instead of clinging around me. My fingers clenched the doused lantern in my hand as if it were a lifeline, and now I could never have been more thankful that it was no longer ignited.

The echoes of voices grew closer, and whoever it was rounded the corner of the sewer. By the sounds they were making, they were definitely soldiers. I squeezed my eyes shut as they clearly came nearer to passing by me.

"I am sick of sewers."

"Shut up."

"There's nothing down here. I don't know why we bother spending our days trudging through the muck."

"Because Skayla Mara requires efficiency. It doesn't matter how small the rumor. You know what can happen otherwise. Now, shut up."

They passed right in front of where I was, and I could feel the light of a lantern on my wings.

Oh please, oh please, don't see me.

They went on, their conversation continuing as they sloshed through the underground.

"If you ask me, she should be more worried about the ghost at the portal site."

This was the last discernable thing I could hear before they rounded the next corner. Even after I was sure they were gone, I didn't move, paranoia keeping me prisoner for at least another five minutes. Then, like some spell, it broke, and I found myself collapsing to the ground and trying not to gasp too loudly as I caught my breath from practically holding it. Then...then a smile took over. I couldn't believe my wings had worked so well.

But now was not the time to revel. I carefully returned the ladder to its place. No longer was I afraid in the dark. Now, I had a level of confidence—and a plan; a procedure. I played with my wings and continued to test the level of effectiveness in their camouflage, surprised by the level of invisibility they could give. I guess I'd never really thought them worth anything except announcing my emotional state to the world. But now...now they could contribute. I couldn't wait to tell Sven.

Sven. I was distracted again when I remembered the soldiers' comments. Ghost at the portal site? What portal site? And what ghost? Surely, if they'd meant Sven, they would have used the full title.

The manhole cover shifted, and I prepared to step out of the light, in case it was *not* Estasia. Fortunately, it was, and in another moment, she climbed back down the ladder and stood before me, looking very pleased with herself.

"You're still here. Good," she murmured.

I nodded. "Barely. Soldiers are patrolling the sewers. They passed by about twenty minutes ago."

"Good to know." Estasia gave a quick look around before turning back to me. She seemed to know I had more to say. She looked at me curiously. "How did you hide?"

I let my pride show just a little bit. "My wings. They hid me. I guess they are pretty handy for camouflage."

She gave an approving nod. "That's something that could come in handy...and you are sure you weren't spotted?"

With a nod, I replied, "Very sure. They were rather distracted...talking about a portal site and ghosts?" I hoped maybe it would make sense to her.

But she only shrugged and said, "That must be the site where the Drogans came through. I wonder what that has to do with anything. We can talk to Sven after we leave tonight."

I cocked my head, confused. "We're not going back now?" What did she find?

"Yes. My contact is going to meet us in the cellar after nightfall, so I figure we can stay here and do a little training and reconnaissance. Besides, if any more patrols come by, we could always do with some more information."

Nightfall...that was so far away. But the promise of training in any form or fashion was appealing. Besides, I could show Estasia just how effective I was finding my wings to be.

"Now, why don't you turn that lantern back on so we can see?" Estasia ordered. Quickly I went over and grabbed the lantern from where I'd set it down, twisting the valve and watching as the center glass stick filled with light. I had been a little too stressed earlier to notice just how different these lanterns were from others—instead of flame and a candle, it was merely a cylinder of glass in the center that, when the valve was turned, filled with a glowing sort of light.

"Are you done staring at the light?"

"Uh yeah. I guess. Wh-what is it?"

Estasia laughed. "It's an old Crafters' invention for safer travel in the sewers."

I wondered why I'd never seen them before, but then supposed that Valdon hadn't really had sewers. Now I just felt embarrassed at the blatant show of how little I knew, and with an awkward cough I asked, "So, what sort of training?"

"Follow me. And don't get caught," Estasia said with a look that told me I hadn't been very good at the subject change. Without another word, she took off like a dart into the gloom of the sewers. I struggled to keep up, and at last, abandoned the clumsy running for the expanse of my wings, finding a way to glide near the top of the surprisingly tall sewer tunnel. Every sense was on high alert as I listened to the darkness around me, trying to discern Estasia's footsteps from the rats and any other strangers or dangers that could be down here. Unfortunately, every sense also meant that my nose was all too aware of the rotting smell the sewage gave off, and I tried not to think of what disgusting waste we were stepping in as we ran through the maze of tunnels.

And indeed we just...kept running. That's when I started realizing: the noises around me—Estasia was listening to them, too. I watched the way she seemed to be a step ahead of translating the sounds around us, and using her reactions as a guide, I, too, began to be able to separate what was a threat and what wasn't. I was pleased when I heard another soldier patrol in the tunnels at the same time as Estasia, and we both took a separate sewer tunnel to keep away—I was no longer trailing behind.

At long last, we stopped, and I landed, panting as I looked around in the unassuming gloom and wondered if we hadn't traveled through the whole city, by now. It certainly felt like it.

"Not bad." Estasia's tone held more of a smile than her lips, as she was busy panting as well. Ha. So she had gotten a workout, too.

"Why did we stop?" I whispered.

Estasia didn't reply in words, instead going over to the sewer wall, where an old iron door stood. She cranked the wheel that was set in the middle of the wall, and I winced at the way it echoed. At last, the door opened. Estasia ushered me inside.

The door shut behind us, and I realized we were in a small, rusted alcove with a ladder that led up to another manhole.

Quietly, Estasia walked over to a spot on the floor and found a metal panel which she pried up and away to reveal a little hollow area.

Confused and undyingly curious, I went forward, craning my neck to see what in Baeno she was getting at and putting the lantern in my hand a little more forward to better illuminate the contents of the smuggling area. Inside the little space were three things.

First, a porcelain doll, painted in rich, dark tones that still shone in the light from above.

Second, a knife, white ivory handle carved with depictions of strange, giant, horned beasts and people that rode atop them.

Third? A small slab of shale rock with an amateurish painting on it. Estasia stared at them for a while.

"What are they?" I asked at last.

This seemed to jerk the woman out of her trance, and she carefully stowed the knife in her belt and the small doll and shale in her vest pocket. "This was where I lived, for a while," she whispered, quietly. Before I could ask further, she shook herself, and the small bit of emotion that I glimpsed was swiftly hidden away behind the bravado and roguishness. "Now, tell me, how many soldiers were there when you hid?"

"I...I don't know. I had to use my wings to hide and couldn't see anything," I said, biting my lip.

"I don't believe you. I told you. Open your ears. You can't tell me you had no idea how many there were. No sense from the footsteps? The voices? Nothing?"

I stifled any frustration, instead doing my best to follow her direction. Voices...how many voices.... "There were three, I think. And they were talking about a portal, and a ghost."

"Good. See? You notice more than you realize. Don't be so quick to dismiss." Estasia gave me a pat on the shoulder, then stretched as if to hide the fact she'd just shown any amount of affection.

I also noticed how she'd been unconsciously rubbing the handle of the newest knife. Was it sentimental? Estasia was a thief, right? So had it been someone else's, or was it actually one of the few things she had owned? The same question was posed by the doll. The painting...the painting was clearly something a child or early teen would have made. But somehow, I didn't picture Estasia sitting down and painting anything. So whose was it?

"Alright. Well. Back to work. We can't go up to the surface today. But let's see if I can get you a little more prepared. You'll need to be on your toes if we do get you out and about in the city." Estasia cleared her throat and sat down on the ground. "Why don't we start working on that with your wings."

I perked up, awaiting further instructions.

"So, show me how you did it before—hid to keep from the soldiers." Estasia made a hand gesture for me to demonstrate.

Nervously twitching my wings, I set down the lantern and then stood there awkwardly for a moment, trying to figure out exactly how best to demonstrate.

"Well, they are currently a very nice shade of...red. So, maybe not the best for blending in?" Estasia's amusement was not exactly helping.

But I attempted to control the embarrassment, taking a deep breath. *Focus.* I thought of the color of the shadows, thinking how I *needed* to blend into the background. Slowly, I took a few steps back to go against the wall of the sewers, covering my wings over my entire body and watching the way they darkened.

"Not bad, Birdy," Estasia said with a chuckle. Slowly, I withdrew my wings from hiding me, allowing the smile to spread from my face to the now gold-tinted wings. I hadn't seen that color much before.

"So how did you do it, then?"

"I, uh, just focused. Really hard," I replied with a shrug.

"Hm. Well, seeing as they're connected to your emotions, I wonder...I bet controlling your emotions is the key to controlling them. Makes sense." Estasia stroked her chin, giving me a scrutinizing glare as she seemed to evaluate every inch of me.

I struggled with the urge to shrink away.

"Aha! See? Try and control your emotions, Baey. What are you thinking right now?"

Blushing hard, I murmured, "How much I hate being stared at."

Estasia just laughed. "Well, I suppose I don't blame you. But right now, your wings, well, they kind of do whatever they want. Hm...how to explain this...."

As she trailed off in thought, I forced myself to straighten, squaring my shoulders and breathing in deeply.

"Yeah, kind of like pretending. That works," Estasia said at last, as if I'd come across some great epiphany. She must have noted how I tried to project the confidence I didn't quite want to feel.

But I wasn't so sure. "I mean...isn't that sort of lying, though?"

Estasia raised an eyebrow, again looking me over. "If it's a choice between that and survival...."

The gaze was uncomfortable, but I stood my ground this time. But pretending didn't seem right. I thought back to Sven's first sword lesson with me, the talk of balance and the pivot point. It felt more like that...like finding the center and remaining stable. Not being pushed over by what was happening around me.

"See? It works."

I smiled, rolling my eyes. "But it's not pretending. I'm still quite uncomfortable. I just have to anchor myself."

Narrowing her eyes, Estasia looked as if she wanted to challenge my differing opinion.

Again, I felt the urge to shrink away, but this time I thought of my hypothesis: of anchoring. I breathed in and looked Estasia right in the eye. It was alright if we didn't always see eye to eye. I could have my own thoughts.

She just grinned. "Alright ,well, whatever works for you, Birdy. The power of friendship and happiness wins."

I blushed, catching myself just in time to keep it from spreading to my wings. I *would* master this.

The rest of the day was spent in different quirks one could pick up on, how to move through a crowd without being noticed, different ways to tell a thief or spy, and tactics for avoiding detection. We tested out my wings a bit, and found I could, in fact, not only change shade but also the appearance of their texture—to a certain extent, at least.

At last, we headed back into the sewers, panic at the tight space shoved to the back of my mind, as I now had a thousand things to notice, listen to, and pick up on. Besides, the way Estasia dodged through the maze of underground tunnels forced a great deal of my worry to be focused on not losing her, rather than the tunnels closing in.

That being said, I was relieved when the tunnels opened back up a bit and we were back to the entrance to the palace. I still couldn't believe a whole day had passed, but Estasia seemed to have a good sense of time, so I trusted her.

Neither of us spoke, Estasia, now holding the lantern, stood very still as she clearly tried to listen. I came up alongside her and did the same. Any moment, Estasia's informant could appear. Hopefully. If nothing went wrong. Oh, so many things could go wrong...but I gulped away the fear. That would do very little except distract me.

Ten or so minutes passed before I heard something. Not daring to utter a word, I simply nudged Estasia to get her attention and let her know. The lady nodded and then looked to me.

"Estasia." I heard a man's barely audible whisper from the surface.

Estasia motioned to get the ladder and I quickly obeyed. Soon, she was climbing up to the opening.

"Illan," she called once at the top. "Down here."

There was a scuffling sound, and then the cover was moved aside to reveal the dim light of the cellar. A lean, worn-looking face appeared through the opening. It was a young man, probably not much older than Tanner. Estasia began backing down the ladder in an express command for Illan to come down, and he obeyed with a distasteful sigh. I could understand the sentiment...I didn't like being down here, either.

Nonetheless, soon he was standing in the murky puddles of the sewer right along with the rest of us. Standing...and, well, staring at me.

It was the wings, obviously. I gave a sheepish smile—unsure what else to do.

"You said you'd explain further tonight." Illan broke the silence.

Estasia gave a brief explanation of what had happened, but very, *very* vaguely. No mention of who The GhostMaker really was, no admission to The Crafter being alive, and no mention of Tanner and the rest leaving. Only that there were allies and we had things to use against Skayla.

"Alright. Now it's your turn; what news, Illan?" Estasia wasted no time in turning the questions on him.

Wearing a blank expression, Illan did not reply, only gave her a small scrap of sorely crumpled paper. His gaze turned from wonderment to suspicion as he once more stared at me.

"She's a friend, Illan. A very important one," Estasia remarked as she handed me the lantern so she could read the paper.

"Aren't they all dead?" he asked, as if I wasn't there.

I winced. "Almost," I answered. "Obviously, I'm still here." I realized that while only a few from Kaedna had known how dangerous I really could be—according to what The Crafters had been told by the Creator— they all had known my race. Sefen had said we were one of the most ancient people in the world. That we'd been angels from another world, come with the gift of knowledge and peace. But nowadays, Esmers were just known to be the first race that was eradicated by Skayla.

"Wait. *Him?*" Estasia interrupted the dying conversation as she stared at the piece of paper. "That's impossible."

"I'm...sorry?" Illan looked as confused as I was.

Estasia grumbled something about backstabbing slimes and glared at Illan. "Have you seriously been giving out information and trusting lowlifes like Temorn? He'll sell you out in a moment if he hasn't already."

"You...know him?"

"Yes, I know him. Now tell me, what have you told him and how much damage control do I need to do?" The paper crumpled in Estasia's tightening grip, and I struggled to understand what was going on. Backstabber? We'd...we'd already had one. My chest tightened at both the reminder and the fear of again being betrayed.

"Listen, Estasia, you haven't been here at Alkemar since what, before Skayla? Trust me when I say if Temorn had wanted to sell us out, we'd be sold out by now. If Lord Atlys trusts him, then so do I. You have no idea what's going on here. I don't even know—and you know that. But if you want help and you want allies, then he's Lord Atlys's contact and the only way to get direct contact with anyone." Illan looked both uncomfortable and irritated.

I knew better than to ask Estasia who this Temorn was, and yet I couldn't help but wonder. I'd almost never seen Estasia this...discomposed? Openly flustered? It was somehow different than the irritation that she'd shown with the rest of our group back in Kaedovarna.

"Are you *sure*?" Estasia's grip tightened on the paper as she asked. "This screams 'trap.'"

"If it was a trap, I wouldn't be here. Lord Atlys saved my sorry hide two months ago. I kept it vague, but I finally told him about the network officially a week ago. We'd actually been trying to figure out how to get ahold of you. He'll be intrigued to know you're here." As Illan spoke, he looked up at the manhole cover, fingers tapping nervously against his leg. "But you still have to go through Temorn to get to Atlys or the others. I wrote it all down. Read it—but not now. If you need me, it will be better to go through him. He has more direct contact with me on a somewhat daily basis, anyway."

I really wished I knew who this Temorn was.

Estasia folded the note and put it in her pocket. "Fine. We'll be in touch." Her shoulders sagged. "Thank you. Be careful."

Illan's head tilted to one side and he seemed as taken aback by the comment as I was. Estasia expressing concern? I wondered if it was Sven's influence, or the items from the sewer.

"And don't get us caught. You know what you agreed to."

Illan's head straightened and he rubbed his forehead. "Yes, yes. I know the drill…" His tone fell away, and then quietly, he asked, "Is Lytho doing alright?"

I watched Estasia as her hand twitched. It was the closest thing to a wince I'd really seen from her. Such a small movement...but I caught it all the same.

"Last I knew, he was alive and well. Now you had better leave before anyone catches you out past curfew."

Illan appeared to want to ask further, but instead, gave a curt nod and headed back to the ladder.

I didn't bother to hide the way I was staring at Estasia, and after Illan had gone, I whispered, "Are you alright?"

The look she gave me was that of startled amusement, but all Estasia said in reply was, "Let's get back to Alenor so I can read this note and burn it before anyone else sees it. Illan is either going to get us help...or get us all killed."

CHAPTER IV: Skayla

Twelve Years Ago
Skayla:

I stood on the balcony of the Royal House, looking over the angered citizens of Alkemar. Threats of harm against the Drogans mingled with frantic expressions of fear until it was a commotion both dangerous and confusing. Moira stood next to me, radiating well her concealed panic. Oh, this was all so tiresome—the endless cycle of hate because of ignorance bringing violence to follow.

The cycle of fear.

As I looked down upon the uproar of the crowd, all I could see were hundreds of ignorant souls who had concluded that our new arrivals looked like Dragons and must, therefore, be monsters. Thus far, however, Ovok had proved nothing but a peaceful friend, and at this rate, we could have the Ice Wars all over again. Did history so frequently have to repeat itself?

"You need to calm them down," Moira said when I still did nothing.

My chest pinched unpleasantly at what was nearly an order. She was right, of course. But I...I didn't want to. It felt wrong. It always felt wrong.

"Patience. You know I must evaluate first." With this, I took another deep breath, and then addressed the crowd. I wished Sven was here to carry my voice, but natural projection would have to do. There was a reason Moira had called for me and left Sven to watch over the Drogans.

We knew he wouldn't approve.... Honestly, I didn't know if I was even strong enough to bear it.

"PLEASE!" I shouted above the commotion, willing the words to flow like sickly honey from my mouth. Honey I wanted to vomit out. I didn't want to be so afraid of all this—so afraid of making the wrong decision. So afraid this was all wrong. "SILENCE, SO ONE CAN EVEN THINK TO ANSWER YOUR QUESTIONS!" At the very first word, the crowd obeyed, staring up at me in submission. Ack. I hadn't meant to so keenly use my ability. Always it was getting the better of me—always I came close to using people instead of helping them see.

I felt Moira touch my arm as if to comfort me, but it brought no such thing. I didn't want to rob people of their choice, and yet so often, they seemed to be picking the wrong one. Moira was right; we walked on a fine line—a fine line that Sven didn't even understand. And yet I wished I could seek his advice. I wished I didn't feel so sick over it, that I wasn't so afraid to make the hard decision.

With it now quiet, however, I could easily be heard across the square. "Would you ignorantly cause war because of the appearance of a weary wanderer?" I beseeched the people. "These beings have been hunted and killed in their own world, and barely escaped with their lives. They seek only peace. If they wanted to harm us so much, would that not have already shown? It has been weeks since their arrival, and still they have kept to where they entered, afraid that wandering could harm them." I took a calculated pause, allowing each face to soak in this information and understand it. I had used just enough of my Gift to help them see my side—and not so much that it would affect their minds. I had done enough of that already. When I was confident I had given enough time. I continued, "I have spoken to their leader, and he says that he, indeed, only wishes for peace. They seem in need of someone to show them mercy. Might we not be that someone?"

With this there were murmurs of agreement, but it was shattered by one man who shouted, "They will kill us all! They have even lulled The Watchers!"

This, *naturally*, caused a whole new clamor and the square was once more a panicked mob. *No! I cannot let this happen!*

"STOP! ALL OF YOU ARE ACTING IN BLIND FEAR. GO HOME, ALL OF YOU." The force in my voice astonished even me, and I instantly wished to take back my words. The square was again eerily silent, and I was horrified when one by one, the people turned around and stiffly began walking away. Their eyes flashed briefly of violet, and my heart rose to my throat. But their eyes returned to their own, even as they left for their homes, as if in a trance. I turned frantically to Moira, "Quick, spin back time! Stop me from doing that," I pleaded, even though I knew that she would already have done so if she could and told me.

There was sadness in Moira's eyes as she quietly said, "I'm sorry Skayla. There was no other way to stop them. I tried."

"Your shoulders hold much weight." Ovok's voice came from next to me. It had been two weeks since the incident, and no one but Moira and I knew what truly happened. Still, I couldn't stop thinking about it. Part of me wished to tell Sven, to give in and just let him help. But I knew how he'd react. Moira and I both knew he was not ready to shoulder this level of responsibility—to have to bend the rules. So instead, I had been brooding day and night, rebuking myself for such disregard for moderation.

"I am simply thinking," I replied. The Drogan and I had talked as often as possible, and now there was no doubt in my mind that he was indeed what he said he was. He had a wisdom I had not seen in another being. But more than that...I felt his sorrow, too. Sorrow and fear. There was something tearing him apart. The weight of his kind on his shoulders.

"Thinking...or regretting?" he rumbled.

The statement appeared both sincere and amused, and I could not help a faint smile from escaping my tight lips. I looked out onto the garden and with a sigh said, "I suppose both."

Shaking his body and readjusting his position on the ground next to me, the Drogan said, "Leading is never easy. The choices we make.... Sometimes we must understand the consequences of what we choose are still less than if we had done nothing at all."

"That's what Moira says," I said with a gulp. "But how do you rectify the two? How can you really know when you are stuck only with the result of your decision?" I surprised myself with the vulnerability in both my question and my tone. What was I doing? But I felt a kinship with Ovok. I felt he understood me more than even Moira. Moira...she controlled time. She...she controlled me. She saw what each path led to and was able to see the result. Me? I was stuck trusting her. Stuck second-guessing. I saw the same sort of regret in Ovok's eyes.

"I see." He gave a swish of his tail—a Drogan's version of a shrug, as I had come to notice.

I watched him closely for a moment, knowing that while I did like his company, he was still very new, and that trusting him was still to be taken with a grain of salt. "Tell me. How are we supposed to help people without harming them in the process?" The question was one I had often asked myself, even before my outburst on the terrace.

"If I knew the answer, then we would not have had to run from our home." Ovok's reply held a mourning sort of growl. "It seems the worlds are intent on hurting each other, no matter what choices are made."

I swallowed hard, murmuring, "That's what I was afraid of."

A long silence followed, and for a while I thought he would not speak. Then, quietly, he said, "A funny word, fear. I suppose it's what kills us all, in the end."

CHAPTER V: The Problems With
Being a Problem

<u>Sven:</u>

"Get them." Skayla spat as she saw the two panicked figures dashing out into the street. I sheathed my blade, still slick with the blood of Lord Ostinar, and without hesitation, jumped off of the mansion roof and into the street after my prey.

I was tired of screaming. It was all one bad nightmare; my mind in such a fog that I could barely do anything except curl up in a mental ball as I played Skayla's puppet, killing everyone I ever knew. Part of me wanted to give up. To just let her wash over me so that I didn't feel it anymore. I was so tired of fighting.

Chasing the shadows in the city was easy, and with one hand on my sword hilt, I ran on. Not many people were in the street, and my hood was pulled low over my face to hide the hideous mask and my violet eyes. The eyes of my sister. The ones I could never be rid of.

My prey made a sharp left and tried to disappear into the night, but I was forced on by my mission blaring over and over in my head.

Get them.

Get them.

I couldn't even wince at the way the words screeched, burning out any other thought that could penetrate this forsaken mind.

I leapt up a ladder and used one of the Rugonian pulley systems to effortlessly reach the top of the flat-roofed buildings, racing across them in the moonlight. Soon, I was ahead of my targets. They thought they had escaped me.

Get them.

I wanted to scream back at the voice in my head. I couldn't do this again. And yet here I was. Still doing it. My weary muscles obeying. My hand reaching for my sword as I jumped down to face my prey.

The lack of hesitation as I drew my sword.

"Darby! Run!" The younger man jumped in front of the blow as I swung for the woman, and a cry ripped out as he fell to the ground, gripping the left side of his face.

Thackeray. I was about to kill Thackeray. I was about to kill Thackeray and Darby—I couldn't. No. Please.

Get them.

I shot awake, sitting up swiftly and being nearly blinded by the light of dawn. It was all I could do to get control of my gasping breaths as my entire body shook. Both hands went to my ears, but I couldn't get Thackeray's cry out of my head. I gripped harder. I had no right to beg the memories to leave, and yet I so desperately wanted them to. So desperately that I didn't bother to take in my surroundings or reorient myself. I only kept my eyes glued shut as I focused on my breathing and not the awful memory before me. Not the fact that I'd killed my best friends. What was worse? I could hardly remember them. I remembered their laughter and their voices, but whenever I tried to zero in on the memory, all I got was their screams instead.

Breathe, Sven. Get a hold of yourself.

It felt like a tortured forever, but I did just that. I didn't have time to have another mental breakdown. I didn't have time to be weak, and I certainly had no right to mourn. It had all been my own, stupid fault.

Slowly, I opened my eyes, the unwelcome glaring of morning light hitting me right in the face as I remembered where I was. I was hidden amid a rocky outcropping above some cliff's edge, shielded by the eyes of any Drogan flying overhead, but still able to be blinded by the sun peeking up from beyond the cliff. I must have slept for two or three hours, at least.

With a sigh, I cautiously made my way out into the open, careful to watch and listen for any signs of Drogans or patrols. I couldn't afford to let my mind get distracted again. I couldn't afford to just fall asleep like that. There was too much to do—too much at stake.

I got a better look at my surroundings.

Right. The portal site. That's where I was. What was Skayla doing?

As much as I wished to stay and investigate, I knew it was a bad idea. It was broad daylight, and my mind was too much a wildcard for me to bet on my illusions alone to keep me safe. There would be too many eyes to potentially see through a ruse, and I was still exhausted.

Throughout the day of travel, I found the airspace to be quite busy. Drogans flew between Alkemar and the portal site, and many had soldiers on their backs or supply bags strapped to them. We had to have been far away indeed not to have seen any of this on the way to or from the boat before.

It was at least two hours past sunset when I, at last, arrived back in the city.

The city gates were shut up already for the night, but I used the sewers, remembering the way back from Estasia's map.

But the sewers were pitch black, making it near impossible to move safely—let alone get back to my mother's house. I found myself rubbing the ring around my finger, realizing all I had to do was conjure up a light, and I could see more. But it had been so long since I had tried to tap into my deeper abilities. Yes, Hytat had been...a start. But the true damage had been a result of my emotions, not control. I couldn't afford to lose control like that; there would be too much damage. I couldn't control the pain brought on by wearing my stupid ring any more than I could change the fact that one sister was possibly dead and the other one *wanted* me dead. At the time, having three relics carved from The Living Stone seemed a good idea. The heart of the world binding three siblings together. Now, it was just another part of the nightmare.

And yet, I really could use a bit of light. So, with a deep breath, I tried to drive all other thoughts except light. The way it bounced off the walls of the sewer. The way it warmed the space. It was more than creating an illusion. No. This...this was real. This was messing with something far more dangerous.

The light burst into existence, dancing like some mischievous fairy off the sewage water and projecting patchworks of unnaturally beautiful ripples onto the curved ceiling above me. It was almost like the twinkling of stars. Funny how it made even the murky water beautiful, in its own way. And yet, it felt wrong to have such beauty come from something I did. Me. The GhostMaker. The thief of lives.

Stay focused. Don't go there. I forced my attention instead on the way I had created my light, and with it to guide the way, I continued.

It didn't take much longer until I reached my destination, realizing with a suddenness that I couldn't remember where Estasia had gotten the ladder. All I could do was sigh. Of course I hadn't thought of asking about the ladder.

Guess I was making a little more than light, tonight. How dangerous could making a ladder be, anyway?

Brow furrowed, I created an illusion of a ladder, putting it up to the seal on my exit. Once in place, I went to climb it. Of course, my hand went right through.

"Come *on*, Sven, get over it," I muttered to myself. If I was going to be of use, I really needed to practice. Illusions were all fine and dandy, but I could do better. I *had* to do better. I deepened my focus. What a pathetic mess I was…. How had I managed to cause such destruction in Hytat, and yet I couldn't even make this stupid ladder real now? I wondered if the others had ever realized what had happened on the docks was more than illusions….

Concentrate. Please just for one forsaken minute concentrate, you fool.

The ladder. I reached out to my illusion before me, imagining the rough texture of coarse metal rungs.

I willed it into existence. I willed it to become reality.

A shiver ran through me as my fingertips came into contact with the cold rung of the ladder, and I dared let out my pent-up breath. I'd done it. Such a trivial little creation. But I'd actually done it without having an utter meltdown.

I hadn't purposefully manipulated reality in a long time. Perhaps I'd hoped it would make me feel a little better—to tap into the true nature of my ring's power—but instead, it just made me feel more empty. If I'd kept my ring and battled Skayla with it, perhaps I would have been able to best her instead of becoming her GhostMaker. I'd been in control then…and yet too afraid of losing and her getting my ring. Now, I'd lost more times than I could count.

As I stared at my small, insignificant ladder, I thought of so long ago, when I alone had discovered that, with the relic made of The Living Stone, I could do more than create illusions. I could bend reality. Just as Skayla and Moira's powers had grown, mine had as well. And yet, I hadn't told them. Not a single soul knew. Perhaps I'd thought my sisters had everything under control and didn't need my help.

Perhaps I had been afraid of what they would want me to do with it.

I'd never know. And now my once-great power was reduced to struggling to make a ladder in a sewer. Pretty pathetic.

With that charming contemplation, I climbed to the top of the sewer tunnel, ignoring the stiffness in my side. The Kovian Fortress still echoed in my body's groans, but I hadn't the time or care to heed them. Carefully, I opened the cover to my exit, and after making sure no one was watching, climbed out, looking back down and willing the ladder to ripple out of existence before I covered the maintenance exit.

Having wasted enough time being pulled into my own head, I quickly crossed through the deserted cobblestone street and made it to my mother's house, my existence erased from any passerby's eyes.

A quick knock was all I needed for the door to be answered, and I was soon greeted by Estasia, practically wrenching me inside before I could so much as take a step.

"Oh good, you're back," she said as she let me in, closing and locking the door behind me. "I was starting to get worried. Did everything go smoothly?"

I fiddled with the ring on my finger. "I ran into a patrol. They...saw me. To a degree," I replied.

Estasia froze. "What of the others? Did they make it to the ship?"

"Yes. They made it. I ran into a patrol on my way back." I winced.

"Did...did they recognize you?" I didn't blame her for the rigidness in her expression and tone.

I shook my head. "I don't think so. Some seemed to think I was some ghost or phantom or something...and—"

"Oh, finally, you're back. If I'd known you'd be back so late, I would have told you how to use my back door—Sven, you're filthy! Go clean up and then come into the living room—you look awful." Mum appeared in the entryway, golden gaze penetrating my weariness with a strange warmth. I'd actually startled at her voice—it had been so long since I'd heard it. So long since I'd given up hope of hearing it again.

"Good idea. And then we can all exchange information. Baey and I were busy, too." Estasia's shoulders didn't relax as she spoke.

Mum provided me with a spare set of clothes, and I was able to change out of my sewage-ridden rags and wash up a bit—an experience I was very unused to.

Soon, I'd rejoined the others downstairs in the well-lit living room, the miniature train model clattering on its suspended rails above. I stopped mid-stride, suddenly stuck on the little steam-powered engine as it wove about the ceiling, and disappeared in a hole in the top corner of the wall to continue its journey through the house. I vaguely remembered how I would sit for hours watching Mum and Da's models.

"You alright, Sven?" Estasia asked as she nearly ran into me.

I managed a mute nod and went over to the fireplace.

"Did everything go well?" Baey asked from where she sat perched on the back of a golden-cushioned armchair.

"Relatively," I murmured as I leaned against the wall and soaked in the rest of the room. The echoes of the crackling fire mingled with the distant whistling and chugging of the train, but my eyes were now drawn to the dark elsdar wood piano that sat up against the far wall. It was just an upright, and yet every inch of it was covered in twirling carved patterns that mimicked living vines. The only part of it that wasn't wood was the glass panel at the front, allowing you to see the hammers and strings.

"So. How did that happen, Sven? Getting seen. Didn't you use an illusion to shield you?" Estasia broke the ambience with the question.

My eyes fell to the floor. "I...got distracted," I whispered.

"Got *distracted?*" Estasia didn't sound as angry as she did confused. "What does that even mean? And how could you have gotten distracted enough to lose focus? Hiding yourself has never been hard before."

Frustration rose, not at her, but at myself. "I'm having some problems focusing," I managed to get out.

"Is your memory...acting up, again?" Baey's question barely flitted into existence. She was hesitant to bring it up.

I disciplined myself into avoiding any physical reaction to the question. Baey didn't need to be discouraged from asking things. I needed to get over it. "No. My memory is fine. I think that's the problem," I croaked.

"Wait. What happened to your memory?" It was Mum, of course.

This time, I couldn't hide the wince. Nor did I look up. "Apparently, Skayla had a few safeguards in case I somehow escaped her MindHold. I had a bit of recurring amnesia for a while." My voice strained against the quietness with much more effort than I would have wished. Somehow, having my mother present reminded me just how much I had changed. Even my voice was harsh and ripping at the seams.

"So, you were in a MindHold, then…. For how long?" That's when I realized I had hardly explained anything to her. We'd been in such a rush to get Sefen and the others to the boat that I'd not had time to really say anything more. I didn't want to relive it again, but she deserved to know.

"I went to face Skayla. Alone. It failed, obviously. She used me to kill the nobility that opposed her. I only just managed to get out of it…um…a month ago, perhaps? But she did something to my mind so that I couldn't really remember much consistently. Not until I faced her again at Hytat and she…gave everything…back." I stuttered to a stop and tried to ignore everyone staring at me. Estasia looked grim, Baey's open concern was evident, and then Mum…Mum looked heartbroken.

And why shouldn't she? Da was…dead, her youngest son was made a murderer by her middle child, and her oldest dead for all she knew.

Wait. *Idiot!* I hadn't told her about Moira!

"This…this is a long story, though. I suggest you sit down and get comfortable," I said, meeting her eyes and forcing myself not to flinch away from her gaze. How could I have left this out? She was suffering enough already.

"Alright," she whispered, going over to a chair and taking a seat. I didn't miss how she clutched the arm.

It took a long time to lay the whole thing out, but at last, the story was told, my throat hoarse by the end of it.

A long silence followed, stretching at least three minutes as we all just watched my mother digest. She remained calm even through the deaths and pain and the news that Moira might not be dead, somehow.

At last, she spoke. "Well. I think for now, you three should rest. If this has been your last few weeks, I think the best thing to do is get a good day or so of rest before we plan our next move."

I shook my head. "No time. We need to investigate what is going on with the portal site and what Skayla wants—"

"Sven." Mum's voice was stern. "You are falling to pieces. You need sleep. Please. I have managed to sit here and wait for over a decade. A day is not going to end the world any sooner, at this point."

I didn't know what to say. I didn't want to argue, and yet I couldn't rest. I didn't want to sleep.

"And...wait. When did you eat last?" She didn't bother waiting for me to reply. Which was probably for the best...because I knew she didn't want the answer. "Never mind. Sit down. I'm going to get you some dinner—sit." The last bit was said forcefully, even as I opened my mouth to argue.

So, I snapped my jaw shut and gave a tense nod. But Mum didn't leave the room until I slowly crossed over to the couch and sat down.

"We've been hearing rumors of some ghost at the portal site, too," Baey commented only after I had gotten comfortable. I had been trying to ignore the stares of the other two.

But getting directed back to business helped the uncomfortable atmosphere dissipate.

"Interesting," I murmured, trying to ignore the way the cushions seemed to fold around me. I really was exhausted. "What else?"

Estasia went on, "I have a list here, as well as some information that we can use. But I agree with your mother. Rest comes first. Acting on anything requires us to have a little more wit about us than you seem to currently have." She raised an eyebrow as she finished.

With a sigh, I ran both hands over my face, wishing I could just blink away the grogginess I was staunchly ignoring. I didn't want to sleep.

Mum reentered, then, with a teacup and saucer as well as a bowl of soup. Without a word, she sat down next to me, only handing over the food when she, too, was sufficiently settled in the folds of the couch.

Her presence was warmer than the tea—which tasted of some faraway memory. I wondered if perhaps it was a childhood favorite, but that all just seemed so long ago, now. I didn't think I could make it that far back without stumbling upon too many unpleasant memories in the process.

So instead, I sipped the tea and murmured a quiet, "Thank you."

She smiled and jostled me ever so slightly with her shoulder.

I really had missed her.

"So…" Baey broke the silence as I began slowly working on the bowl of soup. "What exactly is that thing in the corner?" She pointed to where the ornate instrument stood in the corner.

"It's a piano," Mum replied. Every time she spoke, I remembered she was here. I wasn't alone.

I was so tired. My eyes seemed to droop against my will, and I was losing the battle already to stay awake.

"Sven plays quite well, you know," The voice was as if from a dream. Barely, I remembered my head dropping limply to one side, only to feel the sturdy shoulder of my mother.

I could fight no longer.

Estasia:

"Did...you just drug your *son?*" I didn't bother to keep the apprehension out of my voice. I was paranoid enough as it was.

Alenor's cheeks flushed as she sat unmoving on the couch; Sven's head resting on her shoulder as his chest rose and fell.

"No," she said defensively. Slowly, she reached over and took the teacup to prevent it from falling. "I just gave him some chamomile tea. He must be really tired if he passed out so quickly."

My brow furrowed, but before I could ask, Baey beat me to it. "What is that...?"

Still sounded rather like drugging to me.

"It's not Baenian." Alenor's tone was patient and yet weary. She still didn't move from the couch. "It was...my husband's favorite. From where he came from. He had a few seeds with him when he came, and we cultivated them. It calms you—it *can* put you to sleep, but it's only supposed to help." Her head turned and she looked again at Sven. "It was always Sven's favorite, too. I thought it would help."

There was an unsettling quiet.

"So...wait. Were the Drogans not the only ones that came through the portal? I thought that was an anomaly," Baey whispered, clearly worried about waking Sven.

"It was an anomaly. No one's gotten through besides The Merchant in over two hundred years. Henry was the last, about a hundred years ago." The coolness with which Alenor answered was almost enough to make one think that this was all completely normal.

"Oh. So you are just a hundred years old, then?" I mirrored her calm tone without bothering to hide the sarcasm. But I couldn't stop staring at the way Sven just sat there, leaning on his mother. His *mother*. Like he was a real person.

"Two hundred and forty or something. I really don't count." Alenor made as if to shrug, but thought better of it.

"So, you're only a little younger than Syvil...wait. I don't understand." I could picture Baey's face wrinkling up as she tried to figure everything out. "Are you a Drogan or something?"

But I didn't look at her. I was too busy with Alenor, and the portals...and the fact that the great Sven Mara—the terrifying GhostMaker—was currently asleep on his mother's shoulder.

"No. Just blessed with a longer life. But Sven is not the only one that should be getting some rest. I can explain more tomorrow after you both get some sleep." I watched as Alenor expertly extracted herself from Sven and laid him out on the couch with surprising ease. He didn't stir. I was still pretty sure I'd never be accepting any tea from the woman.

I got up from my seat even as Alenor put a blanket over Sven. Just like a normal mother. Not like one of the great Crafters of Baeno. Not like the world was ending. Just like a mother. Or at least, I guessed—what I'd long ago imagined a mother would do.

Shuddering, I turned to Baey, who was sitting stubbornly perched on her seat. "She's right. Bed and then more answers tomorrow. We need to form a plan. And a proper plan requires proper sleep beforehand."

Baey's eyes were also trained on Sven, and she bit her lip even as her wings twitched, like most people would drum their fingers. She didn't budge from her seat.

"Bed," I ordered. Yeah, no, I wasn't a mother. I pointed to the door. "Before I give you some chameleon tea."

Alenor snorted. I ignored it.

With a sigh, Baey fluttered off the back of the chair and headed for the door, stopping only a moment to murmur, "Will he be alright down here by himself?" to Alenor.

I heard the woman say, "I'll stay with him."

I followed behind, stopping in front of Alenor and again sizing her up.

But then she broke the silence. "Thank you. For taking care of my son."

"It was...no problem." It was definitely a *lot* of sweat, blood, and tears. But she'd heard it all. She knew. And she knew he'd done just as much for all of us in return. It wasn't about debts anymore. Sven didn't do it for the "IOUs," so why should I? Oh boy, what a stupid little conscience I was growing. That thing hadn't been around since....

No. Not now. "Just...don't give me any of that tea, please," I said with a nod, and left, deciding I needed sleep just as much as Baey or Sven. Still, my hand went to the knife in my belt. I'd put the painting up in my room. Along with the doll. Oh, what in Baeno had possessed me to go back and get the stupid things?

It was nice to sleep without having to worry about a Drogan spotting you from the sky, or a patrol ambushing you, or the food running out, or Maeko murdering Sven. It was nice to feel the heat of the Patelaynian air and be reminded that I was, at last, home. It was nice to be far away from the Kovian Fortress. To have my own space—my own room and my own bed.

And yet, as I woke in the actual real, soft bed to the open window and the sounds of the city street, I felt an emptiness. I was home. But it was not the same. It would never be the same. And all the others in the Kovian Fortress...Lytho, Aekon...what if they'd been caught? Punished? I shuddered at the reminder of what Sven—even as The GhostMaker—had saved me from when I'd been thrown in a dungeon all that time alone. What if they hadn't been so lucky?

But I couldn't think of that, now. I slipped out from under the covers and quickly dressed—Alenor had gotten a set of clothes that would fit me—grabbing the knife from the nightstand and lingering a moment to touch the painted shale that rested there. It reminded me of why I didn't like trusting people—why I didn't like friends.

And yet, Baey's trust was louder, Sven's loyalty stronger, Aekon's calmness more reassuring than my skepticism, and Illan's love for his brother a bond knit more tightly than jealousy.

Besides, on the other side of all that was Temorn. I rubbed the hilt of the knife again. I was going to have to face him. Face him, and probably punch him square across the jaw. I'd half hoped he was dead. Half hoped and half worried. But I supposed seeing him would be some good resolution or whatever. Beating him up would definitely put a smile on my face.

Another minute and I was out in the hall, unwieldy hair in need of a good cut. Maybe I'd ask Alenor for some scissors. As long as she didn't offer any tea....

My first stop was downstairs into the living room, of course. Sven was still asleep, Alenor rocking softly in a chair on the other side of the room. Our eyes locked for only a moment and I narrowed them, turning away and heading for the kitchen.

I decided I would get my own food from now on.

I'd grabbed some bread and just about finished it when a sleepy Baey came wandering into the room, wings fluffed and ruffled like bed head, as the feathers stuck in every general direction.

"You still asleep?" I asked as I gulped down the last bit of food. The loaf was still out, however, and I sliced a bit and threw it at her.

It hit her square in the face and she let out a "Mfft" as her eyes actually opened, seemingly for the first time.

She did not catch the bread.

"Well, I'm not cutting you another," I said as she just stared at the bread on the ground. "So, better pick it up and brush it off."

Baey rolled her eyes but picked up the piece of bread, brushed it off, then gave a determined chomp on the piece.

"So, what's the plan?" It was almost impressive how she was able to sound so intelligible even as she chewed a good mouthful of bread.

"I have to talk to Sven." I sighed. "I have to go see...an old friend."

Baey raised an eyebrow. "I thought you didn't have friends."

The smile on my face was both sly and dangerous. "I don't."

There was a flutter, and then Baey was sitting on top of the counter, stretching her wings and sending a few molting feathers around the kitchen.

"Just what I wanted," I said as I plucked a feather off the loaf of bread.

"So, is this friend the guy that was on the list?" Baey didn't quit, and I was glad to see it. Even if I didn't want to answer the question.

"Yes," I grumbled.

Baey's wings flicked as she asked, "So, why do we need him?"

"Well, because according to Illan's note, he is the way to get into contact with Lord Atlys." I was equally as unhappy about *that*. Lord Atlys was known as the backstabbing noble who cowered and catered to Skayla and was permitted his life in return. "I guess they are allies. But it was pretty vague." Paranoia was all that was keeping us alive. In fact, I'd already memorized and burned Illan's note.

Baey bit her lip in thought. "So...who exactly is this guy?"

"Morn? Oh. He's just the leader of the criminal underground, basically." And an egomaniac. And a jerk. I sighed, rubbing the knife. And a backstabber. Why was I thinking so much about this now? It had been an eternity ago. I mean, I'd lived in Alkemar for plenty after I'd split ways with Temorn and his crew. I'd long gotten over what happened. Long stuffed it away. And yet, occasionally, I still wondered what had happened to Eugene.

"Wait. We are going to see a criminal overlord?" Baey's eyes widened.

Ha. Overlord. Morn would just *love* that. "Yes. Sven and I, to be exact." This one was not for Baey to come to.

Baey's wings slumped more visibly than her shoulders, and she tore at the last bit of her bread with a violence.

"Excuse me?" I scoffed, folding my arms and giving her a glare. "What exactly is *that?*"

Instantly, Baey stiffened, swallowed, and muttered, "Sorry."

"I'm not *sidelining* you, Baey. You'd really think that? After everything I've let you do?" I didn't drop the glare.

Baey just shrugged, and another apology slipped out.

"Listen. It's just common sense. If all three of us are out, then that means both the last Mara *and* the last Esmer are out in the open. Sven needs something to distract him, and you can keep an eye on Alenor and get to know her better. There will be plenty of opportunities."

Baey's cheeks reddened, and she fiddled with the ends of her wings. "Yeah, that makes sense, I guess."

My frustration deflated a bit, and I made an attempt at a reassuring smile. "Don't worry. I won't sideline you, Baey. I promise." I walked forward and gave her an awkward shoulder pat.

She sighed. "I know. I do."

"And trust me. I'm sure you'll meet Temorn eventually." If this all panned out, anyway. Illan had better be right about this.

CHAPTER VI: Gadgets and Memories

<u>Baey:</u>

Estasia was right; she wasn't sidelining me. I was being irrational. But somehow being told to stay here was as bad as being shoved down some small, dark hole. I'd already been separated from Tanner; I didn't want to end up completely alone.

"Well, I suppose we should go see if Sven is awake," Estasia said as she slid towards the kitchen exit. I fluttered to the ground and followed, trying to take in every movement. The way she was always rubbing that knife handle made me wonder: Had Temorn given it to her? She seemed to associate it with him, at least. What about the painting?

We both entered the room to find Sven...still asleep, with Alenor in her rocking chair as she had been before. I saw the reluctance in her eyes. She didn't want to wake him. Honestly, neither did I. He looked like he was *actually* resting, and I was pretty sure this was the longest he'd slept in a while. Yet the dark circles under his eyes seemed even more prevalent, and the stoicism had dripped away into something more akin to anguish.

None of us spoke. An understanding seemed to pass between Estasia and Alenor, and the latter got up from her seat and walked slowly over to Sven.

"Careful. He—" Estasia spoke, but then cut herself off when Alenor nodded to show she knew.

Yeah. Sven didn't seem to be really good at waking up. I had seen it a couple times with those in Valdon. They said the battle sometimes never left a person. I wondered what it was like when you were forced to fight it on the wrong side. Well, I didn't want to wonder. I didn't want to know.

I watched as Alenor gently prodded Sven, keeping her distance and calling his name with a softness. A softness that reminded me a bit of Namaya. It stung, the memory feeling bitter as I was unsure what to do with it. Treasure it, or hide it away?

Sven came to with a gasp and sat up, hands going up in a defensive position before attempting to hide the instinct by instead running them through his unkempt hair. He blinked.

"Are you alright?" It was such a stupid question to ask, and yet at the same time, I felt like no one really ever asked him that. Not that he'd answer truthfully. And yet...I wanted him to know I actually did care. That some people saw. Maybe it would help.

Sven blinked again, looking groggy and a bit disoriented as he stared at each of us in turn. When his eyes finally settled on me, he gave an attempted smile. It turned into an ill-repressed yawn.

"Uh. Yes. Sorry...how long was I..." He trailed off as his eyes found a clock on the wall. Right. We had clocks. The ability to actually tell time. I wasn't used to that.

It was just barely past ten in the morning.

"Oh."

Alenor hesitantly touched his arm. "You were very tired, Sven," she whispered. "I wished I could have let you sleep longer."

80

"Yes, sorry. But we have work to do. As you said. No time to spare," Estasia broke in as she crossed her arms, her tone turning to that detached 'it's business' thing she always moved to when she was pretending not to be engaged in the emotion of a moment. Ha. I was catching onto this.

Sven gave a quick stretch and got unsteadily to his feet, Alenor standing with him and helping him balance. I heard her whisper something and he gave some semblance of a reassuring smile as he put a hand on her shoulder. I couldn't tell how much of it was to get his bearings, and how much of it was to comfort her.

"So, where are we going?" Sven turned to Estasia.

"Into the sewers. To see a...colleague."

Funny how she kept changing Temorn's title. Colleague, friend, not friend. I was so confused. And there she was, rubbing the hilt of her knife again...well, until she caught me looking, anyway.

Estasia set her shoulders and added, "They apparently have information about some smuggling thing he has going with Lord Atlys?"

"Lord Atlys?" Alenor sounded a bit aghast. "I was sure he'd been bowing to Skayla."

I latched onto the name Illan and Estasia had mentioned in the sewer meeting. "Who?"

Sven actually looked equally as confused, though I guessed for different reasons.

"He is one of the very few nobles—" Alenor broke off a moment and looked pointedly at Estasia, avoiding Sven. She looked as if she was going to continue with some broader explanation, but Sven was quicker.

He waved an idle hand but turned away from everyone, "That I didn't kill in cold blood." He straightened his coat, then turned around, eyes hiding behind a look of false resolve.

"That Skayla killed," Alenor's reply was barely audible.

Sven said nothing.

I winced. I wanted to help. But there didn't seem to be anything to say. I could tell the other two appeared to have the same dilemma.

"Just. Be safe. Please." Alenor again reached and took Sven's arm, and I noticed the flinch even as I noticed how Alenor didn't retract her hand.

"Don't worry about me, Mum." Sven gave his mother a wink, but then more gently reached for her hand and kissed it. "I'll be fine."

None of us were convinced.

But all the same, Sven turned to me, ruffled my hair, and said, "Don't get too comfortable here, ah? I'm still planning on continuing our training sessions later."

My wings perked at this and I smiled, a bit of my worry dripping away. "Oh, alright," I replied.

"But first you're eating some breakfast." Alenor interrupted the moment as she turned that motherly glare on her son.

"Oh. Right." Sven looked pained, looking to Estasia with a hapless shrug while Alenor disappeared from the room to return with some bread and cheese from the other room.

The reluctance was evident in Sven's sluggard reception of the food, but with Estasia's foot tapping impatiently, it was only a few minutes more before Sven had downed his breakfast and we watched the pair disappear into Alenor's tunnel entrance. The door clicked shut, and I was left behind with Alenor.

"Well…" Alenor's voice held the weary worry I felt. Funny how it was only the morning, and yet I already felt as if a whole day had passed. "I suppose that means we have the house to ourselves, for the rest of the day."

Yeah. All day. I swallowed hard.

"Well, I think this is the perfect opportunity for both a tour, and perhaps some questions on both sides getting answered in a more…leisurely fashion." Alenor smiled and motioned with her head to walk down the hall with her. "Come. We'll start in my astronomy room."

I supposed this would be a sufficient consolation prize. If nothing else, Alenor could use company. I didn't have to imagine being isolated for a decade but *completely* alone? Not even one person to talk to? No wonder her house looked like it did on the inside. All the gadgets and clocks, the turning gears that crawled up some of the walls, the train that wove through the house…creating them was probably the only thing that had kept her sane. At least, I guessed. I didn't know if even that would have been enough to keep me from going crazy.

I matched Alenor's pace as we made our way down into the room that had the giant orrery swinging about it, the glass ceiling above shining with sunlight.

"So…does this also map out the other worlds?" I asked as I watched the planets turn and spin, the groaning of gears and swivels filling the air pleasantly.

"I have done my best to map out what I can tell. Henry and I had tried to figure it out, but our understanding was incomplete. He used his knowledge of his world—Kryso—but we still weren't able to map or understand everything." Alenor walked about the room, ducking expertly between the precariously swinging planets on their charted paths. "Some of the paths of the planets and the placements of the stars could be wrong, but I've adjusted it through the years."

"Right." I tried to make sense of all this. "You said Henry came from...uh...Kryso?" I tried to follow her, but gave up and instead flew up above the orrery and watched her from above, my head a yard or so from hitting the glass ceiling. He'd come from a whole different world? Even before the Drogans?

"Yes." Alenor nodded as she made her way around and to a balcony where a large, pipe-like extension was, reaching all the way to and through the ceiling via an opened hatch. "Come. Have a look," she beckoned.

I flew over, landing in the relative safety of the corner and trying to figure out exactly what this newest contraption was. It had a small lens at the end of it. Alenor bent down and...looked into it?

"Aha. There. Good," she murmured to herself, before facing me again. "Have you ever used a telescope before?"

I blinked. "A what?"

The brief flash of amusement turned sour. "I suppose there are a lot of things that aren't really in the world anymore."

For a moment, she looked just like Sven...ageless and burdened with knowledge and responsibility. I didn't want her to stay there.

"So, how does it work?" I asked, stubbornly determined to drag Alenor back.

"You put your eye to the peephole, and then you will be able to see beyond Baeno and into the great mystery of space." Alenor's lively smile returned as she stepped aside so I could try. "I have adjusted it so that you can see Kryso."

Slowly, I put my eye to the lens, blinking a couple times to get used to the pressure against the corners of my eye.

"Oooh," I whispered as I saw, amid the deep blue sky, a large sphere, clouds swirling around the surface. "So that's...that's like the orrery," I forced myself to back up and point over to her mechanism, "This is how people charted the stars? I always wondered." My smile was broad. This was cool.

I looked back. "What are those...flashing lights? Are they creatures or something?"

Alenor laughed. It was a nice laugh. "Oh, no. Those are flashes of lightning."

"Woah. That looks much cooler from the outside."

"I hear they harness it into an energy form called electricity. So Henry told me."

"Elect-what?" I asked as I tried to make sense of the blurry lights I saw. I could stare at this all day. I...I was looking at another *world!*

Another laugh. "It's a light that does not require fuel, in a way. Henry said it is much like lightning but harnessed. And, actually...we never had lightning before the Drogans arrived."

Huh. I forced myself to look away, curiosity piqued to a new level. "So he just...came here from Kryso? A hundred years ago? Do people from Kryso live longer?"

"No. We both think we lived long because of our charge to care for The Living Stone." Her voice again grew solemn, as did her face. "We had lots of adventures, he and I. He'd come through because of some accident caused on his world. He said Kryso had been tearing apart, and he'd been trying to fix it. Something had happened and he was seriously injured when he came through. Several came through with him...not all made it. I cared for him. The one that acted as our world's guardian before my children—Kassander Knyte. He said he would find someone to bring Henry home. But he left and...and never came back. We never found out what happened. So, Henry and I spent years trying to figure out how to open the portals and get Henry home. But then, when it became clear we wouldn't be able to...Henry decided to stay." The smile was that of some blissful memory. "He was always so kind. And just...good." A sigh, and her eyes dimmed. "Sven is a lot like him." She shuddered; then, with a cough, she said, "Would you like to see some more?"

I gave a smile, determined to try and keep the mood from completely souring. "Sure." Alenor hadn't just been by herself. She'd been...she'd been *alone*. She'd thought the only one left in her family was the daughter trying to take over the world. And even now, all she had was Sven. She needed him just as much as he needed her.

We continued to explore, taking out charts of stars so detailed I was agape—I'd seen a couple in the library at Valdon, but nothing this extensive—and she said, come evening, she would try and show me Eatris—the planet where the Drogans came from.

At last, I dared ask, "So...did you do all of this while you were hidden?"

Alenor had been rolling up the last of the charts, and she hesitated a moment before shaking her head. "No. Many of these charts were made before. Some very old from Henry and my own studies. Some with Skayla and Sven. Sven loved the stars. He and Skayla used to lie out at night all the time and pick out constellations."

Skayla. It was weird hearing her name paired with something so...normal. So...nice. Paired with Sven.

"Was she very different back then?" I didn't know what possessed me to ask.

The sadness had returned to Alenor's features; the weighed-down shoulders, the fallen gaze—and yet there was still love there, too. The smile was sad but still a smile. And she fidgeted with the ends of the rolled-up star chart as if it linked her to a happier time.

"Yes." The word was a breath. "She was always so considerate. So anxious.... They weren't ready." I watched as she set her jaw. "They were so young. Henry and I wanted them to have a few more years before they went into the role, but...."

When she didn't finish, I asked, "But what?"

She sighed. "But it slipped out. And then before I knew it, they were celebrities.... No one even knew they were our children." Alenor paused, swallowing hard. "And soon enough, it was almost like they weren't. Moira never visited. She'd started arguing...and then Skayla. Skayla would come with Sven for a while. But then she, too, started distancing herself."

The story hurt to listen to, and yet...yet I got the feeling Alenor needed to talk to someone, to get this burning lonely pain out, somehow.

With a weary sigh, Alenor leaned against the balcony railing, looking up at the ceiling as if to contain her sorrow. "Sven was worried about Skayla for a while. Not about what she would do, though. Just...she always put so much pressure on herself." She again looked at me, right in the eyes. It was a lot of emotion to withstand. "People were always shouting, she would say. She could tell what a person was thinking, just by how they stood. With the ability to understand how people worked came the pressure to make them all understand." She sighed. "Sven would always be the one to get her away—to get both of his sisters to unwind." The frown turned into a reminiscent smile. "He was always so alive. It was infectious. He'd make you laugh...he did this thing where he'd use his illusions to impersonate others and get into all sorts of trouble. But then when it came down to it, he was often more grown up than his older siblings." The frown returned. "Funny, how he could seem wiser than the ones that had the power of time and mind."

The solemness of all she had said settled heavily around the room, and even my wings seemed to sink under the weight of it all as I digested her words. It was so hard to picture the Sven I saw now as the one that would laugh and get into trouble and help people cut loose. Even to coax a single smile out of him seemed impossible at times, let alone get *him* to crack a joke. I was angry. Angry that Skayla had stolen it all from him—that she'd forced him to do so many horrible things. That she'd not had the guts to kill their friends herself, and instead made him do it.

In that moment, it all seemed to click into place, and whether it was Alenor's words or perhaps the fact I was really looking at it for the first time, I realized what Skayla really had set out to do. She'd tried to destroy him so that even if he ever escaped her, he would be useless. A prisoner to his actions and mind. No friends left in the world, only enemies. Only memories of how he'd made them.

Skayla couldn't win. I wouldn't let her.

Sven:

"So, uh, how are you feeling?" Estasia asked quietly as we made our way down my mother's tunnel to the sewers.

"I'm fine," I replied. I felt less like I would fall over, if nothing else. Come to think of it...sleep had been much more restful last night.

Not so many vivid nightmares.

I shuddered. A pity they came back when I was awake.

"How did you, uh, sleep?" The questions were uncharacteristically awkward. What was I missing?

"I slept pretty well, actually. Why?" I allowed myself to show a little confusion as I turned to give her a look. I felt the nightmares were unfortunately not something I hid well, so it couldn't be that she was just catching up on that, so, what was it?

Estasia raised both arms in defense. "Hey, I just wanted to know how that chameleon tea worked, is all. Don't blame me, it was your mother."

I stopped in my tracks and blinked. "The...what?" Chameleon tea? I was so confused.

Shrugging and stopping with me, she said, "The tea that makes you fall asleep a bit more easily. Apparently, your mother gave it to you. She tried to convince me she didn't drug you."

It finally dawned on me what she was talking about, and with the realization came an unsolicited and undignified noise as I replied, "Did you just call chamomile tea...*chameleon* tea?"

"Did *you* just snort?" Estasia looked more amused than I did, though a good half of it seemed to be hiding the embarrassment of her misspeaking.

I managed a smile briefly before the moment faded, shaking my head as I continued down the tunnel. "Chameleon tea...."

"Shut up." She shoved me, and it took a great amount of effort to not instinctively grab and twist her wrists in defense. The thought was so instantaneous that I was almost afraid I actually *had* done it at first. The GhostMaker was ever present, it seemed.

That sufficiently killed the moment.

"So..." Estasia obliviously broke the silence only when we, at last, reached the end of the tunnel and had arrived at the sewer entrance. "Just. Trust me, and look nice and threatening. You're pretty good at that."

Not really what I wanted to hear right now.

"Exactly like that. Hold that stare and Temorn won't dare pull anything." Estasia chuckled before turning to the door. "Illan had better be right about this..." was the last thing she said before she opened the door and led the way out into the darkness.

The sewers were an extensive system—one my parents had overseen the construction of long ago. In fact, I vaguely recalled Mum once having mentioned the plans to refurbish these bigger main tunnels and create the first-ever underground train system...long ago.

I shuddered.

We moved easily through the dark as my ring both illuminated our path and shielded our presence, alone but for the rats and murky water. At least, at first. As we continued on, I caught sight of a boy running through in the dark, the splashes of his feet echoing about the cylindrical walls. A thief, most likely a lookout for his gang, Estasia had explained. She said she'd been a runner to when she was younger. And then there was a patrol of soldiers, making a sweep through the sewers to apparently check for any criminals who might be hiding down here— Estasia had explained that, too, was normal. But we remained seamlessly undetected, my concentration much more intact today. I had forgotten what a decent night's rest could do.

The more we moved through the tunnels, the more I became acutely aware that I was still feeling the aftereffects of my stay in the Kovian Fortress. It seemed that actual sleep not only had me begging for more, but it made me realize just how stiff I was. It felt like years ago that we'd met Estasia and she'd saved our sorry lives, and yet thinking about it...it hadn't been very long ago at all, had it? A few weeks? I hadn't really been paying attention since leaving Hytat.

"Okay. We're almost here," Estasia said as she pointed up ahead to yet another little child, this one crouching in the shadows of a corner and keeping watch on the sewers. Of course, they didn't see us.

My brow furrowed. "How did we not see them when we entered the city?"

"We weren't in Temorn's territory before. He was always in the southern part. More corners and storage rooms to hide in, and the patrols don't care to come down here," Estasia said with a tight jaw. Her movements had grown more and more rigid as we'd continued on.

I decided it was best not to ask.

Shadows formed from the dark as the light of lanterns pierced the gloom, showing the figures of people with them. Never more than two at a time, and never off-guard as they lurked in the shadows. But they were there, whispering, playing cards or jacks, or sitting watch. My ring kept us from their eyes, but with all the lantern light, it was trickier to hide our shadows.

At last, we arrived at a side tunnel that was guarded by two gruff-looking thugs.

Estasia beckoned me back around a tunnel corner and whispered, "Alright. Drop the illusion so they can see us."

"As you wish." I put up a hand and snapped my fingers—just for her benefit and dramatic effect.

With that, we rounded the corner and allowed ourselves to come face-to-face with the two men guarding the side tunnel.

"Oh, don't bother," Estasia growled as one of the thugs reached for a battered blade. "We are here to talk to Temorn. Let us through—or else."

I clenched my jaw tight as I realized that was a cue for me to look threatening. Hiding my reluctance, I glared at the man that had reached for the blade.

He stopped stiff, eyes locked as the color drained from his face.

I raised an eyebrow.

The man stepped aside. "He's in there. He'll be happy to know you're alive, Esa."

So, they recognized her? I kept my confusion to myself, allowing Estasia to brush past both me and the two brutes.

"Oh, I'm sure he'll be thrilled, Frydrik," I heard Estasia whisper.

After opening the door, we walked through into the surprisingly well-lit and large space, the brick walls reflecting the light of lanterns that hung from pegs that had been jammed in between the cracks. There were cots along the walls, a few chairs or makeshift stools, and a blanket in the back that hung from what looked like a clothesline. It appeared to act as a makeshift wall. The room itself was not exactly abandoned, with a few questionable characters lounging about the cots or standing and talking. I even noted a few dirty, wary-eyed children sitting in a corner or watching everyone else in the room.

Everyone stilled as Estasia called out, "Alright, where's that slimy two-faced sewer rat?"

Well, that was one way to get their attention…. At this point, I acknowledged that I was here simply for backup. This was very out of my depth. And yet, I couldn't help but find my gaze wandering to the children, huddling or trying to appear as if they weren't terrified of our sudden appearance.

They looked so alone. I wanted to help—wanted to do anything. It hurt to just stand here and watch.

"Esa! Why, you backhanded swindler, you. I was sure you'd bit the dust for good!" A tall, dark-haired man from the back walked forward and broke into a wide grin—accented with a few half-rotted teeth with gold caps. His equally dark eyes glimmered dangerously in the lantern light. Like Estasia, he was a bit paler than most other Patelaynians—but that, I guessed, was from the extensive time indoors and below ground.

"Temorn." Estasia's tone was as cold and unfriendly as Temorn's was warm and…slimy.

The man's smile faded, replaced by something akin to hurt. "You can call me Morn, you know."

"And you can call me Estasia. Now I'm here on business, and as lovely as it is to see your backstabbing little face, I don't really want to stick around to stare at it any longer than I have to."

I let her take the lead, watching the few unsavory looking characters that had now formed something of a semi-circle around us. A few of them had weapons, one strongly built woman idly swinging a baton with a grim look in my direction. I stared back until she looked uncomfortable enough.

"Ouch. That hurts, in here." Temorn's smooth, sardonic reply did little to break the growing tension. "Not exactly the best way to get on my good side, Esa."

"*Tasia*. Es*tasia*, Temorn. And I trust you still have enough guilt to tame the tigers." Her confidence never wavered. Perhaps I would have liked to know a little more about what was going on and what we'd walked into...but then again, she'd always pulled through before. Which was more than my own track record.

Yeah. I wouldn't be taking the lead.

"Fine. Estasia. What do you and your boyfriend want?"

I don't know who gagged first: me or Estasia. I pulled my gaze to Temorn and didn't bother hiding how unimpressed I was.

Esastia's laugh was dry. "Ew, that's disgusting—no offense," the last bit was aimed at me, apparently.

"None taken." My voice echoed eerily about the room. Everyone was staring at me again.

You stink. Maeko's words rang in my head. Yeah. I reeked of death. Even the over-confident Temorn appeared to have caught a whiff of it.

"Oh. Sorry, how rude. I haven't introduced my friend." You could *hear* Estasia's smile, it was so sly, "Temorn meet The GhostMaker."

Dead silence.

"*What?*" Temorn at last whispered. He was still staring at me. I stared back, the effort embarrassingly tremendous as I fought to keep from turning my gaze to the ground.

"He was in a MindHold. He's a friend—trust me, I'm less likely to backstab than you are, after all," Estasia hissed back without missing a beat.

When Temorn gave no further reply other than staring back at Estasia, she continued, "Illan sent us your way. Said you were an...ally." She choked out the word like it was venom, and the way Temorn's smile returned at the word didn't seem to help Estasia's mood. "And that you could put us in connection with some more possible allies? Someone a little more useful than you, I hope."

His smile went brittle. "Yes, well, if you want help, you'll have to be a little more genial. I gave you a break before, but if you keep acting like this, I might not feel so guilty anymore."

"Don't push your luck, either, Temorn. My friend here could get the answers out of you one way or the other."

I forced myself not to wince. I could see her ever-so-slight apologetic side glance. She had to put on a show, I understood. Skayla had done it all the time.

No one saw the GhostMaker and lived. That had been my reputation, and seeing everyone I seemed to come in contact ended up getting killed either by me or because of me…I lived up to the reputation.

"Now, tell me, where can we find help?"

"What do you have to offer in return, eh?" Temorn gave a tilt of his head, now actively avoiding me as he stared into Estasia.

"Besides Skayla's prize assassin on your side? Resources. Resources Illan isn't at liberty to disclose and I certainly won't until you prove yourself. I don't know why you've gone all patriotic, but apparently, we're on the same side, again. So helping me is helping you." Her eyes narrowed. "You've always been good at that," she growled.

The tension was palpable, and I, again, found myself looking around to the others that had encircled us. Getting out of here would not be a problem, of course. But if this man proved to be something other than an ally, then he would now know of our presence here in Alkemar. I really, *really* hoped Estasia knew what she was doing.

"Fine." Temorn's reply pierced the air like an arrow to the chest. It sounded as if the one word had caused him about the right amount of pain, at least. "Meet me tomorrow morning at about seven o'clock. I'll bring you to them, and you can be part of the super secret little group." The hand movements added to the mocking. Now *guilt* was definitely something I could recognize, even if clearly this man dealt with it worse than I did. The more uncomfortable Estasia was making him, the more arrogant he was acting. The exasperation that seemed to come from being unable to make amends. The way his eyes had locked on the knife hanging from Estasia's belt.

"Great. Where are we meeting?" Estasia asked, as if oblivious to the frustration in Temorn's tone and gestures.

"Tunnel twelve, near the rear culvert," Temorn replied, jaw set.

Estasia nodded, letting a moment pass before looking around us and asking, "So, can we go now? Or are you really going to try to stop us from leaving?"

Temorn waved a hand, and the group that had encircled us backed off, allowing a clear cut to the exit.

Estasia gave Temorn one more glare before turning to me. "Shall we?" she asked. I gave a slow nod, following her out the door.

"Oh, and Estasia?" Temorn didn't call out until we were right about to pass through the exit. Estasia didn't stop, and yet still there was just enough time to hear the rest of what he had to say. "Thought you'd like to know Atarah's still around. Not that he'd want to see *you*."

CHAPTER VII: Reality Hurts

<u>Estasia:</u>

I didn't let anyone see the way the last statement had robbed me of my confidence, even as I struggled to clutch the dagger at my belt. Instead, I walked straight out of that dark and foul hole of a place, barely registering that Sven followed behind as I desperately fought to keep hold of my composure. And yet I could feel his eyes burning into the back of my head as they whispered a thousand questions. Or maybe it was just me. Maybe I was imagining it, and it was just me trying to justify keeping the secrets.

But no matter how hard I tried, I couldn't get Temorn's words out of my head. Atarah. Eugene Atarah. He was alive. As we passed back through the sewers—Sven having once more hidden us from any unwanted eyes—I couldn't help but wonder what that meant. We'd hardly spoken since...since Eugene. Since I'd left. Since Temorn had—

"So, I guess we're waiting until tomorrow." I broke the silence in an attempt to stop my own devolving thoughts. It was frustrating how this was all coming up now, even though I'd known coming back to Alkemar would inevitably make it all resurface. I just hadn't expected that I'd have to get so up close and personal with the memories I'd long stuffed away, locked in their neat little box in the corner of my mind. But now it felt like pouring lemon juice on a long-infected wound.

Or maybe it was just Temorn's unbearable smile. Funny how his teeth seemed to decay as much as he had.

"I suppose so," Sven murmured, eyeing me carefully as I flinched. I'd forgotten I'd said anything. With that realization, I forced the thoughts away; I could *not* afford to be distracted. I was the one who had to keep a cool head, and I didn't trust anyone else—definitely not Sven's broken mind, right now.

"Stop looking at me like that." I winced at the edge to my tone. That was the last thing Sven needed, right now. But he gave no reaction, only keeping eye contact with me a while longer before focusing his gaze straight ahead. Funny how his silence seemed to have just as many variables as many people's tone of speech had. It was all in how he carried himself, and right now he was irritating me.

"Shut up," I grumbled, wishing I had more self-control.

Sven didn't give any reply. No reaction. A stone, as always.

I let out a pent-up breath. I didn't want to talk about it. I needed to focus. "Sorry," I muttered, in a way that sounded...less than sorry.

"No need to apologize."

I took another deep breath and reoriented myself, hating how much Temorn still knocked me off-balance. I couldn't stand the carefree way with which he pretended he hadn't upturned my life. The way he pretended he hadn't up and got rid of Eugene....

But it had been so long ago. I'd long come to terms with the likelihood of Eugene being gone forever—dead, even—and yet somehow, knowing he was still around was not exactly comforting. If he wasn't dead, that really left only one option.

He was helping Skayla.

No noble had survived otherwise.

Again, I didn't want to think about it, right now. So, with one more deep breath, I shoved it from my mind and settled on the matters at hand. We didn't have much margin for error in our movements.

I used the remainder of our return journey to think through the tunnel system and make sure I would be able to get us where we needed to go tomorrow in order to find Temorn, and by the time we'd arrived back in Alenor's house, I had made a sufficient mental map.

"Oh, good, you're back—and in one piece," Alenor breathed as she opened up the door and allowed us in, her eyes lingering with a quiet fretfulness on Sven as we entered.

As we filtered back into the relative safety of Alenor's home, Baey asked, "How did it go?"

Sven jumped as the door closed and sealed behind us.

We all pretended we hadn't seen anything.

"We have to meet Temorn tomorrow morning." I kept my tone matter-of-fact as we stood awkwardly in the hall. "He says there's some sort of secret group. I'm not sure what he means, but whatever it is, I am guessing they will help us. Maybe give us more resources."

"I see." Alenor tapped her leg in thought. "Well, at least you have a bit more time to catch up and rest. I'm guessing, after tomorrow morning, things are going to pick up speed one way or another."

Yeah. Either we were about to get help, or we were about to get in way over our heads. I had a healthy dose of cynicism for both outcomes.

"Actually, I was going to take Baey back into Mum's tunnel to practice." Sven's voice could be a whisper and still quiet a crowd.

I couldn't help but smirk at the way Baey perked up at the notion. Besides, I agreed with Sven; she needed to be able to defend herself.

101

She wasn't going to sit here forever, and the secure tunnel Alenor had before the sewers was a better place than the house to work on her swordplay.

"Mum, do you have a spare blade lying around that she could use?"

Alenor's eyes rarely left her son, and now was no exception. "Yes. I can go fetch it. But do you need something to eat first? And you should really bathe; you both smell disgusting…."

"Yes to both, please," I answered for both of us and glared at Sven. When he stifled a sigh, I added, "You can go wash up first—and you can bring the food down with you if you're in such a rush to get going."

Sven did not argue. Sometimes, I wondered how much of his eating issue was not *wanting* to eat, and how much of it was simply not thinking to eat. Had Skayla controlled that sort of thing? Maybe he just wasn't used to the freedom of being able to eat when he was hungry or having the responsibility of remembering himself.

Regardless, Sven did not argue, and quickly disappeared to get cleaned up in the washroom. I was provided a towel by Alenor so I could at least walk through the house without making a mess, and so I went up to my room to get ready for my turn to wash. It was only a few minutes, thankfully, and as soon as I heard Sven's footsteps in the hall, I grabbed my things and headed right for the washroom.

I was still not used to cleaning up like this, but I had to admit it felt rather nice. All the same, it only seemed to me like it would make me weak—would my skin become delicate like some posh noble?

I shook the thought away as well as the water from my face, turning off the water and dressing quickly before returning downstairs.

By the time I returned, Alenor had fetched a sword for Baey that seemed pretty suited to her in size, and Baey shoved a plate with a sandwich in my face. Might I get three meals in one day? I would love to get used to this. And yet I was afraid to.

"Don't be too long. We need to be well-rested for tomorrow, and on our toes for whatever it brings," I said, looking more at Baey than at Sven. She would be a better judge of when it was time to stop...hopefully.

Sven—who was holding two small wrapped objects which I guessed were their lunch—gave a near imperceptible nod, and Baey smiled enthusiastically. Soon, they were both gone, leaving Alenor and me in the hall, alone.

"Do you have a map of the sewer system, by chance?" I asked as I took a bite of my sandwich, needing to keep my mind busy and off of Temorn, and off of the sudden desire to go out into the city and find Eugene myself. To see what kind of slimy noble he'd probably ended up as, after what he'd been through.

"Yes, actually. Come with me." Alenor beckoned me down the hall, and I found myself again handling the pommel of the knife Temorn had given me all that time ago. I thought of the painting still in my room, the one I really should have destroyed. Or left in the sewers, along with the knife. Attachments were much better left in the gutter, anyway. Friends never seemed to do anything but let you down or *get* let down. And yet here I was, letting my guard down to Baey and Sven after all those years.

Apparently, I was a slow learner.

Baey:

"You're *sure* I won't get skewered?" I asked, as Sven did a warm-up flourish with his blade. His pointy sword. The sword I would be trying to avoid…. I rather wished I hadn't eaten that sandwich. But at least I was getting used to being in the tunnel.

"Yes, darlin', don't worry. It's just like when we practiced back before Hytat." His eyes were as hollow as his tone when Hytat came up, and yet he kept talking as if he wasn't dwelling on what Skayla had given him back. "See? Watch—" He held his sword up and went to slam his hand into the point. But it didn't make contact, instead passing right through the blade as if it wasn't even there.

"Wait—" I let my confusion show. "But your sword is real. I don't…understand." That couldn't be an illusion, could it?

"Just trust me, Baey. I won't let you get hurt." His voice cracked a bit at this.

I pressed my lips together tightly, if only to avoid asking any more questions. Then, with a tense nod, I waited for the lesson to begin, taking a few deep breaths as I cleared my head and reminded myself the walls wouldn't close in around me.

Sven didn't say anything immediately, and the silence stretched awkwardly before he finally returned to the training session. "Remember the way I told you to stand?"

In reply, I took the stance, trying to keep in mind Syvil's explanation of how to hold my wings. I'd been practicing on the ship a bit, too, which was definitely harder with the thing flying through the air. Hopefully, that meant I'd be a bit more prepared.

I was at least tripping over my stupid wings less, if nothing else.

"Great. Much better. Now..." Sven took a step closer to me, giving his sword one more twirl and taking a stance. "You can put your sword away for now."

Swallowing my confusion, I slowly obeyed, tucking it into the sheath Alenor had provided.

"And now we are going to do the opposite of what we did before. I will act as offense and you as defense. You need to keep your balance and keep out of the path of my blade."

Wait, what? My wings stiffened nearly as much as the air in my lungs. "Uh. I don't know if this is such a great idea," I mumbled.

Sven smiled. He *smiled*. It was gentle, and yet I saw the little hint of mischief before it flitted away to sincerity. "Again, you will not be hurt in any way or form..." But then a hint of slyness arose in his tone. "...I mean. Perhaps your *pride* will take a blow, but nothing worse."

I gave a glare that perhaps would have looked more intimidating had I not been trying to hide a grin.

"You ready?"

It was no easy task forcing my fists to unclench. "Re—"

Yeah, no, apparently I wasn't ready, because I hadn't even gotten the word out before he came at me. I squeaked and froze, the blade slicing right through my head and chest. I'd still half expected to feel the metal, and breathed a sigh of relief even as my wings flicked in embarrassment.

"Sorry," I grumbled. "Guess I wasn't ready."

Sven's chuckle was so soft, and yet it resonated around the tunnel, urging me to relax my shoulders as he again turned away and walked back to where he'd started.

"Don't *plant* your feet. You need to have balance, but don't just become a tree. If your roots go too far down, you won't be able to move in time, as you saw. So. I ask again—" He swiveled around and twirled the blade. "Are you ready?"

I forced every muscle in my body to prepare, tucking my wings in close to me so that I would be able to better leap out of the way. I needed them centered. "Ready," I said, sincerely this time.

Sven again lunged forward.

It was all in an instant. He came at my center, and I used one powerful beating of my wings to throw me back and away, turning to the side so that I ended up to the right of him and a bit more out of range. Without losing his balance or even looking at me, he used his momentum to side kick me. I plummeted to the ground, landing on my wings and back and gasping for air.

His sword was at my throat before I could blink.

"Better. The more we do this, the more comfortable it will be. The goal is to think at least three moves ahead. Predict as much as you can, but don't assume." He withdrew his sword and extended his hand, helping me up and brushing off my one shoulder. "You'll get it, don't worry."

I huffed. "I certainly hope so…" came my less than gracious grumble. It had been five minutes, and already, I was feeling disheartened. Again. I knew it would take time. Really, I did. But it seemed like he didn't even have to try to get past me.

Sven raised an eyebrow and took up his place again. "You will. But it's like practicing anything. Can't be a natural overnight. Took me years."

I wanted to ask who'd taught him, but we went back at it again.

What I guessed was nearly half an hour later, I was panting, sore, and a little more encouraged. He was right. I was getting better. He still always won. I was still always dead by the end, but I lasted longer each time. I'd even been able to predict some of his moves the last couple rounds. It had at last clicked that what Estasia had been saying about body language and observing and all that really came in handy for fighting, too.

"So," I finally got the courage to ask as I sat down against the tunnel wall, "Who trained *you?*"

Sven sheathed his sword and sat down beside me. "I don't remember." The reply was hollow. "But I know I watched a lot of others. Took years and a lot of bad habits."

"So, you didn't have a teacher?" Something struck me as odd that he couldn't remember. Hadn't Skayla given him his memories back?

"I..." He looked perplexed for a moment. "...think I had several."

The answer was simple enough, but the shadow that quickly fell over his expression told me it was time to stop pushing. "So, uh, what's next?"

"Well, you seem to have caught your breath. Why don't we combine what you've learned and try with the sword, now, ah?" He got to his feet and slowly meandered over to get ready to fight again.

I didn't groan. Honestly, I was a bit excited to try and *actually* fight, now. I scrambled to my feet.

At last.

The next hour was...embarrassing. Embarrassing, and yet somehow rewarding. Now, I was determined. Watching how effortlessly Sven maneuvered around me made me wonder if I really could be that good one day. It made me *want* it, and even as I clumsily clung to the sword in my hand, I took note of every move Sven made.

One day, I would be like that.

"Alright," he said at last, putting his blade away. "That's enough for—"

I took the opportunity to lunge at him, abandoning my sword as I dove straight for his legs. He didn't even flinch, stepping to the side so that I found myself hurling face first into the brick floor, only to be caught by the shirt collar just before I did a full on faceplant.

"Uh. What are you doing?" Sven asked as he pulled me up. The thinly veiled amusement showed he knew *exactly* what I was doing.

"I was *practicing* my element of surprise." I gave a mock glare and folded my arms, flicking my wings out to add a bit of dramatic flair to my words.

"I suppose your face was about to be very surprised by the floor, yes...." The grin that slowly grew on his face was worth it.

I playfully punched him in the arm. "Oh, hush. I almost got you."

His eyebrows shot up. "Very mature." He ruffled my hair with his hand.

I smiled. He was what I'd imagined a big brother would have been like. All I knew is I'd give anything for him to stay this way—to see his eyes remain alive and smiling.

But it didn't last. The faraway look returned, and the humor in his expression faded as he walked over and picked up my sword from the ground, handing it to me hilt first. "Why don't you go back? I'll join soon."

My brow furrowed as I took my sword and sheathed it. "Aren't you coming?"

"I'll be along eventually. But...I have some practicing of my own to do."

He was rubbing his ring.

"Oh, are you practicing your illusions?" My wings pricked and I wondered if I maybe could stay and watch. "Maybe I could learn something by watching?" He'd seemed to hint that maybe I would be able to learn to use his ring more.

A shadow settled deep across his face. "No. You go on up. It's dangerous."

Cheeks flushing in sudden annoyance, I barely bit back an argument. Well, I just bit it back because I intended to stay and watch, anyway. I'd get to test just how good my wings were at hiding me.

"Fine." I regretted the edge to my tone, almost surprised I'd let the harsh reply slide out.

"Baey...it's not you. I just need to practice alone for a little while. This isn't something I can promise would be safe. I can't—I just need to be alone."

He couldn't what? Something whispered that he was afraid of hurting anyone more. How bad could illusions be? Regardless, I didn't want to feed into his fear, no matter how unlikely and confusing.

"Alright," I whispered at last, giving a weak smile before heading off up the tunnel, knowing I would just sneak back to watch. I didn't understand, I really didn't. But I knew I wouldn't let him be completely alone.

I walked a while in the dim light of the lanterns, and only when I was sure Sven wasn't paying attention anymore did I come up against the tunnel wall and crouch down low, wings hovering over me and blending into the darkness as I watched my friend.

Sven just stood there, staring down at the ring on his finger and looking like the weight of the world rested solely on his shoulders. I felt like I was intruding on something very private, and yet I didn't want to leave. He didn't know I was here, but I felt like if I left, it would leave him more alone.

He needed someone to have his back.

I felt something strange wash over me—a power that felt like the longing I always got from the watch but now a hundred-fold, and for a moment, my eyes teared up with the weight of it all. Then, everything was still; Sven, the sewers—even my breathing.

Nothing moved.

Sven seemed like a statue for a long while before he knelt down, his hand pressed to the ground. My eyes widened as he...uh...picked...up...the *floor*? It took me a moment to remind myself this was all an illusion, but it couldn't stop the wonder as he created a wall from the floor, only to bend and meld it into a long, elegant looking spear that looked...nothing like the floor. I blinked. Wow. His illusions were...really convincing. That being said, Hytat *had* been really weird.

Again, I thought of the whole sword phasing thing, and again something was missing. Was it really just an illusion?

My attention was drawn back to Sven as he dropped the spear, allowing it to meld back into the floor as if it had never left. His hands were over his ears, grasping desperately as if to block something out, and though he was facing away from me, I could hear him murmuring, "Stop".

Hesitantly, I made to get up. Was he alright? The anguish in his tone instantly triggered memories of Hytat. What was he seeing now?

"Stop!" Sven practically collapsed, kneeling on the ground as his plea echoed through the tunnel.

Yeah, I was going to go over there. I shot to my feet, worry flushing my cheeks and my wings as I got ready to run right for Sven to help.

What happened next was something beyond my comprehension. All I knew was that I blinked, and when my eyes opened again, we weren't in the tunnel. It was as if we'd teleported into a completely different space—one so bright I had to close my eyes again for a second to adjust.

A strange sound filled the air...music. It was music? I'd only ever heard the songs that those at Valdon would sing, but this was...this was a much more beautiful sound. Multiple voices, and not human. It was sweet, maybe a little metallic, and yet the most wonderful sound I'd ever heard. And then there were conversations echoing about the room...and clamor...and….

At last I opened my eyes again, and I found myself in a spacious room with a marble floor and pillars lining every wall. People were everywhere—dancing in the center of the room or laughing and talking with each other.

Woah. It really was as if we'd teleported. Sven must have created a large-scale illusion like he had in Hytat with the crowds. This was insane.

Slowly, I started walking forward, reminding myself that I couldn't actually bump into anyone. I needed to find Sven. Why had he made this? Was it some sort of memory?

"Oh, sorry, miss! I didn't see you there!" A man smiled at me as I...as...as I...*bumped into him?!* What. Was. Going. On? "So lovely to see an Esmer has joined us! Always a pleasure." The man tipped his head in respect.

W-wh-what?

"I...uh...excuse me. I need...I need to get through." I went to the side, passing the confused gentleman as I pushed on through the crowd. I felt suddenly claustrophobic. I could hardly manage to stay oriented with the way people kept trying to talk to me, engage with me, or get in my way. The noise was suddenly too much, the light of the chandeliers above overwhelming, and the people...the people....

They're real?! I was terrified. What was going on? I *had* to find Sven; I had to.

"Let me through!" The words were said with surprising weight, and it was almost magical the way the crowd parted, giving me a clear view to the dance floor and—

Sven.

He was dancing with someone. He looked...so different. He was standing straight, decked in a beautiful white collared dress jacket, a smile on his face as he expertly swept his partner through the dance. A confused but whimsical smile. The dark circles were still there, and the hair was still in need of a cut, but the weight in his shoulders was gone, and the haunted look in his eyes with it. But his eyes were empty in a different way...a very, very *scary* way.

"Sven, come on, loosen up! Am I always going to have to pick you up from the dirt?" It was the woman he was dancing with, her bright personality matching the sparkling blue dress she wore.

Sven rolled his eyes, the grin lopsided and almost youthful. "Don't let it go to your head, Sera."

Sera...Ser...Sera*fina*? I was now fully glued to the floor, completely uprooted and disoriented, and yet riveted at the same time. Were we really back in time? But that was Moira's Gift? I touched the broken watch around my neck and felt nothing. Nothing at all.

I *had* to get to Sven. With a sudden burst of resolve I forced myself to move, running through the dancers and easily getting to Sven and Serafina.

"Sven! What's going on? I don't—I don't understand. Where are we?" I grabbed his arm and wrenched him from the woman's grasp without thinking.

She isn't real. Breathe. She isn't real. Or was she? What was real anymore?

Sven's expression was horrifyingly confused, frantically looking at me as Serafina said, "Who in Baeno is this, Sven? Is everything alright, sweetheart?" The last bit was pointed at me.

Sven's stare had now settled completely on me as he asked, "Who...are you? I'm sorry, I'm confused? What do you mean 'what's going on'?" Sven...he...he really didn't.... Panic again rose up in my throat.

"Sven, it's me, Baey! Please, I don't know what you did but this isn't right. Please. I don't know how to get out!" I grabbed both shoulders and shook him, prompting Serafina to take a hold of me.

"Woah, there, darling. Calm down!" Serafina called. She wasn't real, she wasn't real, *she wasn't real*.

"Sven! *Please!* Look, see, here's Moira's watch!" I tugged at the thing around my neck so he could see, using my free hand to grab at the hand with the ring on it. He needed to feel something. He had to. Everything in here...everything was numb. "Sven!" I screamed.

Something flooded into his eyes, and it all seemed to click as the anguish seeped back.

Everything went dark.

We were back in the tunnel, the lanterns flickering as if nothing had happened, the gloom and shadow restored to all its grim glory. Sven dropped to the floor, breathing hard and choking back emotion as he ran his hands through his hair, distress rippling through his body. "I'm sorry. I'm sorry, Baey. I'm sorry," he whispered, voice breaking at the seams like the rest of him.

"I-I don't understand. Are you alright? What happened?" I wanted to hug him, or do something. I wanted to understand what I'd just seen.

"I'm sorry," he gasped again.

Chapter VIII: The Ghosts I've Made

<u>Sven:</u>

I listened as Baey's footsteps faded into the darkness, even as I felt myself suddenly swallowed up in the gloom. Alone.

The ring on my finger pulsed and prodded, and I wanted to do anything but work with it. Anything but drag up any more of the connection.

But it was time to get to work.

The first thing I did was create a safe space to work. It was something I hadn't done in a long while, and yet I knew if I was really going to experiment with reality, I needed to set aside boundaries.

In case something went wrong.

So I focused, the energy escaping me and rippling through the brick walls and down the way until I knew I had set aside a decent amount of space. To anyone watching, nothing would have appeared to have changed. But anything I did here would not affect the outside world.

Breathe. Stay focused. I hoped repeating it enough would eventually drown out the screaming in my head; the voices that weren't mine. I was alone in the dark with just me and my thoughts, and I didn't like it.

Breathe.

Slowly, I knelt down, hand touching the floor of the tunnel as I reached deep into it. I felt the brick, my touch extending far beyond my hand as I felt the whole floor beneath me. It helped make the illusion reality when I could ground myself to something—like a literal anchor, not unlike the mental one I'd used to keep out of Skayla's power.

Except that one hadn't really worked as well as I'd thought it would. Doubt already started to creep in and I felt my focus flicker, hand shaking even as I stared at the ground.

Focus.

Trying to shut out the whispers of doubt in my head, I grabbed hold of the floor and willed it to fold to my will, the brick crumbling into my grasp as if it were nothing but a fold of silk. It rippled, shimmered, and obeyed, allowing me to pull it up.

My grip tightened around the wall before me and it again rippled and shimmered, slimming down and hardening into a long, deadly looking spear.

Why a weapon? Why was my *first* instinct a weapon?

The screams surfaced again, and I was suddenly staring at my own reflection in the steel. A reflection with violet eyes and a hideous metal mask that made me look more a monster than a man.

My chest tightened. "Stop," I whispered hoarsely, shutting my eyes and yet only replacing the image of the reflection with the all-too-real memories Skayla had given me. Of Thackery screaming. Of so many others.

"Stop!" I didn't know who I was yelling at—myself or the memories— but I barely even registered dropping the spear or falling to the ground. I put my hands to my ears, squeezing my eyes shut as if the tumult tearing about in my stupid brain was actually coming from around me and not inside. As if I could stop from hearing all the pain I'd caused.

Silence. At last. Blissful, beautiful silence.

And then....

"Sven? What in the world are you doing on the ground?" The voice penetrated through my covered ears, and I froze, not recognizing the voice. "Did you trip or something? You look like a lost puppy." Slowly, I opened my eyes, unable to comprehend what I was looking at. Where was I?

"Come on, you promised me this dance, didn't you?" The woman extended her hand, the smile infectious.

That smile....

Where was I, again? Everything seemed a haze, but I couldn't tear my eyes away from the woman in front of me.

"I don't...." I took her hand and let her haul me up from where we were in the middle of the lively ballroom. A song was being played by a string quartet, somewhere.

"You promised Skayla the next dance, so I don't want to miss mine. Come on!" Before I knew it, Serafina had pulled me into the dance.

That's right. Serafina. What was I doing here? And where was Skayla? Hopefully not hiding in a corner, again. Probably why I'd told her she'd have the next dance. She was always such a mess. If only she knew how to breathe.

But why couldn't I remember asking her to dance? Why was everything so fuzzy?

"Are you alright, Sven?" Serafina again pulled me back to reality.

Reality? But why did it not feel...real?

"I...yes...I suppose...I'm tired. A lot going on." Was there, though? We were enjoying peace, weren't we? Nothing was wrong. Everything was perfect...no disruptions. No nightmares. Why did nightmares come to mind?

"Sven, come on, loosen up!" Serafina said with a laugh. "Am I always going to have to pick you up from the dirt?"

Almost on cue, I *did* relax. I was home. Everyone was safe. This was...nice. I rolled my eyes, grinning. "Don't let it go to your head, Sera." Why did the grin feel unnatural, though?

There was a sudden commotion from beside us, and I turned just as someone grabbed my arm.

"Sven! What's going on? I don't—I don't understand.... Where are we?" It was a young Esmer, brilliant colors washing over her wings in seeming panic.

Serafina and I stopped dancing, even as everyone else seemed to move on without a care.

"Who in Baeno is this, Sven? Is everything alright, sweetheart?" Sera asked.

I...I didn't know. I knew a lot of Esmers, but who was this girl? Why was she so panicked? Nothing was the matter.

"Who...are you? I'm sorry, I'm confused? What do you mean, 'what's going on'?" Was someone hurt? No. No one could be hurt. It was safe here.

"Sven, it's me, Baey! Please, I don't know what you did, but this isn't right. Please. I don't know how to get out!" The girl grabbed both my shoulders and shook me.

Serafina stepped in to stop the girl as I just blinked, in a daze.

"Woah, there, darling. Calm down!" Serafina's voice dripped with concern.

"Sven! *Please!* Look, see, here's Moira's watch!" The girl tugged at something around her neck, and I suddenly recognized it: Moira's watch. How did she have Moira's watch?! Was Moira alright?

Before I could register what to ask next, the girl used her free hand to grab mine, making contact with the ring around my finger.

"Sven!" the girl screamed, desperate.

The silence in my mind vanished, and with it the realization of what was going on.

You fool!

And yet, even as I shattered the images around us, I begged for them to stay. I didn't want to be in the dark again. I didn't want to be alone. I didn't want to know *why* I was alone.

Everything went dark.

I slumped to the floor, whole body shaking as I tried to ignore the drowning sensation of being stuck here—in reality. Here, where I knew *exactly* what I had become.

"I'm sorry. I'm sorry, Baey. I'm sorry," I stammered between choked breaths. What had I done? Even without Skayla's stupid voice in my head, I was too dangerous to those I loved.

"I—I don't understand. Are you alright? What happened?" She sounded so scared.

And yet, all I could find to say was another, "I'm sorry." I could only be glad I'd thought to put the barrier up before I'd started. Baey must never have fully left. She must have stayed and been in it when I'd lost control.... Oh, and was I ever glad she had.

"So...so sorry." I wished maybe saying the word over and over would eventually mean something to someone, but words couldn't help what I'd done.

"It's okay. You're alright, I'm alright...I just...Sven, please look up. I need you to look at me, please? I need to know you *are* okay." Baey seemed to barely be keeping control of her own panic.

I took a shaky breath. *Get a hold of yourself, Sven.* I forced myself to look up at her, wincing at the fear in her eyes. "I told you I needed to be alone," I whispered.

"Yeah, sorry."

"No...I...I'm glad you ignored me," I said with a shudder. If she *hadn't*....

We sat in silence a moment longer. I took a shaky breath.

"So...what happened? Those...weren't illusions."

Closing my eyes, I tried to formulate how I wanted to put this. "They were...sort of." I sighed. "Baey...I haven't...I haven't told a soul about this." I opened my eyes and stared at her. "I'm sorry I keep having to make you keep secrets."

She bit her lip. "That's alright," she said weakly. "It makes me feel important."

I tried not to wince at her reply. "Well. This is...this is something I have never told anyone. And I don't want to tell anyone yet, in case I can't get it in a place where I can use it." My hands were shaking. Ack, why were they shaking? "So, when we received our relics, our powers grew. Moira was able to not only mess with time, but also step out of it and wind back up to two or three weeks. Skayla could..." I trailed off. "Well, you know what she can do, now." The nightmare she became. "And then everyone just assumed all that happened was my illusions had gotten more complicated." I gave a brief pause to make sure I still had her. I didn't want to talk. I didn't want to say any of this. It only made my failure that much worse...and yet. I had to tell her. It was clear I couldn't do this alone. I wasn't strong enough. "Well, I thought so, too. And they did. But there was something more that started to happen. I would always take to experimenting on my own—messing around with it. And then, one day, the illusion didn't go away."

The memories felt so far away, clouded by the ones closer to the surface and more painful. It was a struggle to remain focused and not be pulled down. "I couldn't just make illusions. I could...bend reality. Alter things. What you saw me do just now...I...I lost control. Got lost. It was a sort of artificial reality. It was real...but...not. It was based on things I'd seen, I think. My memory of...of...people..." Of Serafina. Before I'd killed her.

Don't go back. Stay here, Sven. I fought the urge to throw the ring far away, like I'd done in Hytat.

"W-why didn't you ever tell anyone?" I looked up to find Baey's eyes wide as she looked me over with some new perspective.

I was just disgusted with myself. "I...I don't really remember, I suppose. I just remember feeling uneasy about it. Unprepared for what Moira or Skayla might ask me to do." I looked away. "But it was some of the reason I gave you the ring that night. If Skayla had gotten ahold of my mind *with* the ring, she might have used me even more." But then, if I'd had the ring, I might have been strong enough to win against her. Or perhaps I shouldn't have gone at all. I should have taken Baey and gone.

Naïve, foolish me had decided to stay. To play the martyr and try and bring her back, even after all she'd done. I had paid dearly for my mistake.

And not just me.

"So, Skayla...she still doesn't know?"

I nodded slowly as I took a shaky breath. "Correct. But the problem is...I can't control it anymore." I waved limply to the dim tunnel around us. "You saw what happened. I didn't even try and do any of that. I can't keep an anchor. I don't—" I didn't have the discipline to stay alert. To stay calm. To stay focused. To keep from wishing this all away.

Baey stared at me a long time before she slowly sat down beside me. She sighed. "I mean. You can't do it alone, is all."

I suppressed a bitter choke.

"And I was able to bring you back. Maybe...maybe I can help?"

I stopped my self-pitying train of thought and pulled myself back, turning to stare at her. "That's...not a bad idea." I *had* to get this under control. If I could somehow master it—even a fraction of what I had been able to before Skayla had gotten me—then we would have a huge advantage against Skayla. "And...perhaps then you can learn, as well." I gave a weak attempt at a smile. It hurt, but I did it anyway.

Baey didn't light up like I thought she would. Only looked me over carefully. "Alright. That sounds like a good idea." There was a pause, and then, "But maybe...maybe for now we just go back to your mother's? Rest sounds nice."

I ruffled her hair, and then my creaking bones allowed me to stand. "Yes, ma'am." I gave a wink despite the heaviness I felt, extending a hand so that I could help her up.

She took it, but hardly used it as she jumped to her feet with her wings aiding her.

We slowly made our way back through the gaslit tunnel, the darkness feeling too close all of a sudden.

"Are you alright?" Baey asked at last as we neared the door that led back into Mum's house.

I stopped the instinctual lie. She would know, and Baey had enough people in her life who had tried to lie around her. I didn't need her worrying that I would do the same. Still, the most I could summon was an honest, "Just tired, darlin'."

And with that, we opened the door and returned back into the house.

Silently, we made our way to the living room, where Mum and Estasia were both residing. Estasia was lying on her stomach on the floor, poring over some maps while Mum sat with a book in her hand and a pair of spectacles perched on her nose.

"Oh good, you're back. Dinner is in the kitchen." She didn't look up from her book as she spoke. Her tone was warm and already chased the shadows away. I didn't think I'd ever get used to her being alive. I didn't know that I wanted to. I wanted her presence to remain this precious. To have this much power.

"I'll get it, you sit down," Baey ordered as she darted from the room. I managed to look faintly amused as she did so.

But I obeyed, nonetheless, sitting down on the couch that had unofficially become my bed. I liked it better than an actual bed. Easier to get out of in a timely fashion if the need arose, with a back to brace against.

Yes. I had thought about the couch a lot, apparently.

"What are you looking at?" I asked Estasia, leaning forward from where I was sitting in an attempt to read the maps. My attempt was not successful.

"Looking over the sewers. Trying to figure out where Temorn could be taking us," she murmured absently as she moved to another map.

"Any luck?" Baey asked, having just walked back in the room. She handed me some soup.

Estasia murmured an absent, "Give me a minute."

I looked down at the soup and decided that I was, actually, quite hungry. I couldn't afford to be off balance. Well. Any *more* unbalanced. The ringing in my ears heightened as my head swam with the disaster of only a few minutes prior. Perhaps eating would help. And rest, the latter of which I really didn't have time for.

"Aha. Here!" Estasia's exclamation almost caused me to drop the bowl, even though it really wasn't loud. I needed to calm down.

Baey and I both leaned over to see what Estasia was pointing at. "Alenor, what's this?" Estasia waited for Mum to get up and come over.

"Oh. That was the beginnings of what Henry and I had wanted to be an underground train station. We'd been planning on updating the sewer system so that it was easier to divert it out to the ocean and then convert the old sewers to an underground railroad and extend them down through all the way to Eknemar."

I lost focus when Da was mentioned again, the lack of his presence just another void in the shadow of my head.

"It's a bit of a jog to get there, though. Some of the tunnels were filled in or destroyed in the assault on Alkemar, as you know," Mum continued quietly.

Estasia nodded slowly. "Yes. I heard."

My eyes wandered along the old blueprints as I tried to compare the relative placement of the station with the city. It was, in fact, a bit outside the city, near the cliffside. I wondered if that was for ventilation purposes, ease of excavation, or for the water source.

"Would Skayla or anyone else know of this, though?" I asked. I couldn't remember. I...I didn't recall this place, but then again, there were still odd gaps in this stupid head. Everything after I became the monster was clear as day. But before? Before was a dream.

"Lord Atlys is the only one. He was helping Henry oversee the construction and provided the workers. Skayla...Skayla killed many of the artisans that we employed." Mum's voice fell away again. I winced, wishing to offer comfort but being unable to give much more than a subtle, sympathetic glance her way. She met it and we held eye contact only a moment before the conversation moved on.

"So then, this would be the ideal place to hide? I mean, wasn't Lord Atlys on the list? This makes sense." Baey only half asked the question. It was nice to see her unafraid to voice her opinion.

"I would say so. If he's smuggling them supplies, then the place by the cliffside and beach could theoretically be the perfect spot. And, I mean, even I didn't know about this place," Estasia replied, tapping her finger idly on the paper. "Regardless," she went on, a bit grave, "We'll find out soon enough."

Estasia:

Did I like this? No. Not really. But then again, perhaps it was more that I didn't like Temorn. Perhaps I was worried he would try and play more games. Or maybe I was still reeling from that stupid off-hand comment he'd made.

Either way, I didn't return the slimy smile Temorn gave us as Sven, Baey, and I slunk to the meeting spot in the underground tunnels.

"Oh, hello there, Birdy." He winked at Baey, and I balled a fist to make it quite obvious what would happen if he did anything stupid. Whether he decided she was a fun little plaything, or something to get rid of like Eugene, I didn't care. He knew better than to cross me.

Granted, Sven was giving some pretty good glares himself.

Then Baey surprised me, replying, "Yeah, great set of teeth you have there. Can we go?" She folded her arms. The raised eyebrow was then added just for effect.

"A little mini Esa, I see." Temorn gave a more brittle smile and then waved for us to follow him as he took off through the sewers.

I had been wary of Sven's suggestion to bring Baey with us to begin with, but with Sven coming along I hadn't argued. He always kept her safe. But now it seemed she was finally growing quite capable of holding her own.

It was a long journey full of twists, turns, and patrols. While the last bit wasn't too frequent, it seemed the city definitely tried to keep the vagabonds at bay. Mainly in the center of the city—well, the underground part of it.

Everyone was silent, and yet screaming in their own way. Sven didn't like Temorn—which was good. I would have been more worried if he *had* liked the idiot—and the way he kept one hand on his sheathed blade was enough of a hint. Even Temorn had taken note of how Sven's hand hovered. And then Baey, while as expressionless as I'd yet seen her, looked tense and apprehensive. She constantly threw looks in my direction, as if I could reassure her.

Unfortunately, I wasn't about to do any such thing when it came to backing Temorn. All I could do was trust Illan.

And, ugh, I hated trust.

The thought only made my chest burn again as the source of much of that only stood a little in front of us, leading the way. Temorn was only out for himself. I'd come to accept that was pretty much the way most people were.

Most.

I turned my attention ever so slightly to Sven, who despite having been sick and imprisoned a few weeks ago, now kept pace with us and hid the last echoes of a limp. I wondered if he'd just grown accustomed to walking it off because Skayla never cared if her toy got injured during missions. Was his lack of ability to take care of himself because he didn't care, or because he'd forgotten how?

I stowed the thoughts away as we made our way, just as I'd predicted, to the outskirts of the city sewer systems, eventually coming to another service door that Temorn opened and ushered us into. It sealed shut behind us, opening up a long, half-finished looking tunnel in front of us.

Temorn still didn't say a word, only led on. The smell grew cleaner— less acrid and decaying—as we moved along the drying tunnel. It was small enough for us to have to go single file, and yet still large enough that Baey didn't have a full-out panic attack. That, or she was getting better at keeping her cool.

Good.

Then came the seeming dead-end, ending with what appeared to be a metal wall. Temorn pressed something along the top left corner of it, and with a hiss and the cackling of gears grinding, the metal door slid to the side in what seemed to be a track that pulled into the half-stone, half-earthen tunnel wall.

Fun.

We continued on.

The tunnel widened again, but it was cruder now. Gone were the bricks and stone, and instead there was now packed earth with scrap metal and wooden beams keeping the tunnel safe. Well, hopefully safe. I really didn't feel like getting killed in a cave-in....

Another door. Of course, there was always another door.

This, however, was again clearly Crafters' work. Though dull and beaten from years of neglect, the metal of the door still shone through from beneath the cogs and gears that covered it from top to bottom. Temorn was already at the door, inserting a key in the middle gear and turning it. The other cogs and gears turned inside the door, and there was an echoing click as it unlocked. The door creaked, and then slid slowly to the side of the wall, groaning as it disappeared the wall to its left.

Temorn beckoned impatiently, and we entered behind him. The door then reluctantly dragged itself to life again and closed behind us.

The last of the pungent odors from the sewers were left behind with the door, and we stood facing a small, building-like hallway made with a low arch.

But I was more focused on the two grim-faced guards in front of us.

I gathered Temorn had already told them of our impending arrival, as they did nothing but stare at us all warily, hands on their mechanical crossbows as a precaution as we passed between them.

Well, this was looking to be quite the sophisticated hideout, huh? Actual guards? Weapons? I was uneasy, but at the same time fascinated. Perhaps Illan really had done well.

Lanterns lined both sides of the brick walls, and a dull rising of noise began filtering through as we walked. It was…almost like the general noise of a city. The echoes were eerie as we went on, and they slowly grew until we stood in front of yet another door—the same build as the other. The only noticeable difference was where the lock was, and I also observed Temorn took out a different key. Smart.

Well. Maybe not smart for whoever was trusting Temorn with these keys. But at least each door had a different one.

The door opened, and I was greeted by an overwhelming combination of sight, sound, and smell.

Before us was a large underground dome, reaching up so high that it must be under the hillside that rose up to the cliff. So *that* was why. I hadn't really grasped just how big this station was supposed to have been from the blueprints. It was…it was big, with brick- and metal-plated walls and ceiling shining and reflecting the countless lanterns that hung among…houses? Yes. Indeed, it was like an underground town, with tents, makeshift houses, and some even more well-built shelters. There were even streets and people walking through them; people in worn-out clothes and a weird appearance of normalcy as they talked with one another, cooked over open fires, even hung laundry on makeshift lines. It was literally an underground city.

"Follow me." Temorn was beaming with self-absorbed triumph as he noted our astonishment. *My* astonishment. I hid it quickly, but it was too late.

I was really getting soft. Not good.

"There...there are children," Baey whispered; she seemed almost rooted in place from where we were standing, overlooking the vast place.

Indeed, I saw a few small figures darting through and even playing with homemade toys on the edge of the city.

"Yes. Come—you'll get a better look, Birdy." Temorn laughed and ushered us down a path that led to a set of stairs.

"Her name is Baey. Only I get to call her Birdy, toothless." Somehow, I really didn't like him using the nickname. It made it sound belittling.

"Well then, *Baey*, come on and get a look while Miss Grumpy grouches in the corner with her shadow." Temorn's smile only grew.

I was remembering just why I couldn't stand him. Once upon a time, his immature mischief had been great fun.

Until the day it had cost us Eugene.

We made our way down the stairs, Temorn leading the way and Sven taking up the rear. It could be easy even for me to forget he was here.

Soon enough, we'd made it down the stairway and into the city. It was odd. Really odd. People looked less wary down here. Well, at least until they noticed us, and then all we got were stares and whispers. But there were no violet eyes. No patrols seeking us out. It was the closest thing to a normal city street I'd seen in almost ten years, and it was *underground*. But Baey was right; there were kids, just running around, being kids. I'd forgotten how long it had been since I'd heard that kind of laughter. Seen smiles.

"Wait here," Temorn said as we stopped in a section near the center of the city, strangely consisting largely of tents. Tents and soldiers. At least, what I guessed were soldiers. *Fighters* was probably a more apt term. Some carried weapons like swords, crossbows, or longbows. But the uniforms were hardly *uniform*, mostly seeming like a stolen hodge-podge of Bethynese garments and Patelaynian guard uniforms.

We waited outside a tent, being eyed by the two guards that Temorn had disappeared behind.

I noted how they especially glanced Sven's way. Was it suspicion? Or did they recognize him as the Watcher Sven Mara? Or was it just how half-dead and grim he looked? Well, that or the way his hand still hovered over his blade.

Temorn reappeared, giving me a wink that made me want to rip out his eyelashes. "They'll see you now." He stepped to the side and let us pass through. First Baey, then me, then Sven. I had no idea who we were about to meet, nor how helpful they would be.

Guess it was time to find out.

Two people resided in the tent: a woman, tall, dark hair pulled up behind her to show a face long marked with the worries Skayla's reign brought with it. Her complexion was similar to mine, one that was clearly meant to withstand the sun, and yet years of deprivation had washed out the richer tones. Next to her was a man, equally tall and well-built, a much more guarded expression rippling across his scarred face. Yeah, that

131

looked like a pretty nasty scar...in fact, it had to have pierced his left eye, because there was an eyepatch covering it.

I made a few very quick conclusions about the pair as we settled in the room.

First, they were clearly siblings. The squared-off jaws, the same hazel eyes. Even just the way they held themselves.

Secondly, I very quickly realized who had given that scar running from forehead to jaw across the man's face. Yes, the man made a nearly imperceptible jump the moment he laid eyes on Sven.

And yet no sooner had we entered the tent than Sven stopped dead. "Y—you're alive?" His hoarse whisper barely crossed the room to the strangers.

There was a moment of awkward silence, in which I tried to deduce what exactly was going on; then the man replied, "Yes." The word sounded forced, but he continued quickly, "But I'm not sure if you are."

So, they knew Sven, and Sven knew them. Knew Sven *and* The GhostMaker. I began realizing these two had to have been of noble birth with how they carried themselves, and wondered if it was a similar situation to Queen Serafina. The question was, when the shock wore off, would they be like Maeko?

"Is it...is it really you, Sven?" the woman asked as she stepped around the large table they had been standing behind. "*Really* you?" She sounded desperate. Lonely. Well, seeing as if they really were nobility then they were probably one of the only ones of their kind left on this forsaken planet, then yeah, I would imagine they were a bit lonely.

All the same, I fought to take a protective step in front of Sven.

"Yes," Sven said, voice a breathless rasp. "I'm afraid so."

"We...thought you were dead," the woman went on, eyes brightening a bit as a smile just barely touched her dark lips. "I mean...you kind of look dead." There was a clear relief in her tone and...was that meant to be a joke?

I wasn't exactly impressed with it.

No one laughed.

All we seemed to be doing at this point was staring at one another as we waited for Sven to reply. Baey's wings twitched with a nervous energy, and I knew she was just as uncomfortable as I was pretending not to be. It was as if three ghosts were all facing each other, trying to figure out how the other had died.

Only, in this case, they were all trying to figure out how they were all alive.

Especially since one of them had supposedly killed off the other two.

At last Sven replied with, "And you look...alive." Was *he* trying to joke? I wasn't sure. He sounded more baffled and lost than in a place to try anything amusing.

The woman offered a genuine smile. "Thanks to you."

Okay. Was this a setup? I looked over the pair of strangers again, dutifully searching for any sign of trickery. The man still seemed nervous in Sven's presence, but it wasn't an angry sort of nervous. The woman really did seem glad Sven was alive, and yet...Sven's luck had really not been good up until now, so I was afraid to believe it.

I turned at last to Sven, to see he was trying to formulate something to say. But nothing came out, and he simply shut his mouth and stared instead.

He stared at the woman, as we all stared at him. He looked like he wanted to wither away from the attention.

"How did you get out?" the other man asked.

"Oh. Um." Sven's eyes locked on the man's scar again, and I could practically see the way his mouth dried up. He swallowed. "I...I got Moira's relic back. It was enough to help me get out. The details are...fuzzy." He flinched. "Sorry. Darbeshay, Thackeray, this is Baey of Valdon—" He motioned to Baey, who like me, had been watching in silent attentiveness. Then Sven motioned to me. "—and Estasia."

My brow furrowed, and I didn't bother being discrete as I asked Sven, "You trust these people?"

"Yes. They're old friends." The reply was empty.

Empty and unsatisfactory. Last time I'd met a "friend" it had been Namaya, who had apparently switched sides three times. We were now too vulnerable to slip up again, and as much as I did put bank in Illan's judgment, I wanted a little more reassurance. "How old?"

"My sisters and I traveled quite a bit for diplomatic purposes. Their family was very close with us." Sven's brow furrowed, and he looked as if he was having trouble remembering again. But what followed next was blunt and said with much more conviction. "And then they were some of the first victims of The GhostMaker."

The silence that followed that statement was heavy, and I took the time to judge Darbeshay and Thackeray's reaction. The pain in the eyes of both was sincere enough, and the wince the latter let slip at the mention of Sven's less-than-savory title.

"I do suppose explanations are in order. Most of you are strangers to us as well." Darbeshay looked from us to Thackeray. "Perhaps you ought to sit?" As she finished, she motioned to the hodge-podge of makeshift seats and stools that littered the room. It took only a few minutes before we were seated around the table, which was strewn with maps and correspondence of various sorts.

Only Sven remained standing. Of course.

Now, I was not exactly about to offer up any information until I knew a bit more about these two. Yes, they knew Sven, and it was clear what Sven had said *was* true. And the scar on the man's face seemed testament enough to how he felt about Skayla, but I'd lived this long for a reason, and that reason was skepticism. We couldn't afford stupid mistakes.

"So, how long exactly have you been down here?" I asked.

Darbeshay and her brother both appeared a bit taken off guard. Yeah, they had probably expected us to go first. They also probably thought Sven was leading this thing, which he had made very clear he had no desire to do. Honestly, he probably wasn't in the position to be spearheading much. He was still recovering from the Kovian Fortress, whether he admitted it or not, and he was *definitely* still dealing with Hytat.

I prepared for some form of argument to ensue over wanting us to share more information first, but instead, all I got was a sigh from Darbeshay before she began. "After things went down in Rugo..." Her gaze flitted to Sven for a moment, who winced and again settled his gaze on Thackeray's scar. But she continued, "We ended up eventually making our way back here. Atlys saved our lives when we were found by soldiers, and he...set us up in this place. He's been helping for a while, but as far as Skayla knows he's loyal to her. Skayla wanted a few, shall

135

we say, token nobles to help keep order. But Atlys used his export and import company to smuggle refugees in here."

I got the distinct feeling she'd skipped over some details regarding Atlys. How was Skayla controlling him?

"Once every month, we get supplies from the exit by the cliff. We only know of you because of Illan coming and almost getting himself caught. Atlys found him, and we were hoping…." She turned to me. "Estasia, correct?"

I nodded.

"Illan told us of your network, and we were hoping together we might do more than just hide people. But then you showed up here, so now I suppose that makes things easier." A faint smile followed the remark, and she again looked to Sven.

"And Temorn?" I asked. "How do you know him?" He wasn't exactly the 'help the good fight' sort of person. And not one to just up and decide to help a couple of nobles.

"He's a contact through Atlys. You would have to ask him how they came into contact. I'm guessing through Atlys's...less than legal activities." She stopped then, surveyed us all, and then asked, "So, what about you? How did you all get here?"

Sven was still staring dead-eyed at Thackeray, so I guessed I would be the one relaying the tale. "Well..." What to say, what to leave out? "I was taken as a slave from Patelayna and ended up in the Kovian Fortress. Events...led me to realizing The GhostMaker wasn't a willing lackey." I felt a sinking feeling upon saying that awful title around Sven. But I didn't break stride in my story, all the same. "And after he saved my life, I started trying to do more than survive. Long story short, Sven got away, but then got caught again. I rescued him and his group, and we made a run for it," I finished, turning in my seat so that I could face Sven, his expression as stony as ever. I tried to make eye contact with him, but he seemed to still stare into nothing—or Thackeray—so instead, I prompted, "But I think from here on you have more information than I do, Sven."

Every expression he gave seemed a variant of a wince, and this time was no different as he tore his gaze from Thackeray; the only form of acknowledgement that he'd heard me. With a quiet clearing of his throat, he spoke at last. "I...I stole Moira's watch, as I said. Made for Valdon. I'd left Baey in their care." He motioned to Baey, who did nothing but watch him with a furrowed brow. "Along with my ring. But my mind was...a mess, and by the time we were on the same page, Skayla had found us. Estasia got us out. I had come to realize that Skayla hadn't been able to kill The Crafters as we'd all thought, and with the help of those at Valdon, we were able to find out where Alenor had hidden." The pause was excruciating. You could hear the pain in it. Or perhaps it was just the way Sven was fiddling feverishly with his ring. "Henry didn't make it, though."

His father. He'd not said a word on the subject, and I had a feeling it was for a reason. For the same reason he never said anything about anything.

There was an all-too-noticeable pause, and when he went on, his voice was a little quieter. "Anyway. We think Moira is still alive. Trapped out of time or some such thing, by Skayla. We sent some others to get The Living Stone in the hopes that we can repair the watch; if we can fix it, maybe we can get her out."

THE LIVING STONE

CHAPTER IX: The Portal Site

<u>Baey:</u>

"Well, that's...a lot." Thackeray said after a long moment.

I tried to quench the doubt gripping my lungs. It seemed like a lot of "if"s: *If* Moira was alive. *If* the others ever came back—let alone with The Living Stone—and *if* I really could use the watch. We didn't even have a way to test it. It seemed like Sven had put a bit more faith in me than I really felt was warranted. But he seemed so certain, it was hard not to trust him.

"So, it's just another waiting game, then?" Darbeshay asked. "What's your plan while you wait for The Living Stone?"

"Or if your friends don't get it?" Thackeray added.

I forced myself to breathe as the thought of Tanner and the others never coming back once more rose to the surface. I barely caught myself in time to stop the fear from shadowing my wings, and I was rewarded when I peeked just enough to see they remained a neutral greyish white. Ha.

But there wasn't time to gloat, and I returned my focus back to the conversation, looking to Sven who was unreadable as ever as he stared intently at our maybe-allies.

"Well, for one, what information do you have on the portal site we saw Skayla guarding?" Estasia took up the initiative when Sven appeared lost.

"You *saw* the portal site?" Darbeshay looked agape.

Sven nodded.

"We've been trying to get information on that for years, but not even Atlys is allowed anywhere near it."

Wings twitching, I faded into the background, knowing that, at the moment, I really couldn't offer anything, but at the same time, feeling the itch of excitement. I'd never been allowed to sit in on this sort of meeting, let alone anywhere near *anything* that was deemed "too stressful" for me to hear. Finally, I wasn't being treated like a toddler, and in this moment, I really, *really* wanted to be able to have something to say. I was done sitting back and letting others figure out the problem. I was brought here for a reason; I knew it. Sven believed I had something to say, so maybe it was time to get up the nerve to say it.

Granted, I'd gotten a little lost in this realization and therefore lost track of the conversation...but it was clear they were still discussing the site.

"So then, maybe they're guarding it because it can be opened again?" I chimed in amid the discussion.

Everyone sort of stared at me. Right. I hadn't exactly said a word before this. I fought the urge to pull my wings around me, but for once I was determined not to act like some nervous little bird.

"Alenor was talking about the fact that Henry came through from the other world of Kryso, but how are the portals opened? And has this one been always closed, or have the Drogans and Skayla been using it for something? I mean, if this is where the Drogans entered, couldn't they leave just as easily? Syvil said Ovok tricked them, but then if he's working *with* Skayla, why?" I stretched my wings outward, willing them to remain open and confident so that maybe I would be, too.

140

"Who is Syvil?" Darbeshay cocked her head, eyeing me intently. But I saw the interest. No contempt. No dismissal.

Oh ugh, now I was in, wasn't I? I felt a thrill run up and down my spine.

"He's a Drogan we saved," Sven replied simply.

Right, we hadn't even told them about the Drogans.

Wow, there was so much to explain. When no one else seemed to take up the task, I found my mouth running almost without permission. "It turns out Skayla didn't put just Baenians in MindHolds, but the Drogans, also. In fact, according to Syvil—who saved our lives multiple times—" I diverted just a moment as I saw the doubt creeping into both Thackeray and Darbeshay's faces—"Ovok tricked them and helped Skayla put them in a MindHold. We don't know if that's the case for all Drogans, or just some, but it sounds as if at least Ovok is of free will."

"So then...Ovok may have come here wanting something?"

"He said he was exiled." Sven's voice sounded like that of someone living a dream. Tanner used to sleepwalk, and the way he'd speak while doing so was way too similar to how Sven sounded now. "When we first talked to the Drogans after they appeared, he'd said 'Our banishment is complete.' He claimed Drogan Hunters had driven them from the world of Eatris and that they were seeking asylum. Skayla mentioned something about the fact that they'd killed one of his daughters and the other had been left behind."

Another bit of silence. Silence which I took as an opportunity to try and think, and come up with any useful theories.

"We need to check out this portal site again," Estasia announced firmly. "There have to be answers there. Baey's right; how do we even know the portal is closed?"

"It was at least for the two years you three had watched it, right?" Darbeshay half-answered, half-asked as she motioned to Sven.

His looked down in what seemed to be deep concentration before replying. "Yes, that sounds right."

Darbeshay looked somewhat confused but moved on. I couldn't help but mirror that a little. Sounded right? Was Sven alright? Then again, it was over a decade ago, and a lot had happened since then.

Discussion continued until it became clear the only way to really get answers was to do exactly what Estasia had suggested: go to the portal site. Sven would be able to help them sneak in, so he was obviously going, and Thackeray insisted on going as well. I didn't like the thought of Sven going alone and wondered if Alenor should go also, seeing that out of all of us, she seemed to have the most information regarding portals and other worlds and all that. But seeing as they seemed to be trying to keep quiet where Alenor was exactly, I decided it was best to wait to ask.

It was probably a good hour or two before we got plans sorted out and were ready to return to Alenor's house for the night. I, for one, was mentally exhausted, and yet beyond exhilarated at the same time. I'd...I'd helped. Maybe a lot. And having done so only made me hungrier to help more.

"You and Estasia should come back tomorrow while they're gone. We need to discuss long-term plans," Darbeshay addressed me as we got up to leave, then turned to Estasia. "Atlys could very well get messages across to your other contacts, and I don't want to just sit here playing detective forever."

So I wasn't the only one tired of sitting and doing nothing. I could see it in both Darbeshay and Thackeray's eyes: they'd hidden for too long.

"Alright. I think I should be able to get here without Temorn's help, next time." Estasia grinned.

Darbeshay's eyebrows shot up, but she only nodded as her brother stepped forward and opened the tent flap for us. Sven was the last to leave, and I heard Darbeshay quietly stop him from behind us.

"Sven...we're...we're really glad you're alive." I felt an intruder for listening, but I couldn't say that half of me hadn't expected her to say something more of a 'you hurt Thackeray and I'll kill you' sort of thing.

"I'm sorry about...."

"Sven, please don't. It wasn't you."

"Yeah." That last reply lacked any conviction, and a moment later he exited the tent, tense and tight-lipped.

I wanted to say something—to coax him back out of the shell he'd hidden further inside after the little reality-bending incident—but no one dared utter a word while in the tunnels.

Temorn had apparently left, but Estasia easily led us back through. I was in awe of her memory. She'd only seen the maps, what, yesterday? And then led through by Temorn only one time?

Once back, we explained everything to Alenor, and after Estasia finished the last bit of the plan, I made my move.

"Shouldn't Alenor go with them, too?" I turned from the now distraught-looking Sven to Alenor. "I mean, you have so much experience with portals and other worlds—we don't have to tell them who you are. They know we had more friends besides us, we could just say we think you'd be good for expertise?"

"I don't think—"

"That's a great idea, Baey," Estasia interrupted Sven, who was looking wide-eyed and almost panicked. "Alenor, are you up for it?" Alenor looked at her son and smiled reassuringly. "I wouldn't pass up a chance to get out of this prison." I realized she had been cooped up here for so long...given just how elaborate her house was and all of the things she'd shown me. The greenhouse had been especially impressive.

Alenor's comment alone seemed to silence Sven, and his shoulders sagged in surrender. I felt guilty for possibly putting his mother in danger again, but I knew it was the right move; and I liked the idea of Sven and Alenor being together. Of Sven having someone close by him when he'd be going with people that were still very new to us.

"Just don't use your real name right now. We're trying as best as we can to keep information from being spread to too many people—Skayla can look in *minds*, after all. We don't want someone like this Thackeray getting captured and spilling it all to Skayla that you're here," Estasia pointed out.

Alenor nodded gravely.

Everything was settled, and with business done, we all convened in the living room for an early dinner. Soon enough, Alenor was sitting in her usual chair, reading a book; Estasia was pensively poring over maps of the city and tunnels; and I was sitting on the back of my chair, stretching my wings out as I watched Estasia. Sven came in after having finished putting away the dishes.

"Alright, Baey, let's get going," he announced with surprising authority as he reentered the room, raising both eyebrows as I swerved my head to face him, confused.

"Uh…." It took a moment to click, but in an instant, I was up, fluttered down to the floor. "Back to the tunnel, then? More practice?"

His smile was as thin as mist, but visible to me, at least. "Yes. Go get your sword and I'll meet you at the door."

"So, today we're going to start with some drills. Then I think you should try your hand at my ring, again," he said as he unsheathed his sword, twirling it carelessly. The movement was empty and careless—and not that *confident* sort of carelessness.

I was momentarily distracted from the motion as I processed what he'd said, and my wings perked. The ring? He wanted me to practice? "And you're going to practice, too, right?" I asked.

He flinched. "Let's just focus on you, right now."

I didn't want him to give up, but I knew better than to press until the moment came. Sven needed practice, too, but he was afraid. At least, that's what I was guessing. I couldn't quite tell, but I did know a thing or two about fear, at least. Estasia said instinct could be good, right? Or was this assuming? Well, I knew *I* would feel afraid after what happened with him last night. Afraid and alone. But he *wouldn't* be alone, this time.

The drills were grueling, and yet the sword didn't feel quite as heavy today. I mean, it was still no easy task trying to manage it, but it was less

145

like trying to swing a pillar and less like I would drop it at any moment. Well, at least it felt better for the first thirty minutes. After that? My arms once again began to feel like jelly, and the only thing Sven let me do was drill without the sword for another ten minutes before picking it up again. Another thirty minutes with it, and then we sparred some. I lost miserably, but all he did was coach gently as he always did. He'd tell me how to fix it, but also say where I did better. It made me hope I really *was* getting better, or at least would be, soon. I didn't want to be saved all the time.

"Alright, have a minute to catch your breath, and then the real work will start," Sven announced at last as he put away his own blade. I didn't need to be told a second time, barely coordinated enough to even guide my sword to the scabbard without poking my own leg instead. My arms and hands were shaking with muscle fatigue.

"Tired?" he asked.

I nodded. "But I'm fine," I added the last bit suddenly, afraid he might rescind the offer to practice with the ring.

His eyes narrowed a little, but he didn't say a word. Instead, the suspicion melted away to something more faraway, and he extended his hand out into nothingness, staring at his empty hand. Part of me wanted to ask what he was doing, while the other part of me worried I'd distract him from...well, whatever it was. I felt a stirring from the watch and that unnatural pull of desire. He was using his ring? I wasn't sure whether to be apprehensive or not, but at least nothing seemed to change—no "full scale ballroom hallucination," at least.

And then I saw it. It was all within a few seconds, really, and I found myself staring in fascination as a glass cup formed in his hand. It twisted and shimmered as if it was alive, and in little more time that it would have taken me to blink, it rippled and glistened into that of a glass cup.

And then, from seemingly nowhere, the cup filled with the purest looking water.

Sven took a sip.

"Is that...safe?" I sat up straighter, enthralled.

Sven met my eyes and held the gaze longer than he had all day. "You want to try some?"

"Uh." I blushed, not sure why I was so embarrassed by my curiosity. And yet not embarrassed enough to say no. "Sure." I made to get up, but Sven—uh—threw the cup at me, and I couldn't help but make an undignified squeak as I lurched forward to catch it.

I almost dropped it in surprise as it found my hand unnaturally. It didn't even spill a drop. Gingerly, I took a sip, realizing my wonderment seemed to feed Sven's ease, so I stopped trying to hide it.

"Wow." I genuinely grinned after having taken a sip. "Uh...that's probably the best water I've had in a while." I wasn't exaggerating either. I stared at the cup, turning it over and trying to find any trace of evidence that showed it as an illusion. "How did you *do* that?" He'd said he manipulated reality, but this was so *real*. It was as if he'd created the water from...nothing.

Sven motioned for me to throw the cup back to him, and so I did. Catching it deftly, he took another sip and then carelessly dropped it on the ground. No shatter erupted. Instead, it scattered into soundless grains of sand and seemed to become absorbed into the stone floor.

I was pretty sure my eyes couldn't get wider.

"The next step about an illusion is believing it's real. It's about understanding and knowing what you want, and having the will to make it more than just your imagination," he explained. "In fact, here: take the ring." He took it off, and with the same sort of carelessness, tossed it at me. It landed in my palm with ease, and yet it still took a moment for me to catch my breath and calm the instant of panic. Last time he'd thrown the relic, we'd almost never gotten it back.

But I didn't want him to know that was what had gone through my mind. "But...you *made* water. "

He motioned for me to stand up, and I obeyed even as he began to answer. "Yes, but I've been drinking water all my life. I am pretty aware of what it tastes and feels like. It's just taking the illusion one step further and making it actually be there. Reality is about how you perceive things...so you just have to have the strength and concentration to change how it is perceived. But I think perhaps we should stick to you trying out illusions before we delve into any of this." The almost bright expression he'd gotten while explaining faded away to something more troubled. "I just needed a bit of supervised practice, and a glass of water seemed harmless enough."

"And you did it no problem," I offered as encouragement as I processed what he had just said. Supervised practice. Did he really think I was competent supervision? I really hoped so. I didn't want to let him down.

"So, are you ready to try some?"

I grinned. "Yes." I was ready. I was ready to help him get past this, and right now, teaching me how to use it right seemed the best way to help him. "So, what first?" It wasn't as simple as sword fighting. I felt like

I should be striking some thoughtful pose or whatnot, and yet I just stood there awkwardly instead. But I wasn't afraid to show that anymore.

For a moment, Sven said nothing, looking deep in thought, as if he didn't really know either. Then at last he spoke. "So, why don't we try with some small illusions and work our way up from there. We can't do it long—this will require a building of mental endurance."

I knew he wasn't kidding. With just the few things I'd tried by myself in the past, I wasn't surprised. I'd tried so hard before and I'd not even made anything good. How was I going to make water out of nothing? I took in a deep breath and tried to focus. Sven had said we wouldn't worry about that right now. Just one step at a time.

"Let's start with things you know. Hold out your hand as if you're holding a sword," Sven instructed, and I obeyed.

"No." His chiding was gentle. "Don't have a closed fist. Really pretend as if you have the sword. There should be room for the grip and hilt."

Right. I felt my wings twitch as I fought with my usual inner doubt, and yet it went away much more easily than usual. I adjusted the look of my grip.

"Now." Sven stepped a bit closer, drawing his sword. "Use my sword for reference, and project that image in your hand. Think about what it felt like to hold the sword before, when we were sparring: the angle, the length, the weight. To make an accurate illusion, one must understand what you are making."

I obeyed as best as I could, closing my eyes as I tried to imagine the blade.

"There you go." Sven's tone was warm with encouragement.

Slowly, I cracked my eyes open. It actually didn't look half bad. No shimmering image. No dissipating. However, a quick inspection proved to find a very obvious error.

The handle was not quite in my hold, but a bit through my hand. At that realization, my focus failed, and the image slowly disappeared.

"Now, try again, this time keeping your eyes open. It will help with reference. It's like singing a melody in your head rather than just playing it aloud. It's harder initially, but it'll eventually train your mind to be sharper than if you simply do it aloud."

I blinked. "I, uh, I actually don't get that one."

Sven looked suddenly lost—that half-in-a-dream state he got.

"Sven?"

With a jolt and a quick breath, he came back. "Right, sorry. I don't really know what I was getting at…. Regardless, you can't go closing your eyes in a fight." He motioned limply with his hand. "Try again. Eyes open."

This went on for another twenty minutes. I made way too many blade replicas to count, each better and easier than the last. After we'd gotten the accuracy down, Sven made me practice speed. The splitting headache started about ten minutes in, but I refused to let on— concentration now in the place of the frustration I had experienced in previous learning sessions. I was beginning to understand the process now. Practice didn't mean failure. It meant progress. The last five minutes were spent with me learning to move with the illusions, and while I failed miserably at it for the most part, I was consistently failing *less* miserably with each new attempt.

At last, Sven called the session to the end, and I wasn't the only one who seemed spent. He looked exhausted.

Grinning ear to ear, I took off the ring—which had changed size to perfectly match my finger; Sven's doing, no doubt. I handed it to Sven.

He didn't smile back. Taking the ring slowly, he ruffled my hair, and together we started making our way back to the tunnel exit.

"So, will we be training you, soon?" I dared ask, with a nosy twitch of my wings.

His shoulders stiffened ever so slightly. A sigh escaped him. "I'll have to. I suppose playing with glasses of water can only go so far."

I was quiet for a bit, wings flexing in and out as I tried to figure out what to say. We were almost at the exit, but I wanted to help. Half the time Sven felt like a father, the other half he felt more like an older brother. But almost everyone else seemed to...I don't know. Not treat him like a person. It was either the great Sven Mara or the frightful GhostMaker. Either way, Sven the *person* was lost in between.

"Are you scared?" I asked suddenly, stopping in my tracks.

He stopped with me. He didn't flinch, or look at me, or do anything. No anger. Nothing. Nothing but, "Yes. I suppose I am."

"That's alright though, isn't it?" I asked.

He took a deep breath. "Yes. I suppose it is." But it didn't sound like he believed that. For all the times he'd said it to me...he didn't sound like he believed it himself.

"And besides, you aren't alone. You have me. And your mother. And Estasia. We'll help." I offered a smile that was left without an echo.

"Thank you, Baey." He shook his head. "You catch on quickly, don't you?"

I gave him a side shoulder. "I try," I replied, even though I wasn't completely sure what he meant.

He elbowed back. Just like a real person. Just like a normal human being. Something I knew he'd been deprived of for so long. Something I wondered if he'd really had even *before* The GhostMaker.

<u>Sven:</u>

I'd been quiet the entire ride. I put it off as concentration. With the three horses all rushing through the forest, it was easy to say I had some work cut out for me to keep us hidden. To keep us from another slip-up that could clue Skayla into our whereabouts.

Not that it was really a good excuse. Mum had clearly been excited at the prospect of being outside, and it made me guiltier over my desire to have her stay in safety. I just…I didn't have the best track record with keeping people safe.

We stopped riding around noon, giving both the horses and us a break. I had tried to hide just how easily worn down I was still getting, and yet both Mum and Thackeray seemed to catch on. I'd been doing well with walking and sparring with Baey, but cantering was still not pleasant on the fresh scars the Kovian Fortress had left behind.

"So, what's the plan once we get there?" Thackeray asked evenly, sitting down under one of the tall, pole-like trees. I looked up at the skies, scanning for any signs of a Drogan. Not that I could see much through the thick canopy of leaves.

"Well, what will we be looking for, Nyta?" I turned to Mum for the first time, and used the false name we'd agreed upon.

She offered a warm smile. A smile that seeped deep but hurt as much as it comforted. "Well, according to Sven, as well as The Crafters' investigations, the portal had been closed upon the Drogans entering. So, I suppose first of all, we need to see if it's opened back up, or they are trying to open it."

"What would that look like?" Thackeray carried on so easily. As if I wasn't standing near him. He'd not so much as said a word on the subject, and I almost wished he would. He seemed caught in the middle, the eyeless scar the eyepatch did little to hide proving I shouldn't be trusted.

You need to focus, Sven. Focus on what matters, not on your stupid self.

"If it's open...well, that will be pretty obvious. If Sven didn't see the portal, I doubt it is, so, we'll be looking for signs of attempts to pry it open. They'll be using some of The Crafters' inventions, no doubt. They're the only people I could picture having technology far enough to maybe produce a portal." Mum fell into her role, not slipping up even once as she relayed the information.

Thackeray's one functional eyebrow drew close to his brow. "So large, weird-looking contraptions, then?"

Mum nodded, taking out her canteen and taking a good swig out of it. "That's right. They shouldn't be hard to spot."

The group quickly fell into silence.

After a few minutes, Mum stretched forward, leaning down to touch her toes as she commented, "Well, I don't know about either of you, but I haven't been out and about on a horse in a while."

I'd noticed how unsteady she'd been upon dismounting. She hadn't sat, though. Only leaned against a tree.

"I'm afraid I am very out of practice, myself," Thackeray said with a stretch of his own. "Darby and I haven't exactly frequented the daylight in a few years. And horses aren't easy to find." There was a wince as he briefly met my gaze, and the expression almost seemed apologetic. Like he felt bad about bringing it all up.

I was going to be sick. He was a *victim*, and he had every right to bring up the horrors he'd had to live through. The scars I'd given and let my sister give.

"Yes, I can't believe you've been hiding in the sewers all these years!" It was Mum, going on in conversation even as she constantly side-eyed me.

"Indeed. We are lucky The Crafters kept the train station project so close to the vest when they were working on it." Thackeray's smile wavered.

"I can't believe I never knew it was down there...." Mum's jaw tightened as she trailed off into some unfinished thought, and I recognized that look well: guilt. She reeked with it even as I reeked of death.

Weren't we a pair?

I wanted to say something—anything to comfort whatever regret she was at war with, and yet I couldn't risk exposing her identity.

"Not even we knew. In fact, I didn't even know we still had allies until Atlys saved us." Something flickered in his eye, and he winced. Was that guilt I saw in him, too? "Skayla likes to make even our friends seem like enemies from afar." His gaze met mine again.

I looked away.

"Yes. Well, we're all here now. And Sven—" She looked at me and I saw her swallow the guilt away. "You need to be drinking."

I blinked. "Hm?" Oh, right. I hadn't been. Quietly, I uncorked my own canteen and took a few swallows. I was a lot thirstier than I'd thought.

"You should really sit, too."

I supposed my legs did ache a little, and yet I shook my head. "Unfortunately, we should probably get going, ah?"

Thackeray sighed and got up. Mum stared at me a while, then stood up straight, stretched, and placed a hand on my shoulder.

I tried not to flinch, and yet she still noticed.

"You alright?"

I nodded. "Yes. Always."

"And by that you mean never, right?"

"Sorry," I whispered in reply, putting a hand up to hers and gently squeezing it even as I pulled it off my shoulder. I was acutely aware of Thackeray watching us. Idiot, we were supposed to be being discreet about who Mum really was. Not that anyone knew who The Watchers' parents had been, but I was not exactly helping keep Mum's identity safe, all the same....

Thackeray cleared his throat. "Ready?"

In reply, I left Mum and mounted my horse. Mum was the only one who verbally replied with, "Yes. Ready."

And we were off again.

Before we knew it, we'd arrived at the edge of the forest, and after securing the horses and placing an illusion over them, we continued on foot across the clearing to the gaping ravine. I was hiding us, of course, shoving any mental weakness to the side as I had to concentrate. But again, it was harder than before. Harder than when I'd struggled to remember anything at all. Now, I couldn't seem to forget.

I felt a hand on my shoulder, and again it was Mum. Always Mum.

I took in a weighty breath and nodded to both her and Thackeray, motioning for them to follow me over to a boulder that sat up against the ravine's crest.

Once we reached it, I took a moment to recollect.

"One of us should take a peek down below and take stock of what we need to get around," Mum suggested.

I was about to volunteer when Thackeray offered instead, "Let me. Will an illusion hold?"

"It would be easier if I went."

"I can manage. And I don't think any of us wish to lose sight of you so soon after the last time you disappeared."

Don't react. Don't react.

"I didn't mean it like that, Sven. I mean last time you—"

"You can go," I cut him off quietly. We didn't need to sit and discuss feelings. Now wasn't the time. It didn't matter what he meant. I wasn't offended either way. I deserved whatever it *had* meant.

Thackeray's lips pressed tightly together, and yet he did not argue, instead fingering the sword around his belt as he asked, "Am I good to go?"

I used my Gifting to secure a mirror-style illusion around him. "You're good. But don't push it. They're messier when I'm not with you to hide you." It would have been easier if I had gone.

"Got it." With that, he ducked around a boulder.

Mum and I waited in tense silence, neither saying a word.

So much for catching up.

It was only a couple minutes before Thackeray ducked back behind the boulder with us, breath even and face lacking any sort of warning signs. So, uh, that was a good sign.

Also, he was alive. Definitely worth letting go of the breath I'd been holding.

"There are quite a few Drogans down there. A whole Bethynese platoon, too, by the looks of it," Thackeray reported. "You were definitely right, Sven. Something is going on."

Why did it bother me so much he was calling me Sven? I felt like there was too little left of the Sven he'd known to warrant calling me that. I felt like there were much better names by which I was fit to be called.

Focus.

"Alright. So now we just have to go down and see if they're probing or if there is anything there." Alenor whispered.

Thackeray nodded, "Right."

I gave my neck a stretch as I prepared to go down. "We ready, then? Thackeray, you'll be able to guide us?"

"I'll do my best."

I was appreciative of the honest answer. No empty promises. Not like I'd made in the past. Promises to protect and keep safe. To save.

FOCUS, won't you? Ugh, Skayla was winning. My *stupid* head.

Both my companions nodded.

"Alright. We are hidden," I said quickly.

And with that, we made our way down, Thackeray leading while my head battled for my attention.

It wasn't too tricky making our way down the ravine. Mum seemed almost in better shape than Thackeray and me, and yet I wasn't surprised—her build was that of a blacksmith long accustomed to work, and it was clear that she'd kept busy cooped up in the house.

Just like that, we made it inside the camp, soldiers and Drogans everywhere. Thackeray hadn't been kidding.

"This way," Thackeray whispered as we wove around the soldiers. Right now, it was better to just stay completely invisible. Bethynese soldiers were too much a risk to try and disguise ourselves here. At Hytat, it had been one thing, but here—crawling with Bethynese—it only took one commanding officer realizing we weren't really part of the platoon.

As we made our way closer and closer to where the portal had been, I noticed the rumblings of some form of machine, and the squealing of some form of steam engine. It was almost like being back in Mum and Da's old workshop.

A weight settled hard in my stomach.

But it had little time to stay there, as my attention was drawn to the conversation of a few soldiers gathered for afternoon rations.

"I still think this site is haunted," the one man said stubbornly, as he slurped up another mouthful of stew.

A younger woman nearly choked on her stew. After properly composing herself and swallowing her food, she said, "You are worse than a grandmother, Kelayos! Ghosts don't exist."

"Then why did we have The *Ghost*Maker as an assassin, hm?"

"Because it's a scary name to frighten idiots like you," the woman replied with a laugh.

There were murmurs of both agreement and disagreement at this, and soon a miniature debate broke out.

But we moved on, passing by another group sitting more quietly by their tent. These weren't Bethynese. *These* ones were in a MindHold, but a weak one, as they seemed still able to talk to some degree, but the conversation seemed stiff and rehearsed. It was as unsettling as much as it was a bitter memory.

"Lady Skayla should be here soon to give further instruction," one said, methodically taking spoonfuls from his bowl.

"Yes. Do we have any portal movement to report?" the other asked.

"Still none."

Skayla? Here soon?

I felt Mum's eyes on me, but swallowed the dread for the moment. We had to finish what we came here for first. Panic later.

Wasting no more time, we made our way to the center of the camp where the machinery sounds were coming from.

And then, like some bad dream, we stood in front of the portal site, the two Drogans guarding oblivious to our presence. The ground where once had stood a blue, disk-like doorway into another world was now fairly unremarkable, but the machines littering the area were what drew our attention.

To the right stood one with a long, arched appendage, like an arm with a curved hook reaching up, holding some invisible force. Another machine lay adjacent, rumbling as gears turned a belt. The machines groaned like some ancient beasts, but for all their work they seemed to be offering no results.

"They got ahold of the designs," Mum said, sucking in a tense breath as she moved towards the things. Her fingers ran along the elaborate metal fixtures, and I heard her mumble, "Oh, Henry."

My fingers felt almost numb as an unpleasant sensation ran up and down my entire body.

"Woah!" Thackeray shouted, jumping in the air where he was standing next to me. I only just masked his sound, but the Drogans guarding outside the ring flinched and one turned around briefly to inspect.

"Thackeray, you can't just—" The reprimand was lost on me as I stared at his pale face and wide eyes.

"You...you didn't see it?" he gasped, pointing a shaking finger to the left of me. The quiet composure he usually held evaporated in the face of whatever had scared him

Mum even stopped working on her inspection of the machines, brow furrowed as she followed Thackeray's finger. "What's the matter?"

Didn't see what?

"Th-th-there was a—" Thackeray's unsettled stuttering was interrupted by a sight that was so startling it could have knocked me to the floor.

There, visible only for a few moments, was a woman, standing as if completely lost, face twisted in desperation.

160

My entire body was shaking, and before I could stop myself, I changed the illusion so only the woman could see me, calling out, "Moira!"

Her eyes trained on me and widened. *"Sven!"* The call was cut off as she disappeared again.

"Wh—" Mum's half-formed question was cut off as Moira appeared again, closer this time and able to see all three of us.

I only barely registered in the back of my mind how the Drogans gave literally no reaction to Moira's cries.

"Sven! Help!" And then, again, Moira was gone.

"Moira, sweetheart. C-come back!" Mum whispered as she lurched forward to where Moira had been, eyes scanning the area frantically before settling on me. "What's going on, Sven?!"

I had absolutely no time to process before the flash of light appeared, and Moira appeared. It was like something straight out of a weird dream.

"Sven, please, help me! I'm trapped, trapped! Sven, he—" gone once more.

"Moira!" Mum again called her name, and I only just had the wherewithal to run up and grab her arm as she tried to run for where the light had been. All I knew was that if Mum followed Moira wherever she was going, we'd have more than just Moira stuck.

She fought against my grip, but only for a moment, reason at least partially taking hold again. Then she stared at me with a fevered expression. "Sven, what is going on?"

I felt as if I were drowning. Before I could figure out how on Baeno to reply, the flash of light appeared again. This time, however, Moira did not scream for help, nor did she vanish moments later. Instead she stayed in place, flickering and fading in and out of focus as if some far away memory.

"Moira?" I whispered, desperation dripping in my tone.

"Sven! Listen, quick before I disappear again—Sven, listen quick before I—" She repeated the words as if somehow forgetting she'd said them in the first place. "Sven listen quick before I disappear again. Skayla trapped me—Skayla trapped me and I can't get—Skayla trapped me and now I can't get back in time. She's—she's trying to open the—Sven! Please help me, I'm trapped! Sven, he—" And then she was gone.

CHAPTER X: Unfortunate Allies

<u>Baey:</u>

"Alright, I don't know about you all, but I'm not going to stand around here all day while they're gone." Estasia broke the awkward silence that had descended as a suffocating cloud upon the tent.

I couldn't help but smile, especially when Darbeshay gave her a slightly baffled look.

"Well," Darbeshay said with a huff, "what exactly would you propose we do?"

Not exactly liking the idea of staying down here idly any more than Estasia, I looked over at her expectantly.

"You've all been talking of Lord Atlys so much, I think it's time I go talk to him myself." Estasia wasted no time in replying. "And you said he's the one with all the smuggling going on, correct? If he's been successfully dodging Skayla all these years, then I feel he's the one I want to talk to." Darbeshay's brow furrowed, and she crossed her arms. "You can't go alone, though. Atlys doesn't trust people. Have Temorn go with you."

Anyone could have seen the disgust in Estasia's features. I wondered again what had happened. Granted, I wasn't exactly fond of the man, either, but this reaction definitely pointed to something bigger.

"You need to bring Temorn. Atlys only trusts Illan, Temorn, Thackeray, and me. He'll kill anyone else, trust me." Darbeshay's laugh was somewhere between amused and nervous. "Atlys hasn't survived this long for nothing."

"What about you, then?" Estasia's question was way too quick not to have been planned. I could see that's what she'd wanted all along. She wanted to see what our new allies were made of, didn't she? I couldn't say I blamed her. While it was clear they knew Sven—and *Sven,* not just The GhostMaker—it was hard to trust *anyone* new, let alone those we *did* know. Not since Namaya. I mean, yeah, they had a whole underground city hiding from Skayla...but Estasia had seemed so skeptical of it all. And what of Atlys? He was a noble left alive under Skayla. That only ever happened if you were already on her side, right?

"I—" Darbeshay paused what seemed to have been a planned rejection. "If we take the sewers...I suppose I could do with a good stretch of the legs. Let me just inform Heldon of our departure."

I smiled. "Great. I'm coming too—right?" I broke off in uncertainty, looking to Estasia.

With a dramatic eye roll, Estasia brought her hand up and rubbed her temples. "Oh, Baey, you're going to need to start being more confident than that if you want to get in on the action."

Darbeshay laughed. "And you're going to need to start figuring out how to talk to people if you ever want me to trust you," she said as she brushed by us both, exiting the tent.

Not exactly looking pleased, Estasia made a hand motion in order to tell me to leave the tent.

"Oh, no. After you. I insist." I grinned as I stepped further away from the door, crossing my arms in defiance. She said I had to be more confident. Well, hopefully stubbornness was a start, right?

Plus, it was funny watching her annoyance battle with her amusement.

"Well done." She punched my shoulder before leaving the tent, and I followed close behind with a huge grin on my face.

A moment later, Darbeshay rejoined us and we were off, making our way to the edge of the city.

"So, Darby," Estasia started right in. "How exactly did you know Sven?"

Darbeshay's eyebrow raised at the unearned nickname, but she didn't say a word on the subject, continuing to lead us through the sanctuary she and her brother had helped create. "We were friends. Sven, Thackeray, Sera, and I."

Sera...that's what Sven had called Queen Serafina.

"And just like that, you forgive him?" Estasia's pressing was a little less than tactful.

I watched the way the other woman didn't give any sort of reaction. Composed. Proper. Hands behind her back and not a hair out of place, which was a stifling contrast to her faded and patched clothes. She smiled at the underground city-goers who we passed and did not waver even in the face of Estasia's questions.

"He saved our lives," she said simply, stopping to accept a pretty little rock from a small girl. "Thank you." The smile was kind but detached. Guarded.

I felt like I noticed so much more now. I was getting, in part, why Estasia always asked things so...candidly. She was looking for the reactions, and Darbeshay's lack of them spoke volumes. I got the sense that she was keeping herself together solely for the sake of those around her. Kind of like Sven. No reaction—only a facade.

"How did he do that? Isn't he the one that killed your parents? Gave your brother that nasty scar, too." Maybe Estasia didn't need to be *that* candid.

Hopefully she wouldn't have Darbeshay at her throat before we reached the exit. We were almost at the edge of the city, now, but with Estasia's question, Darbeshay actually stopped.

The woman looked at me, and then a long time at Estasia. "Skayla killed my parents. She's a coward who doesn't like doing her own dirty work. She likes letting other people live with her mistakes, and that's what she did to Sven. He killed them and chased after us. But after Thackeray stepped in front of me and got...slashed across the face, something clicked. I don't know what—but The GhostMaker just stood there, and for a moment, the violet faded in his eyes. He said, 'Run.' That was all. And in that moment, I knew it was Sven, because no one else in Baeno was strong enough to fight Skayla like that. So, yes. Skayla killed my parents, and Sven saved me and my brother. Now, are you asking this simply to prod and see if you can get me angry, or are you asking this for Sven's sake?" Her tone was even, but I heard the touch of anger behind it.

Even though I'd done literally nothing, I swallowed hard, guilt pressing at my chest.

"A little of both, I suppose. Last person that knew both his identities tried to choke the life out of him, so I'm a little wary." Estasia appeared completely unfazed.

And then I saw the change; the shoulders sagged, the hands came undone from where they had hidden, folded so neatly behind, and Darbeshay's expression softened into something akin to anguish. "I'm sorry," she whispered, and then quickly returned to walking, making it all the way up to the exit with us close behind.

I thought the apology hadn't seemed aimed at Estasia.

"You realize Temorn has told me quite a bit about you, right?" Darbeshay commented after we had been let through the entrance by the guards.

I almost missed the way Estasia tensed. Perhaps I *would* have missed it a few weeks ago. But now, whether because I knew her so well, or because I watched so much better, I saw the small double-take.

"I doubt that. I'm sure he said I was a good little soldier in his gang until he decided betrayal and backstabbing was a fun pastime."

"Should I be worried about him?" Darbeshay asked simply as our steps echoed down the hall.

Yeah...my brow furrowed. Should we? He didn't *sound* like that reliable a person. Estasia seemed to constantly be telling us he was fine when she in turn called him a backstabber. I was really done with that sort of thing.

No more traitors.

"He's fine. He only does it to be petty and in control, and if he helps Skayla in any way, he loses control. He knows that. I know we can trust him because he's out for himself, but he's just as scared of losing his own mind as any of us are."

Somehow, I caught the small catch she'd had before "as any of us," almost as if she'd been about to say "as I am" instead.

I didn't blame her.

We reached the final door that led back into the main tunnels, and Darbeshay again stopped. "I suppose I can't fault him in that." She drew in a deep breath, and then added, "Now we shall need to keep the talking to a minimum."

"No kidding," Estasia murmured.

Darbeshay just raised an eyebrow and looked to me. "It must be fun to put up with her on a daily basis."

I couldn't help but smile, all the more so when Estasia let out a sort of growling huff.

"She's good once you get past the underfed, under-loved exterior," I replied with a laugh.

"I'll take your word for it." Darbeshay's lips tipped up slyly. "You both are going to just *love* Atlys."

We stood behind the house that rose above the rubble-strewn street. The address read 12990c on the barely intact door. Estasia and Darbeshay said this was part of the old city—the part Skayla had destroyed.

I was still *slightly* preoccupied with the fact that I'd actually hidden my wings. Apparently, they could look quite convincingly like a coat if I wanted. It wouldn't go unnoticed if people took a closer look, but at least I didn't stick out like such a sore thumb. Granted, we'd stuck to the sewers as long as possible, only exiting when we'd reached what Darbeshay called "the old city," where apparently patrols didn't really bother going. But still.

But even with the lack of people, I felt anxious, the unpleasant sensation shooting through every nerve and fiber in my body. But it didn't really feel like mine. Was it *really* me? Or the watch around my chest that seemed to burn?

Darbeshay didn't say a word as she walked up to the mutilated back porch and gave a complicated set of knocks.

A moment passed in tense silence before the door creaked opened to reveal a man of about fifty, towering over us in what appeared to be an old military uniform.

"Well, what do you want?" he asked irritably.

"Definitely not that attitude," Estasia mumbled from next to me.

If I'd not been so nervous, I may have actually laughed. Ugh, the stupid watch wouldn't shut up. Was it because Sven was so far away? It had to be.

"Atlys. I've brought friends. Inside?" Darbeshay whispered to the man.

This brought on a huff in reply, and Atlys stepped aside, opening the door wide enough for us to enter. "You shouldn't have come at all, idiot. I've gotten you all out of trouble enough already."

"Noted," Darbeshay replied as she led the way inside.

Even before I stepped inside, I could smell the must, and once in the house, I saw why. The building was emaciated and in utter ruins, with windows smashed and dirt-covered furniture in all levels of functionality scattered or broken about the rooms. Doors were non-existent, and it was almost impossible *not* to notice the gaping hole in the ceiling. It was as if the house itself truly was starved and dead, ravished beyond repair.

I shuddered, sending feathers everywhere as I did so.

"Oh, look, the little bird came." A hint of amusement graced his gruff tone. I stiffened, then realized Illan must have said something. Still not ideal....

"Welcome to my...humble abode." Atlys waved his hand idly and kept walking, going into the open space right in front of us which might have once been the parlor.

"Impressive," I heard Estasia mumble, like some disappointed mother. "I suppose you are Atlys, then." She matched his ill manner to perfection.

"I suppose." He stopped in the remnants of the parlor, turning around and eyeing Darbeshay with disapproval. "You know better than to come here, yourself. Was this really all just for introduction? It's dangerous."

It seemed his pessimism could rival even Estasia's.

"I needed the exercise," she replied calmly. "And besides, we took the sewers, and anyone that would recognize my face is long dead."

"You're bold today. Careful, that's what got you caught when I found you.... These friends you brought had better be worth it." He waved his hand again in our direction.

"I'm Estasia. Illan knows me, and I guess you've been looking for me? I can still leave, though...."

"Feisty little thing, eh?" Atlys gave a dry smile and tipped a musty lounge chair over so he could sit in it. "Chair?" He motioned to the various furniture that littered the floor.

"Thanks, we'll stand." Estasia's voice was cold.

Actually, I wouldn't have minded a chair...but I kept my mouth shut, constantly fighting the distraction of the pulsing watch around my neck. Why was it being so...temperamental? Was Sven alright?

Estasia's refusal of the chair apparently only made Atlys more amused, and he chuckled, "Pity, I wanted to see if any of the other ones were stable."

This man was really starting to seem more and more unhinged. Both Estasia and Darbeshay seemed unaffected, though, so I did my best to do the same. But why was he living in this place? Didn't everyone who worked with Skayla get actual nice accommodations? They said he had the ploy of servitude, so wouldn't he get the perks that came with it?

"Sorry. Do you want some food? I probably have some rodents lying around someplace...." He trailed off with raised eyebrows.

Ew. Definitely a little unhinged.

"No. I want information and a little more civility," Estasia shot back. "Let's start by asking why exactly we should be trusting someone who sold out to Skayla?"

Atlys's face paled a bit and he leaned forward. "She knows how to get what she wants. MindHolds aren't her only weapon, you know. Have you never heard of the holding camps?"

It was rare I saw Estasia look so openly confused. "Holding camps?"

"Yes. Skayla liked keeping a few of the 'old guard' nobility around to keep the cities in check, so she decided not everyone got to die if they said 'no' to her." His smile was somehow even more grim than his previous scowl. "That's where they sent my family."

"Oh. I'm sorry," I couldn't catch the words from spilling out of my mouth, but I didn't try and take them back.

It was unsettling the way he looked at me, his deep brown eyes half-crazed and half-bitter. He surveyed me almost as if staring at some oddity in a cage.

"I've never heard of these...camps." Estasia sounded skeptical.

"That's because no one ever gets out." Atlys's eyes never left mine. But I refused to look away. "And only her most loyal soldiers keep them."

"Do you...get to see your family?" I asked at last.

The smile he gave was cold and humorless. "No."

"Then how do we know you *won't* turn us right over to Skayla if she threatens your family?" Estasia pushed. "You seem the *last* person that should be in charge of any of this."

I didn't like the laugh that came from Atlys. "Because my family apparently tried to escape, and they were killed. But you see, Skayla doesn't know I know that. She thinks I am oblivious and believe my wife is still alive. And because of that, she thinks I'm still a leashed dog."

My heart...hurt. Dead. I understood the feeling, losing everything. And yet I still had Sven and Estasia. And the others—if they returned from Rugo, anyway.

But this man? He had nothing.

Nothing to lose. No wonder he was crazy.

"But anyway. Back to business. Illan hasn't told me much. Said you would kill him, otherwise." Atlys continued on speaking to Estasia as if he hadn't just mentioned his entire family being murdered.

"Yes. I have contacts in other places, but I'm not going to go telling anyone all of them, because the last thing that needs to happen is Skayla getting in your head and seeing them all. But I need to get word to my contacts one way or the other, and Darby says you're the person to do that." Estasia looked around and then added, "Even if you do live in a graveyard."

"Ha! I like that." Atlys slapped his knee and sat back in his chair. "Well, I might be interested. I'm sick of sitting around doing nothing. If you have a list, I can see if I can get some lackeys out to rally the cause," he said with a self-aware artificialness.

"I'll give you one encrypted message to send to *one* person in Hytat, who I will verbally give you the name to. They'll handle spreading it to the rest," Estasia countered, hands on her hips. "I don't like writing things down and giving a list would do nothing but ask for trouble."

Atlys again met my eyes, amusement shining in them even as he replied to Estasia, "Good. That was a test. I suppose competent help can be found every once in a while."

"Now, how have you managed to keep *your* activities secure?" Estasia shot back.

"A few very well-screened spies. And one or two friends."

"Any other nobles among those friends?" Estasia asked. There was something different in her tone. "I hear Eugene Atarah is also still alive."

I couldn't help but be a little perplexed at the out-of-place mention of this Atarah.

Atlys scoffed, "Atarah? I think Skayla's collar suits him too well. I don't trust any of the other nobles. He's got plenty to lose, and I can't afford anyone who's too scared to keep their mouth shut. No. Most of them are my old employees from before the war, and a sea captain or two."

"Great. I will get you an encoded message to give to a name in Hytat. It will inform them both that our phase one is complete, as well as the fact that we have more allies to work with." Estasia seemed so confident, refusing to allow the man to set her off-balance. But I saw the brief flash of disappointment that surfaced at Atlys's reply.

"It shall be done, my lady."

"Lord Atlys! Lord Atlys!" A little boy's voice pierced the air mere seconds before a small boy squeezed through the exposed window frame.

Atlys shot up, allowing worry to show.

I realized my hand had instinctively reached for the blade sheathed at my side.

The tension in the room was palpable.

"What is it, Caspian?" Atlys demanded.

"Sir...Skayla...she—she's in Alkemar."

Estasia:

The words were still ringing in my head as we waited around the map-strewn table in Darbeshay and Thackeray's tent. Sven and the others weren't back yet, and that just left room to idle and worry.

I hated both.

"They should be back any minute, right?" Baey asked, her nervousness pervading the room like a bad cough.

Darbeshay was hiding her fear better than most. "Yes, soon. Don't worry."

I didn't like this at all. Baey said Skayla would be able to feel the relics; she'd know we were in the city. While that didn't mean knowing our exact location, it could be just as bad. Skayla would just camp out here until she found us, and I didn't want to face her again.... I didn't want *Sven* to, either. It was clear he was no match for her, and the last two times had gone badly enough for me to desire no rematch.

"Lady Darbeshay!" A soldier announced as she entered the tent, putting a fist to her chest in some pretense of discipline. But we were all beggars, slaves, and escapees, here. Who were any of us kidding?

"Are they back?" Darbeshay asked as she gripped the edge of the table, throwing out the pretended formality.

"Yes. They just came through the entrance. They'll be here soon."

All three of us breathed a sigh of relief.

But they were back.

Not that it solved our problem at *all*. But at least for now, everyone was still alive and in one piece.

"So, who tells him?" Baey asked. "Should I?"

There was no time to answer the question, however, as three very distraught figures shoved their way into the room almost as soon as the soldier had left it, Sven at the back.

He and his mother looked...shaken. Really shaken.

"So, I take it you already know, then?" I asked as Thackeray came over to his sister's side.

"What?" he said, breathless. "I...oh, that Skayla is coming? Yes, but—"

"No, Thay. Skayla's already *here*." Darbeshay was looking worriedly over her brother, even while I turned to inspect the other two of the group.

"Wait, what?" Sven's voice was barely even a whisper. "What do you mean, she's already here?" Even as he spoke, however, the rubbing of his ring became almost feverish.

He could feel it; I knew it.

"Alright, so then if you already knew Skayla was coming, what happened out there to get all of you so distracted?" I asked. They had made no reaction to the news of Skayla, and clearly that wasn't the reason they were all...well...like this. Alenor hadn't so much as spoken a word, let alone shown any emotion. In fact, she was *almost* as non-emotive as Sven usually was.

And Sven....

He was a nervous wreck. If it wasn't from Skayla, then what was it?

"We found Moira," Sven managed at last.

"*What?*" Darbeshay and Baey both said in unison.

I kept my surprise to myself but only barely.

"She's...we don't know, but she's trapped at the portal site." Alenor had apparently broken her own spell—or maybe it had been Darby and Baey—and at last spoke, hands trembling at her sides. "She seemed to be in some sort of time loop or space out of time. She kept appearing and reappearing...she's the ghost of the portal site. Sh-she is there but not."

"Well, at least she's alive, then," I replied as I refocused my attention on the order of importance. In all honesty, I hadn't believed Sven was right; I'd thought he had just been unable to cope with the loss of his oldest sister. "So she's, what, pretty stable? She's been like that for years? So when they come back with The Living Stone, we can just get her out. This is actually great news." Moira being alive could be a *huge* asset. If Sven was right and Baey could get her out...then all we needed was to hope the group that had gone to Rugo was competent enough to get what we needed.

"Yes. I suppose that's true," Thackeray replied.

Alenor and Sven didn't say a word.

Thackeray thankfully seemed to take it upon himself to continue with their findings. "We also found machines where the portal was. N…Nyta says Skayla is trying to open up a portal." The way Thackeray stumbled on Alenor's fake name and then made eye contact with the woman…ugh, had she blown who she was? If Moira had appeared, then probably. I stifled my own sigh. I'd really wanted to keep that between Baey, Sven, and me.

"Wait. Do the machines work?" Baey asked, turning to Alenor.

"Yes. I think they do, but—" Alenor took a moment to compose herself. "But something's keeping it closed, still. The readings on the devices...they don't make sense. Someone with more knowledge than me on portal devices created these. They're Henry's designs, but they've been improved." She looked apologetically at me before going on. "Henry…Henry and I could never get them to work. Whoever built these machines didn't just poach our blueprints."

Darbeshay looked in shock from Alenor to Thackeray, but her brother shook her head as if to say he'd explain later. I just rolled my eyes. Yeah, Alenor had blown it.

"But you say it's still closed?" I asked, staying on the subject at hand for now.

"Yes. It seems to be experiencing some form of resistance. My theory is it's from the other side. One of the dial panels had a set of readings that weren't on the original schematics. It has to be for the other side of the door—I mean it seems to be a two-sided one, so theoretically it could be locked from the other side."

"Who, uh, who would be locking it, though?" Darbeshay asked, perplexity now evident all over her face.

"Whatever the reason, we need to shut those down," I announced unceremoniously. "Whether it's Skayla trying to flee, expand, or Ovok trying to get reinforcements, it's not good for us. What if she conquers another world? We'd be doubly outnumbered."

Alenor raised a hand and said, "I can dismantle the machines. But it will take time, and I need to make a few tools."

"Great. With Skayla here, we'll need to be careful. I'll have to have Atlys and Illan see if they can find out if and when she'd be going to the portal site. We want to avoid that." Darbeshay began tapping her fingers against the table.

"Sven?" Baey's concern cut the air. "Are you alright?"

Sven hadn't said a word since the conversation had changed from Moira, let alone move. He'd just stood there still as a statue, watching as he always did.

"I'm fine."

No "darlin'," no "don't worry." Just an "I'm fine."

I resisted the urge to tense my jaw. "Yeah, no. You're not fine."

Everyone in the room stopped what they were doing, making me regret my decision a *little* bit. Perhaps I shouldn't have said that out loud.

"I. Am. Fine." The way he drew out each word gave the impression of actual anger, something I'd not really heard from Sven before. "I'm not the one stuck in a time anomaly, or having to deal with being around a murderer day in and day out, so can you all please *stop* asking me if I'm alright, because I should be the least of your concerns right now. Let's get back to the things that will *actually* help people and stop wasting time."

Now everyone, including me, was staring with wide eyes at him. He'd not raised his voice above what would be considered a normal conversational tone, and yet coming from him, it might as well have been shouted. Now the silence was even worse, rending the air like his haunted gaze always did.

"I need some air," Sven growled, only barely cutting off Darbeshay from saying something. Without another word, he stormed out of the tent.

I sighed. I hated dealing with people. "I'll go talk to him," I said, used to the job by now and knowing *someone* had to do it. Alenor was in no state to. At this point, she and Sven would probably only feed off each other.

"If there's any way I can help…." Darbeshay looked as if she wanted to follow me. "We were good friends, once."

"No, I'm fine, thanks," was all I said before exiting the tent. Did I trust myself to do a good job of this? No, not really. Did I trust someone else to? That was an even bigger no. After Maeko, Sefen, and pretty much everyone except Baey and Alenor—when she wasn't processing the shock of her once-dead daughter—I didn't trust anyone to talk to Sven.

And yet, I really didn't know what to do myself.

Now out in the musty, humid air of the Underground, I looked around to see if Sven was still within sight.

I didn't have to look far at all. He was right outside the tent, off to the left and taking deep, unsteady breaths, rubbing that ring like it was going to burn his finger off.

"So, I'd ask if you were alright, but then I would get reamed out again, wouldn't I?" Wait, no, that was definitely not the right thing to say. *Way to go, Estasia. Brilliant.* I really hated people. And talking to them. Gah.

"Would you leave me alone?" Sven's snap was uncharacteristic.

"Look, Sven. I don't understand. You already thought Moira was alive—what's so hard about it now? Isn't this good? And Thackeray and Darbeshay *love* you. I talked to her, myself, they don't blame you at all. She says you were friends before the whole end-of-the-world thing. I thought that's what you wanted; why can't you accept it?"

He ran both hands through his hair, his body seeming to explode in a wave of anguish, frustration, and anger. "Don't you get it? I never *wanted* them to like me, Estasia. I should be the *last* thing on anyone's mind right now, and it seems I am incapable of doing anything except letting you all down or causing worry."

Ugh, I was...not equipped for this.

"Now, I need to be *alone*. I will be fine, and so help me, if one more person asks me that...I...." He broke off again, this time grabbing hold of his ring and constantly taking it on and off his finger like a nervous habit.

My chest tightened. "Please don't throw that away again."

The laugh he gave was chilling—worse than any of Skayla's crazed giggles. "Don't worry, I'll try not to jeopardize us all like that again. Just let me have a minute alone. Please."

I didn't want to. I felt like it was a bad idea for him to be alone, and try as I might, I couldn't stop the worry that he might throw off the ring again. Was it Skayla? Was it her return? I didn't understand. I wanted to help, but I couldn't, and it only made me angry.

"Fine. Stay out here. But don't say I didn't try." I threw up my hands as I gave up, turning back to the tent.

He didn't say a word as I went back inside.

And that's when I began to wonder if those inside had heard it all.

At the very least, everyone was staring at me.

"I give up, I'm not good with people," I growled, not exactly loving the attention.

"I'll go talk to him," Darbeshay murmured, coming around the table.

"I really would discourage that...he said if one more person—"

"I know." She gave a sad smile. "I'll be back. Thay, go over the plan with everyone else."

No one else argued as she quietly slipped out of the tent. The urge to eavesdrop was canceled out by everyone else refocusing on the task ahead of us.

Thackeray explained the remaining pieces of the puzzle I'd missed while I was outside the tent, and with that, we were able to continue onto plans of how and when we would dismantle the machines.

Neither Sven nor Darbeshay returned for the remainder of the meeting, and by the time it finished, I realized that not only was I too spent to go back to our hidden manor, but so was Alenor. While perhaps not having the meltdown Sven was, she had almost completely withdrawn into herself, rubbing her arm and staring at the maps as if they were the only things in the room.

But I was done peopling for the evening. I wasn't even going to bother asking if Darbeshay and Thackeray now knew who she was, because that was just so obvious at this point. I was done.

"Do you think it would be alright if we stayed here the night, Thackeray?" To my surprise, it was Baey who spoke up.

Thackeray nodded. "We have a few spare tents. The buildings are usually reserved for the sick, young, or elderly. But the tents are yours if you want."

Baey's eyes settled on Alenor a moment before looking to me.

I shrugged. I didn't mind it. I'd slept on the ground plenty of times.

"That sounds lovely. Thank you."

With that, we were shown our quarters, and Baey and I settled down into a tent while Alenor got her own.

"I know it's been asked a lot, but are *you* alright?" Baey asked as soon as we were settled.

I sighed. "Yeah, just dandy. Really put my foot in it, this time."

"But you tried. That counts for something, right?" Baey asked gently.

"Right. Tried and botched it up. I think I'll just acquiesce to the fact that people aren't my thing." I was a little more upset over this than I would have liked, and I didn't want to think that maybe there was more to this than Sven and Alenor. That it had to do more with Atlys's meeting and the mention of Atarah's allegiances.

Fiddling with her wings, Baey murmured, "Sounds lonely."

That wouldn't have bothered me a month ago.

Oh, well.

A long silence passed between us, and then Baey got up, "Speaking of trying...maybe I should try and talk to Alenor."

"Yeah. You do that, Birdy." I laughed, shaking my head.

"What?"

"Nothing. Alenor would like talking to you. Go on. Shoo." Speaking of some time alone, I was beginning to want some myself.

Hesitantly, Baey left the tent, leaving me alone, with nothing but the knife at my side. I took it out, fingering the ornate hilt as it shone from the light of the single lantern hanging in the tent. Alone. I liked it because it was easier. But Baey was right—it was lonely. I guess I'd just been this way long enough to get used to the ache.

THE LIVING STONE

CHAPTER XI: Together

<u>Sven:</u>

I just needed to be alone—just needed to get Moira's ghostly image out of my head. Another failure. Another Ghost.

Get it together, Sven!

I barely kept in a bitter laugh. Funny how I made everything about me when trying to tell everyone to *stop* making everything about me. If I'd just stayed quiet and stayed put, then they would have moved on. If I'd hidden it better, then no one would have asked me what was wrong. But no, I had to say something; had to draw attention away from the urgent situation and instead onto me.

Why was I so weak? Skayla had won, *again*. She'd known I couldn't handle my own head, and now I was just dragging everyone down like I did every time.

"Sven?"

I sucked in a deep breath as Darbeshay's voice filtered through the screams in my head.

Right. Not only had I blown up at Estasia, but I'd done it in front of them. How selfish could I be?

"Sorry," I whispered. "That was uncalled for. I'll be right in."

"Sven...follow me. I'll show you where I go to clear my head." She brushed by me as calmly as if I wasn't the person who had killed her parents right in front of her. As if I wasn't the one that had given her brother that scar. As if I didn't give her nightmares.

And yet I followed, unable to argue and unwilling to let my stupid emotional instability get the best of me any more than it already had.

I needed to get a grip.

Darbeshay took me quietly through the outskirts of the Underground, leading me to the far wall where a guarded tunnel lay. We were let in without remark, but I saw the wary glances of the two sentries.

The creaking door closed behind us, and I jumped at the thud of it shutting, finding my hand at the hilt of my blade before I could so much as breathe.

"Sorry. It's just the door," Darbeshay whispered gently.

"You have no reason to apologize." If anyone needed to hand those out, it was me. If only they felt less like empty words. Yes, sorry, I killed your father. Sorry, I helped destroy Baeno. Sorry, I wasn't there. Didn't really fix anything, did it?

I was distracted when I noticed the breeze coming through the tunnel. Fresh air. I sucked it in like a lifeline, catching the sound of distant crashing that was coming with it. It sounded...like....

My thought came to a conclusion as I found myself standing quite suddenly in an opening that looked over the ocean, churning far below us as it crashed against the cliffside.

I closed my eyes and took in the smell of the salty, *fresh* air, the feeling of being trapped slowly melting away with the tide.

"This is where I come to breathe, sometimes. You're welcome to it whenever you want. It's where we bring up supplies from Atlys—there's a path to the left," she explained.

"Thank you...and sorry. Again." What more could I say? "I'll be back in one piece soon. I just…" *Stop. Talking.*

"Do you want company? Or were you serious about being alone?" Her question was asked with such a quiet confidence that it squashed the doubt left behind in my unfinished sentence. "I won't talk, if you don't want me to. But I get the feeling you really don't want to be alone."

"Darbeshay, I can't—"

"Sven, it's always been Darby to you."

I winced. "Why can't you just hate me?" the question tore itself from my throat more violently than the waves crashing against the cliff.

"Sven. How can I hate you for what *Skayla* did? You were one of my *best* friends, and I know if our positions were changed...you would never hate me." Her voice trembled.

"I know. I know I couldn't control my actions under Skayla. But I *knew* better. I should have known better. I made a gamble and I *am* responsible for the result. Don't you see? I could have left and not stayed behind to let Skayla get me. But because of it your parents are dead—Sera's dead. So many others…" And they wouldn't get out of my head. I couldn't ignore them.

Then Darbeshay's voice again cut through the screams. "Not Thackeray, and not me."

My anguish again broke through the thin facade I'd tried to hide it behind, and I felt as if my shoulders would buckle from the weight as I replied, "But why? Why was I not strong enough to stop Skayla every time? Why sometimes? Why couldn't I save them all?"

"Sven, you aren't some infallible being!" The words were passionate but not angry. "Just because everyone else puts you on this impossible pedestal doesn't mean you have to hang from it. You can't be responsible for everything. Anyone else wouldn't have been able to break free *at all*. In fact, no one else *has* been strong enough."

I closed my eyes again, wishing I could be left alone. Not by Darbeshay. No. That's not really what I'd meant by wanting to be left alone, had it? No, I meant the memories in my stupid brain. The nightmare that wouldn't go away.

"I can't afford another slip-up." My voice cracked as I whispered the words. "I just can't."

"That's what friends are for, Sven. To help so that doesn't happen."

I felt a tear creep down my cheek. "But I killed them all."

"Really?" Darbeshay's voice was barely audible. "I'm still here."

"But why can't I remember? All I remember is the pain I caused you. Everything else seems to be hiding behind it…. I-I remember shadows. That's all." Like the one I'd recreated in the hall with Baey. I *knew* Darbeshay was right, and yet I couldn't remember specific memories. Every time I remembered her laughing, it cut to me killing her parents. Thackeray's smile turned to his scar. Sera with….

"Well, I'm not going anywhere. I know it will come back. And even if you don't remember, we can still be friends now. We don't need the past for that."

My chest hurt. "Were we that close?"

"Yes. You were my best friend." She gave a small, half-hearted chuckle. "Though you were a lot of people's best friend, I suppose. Always so genuine."

I knew she was right. I felt it, even if I couldn't draw up any memory besides the one of that night. "I'm sorry I hurt you. I really…I really am." I

188

couldn't gather the courage to turn and look at her as I forced the words out, instead looking at the sea as it churned. Tormented and doomed to batter against the unforgiving land forever.

"Sven. Please. It's Skayla who should apologize." Her tone tipped towards anger at the mention of my sister. "But if you hold yourself to these impossible standards, you realize you need to hold Baey to them, too, right?"

Now I did turn and look at her, confused and a bit taken aback.

The smile Darbeshay wore was sad. "She's the Last Esmer, right? The one you left to save that night? It's clear she looks up to you. And if she's supposed to be the replacement to The Watchers, then she has to hold herself to the same standards as you. Because you were the best of them."

The sigh that escaped my lips was a defeated one, and I looked down. "I suppose." I hadn't thought of it like that. Not that I was the best of us. But she was right; Baey would hold herself to the standard I showed. I winced.

"I just want you to be able to heal, Sven. And...really believe me when I say I'm glad you're alive." She shivered, hugging herself as the wind licked around us. It wasn't particularly cold, but I had a feeling the motion was more for comfort than anything else. "We both really missed you." I felt so empty, and yet there was something familiar now. A memory that tugged, suppressed behind the screams and the victims of The GhostMaker. Something almost comforting.

"Thank you," I whispered. "I must have been very lucky to have you as a friend."

She chuckled, shaking her head. "Well, I am pretty sure everyone was lucky to have *you,* Sven. The least I can do is give it back in return."

I forced myself to breathe, thankful for the fresh air and lack of mustiness that had been so oppressive inside the Underground. I wanted to apologize again, for dragging her out here and making her calm me down, when I was the last person I wanted her or anyone to worry about. But then I looked over and realized she'd closed her eyes, breathing in deeply and letting the wind wash over her as well.

Maybe I wasn't the only one who'd needed some air.

With a suddenness I remembered Mum. I wasn't the only one having a hard time—and I'd left her alone.

"I suppose we should go back," I murmured, catching the regret in Darby's features as she opened her eyes and straightened, returning to the proper version of herself.

She tucked back the stray hair that had been blown out by the wind and nodded. "Yes. I suppose so."

"Thank you," I said again, extending my arm for her to take. A long-forgotten instinct, somehow easier to remember than the memories of my friends, it seemed.

She looked a long moment before taking my arm, but there was a small, genuine smile that made me feel as if the gesture had been at least a little worth it.

"Any time, Sven."

190

After discovering we were spending the night in the Underground and parting ways with Darby, I slowly made my way over to where Thackeray had said the others were staying. He'd said Mum's tent was the one on the far left.

Just as I approached it, however, none other than Baey came out, bumping right into me as I had prepared to announce myself.

"Ugh, sorry—oh, Sven, you're back are you—you look—uh—you here for your mother?" The half-finished sentences might have been more amusing if I hadn't wondered if she was now afraid to ask how I was because of how I had acted earlier.

"How is she?" I asked instead, as if nothing had happened.

Baey bit her lip. "She's okay, I think. I'm sure she'll love to see you though. I don't think she's going to sleep." She hesitated a moment longer, as if again wanting to ask me how I was, but instead just looked at me a long time before walking off, soon disappearing into another tent. I stood out in the damp.

With one more deep breath, I called out, "Mum? You alright if I come in?" It was nice to be able to call her "Mum" again, even if it was the incident with Moira that had led to her true identity being revealed.

For a while, there was silence from inside the tent, leaving me with nothing but the eerie echoes of the makeshift city we were currently in.

"You can come in, Sven," she called, just as I began to wonder if she'd heard me.

With one more deep breath, I obeyed, hoping I could keep myself in check enough now to help.

She looked about as awful as she had when I'd last seen her. Her face was drawn, every muscle in her jaw and face held tightly. Her gaze clung to me like at any moment I might disappear. Like I'd already done before. But more importantly, like Moira.

Quietly, I came over and sat on the cot next to her, our shoulders touching. She sucked in a deep breath and shuddered, but whether from coming back to the present or because she was holding onto a sob, I wasn't sure.

"At least we know for sure she's alive. And where she is," Mum breathed.

"Yeah. That is true." My reply was just as unconvincing. What no one had understood—what I couldn't expect anyone to understand—was that it wasn't about seeing her alive. Yes, believing she was alive and seeing her was different. Seeing her…like that. Knowing she'd been stuck like that for over a decade. Stuck shifting in and out of time.

Stuck watching.

It was a fate I wouldn't wish on even my worst enemy. Really, I wouldn't.

And what was worse? We couldn't get her out. She was stuck there until the others came back with The Living Stone.

If they came back at all.

"I'm sorry," I murmured as I put an arm around her shoulders, and in return, she rested her head against mine.

"No," she whispered. "*I'm* sorry. I'm so sorry. I don't know how this happened. I thought Henry and I—I thought we were better than this. We should have seen Skayla coming. We shouldn't have stepped back like we did. We—"

"Mum." My voice was hoarse as I cut off her rambling. I wished I remembered more. I wished it didn't seem like my mind was wading through a swamp of nightmares just to get to one good memory at the bottom. But the memories of us as children were more real than most. "Whatever Skayla's reasons, it is not your fault. At the end of the day..." I trailed off a moment. "At the end of the day, she is her own person, and she decided to do this. If anything, I'm just sorry you got stuck with us for children."

At this, she sat up straight, turning to me and putting a gentle hand to my cheek. I resisted the instinct to pull away.

"Don't say that, Sven. I love you too much to let you believe that kind of lie either."

I sighed. This wasn't helping her. Again, I thought of the way Darby had pointed out my own high expectations. I didn't know if I could let them go—if it was really fair to. But how could I ask Mum to do it if I myself couldn't?

"Well, you don't believe your lie, and maybe I won't believe mine." I managed a smile as I took her hand and squeezed it.

She mirrored my smile.

"And maybe we can fix this. Together."

There were tears in her eyes as she whispered, "Yes. Together."

Baey:

"Higher!" Sven called just as he came at me again with his sword. I obeyed, barely able to catch his blade in mine before it would have gone straight into my head. Illusions or not—*reality* bending or not—I still felt like I was about to die every time that stupid blade came close to my face.

193

It was like preemptive phantom pains any time Sven got around my guard. I guess if nothing else, it prepared me for the real thing a lot more than sparring blades would have.

"Careful!" Sven's call came right as I allowed him *again* to get around me, and even as he called out the warning, he swept his legs under and behind my own so that I began to fall backward. But unlike the other three hundred times, I *didn't* fall, instead flaring out my wings and using the energy to flip over myself and land on my feet a couple yards away from Sven.

He gave the faintest haunting of a smirk. "Not bad. But remember, flips take time. A quicker enemy might take advantage of an exposed back. So, if you're going to do it, make sure you don't compromise your defense."

I didn't even have time to nod as he engaged again, this time putting his full force into the blade. I *knew* it was full force because my fingers almost instantly went numb with the vibration. Last time he'd done that, my blade had gone flying from my hand.

As it was, I barely hung on.

But I did.

Not that it mattered, because a second later, Sven said, "Dead."

Still locked blade-to-blade, I allowed my indignant confusion to show. "What? No, your sword is *right here!*" I pushed against his blade with mine as if to prove my point.

Sven just raised an eyebrow and then looked down. I followed his gaze.

"Ugh," I grumbled with a sigh as I saw the illusion of a knife sticking in my ribcage. I relaxed, stepping back and untangling myself from his blade.

"You're getting much better, Baey," Sven said, ruffling my hair.

I elbowed him, sheathing my blade. "Right. Because I only die...one hundred percent of the times we fight—still."

He actually chuckled a little, and the sound made me grin against my will, my frustration melting away in the face of his apparent amusement. Somehow, it didn't bother me when I amused him. It wasn't like he was laughing down at me. He wasn't laughing *at* me either. It was as if he was laughing *with* me, even when we weren't sharing a joke, and really anything was worth getting even as small a chuckle as this.

"Yes, I suppose you still die, but that's because I'm not going so easy on you anymore." His voice echoed a bit around the space, but not nearly as much as when we were in Alenor's tunnel. We were practicing in the Underground, today—right outside the city. It was much less stressful, at least. More space to work with, too.

"Yeah, but no one else is going to take it easy on me, either. I mean. I'll still die with them," I pointed out. I knew I was getting better. I just...still felt like I'd end up getting myself killed in a real fight.

Sven sheathed his sword as well, stretching in an apparent attempt to relax. "I don't think you quite understand, darlin'." His expression was poorly masking bitterness. "If you manage to beat me, then there's no one on Baeno who would stand a chance against you."

The statement clung to the air. I suppose I hadn't really thought of it that way. But I'd seen him with Jaythos and Sefen—*without* a weapon. Not even they would have stood a true chance against him now.

Then Sven went on, "Besides, you've already made it through the fight back in the ruins. And you saved me from Skayla. I'd say that's a pretty good streak, saving The GhostMaker's hide—*twice*."

I winced. "No. I saved *your* life. My friend's life. But I'm sure someone would have done it."

"But no one did," he pointed out simply. The sigh that followed was a weighty one.

The statement stuck oddly with me as something deep within whispered he was right. No one else had. Would someone really have stepped in if I hadn't? Back at The Crafters' house—the moment with the knife. Would someone have noticed in time? Had I held my own, even then?

But enough about me. "So, it's your turn to practice, right?" We'd started with illusions before the swordplay—Sven had wanted me fresh and alert—but he'd skipped his own bit of practice.

His entire body tensed, but I supposed I wouldn't have noticed, if not for the fact that he was always so relaxed when he was fighting. It was the only time I ever saw him in any state other than guarded and closed off, and yet still I saw the fear he hid in his eyes as we trained. The fear he would hurt me. The fear that the memories fighting for dominance in his mind would win.

I wouldn't let them. I only hoped he wouldn't, either.

"I suppose you are correct," he replied at last, rolling his shoulders and looking around in an attempt to appear casual. But I knew he was making sure no one was around to watch. Either so no one could see, or no one could get hurt.

"So, what are you going to try today?" I asked as I sat down a little way away, crossing my legs and stretching out my wings behind me. I refused to allow his dread to pervade my curiosity; if only in the hopes that if I was optimistic and curious, maybe he would be a little more so. Maybe he'd be less afraid.

His lips pressed tightly together in concentration, and almost automatically, his one hand went to where the ring rested on the other. Again, I felt the pulsing of the watch around my neck match the rhythm of Sven's nervous twisting of the ring. Not that it had been quiet since Skayla arrived. She'd been searching the city, and with more patrols now in the tunnels, it was hard to ignore that feeling of being closed in upon.

"So, uh, how does it work, exactly?" I piped up, successfully stopping Sven's devolving demeanor even as I tried to shove down my own worries. "I mean, you explained with the water. But like—uh—before." Wait, ugh, I didn't want to go here. Maybe I could make this work.... "How did you make that ballroom so real?"

Sven's shoulders stiffened a bit more, and I held in a wince. But he looked at me, patient and at least mostly still in the here and now. "Well. I'm not...completely sure how *that* happened. Losing control can create all sorts of problems. But part of it was the space we were in. I created it—an invisible wall protecting our area from the rest of reality."

Vaguely, I remembered the weird sensation I'd gotten when I'd crept back to watch him. Had that been it?

"So, now, I'm going to do that—in case something goes wrong *again*. It isolates the damage, but it does not change anything visibly. Not until I take it away. Then everything reverts to how it was before." His shoulders slowly relaxed as he continued to explain, and he reached out a hand around him. "There. Now everything from over there—" He pointed to some nearby supply crates left on the outskirts of town. "—to the wall over on our other side is within a protective field."

I squinted, staring around us and trying to see any difference. Just like before, I *had* felt something. And yet I couldn't see any difference—wait. "I...think I see it? The wall. It's shimmering." It was barely visible.

"Interesting." Sven's tone was more lighthearted than before. "I suppose I shouldn't be surprised at this point. So yes, anything in that field will return to its normal state after I take it back, no matter how much I change things. For instance—" He slammed his foot on the ground, and in response, the entire earth rippled as if it were water. My legs wobbled with it, and I jumped up into the air, hovering above it as the earth churned. Then I looked over to find Sven riding the earth up to meet me while the earth around him remained firm, even as the tidal wave carried him up. When he was to my level, however, the ground froze in whatever state it had been, a petrified ocean of earth.

"Woah," I whispered as I reached down and gingerly touched the ground. It was real. No illusion. "How'd you...do that...."

Sven's smile flickered like a candle near the end of its wick: fighting for every moment of light, and yet still determined to become brighter instead of extinguish. "A lot of concentration. It's taking an illusion and willing it to be real." His eyes looked more alive than usual, and he seemed almost...pleased with himself. Perhaps "playful" was the more apt term.

Since explaining things to me was apparently a fantastic way to help Sven concentrate and actually breathe for once, I continued that angle, happy to indulge my own curiosity, especially when it seemed to help him so much. "So then...is there any limit to what you can do?"

"Everyone has limits, so yes." The earth and brick pedestal that had been holding him shot down with him on it, and soon, he was on the ground once more. I hesitantly followed, sitting atop one of the frozen waves. "I can change how my clothes look." He waved his hand and I watched in fascination as the worn fabric twisted and stretched, his coat turning into a short jacket and his pants mending their holes. "But I can't physically make my own physical appearances truly different in reality. That is only ever an illusion." His clothes reverted to their original appearance. "Messing something like that up—permanently changing how someone *actually* looks—could hold dangerous consequences."

"Then how'd you make an entire tunnel look like a ballroom? And how'd you make people?" I asked, hating to bring the subject back up but apparently unable to stop myself.

That being said, Sven seemed almost wholly unaffected by the comment now, caught up in every question I asked and eager to explain. Since he'd said no one knew about this, I supposed he'd never had anyone to show either.

"That was a mixture of illusion and reality. A, uh, projection of suppressed memories, I think. I lost control, so my mind tried to create a stable environment where I felt safe. The people felt real because they were simply compressed air with the illusion of what they looked like projected onto the spaces. So, still not real people. The tunnel materials then changed to match the rest of the memory. It's so real, even I can be sucked into the lie." He drew in a breath, seeming to realize where he'd come to in the conversation. "That's why I didn't want Skayla to get me with my ring. If she'd found out...." He shuddered.

"Then..." I whispered. "...then we could have been all in MindHolds and not even known it." We wouldn't even have been living in reality. With Skayla's Mind and Sven's Gift, we'd never have stood even the slightest chance. But I could already see him slowly slipping away once more, and so turned the subject again. "So then, how does your forcefield thing work? I mean...this is all very much here...." I knocked on the wave I was currently sitting on.

"Well, let's do something drastic." He snapped back to it, throwing the comment out as if the ground being petrified in waves *wasn't* drastic. He knelt down, a small circle of completely flat earth forming around him as he touched the ground. Then a crack appeared, running along and opening slowly to create a gaping chasm down into nothingness.

Okay, so maybe that was pretty drastic.

"Is that...really...there?" I gaped, shuddering as I was unable to tear my eyes away from the black nothingness below.

"Yup. Really there. Watch." He stood up, giving this little cocky salute. Without another word he hopped into the hole, disappearing as I gave a shriek.

"You had better come back *right now!*" I called as I flew up and over to the spot, looking for him desperately as my skin crawled. A cylinder of earth shot up and I barely got out of the way as he reappeared, having ridden it up back out of the chasm.

He was grinning. Like, really grinning. For a moment, it was almost as if I was looking back in time to the Sven who had rescued me from

Skayla—the one so full of life even amid the sadness. The person I'd always wanted to be like.

I couldn't help but grin back, even as I endeavored to remain angry. "You *scared* me! You can't just jump into holes, Sven."

With a roll of his eyes, he hopped off and to the side of the chasm before us, shaking himself almost like a dog as dirt sprayed everywhere.

Giving up, I laughed, the feeling more refreshing than I could have dreamed it would be. "Stop it! Stop—ew, now I'm all gross! *Sven!*" I hadn't laughed this hard in...in a long time.

I only wished Sven would laugh, too. But he was still smiling very broadly, and for now, even just that was enough.

"Sorry. Did I ruffle your feathers, darlin'?" He arched an eyebrow as if the joke was some extraordinarily good pun.

"Wow. How long did it take you to come up with that one?" I asked with a roll of my eyes.

"About three hours," he replied with a sudden dead serious expression. An expression that didn't last long as a smirk reformed at the corners of his lips.

I just giggled again, unable to come up with anything good or original to say next.

"But *anyway*," Sven went on after I'd mostly controlled myself. "All I have to do is let down the protective field I put around us, and everything will go back as it was. Watch." With a slightly exaggerated motion, Sven brought his hand up and snapped his fingers together.

The change was so instantaneous I wouldn't even have had time to blink. Indeed. The crack in the ground was gone, the waves were gone...even the dirt I'd been splattered with was completely vanished as if it had never been there.

I didn't bother to hide my fascination. "That's...incredible."

Before Sven could reply, however, a voice called over, "You two children done playing with your sticks? They're going over the plan while I go find Atlys, and they could use you both!" It was Estasia, walking towards us. If only she'd come a bit sooner, she would've had her mind blown....

CHAPTER XII: With an Atlys, Who Needs a Map?

Estasia:

We'd gotten a rough plan together, but they'd need both Baey and Sven for specifics while I went on my mission to find out the best timing for things. Theoretically, Atlys would have a better handle on when the best time to raid the portal site would be, and frankly, I didn't feel like leaving Temorn to go get the information. Besides, maybe Atlys would have an idea of what was going on with Eugene. And maybe he'd have insight on Skayla's activities in the city.

"You two children done playing with your sticks?" I called as I made my way up to the pair of delinquents. In their defense, it did actually look like they were finished—both their swords sheathed at their sides. "They're going over the plan, and they could use you both."

Funny how Baey didn't look so clumsy with the blade at her side anymore. It was more a part of her, and it was good to see her not so terrified of...well...life.

I had apparently interrupted *something*, however, as Sven's cheeks had actual color to them, and Baey was looking as if she'd just gotten ahold of herself. As if she'd been laughing. Good. After the other night, I had been worried Sven would get even more lost in his own head. Baey was good for him.

"We'll be right there," Sven said as he straightened, the fun draining out of him a bit.

"Where are *you* going?" Baey's question showed she was paying a little more attention. I was dressed to fit into the crowd, wanting to stay a little more out of the sewers as I was going alone.

I winked. "Out to cause trouble, I suppose."

"And here I thought usually you were the one cleaning up the trouble we made." Sven's joke caught me off-guard.

It was...a legitimate joke. "Woah, Baey, what did you do to him?" I asked as I inched away from Sven. Perhaps I hadn't drained the fun out of him after all.

"Oh, I think the better question is what he did to *me*. My arms are *killing* me." She jostled Sven with one arm, coaxing a genuine smile from him.

"Alright. That's it. Go drink your chameleon tea and be all buddy-buddy somewhere else. I'm going to go play by myself because I think I've *earned* some alone time." I gave the pair a condescending glare as I walked by them, refusing to be awkward or anything like that. Something in my heart squeezed, though, as I left Baey's giggling behind me. Something warned me against participating in it, but at the same time, I wanted nothing more than to join in. Maybe I was done with walls. Sven and Baey were different from Temorn.

My soul still ached from the invisible scar left by the stab in the back, even as I secretly hoped that I'd be able to find out about Eugene when I talked to Atlys.

Part of me wondered if he thought I'd helped Temorn betray him; if he thought I was just as much a scoundrel as Morn. As I walked through the tunnels, I couldn't help but think of those two years, so long ago and forced out of recollection for so long. Perhaps not the sole reason I never trusted or relied on others, but perhaps more impactful than I liked to admit.

I'd let my guard down, and Temorn had let me down in return. Let Eugene down. But was I more angry at Temorn or myself for it?

Yeah, definitely Temorn.

It didn't take long for me to find a sewer exit, but it did take a bit longer to find one that wasn't being guarded, or searched, or guarded…. Skayla really wanted to find Sven, and while she apparently had no idea about the Underground city, she was still covering her bases.

At last, however, I was up on the surface, among the people in the streets as I had once been so used to. It was nice not being invisible—well, invisible in Sven's way. I easily melted into the crowd in *my* way.

Alkemar was home whether I liked it or not, and yet the home I'd known was so different from the one before me now. The houses were now mostly made of brick, identical and plain—and that was only in the parts Skayla had decided to rebuild. Other houses were a conglomeration of salvaged materials shoved together in a vain attempt at repair. Gone was the uniqueness of the villas and the extensive use of glass for people to take advantage of the sunlight. Gone were the many innovations The Crafters had brought. While Hytat had seemed to retain at least some of the inventions, Alkemar was bare and dirty. Perhaps the most ironic thing was the disrepair of the streets. Only half-repaired from the attack so long ago, they held the scars of war almost as evidently as those with violet eyes walking about it.

What was Skayla even doing? For perhaps the first time, I wondered what caused the sudden shift after the Drogans. Before, I couldn't have cared less. The Maras had been the distant and untouchable Watchers, overseers with motivations I never could have guessed or *cared* to guess. But now I knew some of the family, and Sven seemed as puzzled by his sister's change as anyone—as did Alenor. So, if I believed Alenor's claims that Sven and Skayla had been close, how had he missed this? But more importantly, *what* had he missed?

I stowed away the question for now, and focused on weaving through the streets of the city, avoiding carriages and horses alike—albeit there were very few of those about—along with the more numerous pedestrians. The streets were abuzz with a nervous energy that I chalked up to Skayla's arrival, and I noted that those without her mark in their eyes seemed on edge. I also noted the soldiers—most wearing the emblem of the cold and disciplined Bethynese—marching through the streets and knocking on several doors, and even dragging people out into the streets and carrying them away.

I avoided that as best as I could, once being used to that sort of thing. Now I felt like I was cursed with seeing things through Baey and Sven's eyes.

Still, I tried my best to shake off the chaos and fear and reach my destination. The further I went, the more disrepair I saw, and soon enough I was on a nearly demolished and abandoned street, the once-beautiful stone and metal villas mostly reduced to rubble.

At last, I reached the alley behind Atlys's house, and walking up to the back door, mimicked the complicated set of knocks Darbeshay had done last time. I pondered whether perhaps it would have been more prudent to go in through the window, but the last thing I needed to do was startle the man into doing something drastic.

He did seem...a bit on the edge of his sanity.

A moment passed, and soon the door opened a crack to reveal a very perturbed Atlys.

With a grunt, he said, "Oh well, come in, already," and yanked the door nearly clear off its hinges as he stepped to the side to let me enter.

The door shut with way too many sound effects, and I didn't bother to wait for Atlys—showing myself to the room he'd had us in last time.

"What do you want? Where's Temorn? With Skayla here, you really think it's wise to go running around like a disorderly vole?"

I blinked at the rather ridiculous insult but moved on. "Skayla is why I'm here, and this disorderly vole came because she needed to stretch her legs, and she trusts Temorn about as far as she can throw him. Now, I would ask if I can sit, but I'm pretty sure these chairs are more suited for firewood, so instead can we get to business?"

A broad smile that screamed "I'm definitely insane" spread across the man's face, and he shrugged as he went over and leaned against the crumbling fireplace.

"Do carry on." Then his expression hardened. "But in all seriousness, be aware that Skayla knows Sven Mara is here, and she intends to find him."

I stared at him for a moment. He...he knew. How had *he* figured it out?

"Oh, don't look so confused. Darby had shared her suspicions about The GhostMaker's identity, and Skayla now has a witch hunt out for her disappeared assassin—as much as she's trying to keep *that* slip-up quiet. There's no one else on this planet she'd be this paranoid over losing." The amusement and crazed look suddenly melted away to something more faraway. "But when you see him, tell him I'm glad he's alive."

"I will do that," I replied sincerely, glad to see someone else seemed to remember Sven for who he really was. "But to business." I had half-hoped maybe Skayla hadn't found us after all—that the worry had been for nothing—and that all this searching was somehow just routine when she was in the area. But now, all we could hope for was that the maze of tunnels would hide us.

But we had to move forward with plans while we still could. "We're planning a raid on the portal site—to dismantle the machines Skayla's put there."

Atlys's eyes narrowed. "Well, that sounds like the most idiotic plan of the century. The place is crawling with Skayla's Drogans and soldiers."

I sighed. "Yes, but Sven's already gotten us in once. We're worried Ovok and Skayla are trying to get off-world, and the machines at the portal site are actually working. Something is stopping them from the other side, but it's only a matter of time."

"Well then why don't we just let them go and close it behind?" Atlys asked with a frustrated wave of his hand.

"Because if he got here once he'll be able to get here again, and if Skayla goes and enslaves *another* world then she'll have an endless army and any hopes of being free will be over for good. Now, do I have to keep wasting my breath to explain things, or are you going to tell me the ideal time for us to sneak in and get rid of these machines?" As I finished, I folded my arms, giving my best disapproving glare.

The man looked genuinely caught off-guard. "Yes, I think that is sufficient."

"Good. Right now, we need to focus on the portal machines and getting them disabled. But we can't waltz in there when Skayla's there, too, or we'll get caught."

"I can help you, but you need to be careful. This isn't just you at stake. This is the last free bit of the world you're putting up to fail if you get us all caught. While I have nothing to lose, you have it all." Altys's reply was uncharacteristically grave—and perhaps a bit annoyed.

"I have a pretty good track record so far. Better than most everyone else. I think we can handle it." As I spoke, I allowed my arms to unfold, my own frustration dripping out of me as I conceded his point—even if I wouldn't admit it was a valid one. I was so used to living in the face of Skayla's victory that somehow, I had gotten used to the looming reality of how close to defeat we were. I was aware of the risks.

"Yes. Skayla has gone there first and is still there—so you need to wait a few days. I would say a week would be ideal. If you try something right as she's arrived, she'll be expecting it. Let her search all the obvious places first. They change the guard twice a month at the site, and that's coming up in about..." His brow furrowed as he thought for a moment. "...eight days. If you wait for the day of, there won't be much attention paid to you. Sven can hide your presence, I assume? And with so many intersecting Bethynese soldiers, you will be able to get in and out more easily."

"Fantastic. I will relay that information, and we will begin as planned. Eight days it is." I didn't like waiting, but at the same time...waiting was good. It meant we wouldn't be rushing.

"Also—Sven Mara might want to work his magic on the tunnel systems. Skayla's already ordering them to be searched. I've long burned all the blueprints The Crafters had left behind, but that won't stop them from finding the Underground if they search thoroughly."

"Yes...we had noticed the searches down below," I replied sarcastically. But he was right. Sven should help. "I will make Sven aware. Thank you." I paused a moment, then as casually as possible asked, "Also. One more thing. You've mentioned the internment camps and that you and several other of the nobles Skayla left alive have been forced into submission. Any names? Do you know who might be willing to work with us—if we somehow got rid of the leverage?" That was a valid enough question to ask regardless of my intentions, right?

Atlys's entire demeanor shifted, and a shadow passed over his face. "Several. But I'm afraid, at least at the present moment, extracting their loved ones is quite impossible. No one has ever escaped without due punishment. Either to them or the one they were being used as leverage against. No one."

I winced. "Can you at least give me names?"

Raising both hands in a mixture of irritation and defensiveness, Atlys replied, "Fine. But tread lightly, or you'll make more dead men than friends. We have enough of those as it is."

Baey:

The plan was set, and now came the wait. And oh, the wait was hard. We'd been pretty busy in the meantime, at least, with Sven and me working in the tunnels to create illusions protecting the entrance to the Underground, using false tunnels and dead ends to confuse anyone looking for us. Then, on top of that, I still had my grueling training with Sven, and helping Alenor get a small forge set up in the Underground. It was nice to be so busy. Gone were the endless days of twiddling my thumbs at Valdon.

Even when I wasn't *doing* anything, I was tirelessly going over the portal site raid plan in my head. No one would see us—Alenor would dismantle the machines, and then we'd be out without anyone being the wiser. But what if Skayla figured it out and showed up? What if Alenor couldn't dismantle the machines properly? When I'd brought up to Sven the possibility of him simply using his reality bending to dispose of them, he'd said it was too dangerous. Since the machines were actively hitched up to this Doorway or whatever, improperly detaching the machines could create rifts.

My head swirled with all the ways this could go wrong.

It didn't help that I was comparatively idle, at the moment. Now that the immediate work that had needed to be done was settled, Darby was apparently giving us a proper tour of the Underground. It was no longer safe for Sven or me to go wandering around the tunnels with Skayla so close, and now that Estasia was running most of the back and forth between Temorn, Illan, and Atlys, Sven didn't really have much to do if he wasn't training.

And Sven doing nothing was a dangerous thing.

Or so Darby had noticed.

At least, that's what I'd guessed by the way she'd marched in to where Sven and I had been sitting almost sulkily and announced she would be showing us around.

She'd cited it being a holiday. Whatever those were.

"I'm confused," Sven spoke up as we left the area where our tents were, following Darby as she marched ahead of us.

"What? Just because it's the end of the world doesn't mean we don't still have a holiday. It's still the Festival of Chancer." Darby's voice rang cheerily despite the damp dullness in the Underground. I'd learned to tolerate it—but nothing more.

At least it was better than a MindHold.

"Besides..." Darby's voice faltered a moment. "People need something to keep their spirits up. Any normalcy is helpful. Atlys provided extra rations so that the people could actually celebrate and enjoy themselves a little."

"I cannot argue with that," Sven murmured, lengthening his stride a bit to catch up with her, offering his arm without a word.

I smiled, even though I wasn't quite sure why. Maybe it was just because Sven was actually initiating something with someone. Maybe it was because I was pretty sure Darby stole glances at him when he wasn't looking. Maybe it was because it was just nice seeing him act a little like a person.

Nonetheless, I felt strangely isolated as I watched Darby raise a skeptical eyebrow before taking his arm. Like a tagalong.

"Baey, are you coming?" Sven called over his shoulder suddenly, his free elbow extended in a clear invitation for me to catch up and take his other arm.

I didn't hesitate, grinning a bit even as I tried to tuck in my wings so as not to have them sprawled out all the way behind Darby. I still wasn't the most graceful person in Baeno.

"So, where are we going?" I asked, leaning forward and around Sven to address Darby.

"Just into the city. While perhaps a bit lackluster, we still have festivities today. Sven always loved them, so I thought it might be a good change of pace."

Sven looked almost...confused. And yet, just as with every other emotion, he hid it quickly.

"Do you remember that one year during the Carnival of the Midnight Sun in the Ice Lands, when you got Thay in trouble for absolutely spoiling Lady Cheveline's dress with the paint?" Darby's expression was a mix of nostalgia and bittersweetness as she looked at Sven. "You tried to explain to Father that it was you and not Thay, but he wouldn't believe you." She laughed. "But Mother believed you. Father still took away Thay's privileges for a month, and then you and I had to sneak him out into the city at night to do anything."

I turned to Sven, eyes bulging. "Wait, really?" I hadn't realized Sven could be so much...trouble? But then again, I'd seen flashes of the fun whenever I got him going.

The mood was shattered with the utter look of confusion Sven was wearing. He cleared his throat awkwardly. "I, uh, I will take your word for it."

Darby looked...almost hurt. "Oh. Sorry. Yeah, I suppose it was a long while ago. I always remember the stupid things." Her laugh was half-hearted.

There was a tense atmosphere of awkwardness that I was unsure how to break.

Then Darby gave a cough. "So, have you ever seen a festival, Baey?"

Even as she asked, I could hear the symphony of sounds coming from the streets ahead of us.

"No. I've read about them in a book or two, though. And we did celebrate the New Year at Valdon." I tried to avoid the sting at the mention of the name—and the reminder that those that remained were far away, possibly in harm's way or even death's door. I tried to remain light-hearted for Sven's sake, wondering if maybe…maybe he didn't have all his memories after all. It seemed weird that he would have forgotten such a big thing as what Darby had been describing.

"Well, prepare to be amazed, darling. It's good fun," Darby said with a great deal of bravado as we stepped out from the tent section of the Underground and into the wider streets lined with makeshift houses.

But she was right; I was amazed.

The city somehow had transformed from a dismal hodge-podge of forgotten things into a bustling, jovial mess of lantern lights and booths that lined either side of the already narrow streets. There was laughter and smiles, and a sweet yet metallic sound that sung a melody similar to a voice.

"Oh, fantastic, Beatryce took out her fiddle!" Darby exclaimed.

Although Tanner had often talked about the memories of instruments, I hadn't ever gotten to hear them myself, and my wings seemed to vibrate with the melodies that pierced the air.

"Is that a flute?" Sven's hoarse voice somehow sounded over the hubbub as we made our way through the crowded street.

"Yes. Kelti somehow managed to save his father's," replied Darby. But conversation was soon lost on me, and I found myself letting go of Sven's arm to flitter around to all the different stalls and stations. Perhaps

214

I was blissfully ignorant of true grandeur so that such a ragtag festival was a wonder to me, but the stalls of homemade gadgets and clothes and antiques were all so new and marvelous. The smells of freshly baked food and the clamor of laughter and conversation and footsteps overwhelmed my senses in a way that was not unpleasant. I found myself talking to several people at stalls, and before I knew it, it was as if I was really a part of the crowd—a part of the life and the festival. Not watching behind a glass, but *really* part of it.

Even as I wandered, however, I made sure not to go too far from Sven and Darby, who walked slower through the bustling festivities. I saw the way they both garnered attention—Darby with showerings of smiles and offers of gifts; with questions after her health and grateful looks. Meanwhile, Sven was regarded with a more uncertain skepticism. Something out of a disappointing dream. I even saw the fear. But then, every so often, I saw a few awed looks mixed in. A few glances of hope and smiles his way.

All the same, I saw the way he clung close to Darby, almost as if she were some sort of lifeline. He seemed so...lost. He flinched at any sudden sounds and constantly tried to keep his hand away from his sword.

I heard the sound of the music getting louder and blending with stomping and clapping, and as we turned the corner, we found ourselves in a sort of town square, a mill of people running around—no—dancing. A vague memory surfaced from Valdon when Namaya and Sefen had danced to Braed's singing.

I watched in wonder, Darby and Sven coming up beside me as we stood on the sidelines. The fiddle music blended with the sweet tones of the flute, bouncing in a way that made me want to tap my feet, and my wings flexed in the rhythm as I wondered how wonderful it would be to fly to such a beautiful sound.

"You know, Sven was quite the dancer," Darby said hesitantly, as if she was no longer certain of how welcome her comments were.

I swung around, grabbing his arm again, but this time with both hands. "Sven, could you teach me? We could do it here—we wouldn't have to go in the middle. I've never danced before, and it looks so—" I broke off my ramblings, the words having tumbled out of my mouth without a care for decorum or appearance. I was begging, and honestly, most of me didn't even regret it.

Sven looked perplexed. "I...I really don't remember."

I bit back from reminding him he'd done it fine during the ballroom illusion, instead saying, "Alright," even as I tried to hide my disappointment. I turned back to the crowd and satisfied myself with enjoying the sight. I was used to watching, and at least I could appreciate it. "I would probably trip over my stupid wings anyway," I added with a laugh.

Suddenly, someone grabbed my arm and dragged me away. "Oh come on, darlin'." I was suddenly taken up. "One hand on my shoulder," Sven instructed even as he put a hand behind on the small of my back—under my wings.

"Save the next dance for me?" Darby called as we were swept up with everyone else—Sven keeping us still a bit apart from the many other dancers.

I tripped over my wings, but with his strong grasp I had no fear of falling, and soon I figured out exactly how to hold my wings so I wouldn't die trying to dance.

A huge grin plastered itself on my face, and it felt as if my cheeks might burst. I was stumbling and staring constantly at my feet, but Sven's soft instructions and the lively dance music sucked away any anxiety, and soon I found myself able to look up as the world twirled and spun around us. Even better were the intervals where we were called to stop, stomp, clap, or even shout with the music. It was…it was freeing.

I decided that I absolutely loved dancing.

At last, the song came to an end and everyone broke into applause as we hailed the musicians, a moment of pause apparently given for people to find new partners. I was dead tired, panting even as Sven and I made our way through the crowd and back to Darby.

"That...was...amazing!" I didn't care if it was immature, I jumped in the air as I practically shouted, clapping one more time.

Sven's cheeks were full of color, a glint in his eyes and amusement marking the curve of his lips as he raised an eyebrow at me.

"Glad to see that after abandoning us to go crawl into a hole, you still have time to enjoy a good dance, Watcher."

And just like that, the mood was shattered. I didn't know who the passerby was, but I would have decked him if he hadn't disappeared into the crowd of dancers. We finally made it back to Darby's side, but my amazement was tainted by that stupid comment.

"Have fun?" Darby asked, oblivious to what had just transpired.

But then she seemed to guess. If it wasn't enough that Sven was once more as emotionless as a stone, as I looked around I realized he was receiving even more stares than before.

"I think it's best if I don't spoil the mood," Sven whispered to Darby, then turned to me. "Not bad for your first time, darlin'. See if you can try on a real partner, now. I'll be back," he said with a wink, as if that hid the pain in his eyes.

Before I could so much as say a word, he was gone.

My fists balled in anger, and I had half a mind to give the whole group a talking to. Perhaps it was good another dance started up, drowning out my thoughts and any ideas of shouting at everyone.

I felt a hand on my shoulder, and looked over to see Darby still next to me. "Unfortunately, not everyone is as understanding," she whispered. "But I trust they'll come around. I'm sorry it ruined your dance."

I sighed. "Well, I enjoyed myself. And I think he did, too, for a moment anyway."

Darby seemed suddenly more tired than she had before. "We all have to work together. The stress sometimes leaves people looking for anyone to blame. And to stand up for him by reprimanding them would only create division. We've had enough of that in the world already."

She was right, I knew it. It didn't mean I had to like it.

"But the more we normalize him, the better. And they'll see. It took them time to warm up to us, too."

With a sigh, I asked, "Do you think maybe you could go see if he's alright? You seemed like you were really good friends. He could use a friend."

Darby's eyes flashed in doubt. "I don't know. I might make things worse. I...don't know that he really felt the same way."

"His memory hasn't really been the same since the MindHold," I pressed, pieces clicking together. "For a while, he couldn't even remember his own name all the time, let alone who his friends were. I guess we just all thought Skayla gave them back when they faced off at Hytat. But...but I'm wondering if...she just gave him the bad ones back." I couldn't help but remember all the times his mood seemed to sour. The way he seemed unable to remember anything except what he'd done.

Pain was evident in every inch of Darby's body. The way she tensed, the way her brow furrowed. The way she stared at me. "Oh. I see."

"So, I think...I think it's good that you remind him. Even if he doesn't remember. You're the first person who's been really kind to him, other than Alenor. That tells me you were close. I know he'll remember, if you show him." I paused then, looking carefully at her. "And...I think you could use a friend, too."

She shook her head, letting out a sad, small smile. "You're quite observant, aren't you?"

My wings pricked, and I took only a moment to focus and keep their color a neutral grey before replying, "I'm learning." Then I looked again in the direction Sven had disappeared, unable to really see much beyond the festivities and the people. "He's probably gone back to the tents, if I were to guess."

"Actually, I think I know where he went." I turned back to find a strange, lonely look in Darby's eyes. "It's where I go to clear my head. I'd shown him. He'd always liked the water.'"

I gave a nod. "Sounds like you have it figured out, then."

"Yes. I suppose I do. Try and enjoy yourself, Baey. I'll go find him—if you're sure."

"I'm sure," I replied, giving a small shooing gesture.

And with that, Darby left me alone to watch the dancing, a feeling of emptiness pervading my joy. But I refused to let it rule me. I refused to give up. I mingled with the people, reaching out and being a *part* of something, believing that maybe I would get to see a world without Skayla. And maybe then those so embittered would have time to heal. Maybe Sven would have time to heal.

Maybe we all would.

<u>Sven:</u>

The breeze washed pleasantly around me, refreshing after the stuffy underground city. I felt less like I was in a tomb. A little more like I could breathe.

And yet, the ghosts stayed. I couldn't seem to escape the looks and the sideways glances of those that still refused to forgive. I didn't blame them—really, I didn't. I hadn't *just* been in a MindHold. I hadn't *just* been The GhostMaker. I'd been the idiot that had run straight into the trap. The brother of the one who'd ruined their lives. The one who'd let it happen.

The breath I released was a tense one, melting away into the wind and adding more weight to the air around me. It felt less free now. More like the wind was whispering my faults to me.

"Uh…Sven?"

I snapped my eyes open and turned around, looking back at the cave opening where Darby stood, mouth half open and eyes a little wide.

"I'm confused...what are you doing—well *how* are you out there?"

Right.

So, I'd forgotten that I was standing on thin air. I looked down awkwardly at the ocean churning far beneath my feet, and then up at the star-scattered sky.

"Are you—that's not an illusion. How are you—uh, I mean—can I come?" Darby's confusion was now laced with evident curiosity as she took a step closer to the edge of the cliffside.

"No wait, don't— I could drop you!" I took a step closer and reached out a hand in panic. All I'd done was condense the air around my feet to hold me up—like the buoyancy a ship experienced in the water—but I didn't trust myself with someone else. I was done gambling.

Darby stopped. "Don't worry. I wasn't going to do anything unless you said it was safe." The smile was sad. "But I trust you. You just look so alone out there."

The wind blew as if to remind me how many variables there were to this. I knew I wouldn't fall, but what if my mind wandered? What if I did something to drop her?

"I'm fine."

Darby sighed, sitting on the edge of the cliff, her legs swinging idly off the edge. "I wish you'd stop saying that, Sven." The words were quiet, and yet somehow, I heard them.

"I don't know that saying how I am would change anything," I murmured back, now feeling awkward standing out in the middle of nothing while Darby sat there trying to talk to me. But I didn't want to move. I felt paralyzed between the fear of being near anyone and the whispers I was trying so hard to keep out. I wished I could remember the things she kept talking about, and yet all I could remember was the pain.

"It would mean you trust me enough to be honest with me, I suppose," Darby replied. She looked me right in the eye.

I couldn't bear it and quickly turned away, looking instead onto the beach far below. "I do trust you," I mumbled in reply. It was me I didn't trust.

"Then prove it."

My head snapped back and I didn't bother to hide my confusion. "How?" The question was impossible. It took a lot more of the anguish I was hiding with it, and my chest felt tight with the emotion that dragged itself out of my soul when I asked. I realized I wasn't really asking her so much how to prove it as much as how she could trust me. I realized...maybe I didn't believe her. How could she trust me? She said she didn't blame me—Thackeray said the same thing. But they still had scars. Scars I'd given. How could I ask them to get past that? How could—

"Believe me when I say I know you won't let me fall." Darby's confidence rang along the alcove.

My entire body went rigid, and I was barely able to relax my jaw enough to open my mouth and begin to argue. "Darby, no, I don't think—"

"Then you don't believe me," she cut me off, shoulders sinking. She looked...so incredibly sad—sad, and lonely. "Sven, I just...maybe one day you'll see. I just wish you'd stop punishing yourself for what Skayla's done. I wish..." She trailed off a moment. "...wish you'd live again." The last bit was hoarse. Then her fists clenched and she went on, looking almost angry. "Or maybe I should say I wish you'd live *for once*. You were always so much more than your sisters. It's not fair you have to clean up their mess. You deserve to smile and you deserve to have a stupid dance without someone looking at you funny or saying something ridiculous."

I just looked at her, still standing on the air above the ocean in the light of the stars. Away from the world, away from her. And it occurred to me for the first time, perhaps, how alone *she* looked. How tired she was. The dark circles she hid under her eyes. The meticulous way she did her hair and smoothed her clothes so she looked put-together.

"You really want to come out that badly?" I asked at last, trying to ignore everything screaming at me not to be so stupid.

Darby's eyes met mine, and it hurt, but I forced myself to keep eye contact.

"I want you to not feel alone," she whispered.

Because that's how she felt. She'd said we'd been friends, and I knew we had; I could feel it. It was too hard to wade past the nightmares, but I knew she was right, and while I perhaps didn't deserve friendship...could I really deny *her* right to it?

I sighed, extending my hand. "Go slowly, but come towards me. You won't fall." Hopefully.

A smile broke the pain in her expression, and slowly she got up, looking at me once more before taking a deep breath and letting one foot leave the safety of the cliffside.

It held its place in midair, where I'd created the invisible bridge. Darby took another step and let out a small laugh as she now stood completely in the air.

I liked the sound of her laugh. It made the darkness feel less oppressive.

"How are you doing this?" she asked with a wide grin on her face, slowly coming towards me as she looked all around her in awe.

"It's...complicated," I murmured, then realized she hadn't heard me above the sound of the ocean.

"I mean, this isn't an illusion, obviously—we're out on the air—like really on the air. This is incredible."

I found myself unable to take my eyes off her—and not because I was afraid of losing concentration and making her fall. No. Somehow, her wide-eyed wonder made me stop. I hadn't seen her really smile like that before.

"No. Not an illusion," I replied, making sure to be loud enough above the breeze. But she was also closer now. Just a few yards away, her hair tugging out of her bun and pulling around her face.

"Then what?"

"I don't actually stop at illusions. I just...was afraid, I suppose." My eyes fell in shame as she drew closer.

She was standing in front of me. The ocean sloshed and swirled beneath us, and I watched the foam as it crashed against the beach.

I forced myself to go on. "Afraid what I would need to use it for. I don't know. Something else. I don't even remember the particulars. It was foolish, and if I had, maybe we wouldn't have been in this mess."

Darby sighed, "So...if not illusions, what *is* your Gift? I'm assuming it's not flying."

I looked back up to meet her gaze, making what was a way more embarrassed smile than I'd intended. I shrugged. "I may or may not mess a little more with...uh...reality."

She didn't reply immediately. Just stared at me, slowly taking it in.

Then, at last, she laughed. "Well, that makes a little more sense, I suppose." Again, she took a step closer, close enough that I could have reached out to her if I wanted. "I mean. You were never into tricks and illusions. You were always so real. Never fake."

My shoulders drooped. "Yeah, well, it could have come in handy if I'd had the guts to use it."

"And Moira and Skayla could have made you do—anyway, I don't blame you."

Moira? Why was Moira in there?

"Anyway," Darby said, before taking a deep breath and looking around. "It's so beautiful out here. Thank you for letting me come out. It's like the stars are everywhere." She turned as she spoke, looking up at the sky and then over the now calming ocean.

She was right. The sky was cloudless tonight, and the ocean had just begun reflecting the light of the stars in the most magnificent way.

"You know. I never got my dance," she added quietly.

I stiffened. The dance. That's why I'd come out here. The words still stung. What a fool I'd been.

"You deserve to live a little, Sven. There are going to be a lot of people wanting to dance when they get out of a MindHold." Her laugh was now bitter and her smile faded. "It's cruel of them to rob you of your joy. You looked so happy dancing with Baey."

"It's fine," I murmured. It wasn't for her to worry about. Or for Baey. I could handle it.

"You know…you could dance out here. No one's here to judge, Sven. Just me. And it's such a beautiful night."

I just full-out stared at her.

Her cheeks reddened. "Do you want to dance? Or should we go back? We can go back—um—or I can just go back. Sorry, it was silly, I shouldn't have—"

That's when I realized; *she* needed this dance. She needed to live a little—not just me. I extended my hand. "Don't hurt yourself putting that big boot in your mouth, ah?"

Her entire face was red. Even in the moonlight, I could see it.

"So, are we going to dance?" I was pretty sure the only reason I wasn't burning with embarrassment myself was because she was. I wanted to make her feel comfortable. I really, *really* wanted her to smile.

And she did.

It only made me smile more.

"Sounds lovely," she said at last, putting her hand in mine and letting me draw her up in a dance.

"I really am quite rusty. I wasn't even fully aware I…um…*could* dance," I whispered as I tried and remembered how to even start. My feet did all the work, my brain blissfully silent as I looked at Darby's smile. We swayed, dancing along the air as if a glass bridge held us there, her hand in mine, and for a moment, something of a dream came to mind. Not a nightmare. A dream. A memory out of reach, of something almost happy.

"It's so quiet," Darby whispered, head falling against my shoulder. I found myself looking out at the stars, the night so beautiful and…and I allowed myself to enjoy it. I let myself look out into the stars and the ocean and just see how beautiful it all was. Then I closed my eyes, the shadows of nightmares chased away in the wake of Darby's soothing presence.

"Thank you," I whispered. "This is nice."

"Yeah." I could feel her smile even in that single word. Or maybe it was just because the image of her smiling was such a pleasant one that I wanted any excuse to picture it.

I don't know how long we danced, but I could have done it forever.

CHAPTER XIII: Feelings and Stuff

<u>Estasia:</u>

"Where's Sven?" I asked as I watched Baey ghosting her sparring moves at the edge of the Underground.

"He's talking with Alenor and going over the plan." Baey's expression folded deeper into concentration as she did some sort of maneuver that combined a spin with her wings and a slash with the blade.

"I feel like that would only get your wings skewered…." I couldn't help but point out. "I mean. It's definitely fancy-looking, but you don't want a sword sticking through those nice feathers."

Baey's cheeks flushed a bit as she landed once more on the ground, sheathing her blade. But I noticed her wings only barely hinted at color. "Well, I mean, my wings have to be good for *something*. They were good enough to knock people over back in Kaedovarna. I just can't seem to figure out what to do with them, and Sven doesn't really know either."

"I'm sure Syvil will help you once he gets back. Your flying improved rather quickly when he was around."

I apparently said the wrong thing, or so Baey's fallen expression told me. Right. Don't mention the ones gone to Rugo.

Too late.

"Yeah," she murmured, turning back around.

I didn't like the silence, but the last thing I was going to do was try and comfort her or continue to prod the sore subject. So I just sort of stood there, forgetting the question that had started this all, feeling the need to help the child and yet...wanting to run away as fast as possible.

Then Baey spoke. "Do you think they'll come back?" She didn't turn around, still working through some sword moves—but half-heartedly.

"I don't see a point in what I think," I replied honestly, crossing my arms and trying to work through how to deal with this. "I mean, I don't really decide what happens, so...."

Baey sighed, splitting the air with her sword as her workout slowly devolved into flails. "I don't know. Maybe it would make me feel better."

"Fine, then I think they'll come back," I replied helplessly, ignoring the temptation to throw up my hands in defeat.

"Yes...I am...so convinced." Baey gave a wry laugh as she sheathed her sword and turned around. She looked tired. I could see the writhing in her mind, everything tearing her up from the inside out: Sven, those who went to Rugo, the impending mission only a few days away now.

I needed to distract her.

"Why don't you catch me up on what you're learning?" I wouldn't be on the mission to the portal site, unfortunately, but I didn't mind. I didn't really feel like having to deal with that weird stuff, and I didn't need to go get myself killed when I was the only one that could help Atlys with growing the network.

"Sure," Baey said, handing me her sword.

I took it, even as my own thoughts began to spiral out of control. The thought of really taking back Baeno seemed to grow by the moment, and it was almost frightening. Frightening because I didn't know what would happen to me after. Everyone had a life and identity before this all went down. Me? I was just a street urchin. No different than Temorn.

Well, hopefully a little different. But was I? There had been plenty of times I'd used others. What if we still weren't so different after all? What if that's what I went back to? What if everything and everyone just went back to how they were before? How long would it take for the next Skayla to come along?

I shoved all that away as Baey coached me in some steps. At least, I tried to shove them away. But it just seemed to keep coming back, and the knife around my belt just grew heavier and heavier.

At least Baey seemed a bit distracted from her own worries now.

Nonetheless, after a bit I couldn't take it anymore, stopping and handing the sword back to her.

"You alright?" Baey cocked her head, wings flicking and darkening in worry.

I raised an eyebrow. "Yes. Just not as cut out for a sword. I think I prefer knives and other ways of getting the edge on people." I rubbed the handle of my dagger, as if to drive the point home. Oh great, that was a pun, wasn't it? I sighed.

Baey apparently took the sigh as meaning I wasn't *really* fine, and pressed further with, "You've been off since...well, since you went and picked up that stuff in the tunnels." Her eyes were glued to the weapon at my belt.

Okay, so maybe I wasn't fine. But I didn't like sharing. "Well, aren't you nosy." I turned around, getting ready to leave before her words stopped me.

"You know, it's a bit rude that you keep expecting us to give you all this information and all this trust when you hide all the time."

Swiveling to face her again, I gave a glare. "You offered all of that information up willingly. I'm trying to help, and I have given you every bit of information back that was necessary. If you have doubts then go ahead—how exactly am I planning to betray you? Hm? After I got Sven out of the Kovian Fortress? After I helped you *all* get out of Hytat?" I was surprised by the edge to my tone.

But I was more surprised by the hurt on Baey's face.

"Not doubts that you'll betray us," she said quietly. "Just doubts you're really my friend." Her wings drooped, the color greying out into something almost forlorn.

I had no idea what to say.

"And here I thought you had everything so put together." Baey's stare was worse than if she'd looked away. "I just wish you'd trust me like I trust you."

"Look, Baey—it's not personal. I do trust you *more* than most people. We are friends—" That bit was harder to say out loud than I would have thought. "It's just. A thief thing, I guess. It's safer not to trust people."

"Are you really equating us to Temorn?"

I blinked. "What?"

"Come on, Esa. Just because you don't tell me doesn't mean it doesn't exist. I still have eyes—eyes *you* taught me to use."

My entire body tensed, and I glared hard. "Leave it, Birdy."

"Fine. I will. I'll leave it alone. But you know, it hurts."

Again, I was caught off guard. Worse, I found myself wanting to tell her. Wanting *anyone* to know. Someone to tell me that what happened to Eugene wasn't my fault—that I couldn't possibly have stopped it. Someone to drown out the rest of me telling me it was my fault; my fault for trusting Temorn. My fault for befriending Eugene. My fault for letting my guard down. My fault for letting anyone in.

But now, for the first time in my life, I felt what it was like to have a family. Not like the pact with the gang I'd had here in Alkemar. Not the kind that left you looking over your shoulder. Something Eugene had shown me a glimpse of: true friendship. The kind you didn't have to look over your shoulder with—but instead the kind that had your back.

And if I couldn't trust Baey, then who could I trust? "You're right," I whispered at last. "Fine. I'll tell you." I refused to move, instead sizing her up and making it clear I was by no means pleased. "I don't do friends. I never *did* friends. The one time I did do friends, they betrayed each other."

Baey was...unaffected. Her wings stayed steady and relaxed, with none of her typical cocooning, and her eyes met mine with an ease that almost succeeded in making me uncomfortable.

I sighed again. "Temorn is...self-absorbed, if you haven't noticed. But his mother ran the crime ring in Alkemar for years, and her best recruits were always orphans. Temorn was the one who found me and got me out of the workhouse of an orphanage I was in." Watchers or no Watchers, people mistook progress for perfection. They saw the peace from war and many instead became complacent, rather than try and solve the deeper problems that plagued Baeno. It's why I'd always had little love for The Watchers. "He became the closest thing I had to a friend—granted, he was trouble, and I knew it. We both trusted the other to have our back...to a point. It was survival. But then, one summer we both stumbled upon a rich kid who'd run off from his parents. He was from further south, but his family came up here for the summer."

"Eugene Atarah?" Baey asked.

I nodded. "He wanted to stick around—something about family pressures. Temorn thought it would be good fun so we did, telling Morn's mother that Eugene was just another orphan." I winced. We should have just told him to get lost. "Two years went by, and Eugene somehow remained the same—kind. I was fascinated by it, the little kid I was. But Temorn didn't like it. He got jealous. Well, Eugene's parents had put out a reward for him, so Temorn apparently up and spilled it to his mother, and then when I was off on some errand for his mother, Temorn lured Eugene away and collected the money." I growled at the last bit. "The Atarahs left the city first thing next morning, so by the time I realized what happened, I couldn't get Eugene back. He...he wasn't happy at home. The one thing we all had in common was no one loved us. We were the outcasts together. At least, I thought. But apparently, Temorn didn't like that he couldn't control Eugene, and that's when I realized everyone just wanted control. So I left. I started out on my own, and Temorn knew better than to bother me. Usually the crime ring went after anyone not under them, but I was doing just fine until that stupid witch decided to take over the world."

"Oh. I'm sorry." Baey's voice was quiet.

I rolled my eyes. "Don't be sorry. It's how it is. I got over it years ago, and it's been buried a long time. But somehow, I just couldn't resist going and digging up that stupid painting Eugene made. I suppose it just got all those stupid feelings stirred up again, and I started to second-guess myself." Who was I fooling? I'd been hoping deep down that maybe if I could find Eugene, he wouldn't hate me, and maybe I would have at least one friend after the dust settled from this; that maybe it would give me purpose if I let myself try again. Maybe I could try and reach out, the way Baey always did.

"I mean. He's alive, and he's under duress. Why not?"

"Because I don't like people," I spat back, a bit more vehemently than I'd meant.

Baey didn't flinch. The little Birdy was getting bold, apparently. "Well, that's kind of awkward, because I like you," she said. "We are friends, aren't we?"

I stared a long while, a smile sliding through the callousness I hid behind. "Yeah, Birdy. I suppose if I haven't gotten rid of you by now, we might as well be."

"Good." Baey's wings relaxed, making me realize for the first time just how tense she'd been.

With a sigh, roll of the eyes, and a mental note that I really was going soft, I went up and patted her on the back. "You're not so bad for a bag of feathers."

"And you're not so bad for a thief," came the counter.

I laughed. "We'll have to work on your insults, though. Still pretty pathetic," I said as I put an arm around her shoulder and started walking back into the city with her.

"I feel like that's not really something I need to be good at...."

I just grinned. "Oh please, everyone needs a good insult in their back pocket. It's the best way to leave someone speechless." I paused, then, with no attempt at being good at switching subjects said, "Speaking of speechless, why don't we go find Sven."

Baey made a snorting sort of sound and replied, "You are not good at segues."

CHAPTER XIV: Reality Gets a Little Weird

<u>Baey:</u>

I was pretty sure my heart was about to explode with the way it was pounding in my chest. We were here, overlooking the ravine and preparing to go down. Sven was shielding us from the eyes of the Drogans and soldiers, but that wasn't why I was half out of my mind.

I was *here*. Helping. Asked to come. And we were doing something; something to actually combat Skayla and Ovok, even though we still only knew half of what in Baeno was going on. At Valdon, it had devolved into something akin to damage control, leaving me to feel as if we had been nearly stalling.

But not now.

"Ready?" Sven turned to me then his mother.

We both nodded.

"Just don't get yourself killed...again?" Thackeray muttered from the back of our group. He was tasked with staying back; if anything went wrong, we needed someone to send word back to the Underground. We'd left yesterday and made camp not far from the ravine, so he would still have to run back to the camp and grab a horse, but theoretically, if something went wrong, the Bethynese soldiers would be a bit busy trying to restrain Sven. I hoped perhaps I would put up a better fight this time— if something went wrong.

I needed to stop thinking of things going wrong.

Sven did not reply to Thackeray's comment, instead holding eye contact with him for a long moment. Then he nodded and turned back to the rest of us.

Alenor adjusted the sack of tools that was strapped to her back. I agreed—I couldn't sit still any longer, either.

At last, Sven got up, signaling us to follow him as we made our way down and into the camp. It was somehow even more unnerving than in Hytat. We weren't just doing it to get past the gate, and we weren't altering an appearance to fit in with the crowd. We were making our way through a very dangerous camp of Bethynese soldiers and Drogans to try and dismantle a portal to another world that Skayla was trying to open.

Somehow, repeating that in my head did not make me feel better.

As we walked into the heart of the camp, my breath caught every time a soldier came within arms' length of me, or a Drogan flew by, or someone looked in our direction. I wasn't sure I'd ever be able to get used to this, and an eternity of ten minutes elapsed before we arrived at—well, what I assumed was the portal. The huffing, squealing machines and rising steam seemed clue enough. That being said, I had expected to see...I don't know...*something*. Like a door, or a physical manifestation of energy, or something portal-esque. But other than the machines, there was nothing.

Granted, the machines were pretty impressive. If it wasn't for the fact that I was already curbing a mountain of anxiety and trying to keep an eye and ear out in case Sven somehow lost concentration and we were found, I definitely would have just stopped and gawked.

Without a word, Alenor knelt by one of the tall, crane-like machines, plopping her bag next to her and opening it up.

I gave a quick nod to Sven and then flew up to the top of a boulder where I could better watch the camp and make sure we were safe. There was an audible roaring in my ears, and I reminded myself it was simply the watch. As it was, I was dealing with a thousand knots in my stomach—an incredible yearning for something so close. Sven had warned me it would happen, what with Moira so close. I tried to focus instead on watching the soldiers and Drogans watching the perimeter, but I couldn't help but also try and catch a glimpse of Moira.

The ache in my chest turned to burning, and became so intense I almost wanted to rip the watch off to get a brief reprieve. But I pushed it to the back of my mind, again scanning the surrounding area for any sign we might have been made. But we hadn't, of course. Sven had made sure of that.

I found myself in a pattern: scan the camp, look behind at the other twos progress, then look for Moira. I'd not felt something *this* intense before from the ring *or* the watch, and it was like a mixture of anxiety, longing, and apprehension all balled up in one. I'd guessed it would be an unpleasant experience, but somehow hadn't thought it would be *this* unbearable. I wanted to scream.

But I didn't. I just kept my post, the tension of time passing only adding to the stress as Alenor dismantled one machine after another. I'd asked Sven why we couldn't just have him destroy them and be done with it, but apparently doing something like *that* would only destabilize the portal.

Well, the portal everyone was *saying* existed. I still couldn't wrap my head around it. I'd expected the area to look a little less...empty? A little less like the portal devices were just taking up space awkwardly.

"Wait, what's that—Mum did you—"

"No, this isn't me—I don't—"

I turned around even as I began to hear the squeals of the machines and creaks of metal magnify to an alarming volume, and suddenly a blast of light enveloped the space in between them, knocking Sven and Alenor back.

I jumped off and ran over to Alenor, but my attention was almost instantly grabbed by what I was staring at. The light—the brief rectangular doorway that had opened up—had vanished, leaving behind a man.

"Oh...uh..." The man said, as he looked not at us, but the machines to his left and right.

"*Grenedil?* What in the world are you doing here?" It was Alenor, staring in disbelief at the stranger.

"Alenor? What is—"

There was the sound of a screeching Drogan from not too far off.

"Baey—check the perimeter," Sven ordered as he got to his feet. "You—I have no idea who you are, but unless you're friends with Skayla, I suggest you make yourself scarce with us before her soldiers find us, after the display you made."

"Sven, don't worry, he's an...old...friend—but Grenedil, of all the times to show up, this is by *far* the worst!"

Confusion mingling with the panic, I took to the air, not needing to go far up at all before I saw the soldiers running from the camp and in our direction.

"Sven, I think we have to hide—or leave," I called down. We were all hidden, but regardless....

"We can't! Not until I finish—the readings on the last machine indicate the portal didn't fully close. We leave now, and Skayla might be able to open it."

"Wait. Skayla? What do you mean—" The completely unasked for question came from our *uninvited* guest, who was scrambling to wrap his head around something.

Maybe it was that he'd just appeared from a portal. I really didn't bother trying to figure it out at this point.

"Mum—be quick. You—do what we say unless you want to end up as Drogan food." I'd never heard Sven utter anywhere close to a threat before, let alone one so...intense.

"Wait, what? Ew, they don't *eat* people, what are you, crazy?"

"As a matter of fact, yes, I think he is, a little bit." We all turned around at the voice that cracked open the tension like an egg.

I now knew why the watch had been going crazy, and it *wasn't* Moira.

"You're so *loud*, Sven." The laugh that followed the comment was purely demented.

Skayla.

Ugh. In the panic and the portal opening, Sven's concentration must have wavered somehow...and I had been so busy with the stranger, I hadn't noticed we weren't invisible anymore.

Now two Drogans flanked us on either side: one a large, dark green with silver edging its wings, the other a brownish red. I didn't think the colors would matter very much when they ate me, of course.

"Mum, don't stop!" Sven shouted even as he drew his one blade and made the second materialize out of nothing.

241

I drew my own and gripped it hard. No more training—and no more faking my way through.

"Drop it, Sven. *Now.*" There was no charm in Skayla's voice—no attempt to make us lower our guard. This was vehemence through and through. That being said, the soldiers filing behind her and the Drogans were proof that there was no emptiness behind the threat in her tone.

"No."

Chaos erupted. The soldiers jumped forward, and even as Sven worked illusions to keep them disoriented, I took to the air, intending to strike them from behind. But my fear of being eaten became suddenly very real as the green Drogan lurched upwards, mouth gaping as if it intended to swallow me up.

Whoever that stranger through the portal was, he didn't know the next thing about Drogans, because this one was *definitely* down for eating people.

I managed a very strange airborne roll to the side, my wings tucking close as I reeled in the air, somehow finding myself landing on the Drogan's back. I didn't waste another minute, plunging my sword into its back between the wings, then springboarding off of it just as it jolted back in pain. I barely gripped my sword hard enough to get it dislodged as I took off.

It was hard to tell what was going on anymore, and my vision was almost tunneled as I landed on the ground, attacking from behind the line of Bethynese soldiers. I ducked, guarded, and beat my wings when necessary. All the while one question rang in my head; where was Skayla?!

A tail came out of nowhere and swept me off my feet. The Green Drogan was injured, but still apparently struggling to carry on in the fray as it turned its narrowed eyes on me. I wondered if it had a choice to keep going, or if Skayla made them fight to every last drop of energy.

Before I could remind myself now wasn't the time to be getting distracted, something came at me from behind, and I instinctively used my wings to block *exactly* like I'd been warned not to do. The pain seared up and down my left wing. I only barely registered that it had missed the bone as I kicked back as hard as I could and sent whoever had stuck me flying. The sword unlodged itself and was carried with its master, leaving me to let out a scream. Another soldier was upon me even before I'd fully gotten rid of the other one, however, and through my clouded vision and pounding head I got past his guard and felt the sickening sinking of my sword in his chest. There was a gasp as his life drained from him, but for once I knew better than to look twice, taking to the air even as I wrenched my blade from its victim.

Ugh, my wing did *not* like flying. It was hard enough to stay in the air, let alone keep focused as I battled the pain. But to allow it to overcome me meant death—and so I refused to let anything be an option other than continuing on.

My decision to do as much was *really* about to be tested, as the green Drogan again came right for me.

Ugh.

"LET HER GO!"

The voice shook the entire world; or at least, that's what it felt like. Everyone stopped. The Drogans. The soldiers. Me.

I looked down to where Sven's scream had originated, the blood draining from my face as I saw Skayla about to plunge a blade through the back of her own mother.

Sven:

I wasn't sure which emotion was stronger: fear or fury. I didn't know that I cared, at the moment. In mere seconds, all my plans to keep my true abilities hidden flew out the window in the face of the reality that I might lose my mother, too. Gone was my ability to think, something more primitive and vicious taking hold.

The earth shuddered and split between Mum and Skayla, sending Skayla flying backwards and Mum to the side. My eyes settled on her only just long enough to see her get up. I had one goal now.

"You would kill your own *MOTHER?!* What kind of MONSTER are you?!" The earth was rippling beneath us, causing everyone to stumble. Surprised shouts rang out around us but I was gone, almost oblivious to the way the earth was crumbling around me, floating in the air as even my own feet failed to touch the ground.

Skayla had tried to kill Mum.

"Oh please, don't lecture me, *GhostMaker,* you ha—" Skayla never got to finish her sentence, as with a mere snap of my fingers I sent her shooting across the way until she finally slammed against a boulder, the wind knocked out of her.

"Hm? Sorry? Didn't catch that, *murderer.*"

Terror. Terror was in her eyes. And I wanted it to stay there. To get a glimpse of what I'd felt for the last eight years.

I wanted her to pay.

The Bethynese soldiers seemed to have gotten ahold of themselves, trying an organized charge on me as I hovered a few feet above the ground, standing on invisible air, eyes burning as all I could do was stare at Skayla—at the one who'd caused all of this. I flicked my hand and the soldiers coming towards me sunk waist deep in the ground, screaming.

"H-H-How are you—these aren't—"

"—Illusions?" I spat, interrupting my sister as I walked up to her, willing the boulder to fold around her wrists and ankles so she could merely struggle like a worm caught in the beak of a bird. So that she could still move but go nowhere. Just like me. "When we got our relics, you and Moira weren't the only ones whose powers increased." I smiled in a way that might have made me sick any other day. "I don't just make illusions, Skayla—" I was up close to her, pressing the edge of my sword up to her neck. I saw the way she was straining for her knife with her one hand, and allowed the rock restraint to break. But as she tried to drive the knife into my side, it simply crumbled to ash.

Her eyes were wide.

"I bend *reality!*" I pressed the sword harder against her neck, unexpected tears streaming down my face as I still somehow hesitated in ending her life. "And you made mine a living *HELL*—you took *everything* from me and I don't even understand why!" I thought of Mum and Da, of Moira. Of the broken watch around Baey's neck that I had to look at day in and out.

The watch. It had been cracked and rendered useless. Something clicked and I turned my eyes on Skayla's armlet.

Skayla continued to squirm, desperate. "Sven, please, stop! You don't want to do this!"

"I'm sorry? What? Did you want me to stop? You choked the life out of me, why shouldn't I do the same for you?!" I shouted, training all my focus on the armlet even as I felt the very will of The Living Stone fighting against me. I knew what I had to do.

"Sven. Sven—no, what are you doing—SVEN! Sto—" The first of several audible cracks rent the air.

And then...then I lost all concentration as Skayla's entire facade changed.

"Sven, please no, I can't do this without it!" Her eyes flashed, and for a moment the twisted maniac I had seen for the last decade blinked away to show a desperate, terrified sister.

Without warning, something struck me in the side and sent me flying, moving me out of the way just in time as a heated tumult of acid-like fire exploded where I had just been. The thing that had saved me was none other than Baey, and the thing that had tried to kill me was none other than a Drogan.

There were five of them now—and more soldiers had arrived.

One of the other Drogans freed Skayla and she encircled us, Mum and the new stranger coming up beside us.

"Well, the good news is...I killed the machines." I barely registered the voice as Mum's.

"The bad news is, I picked a really bad time to show up, didn't I?" The stranger sighed in what sounded like tired exasperation.

"What have you done, Sven?!" Skayla screamed, almost...twitching? She laughed that crazy laugh, but it seemed to spastically change to crying. Her face contorted in a mixture of fear and anger, and a tear rolled down one cheek.

Baey gripped her sword tighter, and Mum as well as the stranger held swords they'd clearly gotten off soldiers.

But we'd be no match, and I could feel myself draining even now. We had to get out of here.

I took in a deep breath.

This...might kill me.

I had never tried to bend reality to the extent which I was about to, and I was not completely sure it would work—or that I'd make it through the other end. I was already sorely drained from my earlier power display, and yet if I couldn't do this, we'd all be done for. I had to try.

I was a reality bender, right? Theoretically I could bend distance...it was all part of it, right?

This was a stretch, even for me. But seconds before the soldiers around us made the final assault, I took a deep breath and willed the ground around us to invert like a turntable, and to my shock it actually obeyed. What followed was the oddest sensation I've ever experienced.

We were turned down into the ground, but what should have ended up with us hanging from the ceiling under the earth instead found us upright and...in the Underground.

"Wha—how—" I honestly had no idea who was speaking, because even as my eyes adjusted to the darkness and I registered we were indeed safely back in the underground city, my vision tunneled and the roaring in my ears drowned out everything else.

THE LIVING STONE

The last thing I remembered was someone calling my name.

CHAPTER XV: What in the Worlds...

<u>Grenedil:</u>

"Are you going to help us?!" The girl's shout came even as I struggled to register the logic of what had just happened. Where in the worlds were we *now?!* I turned to find both the girl and Alenor Mara struggling to hold up the man—Sven Mara, if I was correct. But I had apparently a good streak of being very *wrong* as of late, so….

"I—right." I cut off any attempt at voicing the thousands of questions that were drowning my already muddled brain and limped up beside the girl—an Esmer—taking her place at Sven's side. I only just began to register we were in some sort of underground street when the Esmer began shouting, gaining the attention of the ragged city-goers.

"HELP! Someone get Darbeshay!"

I saw a few people in the crowd take off, but I was a bit preoccupied at the moment. Only barely did I register that the ground had been shaking, or that I felt rubble sprinkle against my shoulder. I was in a haze, unable to catch my breath as I struggled to overcome the just absolute shock of the last hour—days—weeks—years—I was having a hard time keeping track, let alone keeping *up*. Was it me or was this whole cavern spinning?

And somehow, amid this panic and the fact that I was trying to hold up Alenor's unconscious son in the middle of some underground city, I remembered the fact that I still had no idea if Mitheau had made it to Litash with Astra.

"W-why is everything…spinning?" The Esmer girl asked *right* before she fainted, blood dripping from her mangled wing. I tried and failed to catch her even as I held onto Sven, but fortunately for me, a woman came running in through the crowd just in time, snatching up the girl before she hit the ground and giving me an utterly confused stare before her eyes landed on the burden I was helping Alenor carry.

"Baey, come on, stay awake, Birdy." The woman hoisted the Esmer—Baey—up and helped her stay on her feet. But she was swaying.

And my arms were giving out.

"What happened? What's going on?" Another woman followed by a rag-tag group of what I guessed were supposed to be soldiers appeared as the crowd parted for them, and soon both Alenor and I were relieved of the unconscious man we were holding up. I noticed I wasn't the only one struggling to stay on me feet, though. Even those standing in the city seemed unsteady, like the room really *was* spinning.

"Sven he—he did something. Got us out in time, but I think he…I don't know."

"Alenor, where's Thackeray?" The woman that had arrived with the soldiers addressed The Crafter, eyes widening in confusion as her gaze wandered to me.

"Thackeray should be fine. The—the portal is shut off. Please, let's talk somewhere private," Alenor looked around at the crowd, "and then hopefully by then, my son and Baey will be recovered."

And I would be caught up to this newest disaster. What was going on? Why exactly was Ovok trying to *leave?* Or at least, I was guessing that's what they'd wanted, as they'd been attacking the portal when I arrived. But why were we underground?! The last underground major city I'd known of in Baeno had been several millennia ago, and if I didn't know any better, I'd say these all looked like...refugees.

"Who is *he?*" The woman pointed directly at me, doubt and suspicion dripping from her tone.

"Believe it or not, a friend of sorts. But please, not here."

At least Alenor remembered me—which was fairly impressive since I hadn't seen her in over twenty years.

Finally, things stabilized, and only when it stopped did I realize there had been this low rumbling-like groaning, as if the very walls of the expansive cavern had been struggling to hold together.

"Alright. But quickly; right as you appeared…the city moved. Like an earthquake, almost. I don't know, but things are…nothing's in the right place anymore. Follow me," the woman with the soldiers said with wide eyes.

We were ushered away from all of the commotion, through the streets of panicking people. I barely registered the way some of the buildings looked like something out of a fevered dream. Spliced together as if one had been transported halfway into another. I'd noticed none of the architecture we'd passed had come anywhere close to Baeno's usual refinement, only making me panic more. I must have come in on the edge of a warzone. But why would Alenor be putting herself on the front lines? Surely The Crafters would have been better served behind, where it was safe. And where was Henry?

"Alright. Why did the Undergound just completely re-order, and are you're *sure* Thackeray is safe?" asked the woman who was clearly the leader—another odd reality, as I would have expected Alenor to be the one in charge—or at least one of her children.

Which only made me remember Skayla.

I was pretty sure I was going to lose my mind.

"The portal opened while we were shutting it down. Skayla...." Alenor trailed off, but even as she did so, the woman picked it up.

"Skayla apparently left for the portal—Atlys sent us word only half an hour ago, but it was too late to warn you. I'm sorry."

"Yes, she was there, but we did successfully shut it down and rendered the equipment nonfunctional. That being said, if they've built them once, they'll build them again. So I don't know how much time we have."

I wanted to scream. This was a nightmare. "Alenor, *what* is going on?" I decided I could no longer keep myself quiet. "Why is Skayla attacking you—what are the Myrandi doing, and why are we huddling in some underground shelter like it's the end of the world? I know I have really bad timing with showing up, but this is...what in the worlds, Alenor?"

"Honestly, I could ask you the same thing. Where did you disappear to, and what in the world is going on? One day the Myrandi—Drogans, whatever you wish to call them—show up saying they've been hunted off of Eatris and are seeking shelter, and the next minute my own daughter has betrayed her entire world and is helping the Drogans destroy it. We only just found out at least *some* of the Drogans are being forced to help against their will, but from all accounts, Ovok has somehow orchestrated all of this. None of us know why, and I can't even fathom the motivation of my own *daughter* who, by the way, made her older sister a practical ghost outside of time and her younger one a forced assassin for the last eight years!"

Ovok...what? While after the stunt he pulled on Cyl, I wasn't exactly surprised with him being, well, self-motivated; I didn't picture him destroying a whole world on a whim. I'd assumed he had been trying to get the Drogans somewhere else to escape the Nythrilians. I thought the erratic behavior and the attack on Cyl had been because of the death of Rhioa.

"I...I'm sorry, I had no idea. This is...bad...." I ran my hands through my hair as I desperately tried to process all of this.

"Bad is an understatement," the other woman added.

"I'm sorry, I was—I was trying to find Cyl. The keeper of the Doorway. He—I thought he was dead after Ovok forced his way through, but I only just found him, and he's been apparently keeping the portal sealed so Ovok can't get back in for...whatever reason he wants to get in. We don't know, and Cyl is still so tremendously ill that the best he could do was keep it shut. I have been...*everywhere* trying to pick up the pieces and mess between the worlds, and while I knew Baeno was a bit of a mess, I was thinking political mess. Not...not this. How much have Ovok and Skayla taken?" I felt breathless with the weight of it. I'd only just found Cyl, battered and bruised as if the battle in The Maze had happened yesterday—not over a decade ago. I hoped that with Alenor apparently dismantling the portal devices, he would be able to restore some of his strength. But I had to leave and check on him...which would mean trying to find a backdoor into The Maze, which could prove tricky if *apparently* Ovok was trying to get off of the world, too.

I suddenly realized I was being stared at.

Alenor looked sympathetic as she said, "Grenedil. It's not *how much*. It's *how long*. Baeno's gone. Skayla has everything. She's had everything except one corner of the world for years now. And that last corner—Kaedovarna—just fell a month or two ago."

Life itself seemed to leave me as my shoulders sagged helplessly. "What?" No...no, this couldn't...."

"I'm afraid so."

"Alenor, I'm so sorry, I had no idea—I'm really trying. The worlds are a mess and I still have no idea what Ovok wants or what's going on. I just left a friend to quite possibly get eaten by a monster as she tries to fly a girl across a very dangerous forest to hopefully get help before she dies because Ovok's son-in-law is going crazy and I have no idea why and no idea what *he* wants either and whether it's connected or if this is all an unhappy coincidence...and I still have been unable to locate my *stupid* brother, whose tool bag we could really use."

"You still haven't found him?" Alenor's brow furrowed.

I threw up my hands in exasperation. "No, I haven't. For all I know, he could be on Kryso. I was hoping he would be on Eatris, but that was a no, and so I thought maybe he'd be here, but...somehow I doubt he would be, with Ovok going on an apparent rampage." My throat stuck and I took a shaky breath. There was no clearing my head. This was even worse than the worst-case scenario I'd conjured up. And if that wasn't enough, I couldn't forget Mitheau, trapped in that box of a prison before we'd gotten her out. What if the fate she'd flown off to was even worse? What if Astra *died?!* What in the worlds would I do then?

The next few hours were spent catching us all up on what was going on. The woman—Darbeshay—was most gracious in taking this all in stride. Baeno, at least, had more knowledge of the fact that their world was not the only one, and so it was a little less of an overwhelming process than when I'd tried to explain the situation to Astra and Louko. But the bigger problem was that what Darbeshay and Alenor needed explained were all things I didn't have the answer to. I had no idea why Ovok had left. I had no idea why he was working with Skayla. My best guess was The Living Stone—as Alenor said The Creator had told her to hide it before things really went downhill, and that...that Henry had been killed protecting Alenor's whereabouts.

So many dead. So much destroyed. I still couldn't believe Ovok had done all of this. And for what? It didn't make sense. Ovok had been all about protecting the Drogan race in the last several decades, and yet, apparently, he had willingly let Skayla put a MindHold over at least a few of them? Alenor had asked if Ovok might also be under one, but I knew that was impossible. There was no way a being over two thousand years old would have been so gullible. No. There was something going on, I just didn't understand what. But somehow, I knew it had to do with The Living Stone. I would have thought it had to do with the prophecy of the new Guards that would replace Ovok, but no one except Alenor and The Merchant knew of that.

The Merchant, otherwise known as my selfish brother.

What were the worlds coming to?

CHAPTER XVI: Death's Toll

<u>Baey:</u>

I was in the medical ward for a couple days, but overall, the scrapes and bruises I'd been given were nothing too major. Thankfully, the wound to my wing was also a minor issue, between my thick feathering slowing the blade and then it having missed anything that could have permanently damaged my wing. But the thrill of knowing I'd truly held my own in a fight and survived to tell the tale was drowned out by the fact that Sven was not awake to tell it to.

It had been a week and a half, and he was still unconscious. Alenor said she was afraid he might never wake up. Apparently, he'd stretched his abilities too far—dug too deep and quite possibly had drained himself of his very life force. Since all abilities were linked to The Living Stone—especially his powers—he had drawn deep from his own life to save us.

What an idiot.

But what was even worse was the price his move had come with. Apparently, Sven hadn't just moved us through an impossible distance. He'd moved…everything. We didn't know to what extent, but the Underground had been shaken and torn up only to be spliced back together. Buildings were meshed and combined, and we'd even found buildings that belonged on the surface now were with us below. And that wasn't all; Alkemar was a mess. It was as if it had been picked up, folded in half, squished together like dough and then dropped back down. Sven had altered the reality of the very city, and it sounded like there had been a few deaths. Deaths I didn't want to tell Sven about.

If he ever woke up, anyway.

But I didn't have time to sit and mourn him being gone again. I'd taken his place in our planning. Alenor had caught me up with regard to Grenedil, but my usual curiosity was ruined with our situation. We'd still heard nothing of Tanner and the rest, and I was beginning to worry that they, too, were gone forever. The disaster that was the surface city was still crawling with soldiers, so much so that Atlys had even cut back on giving supplies, and no one had been allowed to leave the Underground unless there was a very, *very* good reason.

At least they couldn't trace us back to the sewers—which had completely reordered themselves like the rest of the city—and the Bethynese soldiers didn't seem to have any idea that an entire city was hiding underground. I wondered how long that would last, though. And then there was Skayla. Or perhaps…the fact that we hadn't *heard* from Skayla, and Atlys had heard whispers of something being…wrong with her. Of her struggling to keep a hold on her power. That Sven had cracked the armlet, and her with it, and of riots taking place in other regions of Baeno. Could her hold on everyone's mind really be slipping?

"Baey!" Estasia had found me practicing my sword drills on the edge of the Underground, and my concentration broke as I caught the concern lacing her voice.

I turned around to see what was the matter.

"I figured you'd want to come see yourself—the guards posted at the back tunnel to the shore just spotted a Drogan crash land on the beach. It's dying. They are going down to investigate and wanted you."

Why did my heart sink to my feet? "Wait, what? What was the color of it?" I asked before even comprehending why.

"They didn't say." But the look in Estasia's eyes proved I wasn't the only one worried about what the answer might be. We hadn't had any run-ins with Drogans recently. So how would one be injured and dying on the beach?

I followed Estasia through the city and to a door on the opposite side of the wall. Without a word, she clicked the key into its hole and opened the door, giving a nod to the guards before disappearing into it. I followed closely behind. The smell of salt blew lazily up the tunnel as we hurried down it, and it would have been refreshing if I could have gotten past the knot growing firmly in my stomach.

The tunnel split into two entryways, one that led up and one downwards. We took the latter, and a few steps later it opened up into the evening seaside. I found myself on the soft sanded beach, bathed in the light of the two moons and the fascinating, scattering blue and violet aurora streaking across the sky.

But the beauty was lost to me as I stood with Estasia, the guards on either side of the exit pointing us to where a small group had gathered further down the beach. A little further from them was a large dark mass, its sides heaving in and out heavily where it lay on the sand.

I ran, instantly left behind by Estasia running more skillfully up to the group standing not far from the dark mass on the shore.

It was Darby and Thackeray, brows furrowed as they looked at the creature on the beach. They seemed to have only arrived at the site a few minutes before Estasia and I had.

My eyes followed the stares of others to the creature just beyond us. In the pale illumination, I could just make out the glint of golden scales.

"Oh, no." I barely registered Estasia's murmur.

"Syvil!" I shouted, breaking through the small crowd of people and running to his head. No, no, no, no! "Syvil! Are you still there? Wake up, please." Tears began filtering down my cheeks as anguish set in. Where were the others? What had happened?!

The Drogan's eyes flickered ever so slightly open to reveal a dull, faraway expression. He gave a soft moan, trying to move his head. Slowly, his body shifted, shrinking and morphing lazily into his human form. "Baey?" He croaked between a cough, shivering where he lay on the beach.

I reached forward and clutched his hand. "That's it, you're alright." I soothed through shaky breaths, trying to see where the wounds were. There were too many to count. Why hadn't they healed like before?!

"...Ovok..." His voice was weak, every breath labored and each syllable accompanied by a wince. "...Took...Living Stone...trapped...trapped...." He gave a shuddering breath followed by an unearthly groan. "...please don't—don't leave me—alone. I d-d-don't want...I'm sorry. I'm sorry—I couldn't. I'm not—" His eyes stared out into nothing, coughing interrupting each sentence.

"I'm not going anywhere." I squeezed his hand even as I screamed back at the others, "Someone get help! Quick!" Then I turned back to Syvil. He was so pale. "Please. Please, Syvil don't go. You can't leave."

"I'm sorry—I'm sorry—I tr-tr-tried to tell you I...I wasn't...wasn't a fighter...wasn't strong...I'm sorry...." Then he laid still. Deathly still.

"Syvil?" Tears streamed down my face. "Syvil? Please say something."

But his eyes were wide open now, empty. Lifeless.

With a shocked gasp I fell backwards on the sand, swallowing the tears with limited success and unable to tear my gaze from Syvil's body. The Drogan that had risked everything for us. The one who had been so afraid to die. Only barely did my panicked mind turn to an even worse horror: The others—Tanner, Sefen, Jaythos—where were they? I felt a hand on my shoulder, but my vision around me was too blurred with tears to see who it was. All I could do was mentally repeat the tortured words Syvil had uttered.

Ovok took The Living Stone. Trapped.

THE LIVING STONE

CHAPTER XVII: Skayla

Eleven Years Ago

Skayla:

I stood before the mirror, uncertain if this really was the right decision. Ovok had taught me much since his arrival, and his people even more. The biggest was how prejudiced and afraid our world still was. The Drogans had been greeted with so much unease, and riots had even broken out in some regions of Alkemar. I had calmed them, but days later, I would see the same people at it again, having learned nothing. Ovok was right. Our world was a mess, unable to understand a bigger picture or accept anything new, and I was too afraid to change their minds. Even when I told myself to push my power and try and truly get them to see, I would back off in fear.

So, here I stood, in front of the mirror. I stared at the reflection on the other side; the deep violet eyes so uncertain.

"Don't be afraid," I told myself, breath shaky.

Nothing happened.

I winced and looked away from the image, again, too afraid. No. This wasn't right—this couldn't be right. Perhaps there was another way to give me the strength and the courage I lacked. Again, the thought of my siblings surfaced. I had told them nothing of my fears, especially Sven. He'd been as unsure about the Drogans as some of the others, doubting Ovok's intentions with a fierceness. He didn't understand—how could he?! Again, I turned back to the image in the mirror, now confidently looking myself in the eyes.

"Don't be afraid," I ordered, using my Gift. "You will make them understand. But you can't be afraid." I shuddered, wishing to feel afraid and suddenly unable to be. I continued. "You and Ovok will change the world, for the good of all. Once they see, they will understand. But you cannot be afraid to use your power." My mind began to feel numb as the icy waters of the Thaesha River, and I found myself oddly at ease. A smile crossed my face, and I even laughed. Turning from the mirror, I smoothed the folds of my dress, setting my shoulders in confidence as I prepared to meet Ovok like we had planned. It would be worth it. A life was at stake—and the world in need of change. They would thank us for this.

END OF PART ONE

CHAPTER XVIII: Rough Seas and Worse Company

<u>Tanner:</u>

The eerie laughter echoed about the halls, twisting and turning until they shot down every corridor and filled them with a chilly wickedness.

"Motttttther, Fattttther, where arrre you?" More laughter. Fear. Panic. Footsteps running up and down the house. I heard screams and shouts then silence. Everywhere there was the smell and ache of death—the walls were rancid with it. Then fire and the shadows of beasts. Rubble.

Everything blurred together and then rewound, repeating itself over and over even as I voicelessly screamed for it to stop. Even the pleasant memories of the house were tainted by Skayla's wild giggles, and all was tainted and torn.

"Motttttther…."

I woke, bolting upright as the boat lurched lazily to one side. Cold sweat poured down my back, and I breathed a sigh of relief as the acute smell of salt and sweat wafted unpleasantly into my nostrils.

I rolled my eyes, a mixture of thankfulness and nausea battling inside of me. I *hated* the sea.

But I hated that memory even more.

With a yawn and a stretch, I got up, slowly finding my way about the dark and cramped quarters as I tried to reach the steep stairs at the far end. Maeko's cacophonic snore ripped through the silence, and I heard him adjust in his hammock. How lovely.

A few more steps and I made it to the exit, carefully stumbling up the steep stairs and into what many would call "fresh air." The air that hit me only felt cold, rough, and smelled of the sea, reminding me once again I was stranded on a flying boat.

Not fun.

But I was complaining, of course. Really, I was doing the exciting part, while poor Baey was forced once more to stay home. I was a tool, a thing you could use and not be afraid of breaking. Baey—for all of the smothering and unbearable coddling—was at least loved. No one cared enough about me to lock me safely away. I was just their best intelligence device, a built-in mind-reader.

The boards beneath me gave the usual unnerving creaks and groans as I walked across the deck, nodding to Sefen, who was at the helm, but not desiring any form of conversation with him. No one really wished to talk to me unless it was part of the plan, anyway.

Making it to the end of the ship, I leaned against the railing, looking at the dark silhouettes of waves passing far below us and trying not to throw up. Maybe I'd picked up motion sickness from some random person I'd pickpocketed a memory from. Sometimes it was hard to distinguish what was me, and what was everybody else cluttering my brain. No one bothered to ask if the memories I took ever went away, and, so far as I had experienced, they never did.

Folding my hands to keep from fidgeting, I thought of the tasks ahead. I had to keep the memory alive of how to get to The Living Stone. While Alenor had hidden The Living Stone itself, her husband had hidden the key, and Alenor had very reluctantly given me the spectacles so that it wouldn't be so hard to recollect the memory of where it was hidden. Still, she was understandably pained about it, so I wanted to bring them back in one piece. But memories weren't an exact science, especially when relating to inanimate objects. All I knew was that the key lay in the city of Veka, the capital city of the Isle of Rugo. And a quite literal key it was.

The boat lurched ever so slightly in its flight path, and I gripped the railing as I looked down to the dark waters far below. "Stupid boats," I murmured with a groan.

"Are you alright over there?" Sefen called out.

"Absolutely," I replied, even as I fought the irritation of being watched. Sefen was paranoid. I suppose I couldn't blame him, though. Between Namaya, his children, and his brothers...I'd be paranoid, too.

Shivering from what I decided was the wind, I let out a yawn. Two more days, Maeko had said. Two more days of absolute torture. Maeko hated Syvil, Jaythos hated...well...everybody, and Sefen was still acting as if he was the leader. The problem was that everyone was realizing how bad of a leader he was.

About time.

I stayed on deck until the sun slowly reared its face and everyone else began stumbling up top. Maeko took Sefen's position, and the latter went down to rest below. In the meantime, Jaythos was sitting atop a crate by the stern, and Syvil had just come up from below.

"I'm going to go fishing," the Drogan announced, eyeing us all with a good measure of distrust. He was still recovering from his wounds, and yesterday had been the first time he'd really been on deck instead of sleeping most of the day away in seclusion. I half wondered if there was a part of him that had simply been trying to avoid everyone else's company, and the way he held himself and flinched at every sound seemed to indicate I wasn't far off.

"Get something for the rest of us, ah?" I called as he shifted to his Dragon form, only just catching him before he dove over the edge of the ship and into the air.

I hated how other people always seemed to worm their way into even my speech pattern.

A few minutes later, there was a loud reverse splash as Syvil sprung from the water, still in Dragon form and about the size of a large horse. He landed on deck, looking very full and pleased with himself as he plopped a really, *really* big fish on the deck. It was at least as long as I was tall, silver and green scales glittering in the morning light.

"Be human or get off! No room!" Maeko shouted as he waved his arms at Syvil, coming back over to us.

I saw what appeared to be a Drogan version of a smirk, and suddenly I realized what Syvil was going to do.

I ducked for cover just in time, hearing Maeko's indignant cries and Jaythos's dry laugh as the Drogan shook himself vigorously, giving Maeko a bath in the process.

Maeko just grumbled something about animals and went back to his post at the helm while Syvil dragged the fish over to a corner and then returned to his human form, fresh scars shining in the sun. I flinched, feeling as if I could still feel the fear Ovok had caused each one of them.

I shouldn't have touched him after Hytat. It was like I was processing his terror right along with him, unable to rid myself of the memory of

Ovok's massive form. Of the knowledge that I'd gotten away out of pure luck. That a few more minutes and I never would have felt the wind against my feathers again.

Syvil's feathers. Not mine. Him. Not me. I shuddered, coming back to myself and looking away from Syvil as he inspected his catch. Instead, I turned to Maeko. "So, we have about a day and a half left?"

"You ask every day," Jaythos murmured.

I rolled my eyes, giving him a very childish expression to show my disapproval of being called out. It wasn't like Jaythos had any more patience than I did.

Fortunately, Maeko humored me. "Two days, more like. The wind is not good on the first trip, and Rugo is further down than Hytat."

By down, I knew he meant south. "Are you sure you know a safe place to dock?" I once more asked. Sven had kept the boat hidden from sight, presumably, but what if something happened and the illusion fell? Regardless, we needed to find somewhere where our boat wouldn't just be accidentally bumped into...all while trying not to be too far from the route to The Living Stone.

"Yes, he does, now stop asking," Jaythos answered for Maeko.

How had we ever gotten along in Valdon? Oh yeah...we hadn't. I'd just been better at shutting up when Baey was around—of letting the illusion stand so she didn't see how much the rest of the group grated on my nerves.

I decided not to engage, instead returning to my position on the railing. It was a more advantageous spot, and one where I could continue to watch Syvil. He still seemed shaken. I wondered what it must be like to be helping a bunch of strangers. What it was like to know that you'd killed your own friend for them.

Then I shuddered as his memories whispered answers, reminding me I didn't have to wonder.

In an attempt to get my mind off of *that*, I closed my eyes again, allowing a very different memory to wash over me as the waves against the ship. The one that actually mattered—the one that would lead us to The Living Stone.

"Alenor." The voice echoed suddenly in every corner of the memory, faraway and nearby. "You must hide it. A great power seeks to possess The Living Stone. Bring it back to the beginning." I had never heard a voice like it before, strong yet gentle, stern and soft, loud and silent. It couldn't be described.

The scene came into focus more, but too quickly, and warped. I felt raced across a great sea to a flat island. The sound of birds drowned out senses, and panicked voices rose only slightly above them. A cave...or was it a house? I hated distorted memories.

Below or was it above? In the memory went, winding through passages and endless rooms, up down, around, then right before we came to the end of the tunnels we went backwards, and the journey across the ocean was replayed again, though more slowly. Different things I had not seen came into view.

Big ships larger than mountains, people thicker than trees. Tanned and muscular, no voices escaped them. I put the very warped images together. I knew where we were.

Again we jumped, past the island and passages and back across the ocean to here. Hiding, frightened, torn, and full of remorse. Fire, flight.

"I'll distract them. Run—they must not get you!"

"Henry!"

"I love you."

I took a shuddering breath as I came out of the memory so vividly replaying in front of me. Emotions that were not mine tumbled and rolled, and I found myself drumming the railing with my fingers. With a sudden frown, I stopped, staring down at them. Great. I'd picked up yet another person's quirk.

Jaythos:

Hands firmly gripping the helm, I tried to keep a wary eye out for anything on the skyline. We were only a day out now, and I was finally getting better at handling the ship, but it was difficult to stay focused on keeping it steady as well as scanning the surrounding skies for Drogans. It was a wonder we hadn't seen any so far, but if we did run into one...I knew I would be grateful for Syvil. I was still not quite sure what I thought of the Drogan, but he had saved our hides more than once and probably deserved all of our trust. Still, I found myself hesitant. Perhaps it was just that after Namaya, I found myself struggling to trust *anyone.*

Or maybe I was just jealous that he and Sven had such a good excuse for the things they'd been forced to do. Unlike my family.

I was torn from my musings by the presence of someone coming up beside me.

It was Maeko. We hadn't spoken much since after Sven had been revealed as The GhostMaker, and he hadn't really taken well to my opinion on the matter. I knew he'd just wanted someone to blame; someone he could hate and kill to avenge the death of Serafina.

"I suppose I owe you an apology," Maeko addressed me in Rugonian.

Unsure what to say, I simply continued to look forward, not quite sure what he was apologizing for.

Maeko sighed. *"You are going to make me say it, I see."* Just as I was about to give up and ask what he was talking about, however, he went on, *"Sven is not the one that killed Sera. Skayla is."*

I breathed in, turning around and looking him at last in the eye. I saw the guilt; he meant it. *"Well. I hope you live long enough to tell that to Sven, because I am really not the one you should be apologizing to."*

"But I blamed you for siding with him. And for that I am truly sorry."

I allowed myself a small smile. *"You are always forgiven, my friend."* For that was what he was: my only friend. In this entire forsaken world, I had found few cared about a Bethynese turncoat. But Maeko always had. When I'd defected from Bethyn to Rugo, he'd been the only one to stick up for me and believe me; the only one that thought the personal guard of a Bethynese diplomat could actually want to be free of the strict government of the Bethynese. For that, Maeko had my gratitude and friendship forever, despite any insults or threats he'd thrown my way when I'd called him out over Sven.

"Thank you." Maeko placed a hand on my shoulder as he replied. But I felt the awkward silence and knew what he was about to say next. *"And are you going to be alright? You know who was posted in Rugo's capital."*

Gripping the helm a little harder, I said simply, *"Yes. I doubt he's still there—and even if he is, we're trying to stay clear of any confrontations, so I don't need to worry about seeing him."*

"Just be careful. It's been a long time. He's no longer a kid, Jaythos."

The urge to snap back at him was crushed by the fact that I'd been spending the last few weeks criticizing him for doing so against Sven. *"I know. And he's on the wrong side."*

"You did everything you could."

I let the conversation die out there, the words echoing relentlessly in my head, because deep down, I knew they weren't true. I hadn't done all I could. I'd taken the one shot at being free I had, and in doing so, had betrayed my own family, and now I wasn't sure what I would do if I had to stand face-to-face against *him*. Wrong side or not, he was still my little brother, and I didn't want to think that I might have to choose between killing him and letting him kill my friends.

The day wore on, and at about noon, Maeko took my place. Everyone was doing their best to avoid each other, and it was frankly one of the most peaceful days we'd had so far, making it extremely insufferable. I was done idling and waiting around. So, dodging down below, I grabbed my crossbow and an bolt and went back on deck. I needed to keep in practice, especially with the way the stupid arm wound had affected me.

But we were all beaten and bruised one way or another, and we needed to be as in-shape as possible.

"If anyone wants to get stuck with a crossbow bolt, let me know, otherwise stay in the stern," I announced as I made my way to the back and perched myself on the railing of the raised stern. The ship was so tiny that even from all the way back here, I felt I wouldn't have much of a challenge. Bethyn had always had such large airships that this one was a bit of a disappointment. Still, better for stealth, I supposed.

"What if we don't want to move?" Tanner asked queasily from his spot in the bow.

In response, I growled, "Then prepare to be skewered."

He moved without another word, clutching his stomach as he did so.

I sounded like my father…. As much as I tried to distance myself as much as possible from my family, I still ended up acting like them. Which only put me in even a worse mood.

Good thing I had some target practice.

I loaded the crossbow in one smooth motion, targeting one of the cargo boxes that had come with the ship. Aiming for the knot in the bottom corner of the wooden side, I fired, hitting it right on the mark.

"Good shot," Maeko called from his post.

Not a challenging one, however. I huffed in discontentment and swiftly went over to gather up the bolt. Usually, the bolt would be fairly used up, so deep in the wood it would be impossible to reuse, but these were made of Bethynese metal, resilient but easily recovered. I pressed my thumb down on the pin-needle-like button up near the fletching, and the inner contraption narrowed the tip of the bolt so that it would be a little easier to retrieve.

After tugging the bolt free, I again returned to my perch and picked another target. This continued for a couple hours, with me constantly coming up with more difficult challenges. Loading and shooting while climbing up one of the rope ladders meant for balloon maintenance, shooting while hanging half out of the net...pretty much anything that would distract me from the forced stagnation.

Finally, completely bored of being a good shot, I wandered back to Maeko. *"I can take over again,"* I offered, switching to Rugonian.

Maeko responded with a lifted eyebrow, giving an odd and unnatural look to his emotionless features, and replied, *"You are not the only bored one, you know."*

"Yes, but I am a bit more dangerous when bored."

Maeko hid his amusement.

I took a deep breath, turning to the question I really wanted to ask. *"And it's my turn to ask; are you going to be alright going back?"*

Maeko's entire body stiffened, each muscle showing the visible tension my question brought with it. *"It is touching that you are concerned."*

"I just wanted to know if I had to be worried about you freezing up. But if it makes you feel better, sure. I was concerned for you." I covered my tracks quickly with the sarcastic remark. But I really was concerned, even if I was bad at showing it. We were both going through similar things; we'd both lost family and were returning to a place that would dig it all up again. Though perhaps my loss was a bit different than the queen he'd treated as a daughter.

"I will be fine. Thank you for rubbing it in." Maeko returned to looking forward, out into the blue skies around us.

"If you are certain."

"You didn't seem to question Sefen twice when his own wife betrayed us and died. Yet you question my ability to hold it together?" Maeko pressed the issue, gruff and annoyed.

I sighed. *"I always question Sefen. I usually don't have to worry about you."*

The man's shoulders slumped ever so slightly. *"I know. But I won't let it cloud my judgment. Not this time."*

"So, how do we sneak into the city with no one seeing us?" Syvil's question intruded upon our conversation.

Yeah, I suppose we did have to figure that one out sooner rather than later. "Ideas are welcome," I called over. Sefen and I had talked about it last night before he had taken over, but we had come up with nothing. I never liked Sefen's plans to begin with, and all of the madness at Valdon's collapse had only made him worse.

"Well, I could sneak in easily enough, but I'm not so sure about the rest of you." Syvil came a bit closer, his nervousness abated with the realization of the dilemma.

"And how would you do that?" I asked. We didn't have passports, and while Maeko would perhaps be able to get in, even Syvil looked nothing like a Rugonian.

Syvil shrugged. "Rugo has deep canals, yes? For the city's cooling system?" He cocked his head, directing the question towards Maeko.

Maeko gave a taut nod in response.

"I can swim in that way. If I do so at night, I won't be seen." The Drogan gave a small shiver after he spoke, and I saw the hints of fear in his eyes; fear I was not in the mood to deal with, and fear that would buckle under even the smallest weight, should we be caught. I wondered if we could count on Syvil not to betray Sven and Baey's whereabouts if we were captured.

"Not a bad plan," said Maeko.

The Drogan just smiled, hiding his nerves beneath it as he rubbed his right arm. I, however, was more preoccupied with the fact that, once again, the Drogan easily solved our problems. I put it off as being the hundred or so years of extra experience, even as I wondered if we all were really just *that* incompetent.

"It's a good start," I replied simply. There were, of course, many finer details that would have to be figured out, but this was slightly more than we'd had five minutes ago. Granted, we would all still likely die. Especially since the Drogan would pretty much be the basis of the plan succeeding.... Maybe I was more worried about the fact that I felt more confident in a Drogan we'd befriended a few weeks ago than in the companions I'd been with for years.

"What's this?" Sefen's voice came from the hatch to below deck, and a moment later, his head popped up.

"While you were getting your rest, old man, we were figuring out how not to die," I explained without skipping a beat. Sefen did not appear impressed. But then again, since Valdon, the humor had been wrung out of him.

"And what have we come up with so far?" Sefen asked, taking a seat.

Sefen was quickly brought up to speed, and what transpired next was an actually civil conversation plotting out several scenarios of how to get into the city. Tanner said the key was hidden in the Hall of Merceri, a grand museum that had only just finished construction one or two years before the Drogans had arrived. The problem was...we didn't know *where* the key was hidden. Tanner said the key had been handed off to the curator of the museum: Runin. Both Maeko and I had been vaguely acquainted with the elderly man, and all I could think of was the likelihood of him being dead. And on top of that, how would the museum even still be standing after the destruction of the war? Rugo had been occupied by the Bethynese for at least six or seven years, and if Runin had been found, wouldn't Skayla have found the key by now if that's where it was hidden? The Maras had never struck me as dumb—especially Skayla.

And then there was that.... What happened if Skayla already *had* the key? We knew she'd apparently been looking for The Living Stone for a while, now. So what if she had gotten the key and just needed the location? What if we led her right to it? I was trying not to be paranoid, but with our track record, it was hard not to be. And if I was honest, I wasn't sure if I could trust the others to have my back anymore. How had Sefen not realized his own *wife* was a traitor? How had Tanner not seen it? Surely the kid was always sneaking into other's heads and trying to acquire information. How had we missed it?

I sighed. They were no Bethynese cohort. Zeal could not replace discipline, and as much as I'd tried to reconcile that fact, I couldn't help but find myself still irritated with Sefen. I felt all the years at Valdon had been wasted, and I wondered if Maeko and I shouldn't have just stayed in Rugo to organize some rebellion and fight back.

I shook my head, clearing the air. Maybe I wasn't the one who was in the most danger of freezing up in Veka.

Everyone had long since gone to bed, once more leaving Maeko and me to tend to the ship in the night air. I had hoped it would clear my head, but instead, it was clearly only making things worse. I needed action. I'd thrived on it—been reliant on it to snuff out all the doubts still ringing in my ears after over a decade.

"Things are quite different now, aren't they?" Maeko's question split the air.

"Yeah. I'm really not sure if we're closer to the end of the world, or further from it, at this point," I replied, giving a weak attempt at humor.

Quietly, I walked away from the rigging I'd been pretending to tend to and went over to Maeko, breathing in the night air and watching the Glaedus Aurorus as its streaks of blue and violet chased each other in the night sky. I hadn't seen the aurora in so long, I'd nearly forgotten the beauty of it.

"I don't know. The dead have been raised…but friends have been lost, as well." Maeko's reply did nothing but bring up the memories of everyone we'd lost in the last month. With the way things had moved so quickly, I'd hardly had time to even process that all our companions that had gone to Kaedna to help Emarian were now dead. Well, dead or in a MindHold. But most likely dead.

"It doesn't feel real. At this point, nothing does. After all, Sven Mara came back from the dead…I don't even know what is happening anymore," I replied, shrugging it off even as the words sank deep.

"Do you miss them?" Maeko asked.

Looking up and out at the sky, I said, *"Yes, but I guess I'm just used to it, at this point."* I realized that they might not all be as accustomed to it as I was. You were used to casualties when you lived in Bethyn. If someone didn't make the cut—if someone was too weak—they were sent to the Isle of Curr. If someone hesitated in battle? Executed. Only the strong survived. It's why I'd never allowed myself friends. When they could be gone the next day, what was the point?

"I am afraid of that, more than anything." Maeko's comment caught me off guard. *"And I don't think you're as used to it as you think. Otherwise, going to Rugo now would not bother you."*

He just had to bring it up, again, didn't he? *"Well then in that case, don't let anything happen to you, because then I really won't have anyone."* I gave up and turned to face him, staring at him until I hoped it made him feel uncomfortable. I needed him to know I was dead serious.

"I am happy to remain your babysitter," he said, doing nothing to hide the grin that had slid onto his face. *"I'm pretty sure I'm the only reason you're alive at this point."*

I rolled my eyes. *"Oh don't go getting a chip on your shoulder. I'm still winning the count on saving your rear."*

"I beg to differ. I believe the account with your arm led me to take the lead."

"But then during the ambush, I was the one that stopped the archers," I countered.

Maeko just laughed. *"I think the Drogan would argue that he was the one that saved everyone's hides that night."*

True or not, I still gave Maeko a hard glare, refusing to concede the point. But it was nice to have the banter and the slightest bit of normalcy amid all this chaos. The question was, how long would it really be until another one of us fell?

CHAPTER XIX: Do We Have a Drogan or a Sea Horse?

<u>Tanner:</u>

The next day we'd finally spotted land. But it was early evening when we found the secluded lagoon that Maeko had pointed out, and lowered the boat's altitude enough to sink low to the ground until we were satisfied with the way the trees hid us should the illusion somehow give way. According to Maeko, at least, no one ever came around here, so the chances of someone physically running into the invisible boat were also unlikely.

Maeko and Syvil had concocted a plan for the Drogan to sneak inside the city and then let us in—Maeko's knowledge of Veka had proven extensive, as I would have expected, and he gave a detailed list of which districts were most likely to hold trouble and a few spots that held likely hideouts for us.

"Why not get going and have time to be prepared?" Maeko practically ordered Syvil after we'd gotten the boat secured.

Syvil flinched at the order but didn't say a word.

Jaythos gave a grumbling sigh and added, "Just be careful. We don't need you back to trying to eat us."

I knew it was Jaythos's way of saying "don't die," but I couldn't help but wince, remembering when I—when Syvil had been forced to hunt and kill like some monster.

But Syvil didn't say a word about it, only shifting quickly into his Dragon form and jumping off the deck. Soon, he was lost, submerged underneath the warm, shadowy water. I shuddered and fixed my gaze on the dim light of the city, the thousands of lanterns having probably just been lit with the setting sun. Hopefully, Syvil would go undetected.

Every inch of me crawled with anticipation, and yet it was strange that nothing felt new or unfamiliar. I'd never been in a city before—besides Alkemar—but the memories I'd experienced through others made it feel like I'd lived in one my whole life. Meanwhile, Baey, who would have loved to have seen a city, was stuck inside yet another house, waiting once again. How I would have loved just once to be told I was too indispensable. Too loved.

"So, now what?" I asked aloud in order to get rid of that thought. Syvil was gone, and we had to wait until well after sunset before trying to get in through the wall. Maeko had given the spot where it would be possible, and we were to meet there. But he hadn't been in the city for years—how did he know things hadn't changed? Sure, Veka had surrendered after Serafina's assassination, but as I'd pointed out while we were planning, Skayla had still laid siege to the city for a week before that. Much of the wall had been damaged, and while the southern part of the wall had remained intact—I knew this from Maeko's memories—could we really trust that it would be the same?

"We should scout around a bit as well." Sefen was naturally the first to speak up, causing my panic to be replaced by irritation. We weren't in Valdon anymore, and I, for one, wasn't keen on following his lead. Even Maeko appeared a little ill at ease with Sefen's constant belief that he was still in charge.

"I'll go," Jaythos announced as he already began to disappear into the long shadows of the nearby trees. No one bothered to argue, of course.

Minutes stretched out until at least an hour had passed, and to say the least, I was growing incredibly bored. Bored, anxious, and warm. From the moment we'd landed in the lagoon, I'd noticed the humidity. Now it was overpowering even in the cool of the evening, and something told me it only got worse during the day. The mosquitoes were enough to drive me crazy, even without the heat.

In an attempt to distract myself from the hordes of bugs attempting to devour me, I looked over again to the towering city in the distance. Even with the sun having set, you could see the lantern lights and the shadows of buildings. It was so...tall. Vague echoes of memories surfaced even from just looking at it, and for once, I let them. I didn't care about getting lost in a memory right now, because it was still better than the bugs.

The intense longing and pain of nostalgia grew in my chest, and I found myself reminiscing over the beautiful, glittering canals and the layered roads that wove under and over each other. It had been like a puzzle, towering higher than any other city in the world with the maze of streets winding up and down the sky. Would it still be that way? Or had Skayla ruined it like she'd ruined so many other things?

Just when I was sure Jaythos was somewhere dying in a ditch, he returned and gave a brief, uninteresting report. Silence returned. I focused my attention to where the key was hidden—the key that would lead inside Kayta Mountain.

If this memory was accurate, Baey would have loved the Hall of Merceri. Honestly, even I was rather intrigued. If it was still there, anyway.

The idea of artifacts from hundreds of years ago out for display wasn't nearly as interesting as the thought of touching them to see what secrets they hid. As crowded as my brain was, I would happily shove a few more memories in there. At least then I'd have ones I actually *wanted*.

"So, how long do we wait?" I asked. Apparently, I was the designated pesterer, and it wasn't by choice. This group was one argument away from anarchy and even worse was our lack of clear communication. I knew all the secrets they hid from each other—all the meaningless issues they kept to themselves. It only fueled the fire, and I couldn't stand the way they each assumed the others would just follow along. It would be nice to at least have *everyone* on the same page for the plan. But no. We were always off in our little groups, whispering and debating.

"One more hour," Maeko replied. "When the clock comes to eleven will be when Syvil is in the position." Of course, I understood he was talking about the giant clock tower in Veka.

I hated waiting. Problem was, at this point, I couldn't tell if *I* genuinely didn't like waiting, or if I'd just picked it up from one of the many people I'd absorbed. Like Jaythos. I started drumming my fingers nervously against my leg only to stop abruptly and stuff my hands in the pockets of my ill-fitting breeches.

Waiting would be the death of us all, one day.

Despite that gloomy prediction, we all survived the wait, and after the predetermined hour was up, we made our way carefully through the darkness and up to the city wall. It was unremarkable in the night, but I could still see the twisting pipes that wove up and down the length of it. The wall seemed to be constructed so that guards were posted inside as oppose to on top of it, but I saw light from windows on the higher level of it. The darkness of night shielded us, but only barely, as we crept along the base of the wall, making our way to the southern gate where Syvil was supposed to be opening a small side door.

I sure hoped the stupid blueprints were the same.

"Here," Maeko whispered, halting at the front of our group. I blinked a few times and leaned forward, just barely able to catch the outline of a door not far ahead. Now we just had to wait for the clock tower to chime eleven o'clock. I guessed the strange hour was to avoid changes of the guard. After all, Skayla guarded these cities like no tomorrow: We'd never taken one back. I shuddered, a foul taste in my mouth as I recalled Kaedna. The horror of the battle, those crazed violet eyes.

The tolling bell was much louder than I'd expected, and I would have jumped straight in the air had Sefen not put a hand on my shoulder to stop me.

The bell tolled on but the door did not open. The way Jaythos was fingering his crossbow was not exactly encouraging, either, and I found myself struggling to breathe. Yeah…watch us all get caught before we even so much as got the key to what we needed. What fine warriors we were.

Then, just as the ninth toll rang, there was a squeaking groan, and the door opened inwards to reveal a hand motioning wildly for us to enter.

Everyone must have been insane for just straight up obeying the hand and entering. Insane or desperate.

And stupid. Definitely a little bit of stupid.

Fortunately for us, it was indeed Syvil's hand that had gestured for us to come in, and soon, we were all huddling in a dark hallway inside the thick wall of the city. And we had no Sven to hide us this time.

"Quickly. We have about two minutes before the guards make another pass down this hall," Syvil whispered vehemently.

No one argued, and Syvil led the way down the corridor, which went on much deeper than I would have expected a hallway in a wall to go. In fact, there were one or two off-shooting halls that even went in other directions, showcasing what I already knew from Maeko's memories: The inside of this wall was quite a maze of corridors.

No one spoke as we hurried through the interior wall, but it didn't really matter, as there was plenty of noise around us. Besides the echoes of soldiers patrolling the halls, there were also the pipes that ran along the walls, squealing and sizzling as water from the ocean moved inside the pipes. Henry had come up with the idea—of taking the ocean water and purifying it so that it could be used as running water throughout the city.

Henry was dead and you didn't know him. I tried to remind myself who I was, but with the way we were already on edge and running around in the heart of enemy territory, there was little time to get my stupid brain in line.

And it was just *so* hot. Steam was everywhere and the roaring of furnaces bounced off the walls. I hated sweating.

"Tanner, keep up," Maeko hissed in my ear as he pushed me forward. I had been dragging, leaving him and me to lag a bit behind.

Right. Enemy territory. I sped up my step and then had to readjust so as to not run right into Sefen.

Suddenly, I heard footsteps coming from a side hall we had just passed, and that's when I realized we really were lagging behind the rest. Maeko pushed me and I practically fell forward into a run, my shirt tearing on a protruding valve as I struggled to keep my balance.

The footsteps grew closer.

Maeko and I rounded the corner to find Syvil motioning with wide eyes for us as he reached the apparent dead-end. Well, dead-end with a door.

Fumbling with the latch, the Drogan seemed about as nervous as I was.

The footsteps from behind us came to a halt, but now I heard confused voices.

"This cloth can't be from us, and there was no maintenance today."

"Check the exit!"

The footsteps resumed—faster this time. They would come around the bend any moment now. We'd be spotted and dead in seconds.

There was a groan as the door Syvil was fighting with opened, and we all winced at the noise it brought with it.

"What was that?" I heard the question from right around the corner.

Syvil practically ran into the darkness that lay beyond the door, and we did the same. Maeko closed it hastily behind us, and together we stood once more in the shadow of the wall. But now we were inside the city.

"Quick, they'll have heard that!" Syvil whispered harshly as he motioned for us to follow him. We were doing a lot of that lately. But seeing as all of our miserable lives depended on it, we ran on without question, and honestly, I trusted Syvil more than Sefen.

"They'll be searching this whole city before the night is out," Jaythos commented as we dove through the dark streets.

"Trust me," was all Syvil said in reply.

I panicked as a dark shadow passed overhead, expecting to see a Drogan circling us. I sucked in a deep breath of relief when I looked up and back to find that it had merely been an overpassing road resembling something of a bridge. The relief was a bit short-lived as I looked forward just in time to smack right into Jaythos, who grunted unappreciatively.

More shadows passed overhead as we ran through the base of the great city, built almost like a maze of levels, with bridges and overhangs crisscrossing above us. I even heard the footsteps of soldiers running across some of the bridges overhead.

I tried not to let panic set in as the otherwise empty streets echoed with the sounds of searches for us. This wasn't like Valdon. There was no backup—no chance of escape if we got caught. It would be the end of everything for us. I didn't like the idea.

We barely avoided the patrols as we climbed from the ground up to the third story of the city. Maeko had taken the lead with Syvil, and I guessed that it was to help make sure we didn't get lost finding wherever Syvil had discovered to lie low.

I didn't really even take notice of the giant clock tower until it was overshadowing us completely, the lantern light alone casting enough illumination to really see the massive structure's ornate trim and metal ribbing.

"This way," Maeko muttered as he and Syvil led us down a suspended road that ran right up alongside the tower. There was a small diverting pathway that led up to the back of the structure, and I realized it was a maintenance entrance into the clock tower. Syvil took out two small metal pins and picked the lock as if he were a master. I wondered if Estasia had taught him while we were on the boat, or if that was just one of the random things you decided to learn when you lived several hundred years. For once, I didn't have the answer off the top of my head.

I decided now was probably not the best time to ask.

A few seconds passed in quiet tension, and we slipped in just as I began to worry some city guards would stumble upon us.

The inside of the clock tower was like an old friend, familiar and comforting. I was suddenly lost in the massiveness of it, the loud mechanical clicks of the clock high above echoing down the hollow interior. As we climbed the stairwell and the clicking became louder, I found myself becoming lost in the memories that haunted the place. Echoes of work and a time long lost. Of artistry being shared. Of the time when there was more to life than avoiding Skayla's eyes.

I thought of the long hours I'd put into the planning just to have it sit and waste away here, alone and ill-cared for by the looks of it.

Wait. I'd not put any time into it. I was getting lost in Alenor's life. If I wasn't careful, I was going to drive myself into an identity crisis again.

I forced myself to concentrate on my breathing—or rather, wheezing—as we climbed the stairs, trying to keep going despite my exhaustion. Just another step. One more. Then another. Keep your mind on the numb repetition. Avoid the whispers that called to me from the walls of the building. Avoid the memories that weren't mine. I had enough to deal with without having to deal with everyone else's trauma.

Just as I was sure my legs would fall off from their burning, we reached the top of the clock tower, coming up into a large room where the clock faces were set. There was a sort of boardwalk all around the large square space, with the center still hollow like the rest of the building. Only not quite hollow, for it held a mesh of cogs, gears, and pulley systems that ran up to the ceiling and around the room to the four clock faces that looked out over the city.

"Well, the bell will be a pretty unwelcome reminder of our staying..." Sefen murmured as he wandered about the room, taking it all in.

"There are no bells anymore," came Maeko's dry reply. "It was long taken." He pointed up to the ceiling and I somehow knew that the ornate bronze bells had once hung there to chime away the hours. You'd think one would get used to all the marred beauty Skayla's destruction had caused. But somehow, it only ever made it harder.

"Wait, then what did we hear—"

"The small watchtower clock on the city wall. It's useful to Skayla," Maeko growled, leaving everyone to ponder how raiding one of Skayla's mother's great masterpieces seemed the reason for the lost bell. An excuse to destroy her legacy.

Then Jaythos broke the grim silence, his voice cutting almost as clear as a bell would have. "Well, I'll keep the first watch. You beauties get your rest. Long day tomorrow."

I blinked awake, the sunlight pouring in from the clock face and shining unpleasantly in my eyes. Still groggy, I sat up, looking around me and finding the others sitting or standing in a near unnatural stiffness. I was just about to ask what in the world was the matter when Jaythos locked eyes with me and put a finger to his lips.

That's when I heard the groaning from outside—like something was putting immense stress on the clocktower's framework. A shadow swayed over the clock face to my right, and all in a moment, it dawned on me why everyone was so still.

There was a Drogan on the tower.

My lungs seized as I mimicked everyone—freezing in place and afraid to even breathe. Did the Drogan know we were in here? I dared move my gaze from Jaythos to Syvil, the former of whom was giving me a glare that masked fear, just as it always did.

The minutes dragged by and the silhouette of the beast outside remained, its breathing actually audible from inside the tower. I wondered with a pit in my stomach if it was someone I knew. Maybe Lyri or Phaela—

Get out of my head, Syvil. I just barely remembered not to make an audible sigh as frustration poured in to mix with the panic. This stupid brain was getting way too crowded. Sometimes, I wondered if there was any me left inside.

But what was I even like?

Drogan. Focus on the Drogan, Tanner.

As if on cue, the Drogan shifted, the creaking of the building under its weight echoing through the lonely chamber of the clock tower as everyone flinched. Then the shadow of wings appeared, and with a final crunching groan the building was rid of its living gargoyle.

The Drogan was gone, but no one was exactly sighing in relief.

"Does everyone remember the plan?" Sefen asked in a whisper. As irritating as it was that he was once more proclaiming himself in charge, we did have to get moving.

"Yes," I grumbled in reply. We had to find this Runin fellow and get the key. If he was even alive. If he was even on our side. There was no way to tell if Skayla was even looking for the key or if she was going right for The Living Stone, and no way to tell until we stuck our heads into a possible death sentence.

But hadn't that already been the last two months of our lives?

"Don't. Say. A word," Maeko murmured for about the two hundred and twenty-fourth time.

He'd gone out into the insufferably humid streets first to purchase proper disguises so we wouldn't look so foreign, but there was only so much you could do to fit in when you looked pale, underfed, and very much like you had been on the run for far too long. That and the thick, dark hair and sun-touched complexions of Rugo hardly matched Sefen or me. Because of this, we'd decided it best to split up. And by we, of course, I meant Sefen. Granted it had been a decent idea. Jaythos had a complexion closer to an islander—having come from Bethyn—and so separating Sefen and me would help us stick out less. Plus, I couldn't sit away hiding…being the only one with the information on the key and all.

But I couldn't have cared less about our splitting up. I was more focused on all the violet eyes. So many. Just…so many under Skayla's hold. How did Skayla keep them under her control? I could hardly keep all of my own brain intact, and all I had were the memories of others—not their very *minds*.

The thought was an unpleasant reminder of my situation as well as Skayla's presence, and again I wished I could ask how much farther to the museum. But of course, Maeko had made it very clear that talking would not be tolerated. Just had to rain on my parade.

I decided the best thing to do was quit trying to think altogether and instead focus on not losing Maeko as we wove through the city. And indeed, there was a lot of weaving. Not just between the people, but the levels of the very city. Roads seemed to be everywhere—suspended by complex cables and archways, and allowing for much taller buildings than were once found in Kaedovarna. But what I loved the most about the city was that *water* was everywhere. The city had giant fountains all over the city, as well as sprinklers in wide, suspended garden areas and parks that created shade from the warm air. Vines dangled from the railings of the roads and even wove through trellises arched over to other adjacent roads, helping to provide shade as we passed underneath.

"Here," Maeko announced. Casting a large shadow over us was a magnificent building, reaching far below and far above us as at least a good dozen roadways all came to connect to the various entries to the building. Falling into disrepair as it was, it was still a beautiful remnant of a once-glorious time, with a glass dome rising above the fused marble and metal columns. I again felt the whispers of memories and hauntings of thoughts left behind by those that had walked here, and with a sharp inhale I willed them to leave me alone.

I don't know why I'd thought the museum would have been guarded, but it wasn't. Almost no one was going in or out, and as we came up to the entryway, I noted the disrepair even more. The doors held the scars of having once been burned and broken; the walkway scraped with the deep gashes left behind by Drogans' claws; and the hallways echoed of screams and terror. Things were too loud to ignore here.

As we walked down the long hallway, I couldn't help but wonder why exactly no one was guarding this place, and why people were even allowed inside. For indeed, we actually passed one or two people on their way out, no violet eyes, and no smiles. It was like this place was more of a tomb than a museum.

The hallway opened up into a spacious vestibule, and light filtered in through the cracked glass dome above. The imperfections in the ceiling created an interesting pattern on the marble floor. But I was drawn to the three gigantic statues, each guarding one of the floor-to-ceiling entrances that led to the various wings of the museum: statues depicting The Watchers.

To be frank, I really already disliked Skayla before seeing a two-story high marble statue of her glaring at me.

"This way," Maeko murmured as we went for the entrance beside Moira's statue.

"Do you even know where we are going?" I couldn't help but ask as we rushed along.

The only response I was dignified with was a "No."

Our footsteps echoed across the marble and metal halls, and the cracked floor spread before us in a vain attempt to remind us of the former grandeur of the place. I had never seen a museum before, and yet the wonder of new things was ever overshadowed by the relentless sense of familiarity. It made everything feel haunted—as if I was living someone else's life. Even as I stared at the rows and rows of paintings and objects that lined the walls, I only had the reminder of how this place had once been: bustling, full, and alive. I knew exactly what had once hung in the empty spots, and I could see the damage done to some of the artifacts that still stood on their pedestals.

A propeller from some of The Crafters' early experiments, the ring of Castyle West, the first pair of spectacles.... I noted a glaring spot on the wall where two metal hooks protruded. Unlike some of the other plaques that still informed you of what was missing, there was none for this one. But I knew it was the Sword of Eknemar. Whatever that meant.

We made a left and then went up some stairs, and soon the hall was filled completely with portraits. Unlike many of the other halls, nothing was missing here, and as we walked, I realized why. And I realized exactly why the museum was allowed to remain.

It was a reminder. A reminder of just how powerful Skayla was. For each portrait on the wall was someone who had died. Because pretty much every noble or important figure on Baeno was dead. We passed Alenor and Henry, Lord Emarian and his sons Darian and Edmond, and many others that had been part of the Great Coalition formed by The Watchers. Further down the hall we found the paintings turned to actual photographs. I'd only seen one or two that were kept in Valdon, as those types of portraits had been a newer invention. The very first three were enough to make my breath stop for a moment.

Of course, The Watchers would have been the first to be photographed. The picture of Skayla was very different from the Skayla I had seen on the harbor of Hytat. This version of Skayla was much younger and severe. Almost...perplexed. Like something was tearing her up inside and she was trying so hard to smile and seem like everything was fine. In that moment, I found myself in her as I related all too well to that facade, and maybe it scared me a little.

The picture to the left of hers I instinctively recognized as Moira, a more regal appearance—again, forced and unnatural. I felt a guardedness as my eyes brushed past the photo, and yet I wasn't able to think long on it as my mind was almost shattered by the image of the last Watcher: Sven Mara. Besides the fact that he somehow managed to look three decades younger, there was something more to the picture that set it apart. Where Skayla and Moira had looked serious and stately, Sven looked at ease and full of life, a huge, impish smile on his face and a genuine, lively glimmer in his eye that one could see even in a simply black-and-white photograph: sincerity.

It was at this moment I registered that the reason I'd been able to stare at these pictures for so long was because Maeko had stopped just ahead of me.

He was staring at the next photo down from The Watcher, one of a very stately looking young woman. I took a few steps forward and the dawning of realization was nothing compared to the wave of grief that washed over me. It was Queen Serafina. I tried to remind myself I hadn't ever met the woman, but I was still stuck with all the emotions that went with having known her. What I would have given for my head to be empty.

Then Maeko sucked in a breath, jerking us both out of the silent grief, and we went on.

But even after we had left the portraits behind, they haunted our hollow steps and the emptiness of the halls. I wondered how long it would be until we actually found this Runin fellow. With a building this big...it could be forever. I didn't like being here.

But there was hope. As broken and in disrepair as this place was, there was a lack of dust and mildew. Someone was *definitely* taking care of this place—at least as best as they could.

"Can I help you?" a woman's voice called in Rugonian from behind us, and both Maeko and I swiveled around. Maeko only barely kept from unsheathing his sword, and I had to remind myself that people were technically allowed to be about the museum.

"We're looking for the keeper of this place. Runin Vaers?" It took me a moment to process Maeko's response was in Rugonian. It hurt my brain and yet I was still understanding what both he and this stranger were saying. I hated my head.

The tall woman eyed us carefully, dark brows settling deeply over her equally dark eyes as she seemed to size us up. I didn't like this. Most of my life had been at Valdon, doubting anyone that wasn't from our halls. And now every instinct told me to run.

And yet something took hold of me, and in that instant, I recognized her. "Ma...Marion?"

The woman's face paled, and her hand went to her side as if a weapon was there. "Who are you?"

"It's Syvil, it's—" Wait, idiot, get back in your own head. "I mean that...he's...he's with us. He got away from Skayla. How are you...here?" It was a funny thing the way the memories could so easily take over and gain a life of their own. Ones I'd never even consciously acknowledged before.

It was as if she'd seen a ghost. "Don't talk here. I'll bring you to Runin—but no more talking."

CHAPTER XX: The Key to Everything...Annoying

<u>Jaythos:</u>

Why was I so concerned? Oh, because for some reason Sefen had decided that allowing Maeko and Tanner to go alone to the museum would be a *good* idea. Because Maeko would definitely be able to keep Tanner from doing anything stupid. And Tanner could always stop Maeko from doing anything rash. And I could always impale myself with a sword, and it would be fine. At least, according to Sefen's logic.

But no, Sefen wouldn't go with them because he didn't want to leave Syvil alone, and he didn't want me to go because...actually, I didn't know the reasoning for that. All I knew was we would no doubt be pulling them out of a dungeon—or worse—by the end of the day.

But I couldn't dwell on stupidity. I was too busy staring down a merchant.

"Two ques." The man's expression didn't change as he spoke, beady eyes searching me out for even the slightest spark of weakness.

But he would find none. *"I said thirteen quitts, and that is final."* I replied in Rugonian. I was sporting the Bethynese attire Maeko had acquired. I'd decided it had been best not to ask questions over that one, only be glad he still remembered enough of my people's custom to grab the excused absence lapel meant to indicate a soldier who was on his day's leave of absence. Otherwise, I would have been easily caught for abandoning duties.

THE LIVING STONE

"One and a half bafa?" The merchant tried yet again.

I said nothing, instead slowly straightening and preparing to leave. We couldn't seem desperate. Rugo was deep in Skayla and Kovo's territory, and we were being hunted. News of desperate strangers could spread like wildfire. Besides, if I was to act as one of the Bethynese soldiers occupying the city, I needed to appear as if I was just spending my soldier's allowance. Not stocking up for a journey. But I also didn't want to seem naive to the merchant—hence why I'd chosen to speak Rugonian instead of Varnian, the more common language used in trade.

"Wait—wait. Thirteen quitts is more than generous."

A coy smile found its way on my lips, and I turned around, slowly taking out the coins we had agreed on. While I handled the money, he counted out what was due to me and put them in a small sack, placing them on the table. We exchanged the money and items, and I walked away, extremely annoyed.

All that for a bag of apples.

I should have gone with Maeko and Tanner.

But I wasn't, and so would instead wander the marketplace doing errands for Sefen while he and Syvil got into who knew what sorts of trouble. As I walked through the somewhat busy streets, I noted not those in a MindHold, but those free. In my opinion, anyone who wasn't in a MindHold and was still free to walk the streets was either weak, or didn't really care who was in charge. There were far too many of the former. That was Baeno's true problem; we were soft. Soft and too willing to take the easier path.

Guilt pressed hard against my chest.

But I didn't have time to angst, because apparently, I had to go play butler and do something useless…. In my opinion, Sefen and Syvil would have been more use here than whatever else they were doing. Never had I wished for Sven to have come with us more. But then, reining in Maeko would have been impossible.

I wandered about the streets with a wary eye, carefully avoiding any direct contact with other Bethynese soldiers. It was perhaps an irrational fear, but what I was truly afraid of was not being caught as a fraud but rather being recognized. Being recognized or recognizing someone else. It had been over a decade, and yet I still wondered if my brother could recognize me, or if I would even recognize him.

Frustration continued to build, egged on by the growing tightness in my chest. I needed to get a handle on myself. I still had at least two hours until the market wound down and we were expected to meet. The last thing I needed to do was draw attention to myself by staring at the other soldiers, and what exactly would I have even planned to do if I saw him? *Nothing. You would have to do nothing. Just like you did before*. That thought pleasantly rooted in my head, I wandered the market and kept an ear out for trouble, trying to see if I could catch any gossip related to our entry last night. But after about half an hour of being 'good' and *not* getting into any trouble, I decided that I couldn't stand it any longer. All I could picture was Maeko and Tanner getting carted away for questioning when they were found wandering around a stupid museum. Or Maeko being drowned in the bitterness of what we'd lost.

"So, you're sure the seaman saw a Drogan in the aqueduct last night?" The voice speaking in Varnian cut through the commotion of the marketplace and found its way to my ears. But with the commotion of the city, it was hard to discern where it had originated from. Carefully, I searched the crowd to find the source, and soon I caught sight of the group of Bethynese soldiers not far from me, thoroughly occupied with their conversation.

"Yes, sir. He was positive. They said it entered from the lower waterways."

"Then we need to inform Kovo and cover all exits. It is most likely the one we have been looking for." The crimson stripes on the man's uniform gave away his rank as captain. Something in me began to drop. I hadn't really thought I would see him.

Come on, turn around. I condemned the thought immediately. I realized I didn't want to know. I didn't want to have to deal with the fact that he could be hunting us. But he probably thought I was long dead anyway. I forced myself not to put a hand on my concealed sword, knowing that would most definitely draw attention. Instead, I took an apple from the ones I had just haggled for, and began chomping on it, keeping my hand free as well as appearing at least a little more natural. I knew I should leave, but I also knew they were talking about Syvil and how he got into the city...and now they were talking as if Kovo was here. This could mean Skayla as well, and without Sven with us, I was a little more worried about how our group of idiots would fare if we had to face her. Not well if we listened to Sefen, definitely.

"We should double the guards at the entrances to the city. The night guards heard and found evidence of someone in the wall last night, and if the Drogan did indeed join Valdon's remnants, then it could have let them in. Obviously, the beast itself isn't still in the city, as we haven't spotted it. So why else would it have tried so hard to get in?"

Great. So now we were trapped in this city, and it would only be a matter of time before someone slipped up and got found.

I needed to find Maeko and Tanner.

With one last bite of my apple, I prepared to make for what I hoped was the direction of the museum.

That's when the biggest blunder on my end of this stupid plan took place.

Just as I began walking past the group of soldiers, the captain took that moment to turn around, and in the crowded area, ran smack into me. I looked up, half a life story already invented to accompany the lies I was about to spout when I found myself standing face-to-face with none other than my brother.

Older, yes. More battle-worn and hard, definitely. But there was no doubt. Those ice blue eyes belonged to no one else but Kearn, and in that moment I could do nothing but stare at him as all the things that had gone unsaid sprung to my mind.

"Soldier, explain your blundering—" Kearn stopped dead in the middle of his sentence as he locked eyes. "You." The whisper was vehement and for a moment time seemed to stand still.

And then as Kearn reached for his sword, I realized just what a mistake I had made.

"Get him! He's with them!" he shouted above the clamor even as I broke my own stupid trance and bolted for it, the bag of apples left forgotten at the feet of my brother.

Shoving my way through the crowd of people and animals, I used my one free hand to begin pulling off my jacket, desperate for anything that would help lose me in a crowd. Everything and everyone seemed to be shouting now, and I saw the terrified looks of people as I ran past them, which wasn't exactly helping with my "disappear into the city" plan.

I dared not look back. But I didn't need to in order to hear Kearn's yelling above everything else as he pursued me.

My coat finally off, I wasted no time in throwing it in a nearby trough, grabbing someone's top hat off and ignoring their cries of "thief!"

I was making ground now, pushing a few unsuspecting people in the way behind me and jumping down a few side streets. I didn't miss a beat as I dodged through the city. At least I still knew my way around here pretty well from my time with Maeko. I chanced a look back and found that, while Kearn was still in hot pursuit, I was far enough ahead that he didn't have me clearly in his sights. Now was my chance to get out of this. Swiping a coat from a merchant's stand, I made another hard left and then snatched up a neglected cane leaning by its distracted owner.

"Jaythos!" The voice pierced through everything else; the sounds, the sights, the aromas...all other awareness seemed to fade away at the realization that both my worst nightmare and most desperate hope had come to pass. It was Kearn. My brother. And he wanted me dead—I had seen it in his eyes. Dead...or to at least make me pay for leaving him.

I caught sight of a ladder to the left, leading to the next road tier up, and I knew this was my best shot. I practically launched myself at it, jumping and skipping the first four rungs and hauling myself up to the wide road that turned out to be a carriage lane. Perfect. As the rattle of carriages pulled by people instead of horses drowned out the commotion from the ground level, I forced the last of my energy into a sprint and ran to the other side of the road, barely missing being run over. Without a moment's hesitation, I put on the hat I had stolen, finished putting my coat on, and somehow had the time to jump onto the back of an intricately hand-painted carriage, landing as lightly as possible so as not to cause the muscular man pulling it to be jolted off course. I then tipped my hat over my eyes with my cane-ladened hand and was just able to lean over and catch sight of my brother running underneath on the previous level of the city. He looked up and I forced myself to look at my feet, hoping he hadn't caught me looking at him. I looked entirely different now, but fear was still an unpleasant companion. I heard no shouts to get to the next city level, and as I clung to the carriage, and it twisted further down the road and upwards higher into the city, I allowed myself to breathe a sigh of relief.

The carriage levels of the city were a lot wider than the other levels of the city, but the nice thing about them was the frequency of main stops to allow for city-goers to switch road lines. The higher levels were clearly not made for carriages, so most of the long-distance travel across the city was made on this level, and one simply got off at the stop they desired. That being said, as much as I wanted to immediately make for our meeting place, I dared not until I was absolutely sure I'd shaken Kearn and the other Bethynese soldiers, and so instead hopped off at the sight of the wide staircase that connected the carriage road line up to the residential suites.

I hopped a few more road lines and finally ended up on the third or fourth level before, at last, heading back to the center of the city where the museum was.

After making one last careful check that I hadn't been followed, I dodged inside, taking deep, steadying breaths in order to keep my heart from exploding. I was lucky not to be caught, which was ironic after how convinced I'd been that Maeko and Tanner would do just that.

I was not looking forward to explaining this to Sefen. But I would have to—especially with the city quietly being put in lock down. Getting out of here was going to be a blast.

I forced casualness in my step as I made my way through the museum. The artifacts and paintings along the halls were grim reminders that I had no desire to see, but I wasn't about to just breeze by and alert anyone who was in the halls that I was here for something other than exhibits. Not that there was really anyone else here. But after my carelessness earlier, I was in no mood for another gamble.

Maybe I had been worrying about the wrong people getting caught. Clearly, I was the weak link here.

That lovely realization now at the forefront of my mind, I walked across the cracked marble floors and passed by the decaying artifacts, feeling they all resembled Baeno's state a little too well. Perhaps that was why Skayla had allowed it to stay in place. To remind us just what we had lost. Worse, it made me think...and I couldn't help but wonder...if it also mirrored how truly impossible it was to save this stupid world. Even if we did defeat Skayla, then what? My brother was still on the wrong side. What exactly would happen to him?

This was about when I knew for sure there was a lady following me. I'd gone into two rooms and down a couple of halls, and I had noticed her in most of them. It was the eye contact that made me most uncomfortable. Of course, by her giving eye contact, it meant running wasn't an option, and at this point, I probably wouldn't make it far after my escapades in the city.

So that all decided, I determined to just get this over with. Slowly, I walked over to where she was pretending to admire a set of small photos. Looking at what I realized were portraits of the Maras, I asked, *"How can I help you?"* in Rugonian.

"You are Jaythos?" She didn't look at me as she replied with the question, only sighing and adding, *"Maeko said you'd be meeting them here."*

Tanner:

I found myself drumming my fingers against my leg as I tried to concentrate on the flame flickering in the gas lamp, impatient for the others to arrive. Maeko and Runin had been talking in Rugonian for the last ten minutes, and it was beginning to make my head hurt.

"So Syvil told you about me?" Marion asked as she stood across from me, giving me the same skeptical look she'd been throwing at Maeko. She was tall like Syvil, shoulders squared and head almost constantly tilted ever so slightly—as if she was always evaluating you. I could tell the way she was listening and watching everything in the room, but maybe that was only because we had all been doing the same for what felt like a lifetime.

"A little," I replied at last, trying to stay vague. I didn't feel like explaining I'd been in her friend's head. After Skayla, the Drogans clearly distrusted the very idea of a human poking around there. "But...what are you doing here? Last he knew, you were still in a MindHold like everyone else?"

"I was never caught. It's a long story, and I don't trust either of you. I'm waiting until Syvil arrives. You said it shouldn't be more than an hour?"

"Yes. Hopefully. But don't expect me to answer questions if you don't feel like doing it either," I mumbled, turning back to where Maeko and Runin were still talking. I wanted to listen, but my brain just hurt so much, and it was like trying to listen to a conversation happening underwater.

"I am simply trying to gauge how much Syvil trusts you by how much he has told you." Marion's reply was so calm and collected that it was like we were having a simple conversation—not an argument.

"He told us Ovok helped put you all under Skayla. We honestly haven't had much time to talk since we've all been fleeing for our lives. Sven was the one who saved Syvil, so—"

Marion tilted her head further in clear interest. "As in Sven Mara? He isn't dead, then?"

Oh. Oops. I shouldn't have said Sven's name, should I? Too late now… "No. I suppose that's what Maeko is explaining to Runin. Alenor is alive too. We're trying to get the…" I paused again. Why was I telling all of this to a Drogan I didn't know?! Only a month ago, they'd all been written off as easy enemies.

"The…?" Marion waited for me to finish the sentence.

She had always been the curious one. I shook my head in an effort to disentangle Syvil from myself, but that only seemed to confuse Marion further. So, I added quickly, "The Living Stone. We need it for the next stage of planning." I was letting Syvil's trust become my own, and I needed to be more cautious.

310

"Alenor and Henry hid it for a reason, Runin says. Skayla and Ovok have been looking for it for the duration of the war. Is it really wise to expose it now?" Her tone never changed, and it was fascinating. No wonder she always won the arguments with Syvil, the calmness was—

Please go away. I was beyond frustrated with the wandering; it was like I could never focus. Or be myself.

"Are you alright, child?"

I wasn't sure whether to be insulted by the term. Part of me longed for it, and I couldn't pin down whose memory sought after it so.

"I, uh...yeah, I'm fine. Just tired." It had, after all, been a long couple weeks.

"Well, then!" Runin announced in Varnian as he turned around, his dark wrinkled face spreading in a disarming grin as his eyes set on first Marion, then me. "This is quite a turn of events, then. You will have to give Alenor my regards when you return to her."

I knew she would like that. But I couldn't help but wonder if Runin would be alive by the time we returned—if we returned. Everything was falling apart lately.

"And Marion—" Runin went on when I didn't reply. "I need you to go back to the art gallery and wait for the rest of our guests. It should be a Bethynese soldier with a paler complexion than most of the ones we see around here and dark hair, and then your friend Syvil and another will be coming also." The old man's smile softened as he tapped his cane thoughtfully against the floor. "But we must be careful. You know we're still under the occasional surveillance."

"*You* be careful," Marion said even as she moved towards the exit of the study, eyeing Maeko.

Runin's laugh was warm. "I always am. How else did I get to this age in a time like this?"

Marion arched an eyebrow as she stood framed in the doorway, a smile playing on her lips. "Oh, please. You're still an infant to me," And with that, she left.

Oh, right. She was older than Syvil, wasn't she?

The silence was awkward, and I didn't like silence. I didn't like doing nothing. But then again, we'd been running for so long that there was a part of me that didn't mind the chance to breathe.

I continued to watch the flame, allowing myself to be pulled into the thoughts of iron forges and evenings by the fireplace...of stories told to young children as they giggled and leaned in to hear more. I knew they were Alenor's and not mine, but I let myself pretend they were. Just for a little bit.

"Found one of them, anyway." Marion's abrupt re-entry startled me out of my thoughts, and I looked quickly over to the clock to find that an hour had passed.

"What is going on?" It took me a good minute to realize the man that had entered was, in fact, Jaythos. Only the irritation in his tone gave me the proper clue. He looked...very different. Top hat, dark coat, cane...he looked more like some posh gentleman than the Bethynese soldier he'd been dressed as earlier.

But I was more distracted by the worry on his face. The worry that was in no way alleviated upon seeing Maeko and me.

"Is someone going to explain what's going on?" he asked, as Marion left once more to wait for Sefen and Syvil.

"I'm Runin. Pleased to meet you. We decided it would be more discreet for Marion to wait on the rest of Maeko's companions, as things are never safe these days."

This didn't seem to satisfy Jaythos very much, but he nonetheless took Runin's extended hand and shook it. "Sefen and Syvil are not here yet, then?"

"No. Not yet," Maeko replied.

"What do you need to tell Sefen so badly?" I didn't bother with pleasantries. Something was wrong, obviously. Jaythos was always blunt, but the more trouble there was, the blunter he became. Plus, he didn't have the supplies he was supposed to have bought, *and* he was clearly wearing a last-minute disguise.

Jaythos's glare turned on me, but I met it with equal callousness. I knew the doubt that went on behind the bravado.

The glare dissipated, and instead Jaythos looked doubtfully from Runin to Maeko. "We just have...a situation."

Great. I was used to being kept out of the loop even when I was meant to partake in it, but lately, it was getting harder to tolerate it. Baey wasn't around to commiserate with either.

"Were you followed?" Runin's tone touched on actual worry, and his hand clutched his cane a little harder.

"No." The curt response was clearly a cut-short insult. "But getting out of the city is going to be a blast."

Conversation was interrupted then by voices, and the door opened to find Syvil...smiling. Smiling and talking to Marion like an unashamed schoolboy.

I didn't know what that was supposed to mean....

"I can't believe you're alive—I should have known you would escape Ovok."

Marion was also smiling relief glimmering in the joy her expression held. "Yes, well, I could say the same for you. I should have known only you would have ended up with a bunch of idiots like this."

Sefen followed close behind, looking extremely displeased as he closed the door behind him.

"We're all here, then?" Runin asked.

"Yes," replied Maeko, giving a short nod to Sefen.

Marion and Syvil stopped their excited chatter.

"Good. Then let us get down to it. You need the key to the mountain, correct?"

Everyone looked at me, and I couldn't help but roll my eyes. Yes, I was useful again, and therefore, was allowed to exist once more. The walking, talking relic. "Yes. I know where the entrance is, but Henry hid the key with you." I knew Maeko had explained this all, but it seemed Runin wanted to make sure.

"I still do not understand the wisdom behind this plan..." Runin's brow furrowed, even as he reached into his vest pocket. "But I trust Alenor would not have given you the information unless it was completely necessary." With that, he produced a small, quaint looking key with prongs that depicted a castle. He handed it to Maeko.

With that same foreign sense of familiarity, I realized it was because Maeko had often come to the museum with Serafina. He must have known Runin—even if that familiarity didn't so easily surface.

Would explain why he had been so quick to trust the old man.

314

Sefen didn't seem so willing. "How do we know he's not turned to Ovok? After all, there is a Drogan with him…" he said unpleasantly.

"You are so ignorant," Syvil muttered with a sigh.

But now the spell of temporary trust was broken, and everyone was looking at each other with uncertainty.

"Tanner?" Sefen's one-word question was painful. I felt the resentment building, and I wanted to say no. I wanted to let them figure it out instead of playing their human lie detector.

"I mean, wouldn't he have given Skayla the key by now? I don't see the need to split hairs when we're already short on time," I argued, Runin and Marion looked confused and now very on-guard. Syvil stood a little closer to his friend, the distrust in his eyes hardly on *our* side.

I didn't blame him.

"In Sefen's defense, how do we know Skayla isn't just waiting until we get the key—she doesn't know where to put it, right? Only Alenor knew. And now Tanner knows. So why not just wait and keep the key here to wait for someone to take it and lead her to where she needs to go?" Jaythos's reasoning was far from helpful.

Runin bristled, straightening his ancient body and looking a good ten years younger as indignation showed in his tight muscles. "I would never betray Alenor. What are you implying?"

"Nothing. We are just requesting that you allow Tanner to search your memories to confirm that you are indeed on our side still, Runin. It's been a long few weeks. Friends have turned on us. We don't know who to trust anymore." Jaythos toned down his brashness to at least try and sound sympathetic.

315

Maeko sighed and put a hand on the old man's shoulder. *"It's true. Nothing personal, Runin. Sefen's own wife tried to turn us over. Tanner is our only way of truly distinguishing friend from foe."*

"I don't like this." Marion's hand was over her skirt again, and I was becoming fairly certain she had a hidden weapon under there.

Runin sighed. "Fine then. If it will satisfy you, I have nothing to hide." He looked to me. "Do what you must."

I wanted to shrink back and refuse. But we would get nowhere otherwise, and this was the only reason I was here, after all.

"I'm sorry if I'm a little unwilling to yield my personal memories to a stranger, but I really don't feel like allowing some boy to search through my head," Marion interjected.

Syvil leaned in then and whispered something in her ear. Her lips pressed hard together, but when they finally opened, they let pass a single word: "Fine."

I rolled my eyes and walked forward, first to Runin. "I will require your hand," I said simply, mentally preparing myself to take on yet another soul's identity.

What were a few more memories in this tattered brain, right?

CHAPTER XXI: Getting Acquainted

<u>Jaythos:</u>

"They're good." Tanner's announcement was a whisper, and did I imagine the slight tremble in his hand as he shoved his hands in his pockets? What had he seen?

I wondered if maybe I should be concerned; Tanner rarely showed any sort of hesitance, and yet recently...recently, he'd been acting stranger and stranger. Was it hard for him to be separated from Baey, perhaps? She had, after all, been the closest thing to family he'd really had.

"Well, now that we're on the same page, I think there's something you all should know," I said, after no one said anything. Tanner was rarely wrong, and if he said they were good, then I trusted them.

"Great, what now?" Sefen asked, giving me a look that showed he was prepared for the worst.

In all honesty, he probably wasn't prepared enough. "We're trapped in the city. I...ran into some Bethynese soldiers in the city—" I briefly locked eyes with Maeko just long enough to silently confirm that my worst fear had come true. I was sure we'd have a conversation about this later....

"*What?*" Sefen looked panicked.

"Well, isn't this wonderful?" It was the other Drogan, Marion.

I winced. "And...apparently Kovo is here, also."

A stillness settled over everyone. But perhaps what was most unexpected was the way the two Drogans were staring, terrified.

"Wait. *Ovok?*" It was Marion.

"No." I shook my head adamantly. "I said Kovo. You know, Skayla's advisor?"

Syvil blinked. "You realize…that's…wait, had you not put this together?"

Everyone was staring at them now.

"What are you trying to say?" Sefen asked, tone thin.

I heard Marion mutter, "Humans are so dumb…" before looking me square in the eyes. "Ovok *is* Kovo. He didn't even bother hiding it—I mean, it's literally his name backwards. Drogans have two forms, that's why he had us keep that a secret. He wanted to be able to move around undetected."

She was right. We were kind of dumb. "Well, I guess this means Ovok is here…which is…admittedly much worse."

"Well…why don't we discuss the rest of this over some dinner then? You all look like you haven't eaten well in weeks," Runin announced, cutting through the dark mood that had settled.

Ovok was Kovo…why did this make so much sense? Why hadn't I immediately thought of it when Syvil had first shifted into a human? And if Kovo was really Ovok, then what else was going on that we didn't know? He had always been with Skayla—always in her ear.

And not only was he in the city, but he was the most dangerous Drogan on Baeno.

318

As much as I hated the thought of sleeping without one of us staying awake to keep an eye out, I found myself beginning to realize just how tired I was. Besides, we were as good as trapped in this city anyway, with Ovok apparently scouting the city for us. So, to be honest, it was the only reason I didn't argue about staying the night. The museum would be the last place anyone would think to look, and we would need more than a half-baked plan to get out of here.

I just had to convince my instincts to let me sleep, and maybe my mind to stop racing through all of the unknowns that were constantly coming up.

First, Ovok. Syvil and Marion were both terrified of him, and after what he'd done to Syvil in Hytat...I understood why. I couldn't stop thinking over the implications of this—of the fact that this meant Ovok was definitely not a victim of Skayla. He *had* to have something to with Skayla's abrupt change.

Second? Runin's concern over us getting The Living Stone. He was right. Was this really a risk worth taking? Especially now that it was clear Ovok was here…. How did we even know for sure Moira was alive, or that Baey could even use the watch? It was all so theoretical that I was beginning to doubt it was worth the risk.

But these two problems were far overshadowed by my own selfish concern for Kearn. I'd told Sefen I was spotted but not by whom. I hadn't even spoken of it to Maeko, even though I knew he must have guessed who'd spotted me. I just...I couldn't get Kearn's face out of my mind. He was so much older. So...Bethynese. Last I'd seen him, he'd been a kid, young and desperate. The last I'd heard from him was after the war had started and he'd replied to my letter saying he would be staying in Bethyn. The vehemence with which he'd chased me was a bitter reminder of just how much I'd failed him, and I couldn't help but wonder what would happen if he actually caught us. If we actually had to face each other with no chance for escape. Did he really hate me that much?

I sighed and turned over on the mat Runin had given me. At this rate, I was never going to get some rest. But no matter how much I tossed and turned, all I could do was think about Kearn and my numerous other failures.

So, giving up on the idea of sleep, I got out of bed and walked over to the window, peering out into the night and hoping to catch a glimpse of anything: Kearn, some way out, Drogans, anything.

But all I saw was a city, standing in the night, conquered. Exhaustion and anger welled up inside when I remembered being in this city with Maeko all of those years ago. Then, everything had been simpler—comparatively. We'd had each other's backs. We'd been friends. Now, I felt all too often we were too busy staying alive to be anything but fellow soldiers. But honestly, what hurt more was the reminder we didn't have anywhere to even pretend to call our home. No Valdon. No Kaedovarna. Skayla had won. We weren't fighting a war anymore. We were leading a rebellion. A pathetic, dysfunctional rebellion of about...a dozen or so people. A dozen people against an entire world. Who were we kidding? We had been fighting so furiously at Valdon that I hadn't realized just how much Skayla had succeeded, and now I wondered what Kaedovarna was like. Emarian was most likely dead, or at best in a MindHold, and the people and mountain city now reduced to the state of this place. I looked out again to the Rugonian city, remembering the violet eyes I had seen all around me in the marketplace. Hundreds—thousands, even—with no true free will; only living on the outside. I'd seen what it had done to Sven. True, he had suffered in a unique way, but really, how many others were suffering similar fates? Skayla's body guards were made up of those in a MindHold. And those in a MindHold in this city would hand us over in a heartbeat, with no other choice. And what would even happen if we won? Maeko had barely even been able to forgive Sven—Sven Mara, the last Watcher of Baeno. So, if we could barely forgive the best of us...then what would happen when all the others were freed? Even if we killed Skayla, would we ever be able to put this world back together?

It was at this point that I heard muffled voices. It was from below my room, where the kitchen was. Syvil and Marion, as I gathered. The faintest of light filtered up from the floorboards.

"Did he kill you, too?" It was Marion's voice.

I was beginning to feel like Tanner spying on someone's memories, but still, I could not make myself ignore their voices. In the stillness of the night, they rang all too clear through the floor, and I was just so tired.

"No. Sven Mara helped me."

"Get out of a MindHold?"

"Yes."

"So you still have both forms?"

Silence.

I should go to sleep.

"Runin found you?" Syvil's ignoring the question led me to believe he had either given a non-verbal answer or was ignoring it altogether.

"Yes. We rather found each other, and he convinced me to wait here and gain information on Ovok instead of trying to take him down myself."

"I do not even know if he can be killed." Syvil sounded weary. "He still has Ckaknimaen."

Again, silence.

"That stupid blade…."

That was it. I couldn't stand eavesdropping. I wasn't a child, and this was ridiculous. So, without a second thought, I left my room and quietly made my way downstairs. Syvil had more information, this much was clear, and it would seem if we wanted it, we would all need to be more civil to him.

The least I could do was explain that he and Marion were not exactly very good at having private conversations.

I knocked quietly at the kitchen door, the silence following somehow louder than my knock.

"Yes?" Marion's voice ran through.

Entering, I nodded to both of them and then found the nearest wall to lean up against, saying, "My room is right above this, and the boards are very thin."

Both figures became stiffer than marble pillars.

"So, you are also a Drogan?" As they were not obliging, I decided to begin the conversation, trying to tread lightly and keep a conversational tone. But I didn't really know how to do that, and so ended up stating the very obvious.

Marion raised an eyebrow, then leaned against the countertop. "Yes."

I pressed my luck. "How did you get out of a MindHold?"

Marion's smile was sad. "I didn't. I was never in one."

The answer was intriguing, but I was unsure how to press forward. But if I didn't keep it up, we wouldn't get anywhere, and our group would continue to keep secrets from one another. Not that I was exempt from that accusation…. "What does that mean?"

Marion's expression was difficult to read, but there was a bitterness in the pain. She did not speak to me, however, instead looking to Syvil and asking, "How much did you tell them?"

Syvil shrugged. "Only that which would not make them feel it was a lost cause, I suppose. And only that which I knew for certain."

"Well, that doesn't sound like much at all." Marion turned back to me. "Where were you when the Myrand—we came?" she asked.

"Here," I replied honestly.

"Do you remember the pretense for peace we came with, or were you tainted with the lie that we came to make war?"

My brow furrowed at the way her question was asked, but I replied with "Both."

"Hm," Marion grunted, moving on. "Many of us did come to escape Eatris—the world we came from. Ovok convinced us here would be better, and I think it could have been. But Cyl and Grenedil had been right…he had been deceiving us."

I knew better than to interrupt. "Go on."

She appeared to appreciate the encouragement and continued, "Not long after the small riots broke out in Patelayna, Ovok declared this place would be no different, but that we could change it, and the Maras would help. When it became clear this meant war, Syvil, I, and a few others wanted no part in it. I was going to warn *someone*, but if the Maras were in on it, then who was I supposed to tell? We kept quiet but did not intend to take part. Then I realized what Skayla was doing to the Drogans. She would come and talk to them, and then they would be...different. A MindHold. All of the others who had been opposed to fighting either disappeared or suddenly changed their minds. Then I found out why. Skayla and Ovok found me one night...Ovok tried to pin me down, but by luck or The Creator's mercy, I struggled harder than Ovok anticipated. In the struggle, he landed a blow—by accident or on purpose, I don't know—and I died. I'm not sure if Syvil explained that Drogans have what you might call two lives. My Dragon form died, and now I can only live in this form, trapped."

Vaguely, I remembered the night when Syvil had saved all our lives. I remembered how he'd killed one of his own. How in that moment, I had understood his position more than perhaps any of the others could.

"When we die, we reappear next to the person we are closest to. I woke next to Syvil...but he was already in a MindHold." Marion paused, locking eyes with her friend as a sad smile traced the edges of her lips. "But he still had the will to do nothing as I ran for it. I was in shock, but somehow, I made it across the sea and to Rugo. Runin found me and helped me. But by the time I was really able to come to my senses, it was too late. Skayla and Ovok had already taken Patelayna, and the war had begun. Runin kept me safe and convinced me The Creator would send someone to get the key and help. And so I waited." She paused again, looking me over very carefully before asking, "So, any questions?"

"So...what exactly made Ovok leave your world—Eatris?—in such a hurry?" I asked, looking from one to the other.

"Eatris was full of death. There were Drogan Hunters, and we were forced to stay in the shadows. Ovok—well, he kept us safe for a long time. But the last straw was really his daughter, Rhioa. She was killed. And after that, he claimed we would all be killed, eventually."

Tanner:

That sweet sound filled the air—music. Stringed instruments, brass, all ebbing and flowing together in one smooth rhythm. I loved the sound of music.

"Please, how are you such a good dancer?" Darby laughed.

"Too much time." I rolled my eyes and smiled as we skillfully swept across the dance floor. I caught sight of Skayla again, looking overwhelmed as she hid in the corner. I would ask her for the next dance, of course, but this one had barely begun. Not that I minded Darbeshay's company. I only knew that Skayla needed to unwind. A dance would do her good, even if it would take some coaxing to get her to agree to one. I knew parties overwhelmed her with all the stimulation caused by other people.

"Really? Too much time? Father and Mother talk of nothing but how busy The Watchers are. I mean, you travel the world, Sven. It must be exciting."

"It is quite the experience." I laughed a little as we turned about the room.

I was at a table, several others older than I standing around it.

Emarian's face was grim. "She's taken Patelayna."

I couldn't believe it. "Has anyone located The Crafters?" I asked again.

"No."

"Has anyone found Sven?" Sera asked, gripping the railing of the balcony as she looked out to the city.

"No, My Lady. I fear he has still not returned." I tried not to betray the fear I felt.

"That stupid boy. Not everyone can be saved...he shouldn't have gone alone. He shouldn't ha—"

There was a buzzing sound as a crossbow bolt flew inches from my face. It didn't feel real even as I jumped to her side, grabbing her as the stain in her dress grew rapidly bigger from where the crossbow bolt protruded.

"Serafina! My Lady! Sera!" I knelt beside her, cradling her and desperately trying to get her to reply. But it was too late. She was already limp. In blind panic, I looked frantically around, barely able to catch a glimpse of a shadow on the rooftop not far away. I would kill him. Whoever it was, I would find him, and I would kill him.

Gasping for air, I woke up, sweating like a pig and breathing like one about to be slaughtered. *Deep breaths, come on.* Side effects. I hated side effects. Always getting worse. I wanted it all to just shut up and go away. Oh, but it was such a *useful* Gift. So good for everyone at Valdon to use.

It was a curse, that's what it was.

I wanted nothing more than to switch places with any of the others, even for a day, and see how they felt being stuck with everyone else's trauma.

In an effort to reorient myself, I closed my eyes, running my hand through my hair and tapping my leg with my other free one. Was that what I did when I was nervous? Is that how I calmed myself, or was it someone else? I didn't even know if I cared anymore. I didn't even know that I cared I didn't exist behind the masks of everyone else's memories. It wasn't worth crying over, because at this point I was as good as lost anyway.

Just a tool. Just a way to bypass trust.

Grumbling and at the end of my mental rope, I got up from my mat, got dressed, then sat back down, closing my eyes again to try and fully awaken. It was not yet dawn, but I would not go back to sleep.

I will kill him.

Maeko's anger was overpowering, and I quickly opened my eyes. Nope. That wasn't helping.

But then I was distracted. Who belonged to the other memories I had seen in my sleep? Curiosity was the only thing that kept me from pure insanity, and I couldn't help but idly wonder who they belonged to. Whose were they? The last, again, was Maeko's, a memory I had experienced many times. But not the other ones.

They flitted just out of reach, and I was left to shrug it off and shove myself back into the problems we were facing now.

I heard a faint noise from downstairs, and suddenly the thought of food was all that was crowding my mind.

Food was good.

With that, I got up and headed for the kitchen, finding myself thinking about dancing and how I missed hearing the music and the laughter.

I stopped my train of thought and tried to reorient myself.

Just go away, please?

I was so befuddled, in fact, that too late did I realize there were voices coming from inside the kitchen door, and before I could even think I had opened it and walked in. If I had been thinking, I would have eavesdropped. Pity.

"Good morning, drowsy," Marion piped up, as if I had slept the day away...but it wasn't even sunup yet. Charming.

"Mm." I rubbed the back of my head, feeling a monstrous headache beginning to form. What a day this would be.

"I'm sure you're hungry. Sit down at the table and I'll get you something to eat, child." The way Marion said that made it sound like she actually did think I *was* a child.

Without a single word, I sat down across from Syvil at the table.

"I assume we'll be leaving as soon as possible, then?" Marion resumed the previous conversation; it appeared I would not have to wonder what they'd been talking about.

"Yes. You said Estasia's contacts inside the city could help us sneak out?" Jaythos was, as always, lingering somewhere in the shadows, but it took me a moment to get who he was talking to. In fact, I didn't understand until Syvil was the one who responded.

"That is correct. But it is, at best, a very risky move. Not that anyone has any better ideas." The Drogan sighed and swished a cup full of what looked like tea but smelled a little...bitter?

"What is that?" I couldn't help but ask as I peered over at him. The aroma was vaguely familiar, but then, everything looked or smelled or felt familiar. I hated that.

Marion came over and set a plate of eggs and toast in front of me. "It's coffee. Very helpful for waking up. Would you like some? I think it is one of my favorite things about this world." She paused and frowned. "Which I suppose isn't saying very much."

"Er...sure." Waking up sounded nice. I still had this inexplicable desire for tea, but honestly, anything that could get rid of this awful headache.

She raised an eyebrow, and without another word, went back to the counter, presumably to make this coffee. I turned back to Syvil and Jaythos. "So, we're going to leave this morning?"

"Or get caught." Jaythos's reply was not helpful. "Ovok is here, after all, and he and the entire garrison of this city knows we are, too."

"You really are a ray of sunshine, aren't you?" I mumbled as I took a bite out of my toast. The jam on top was a pleasant sweet addition to the bread, as the last few days had been biscuits and cheese with little flavor left in them. I savored it as long as I could, knowing this would probably be the best meal I would have for a while. Or ever. I shuddered. Great...Jaythos's attitude was catchy.

Just then, Marion returned to the table, plopping a steaming cup of the coffee drink in front of me before taking a seat herself. "We have to make sure everyone is in the loop before we try anything, however."

"Joy," Jaythos murmured.

"In the loop of wha—ah! That's hot," I interrupted myself as I took a sip of the drink, nearly spilling it in surprise. Sure, it had been steaming, but I still hadn't expected it to be *that* hot. Why did they need hot drinks in such a hot and miserable place, anyway? Wasn't it insufferable enough?

Everyone looked at me, and Syvil's amused expression did not help my pride. As best I could, I tried to recover, asking again, "In the loop of what?"

The silence lasted only a moment, with me soon breaking it as my fork scraped against the ceramic plate in a pitiful attempt to catch my scrambled eggs. I was being so awkward. Awkward like Baey.

Get out of my head, won't you?

Then Jaythos spoke, "We are going to have a problem with blending in, seeing as I have been recognized by some of the local Bethynese soldiers."

"Oh right," I mumbled. "Was it Kearn?" Oh boy, this headache. I took another ginger sip of my coffee, now a little cooled.

"I'm...sorry?" Jaythos's aghast tone was the only thing that clued me into the fact I'd said something I shouldn't have. Only, I couldn't figure out what.

Thankfully, he didn't leave me wondering.

"How do you know that name?" He was leaning forward now, staring at me with a dangerous look in his eyes.

"Of course I know about Kearn, idiot. I've had to see in your head like five times. What did you expect?" I didn't bother keeping my tone civil. "Look, I'm tired and I have a headache and I really just don't feel like putting up with you all, and I'm sorry if I can't remember what I'm supposed to know and what I'm not—it's just floating around in my head and you can deal with it. Just leave me alone." Part of me wanted to apologize, but that part was probably Baey, so I didn't bother taking back the words. I only sipped my coffee and thought how much harder it was getting to keep my tongue in my mouth.

No one said a word for a long time, but everyone gave plenty of looks.

Naturally, Jaythos was the one to move on and act as if nothing had happened. "Syvil said Sefen got in contact with one of Estasia's contacts here in Veka, and the source confirmed that Ovok is here. I guess Skayla sent him here to see if we'd seek shelter here. So, at least they don't know where Baey and the rest are," Jaythos finished after the awkward pause.

"What makes you think Skayla's the one calling the shots?" Marion asked, with a good dose of incredulity.

Every time the name Ovok was uttered, I felt a shudder run down my back. I remembered how terrified Syvil was of him—and even now, I saw the way he shrunk a bit into himself.

"What makes you think Skayla isn't?" Jaythos asked, apparently genuinely. No sarcasm, for once.

Marion's scoff was like that of a mother gawking at her child's ignorance. "It's hard to believe a several-thousand-year-old being was fooled by a pup of a human. Ovok is more than happy to play a part. I am only confused why he is playing this one. No matter his methods...he has always kept us safe. The worst thing you can do to a Drogan is debase us to the role of an animal, so I don't understand why he allowed this." Her eyes wandered to Syvil, and something passed between them. She shuddered. "Anyway, Ovok is here, but Skayla is not. And he is more dangerous than her, trust me. But regardless, this means—"

"—It means Skayla could be anywhere." Sefen's voice now came from the doorway. I turned and saw he had just barely entered, looking groggy and out of sorts. Nothing out of the ordinary then.

"Food's over there." Marion pointed to the countertop, suddenly in no mood to get up, it would seem.

Sefen nodded and went over to help himself. The conversation had come to an unceremonious halt now, and so I busied myself with eating and gulping down the bitter coffee that I could only hope would help my headache.

"While you've been sleeping, we've been coming up with a plan to bypass the Bethynese soldiers," Jaythos announced.

Sefen didn't bother getting a seat, grabbing some food and scarfing it down as he replied, "Great. Well, might as well hear it. We shouldn't stay in one place too long."

CHAPTER XXII: Less Than Graceful Getaways

<u>Jaythos:</u>

Of course, Sefen didn't like the idea. He never liked anything that wasn't *his*. But for once he was outnumbered, and so we'd gone with what Syvil, Marion, and I had concocted for a plan.

If this didn't work, Sefen would never let me live it down.

Good thing we'd all be dead if it didn't.

"This way." Marion led Tanner and me through the layers of streets with ease. Maeko had taken Syvil and Sefen. We were too large a group to travel through a city together, and so we had split to get to our destination.

As we made our way about the city, I found myself constantly searching the faces of some of the early risers, looking for Kearn. If he saw me again, we would be done for, and I couldn't let that happen. Yet what was I doing? Searching for him. What an idiot I was.

We were heading not for the port, but for the factories on the ground level. Well, work *ruins* now. There was more than one reason Sefen hadn't been for this plan, and at least partly, I could sympathize. It wasn't going to be a "clean" getaway, at the very least.

Eventually, the houses turned from new to old warehouses long abandoned. Roads had dead ends or makeshift wooden patches, and traffic was few and far between. It was eerie, to say the least.

Sefen had given us a place to meet up here, and it didn't take long to find it and the rest of the group. Sefen still looked less than pleased. But we'd been in worse spots of late.

"I'll return," Sefen announced without any further need to loiter, entering the decrepit and deteriorating, factory-looking, brick building and disappearing among the permanent clouds of dust and mildew.

I forgot how much I hated Rugo. The tropical atmosphere was oppressive, and it reminded me vaguely of home—which, of course, only made me hate it more.

I tried to busy myself with keeping watch, straining for any sound that could be out of place. Few people were about the streets this early—especially this section, and so there was less to hide an intruder. There was also less to hide us.

Sefen came back out of the building, his footsteps upon stone jolting all of our nerves. Or at least, so I guessed by the way Syvil and Tanner flinched.

"We're clear," was all Sefen said, urging us into the ruined building.

It was hard not to choke on the dust, but the fear of drawing attention was stronger than the urge to cough, and no one made a sound. But the warehouse did. Our footsteps creaked along the rotting floorboards as we drew further into the building, setting my nerves even further on edge.

Another few steps and we found ourselves in what was once a large factory room with old, rusting machines that creaked for no obvious reason. Sitting on a rotting work bench was a firmly built man, a belt of tools hanging about his waist. "Aha. This is the rest," he said in Varnian, albeit with a thick Rugonian accent as he looked all of us over.

"Yes," Sefen replied as the rest of us filtered in the room. "So, can you get us out?"

The man got up from his despairing throne, revealing his tall but rather skinny frame in the process. He eyed each one of us, stopping at Marion. "He says you have your own way?"

She nodded. "It's best we don't all leave together. Sefen, Syvil, and I will leave by a separate method, since no one is looking for our faces. Runin had a spare pass."

The Rugonian turned to Tanner. "You're a scrawny one. But some grease should help make your hair darker, and clay will hide the paleness."

Tanner looked displeased but did not argue.

This settled, the man turned back to us. "Maeko will be the easiest. He is Rugonian and not hard to pass off here. You—" He turned to me. "You are the one they are looking for?"

I nodded.

"You will be in the cart. We have a false bottom. It will not be pleasant but better than dead. Ice breakers often have large carts, and I have made sure to use this one regularly so it is no change in routine." Ah. So he was an ice harvester from the northern mountains. That explained a lot. By the looks of it, a glorified slave who traveled to the mountains to retrieve ice for the pompous cowards ruling the city for Skayla.

The ice harvester went on, "So, you and Maeko will be out with me. We will say we are going to Lord Dako's Manor outside the city. I am due to take inventory there and get the next order anyway, so it will be believable. He gave me enough city passes for two besides myself, so it should be little trouble getting out." He paused then and made a face. "Well, less of a problem if not for yesterday."

I maintained a straight face, though feeling partly responsible for the raised number of guards. Of course, Syvil had been the one spotted first, but I was the one that had hit the final nail into the coffin.

"Then it's settled?" Sefen asked.

Our newest addition nodded, looking again at each one of us before answering, "Yes."

"This would be a lot easier with Sven…" I heard Maeko mumble.

This was somehow even more unpleasant than I'd pictured. When the man had said they had a false bottom, I had underestimated just how small the space was. They'd done a great job at hiding it, but a really horrible job at it being actually usable for someone my size. I was pretty sure my ribs were permanently flattened, and my neck was beyond stiff as I was stuck looking to my right so as to not have my head squashed.

"Silence," I heard a murmur by the cart and caught the drift. We were at the gate.

I only hoped Tanner wouldn't stick out too much. The harvester had done a good job at covering him up and altering his appearance, but I still worried.

The cart stopped.

"Where is your pass?" Even from the cart I recognized the distinctly clear tone that rang out above the rest of the general clamor, and it was hard to miss. He was probably betting on being able to recognize me.

"We're looking in the cart." Kearn commanded sternly, and I tried to take a quiet, deep breath. The latter was impossible with the way my lungs were practically crushed from the narrowness of the secret space.

We were going to get caught. I was about to get everyone killed.

Joy.

I found myself closing my eyes as someone rummaged around the cart, taking out the various pieces of equipment that the harvester had placed in the cart over me.

Don't move. Don't breathe.

"Where are you going then?" Again, it was Kearn.

"Lord Dako, sir."

There was a long silence, making me even more paranoid about breathing.

"Everything is in order. You're free to go."

The cart lurched forward, and I couldn't believe that the ploy had *actually* worked.... Kearn would be livid if he ever found out just how close he'd been.

There would have been a time when I could have rubbed it in his face.

Tanner:

"That was insufferable," Jaythos announced between coughs as he was let out of the cart. We were out of view of the city, waiting in the forest for the other half of our group. I did not envy Jaythos his hiding method at all, especially knowing Baey was claustrophobic...and I was having such a tricky time keeping out of people's heads.

Maeko chuckled. "At least you're alive."

"Oh, shut up. Next time, why don't we stuff you in a coffin and see how it feels?" Jaythos growled, brushing himself off.

"Quiet, both of you. Quick tongues are quicker caught." said our stern guide, who had been replacing the false bottom on the cart and putting the other items once more atop it.

He was right. In fact, every minute we stood out here I felt exposed— like we could be caught at any moment. Sure, there were lots of trees to hide us. Trees that were too sparse to hide under…. Trees Baey probably would have been fascinated by, and trees I couldn't care less about. I found myself drumming my fingers against my legs, wondering if any of us would live long enough to see Patelayna again. I thought of Baey, and how she would be so torn up if any of us got ourselves killed. But what were the chances of that not happening? I briefly glanced at everyone around, and against my will wondered which one of us might not return.

Joy. Just what I needed. Someone's gloom tainting me and making me lose my train of thought in fretting. What in Baeno was I doing, thinking someone was going to die? I was tired, and that definitely was contributing to the uncontrollable use of other's habits and thought processes. Lately, I was feeling less and less like myself and more like everyone else. I thought of Skayla, hiding in the corner and overwhelmed. I wished I could just hide in the corner with her.

"I must go now. If I do not continue on to Lord Dako's, I will be too suspicious," the ice harvester said. "Good luck, and may you have success in whatever brought you here." I couldn't tell if the look he gave us was hope or dread. It was some sort of mix between the two. He was one of Estasia's contacts, and he seemed to understand the stakes.

It was a long while before we no longer heard him pulling his cart away, but the eerie quiet that settled in its place was equally unpleasant. Just when I thought I couldn't handle it any longer....

"There you are," Jaythos piped up, and I looked over to see him greeting Marion, Sefen, and Syvil.

Sefen said nothing, only walking to the center of our group and dropping a large bag down where all could see. He opened it up, grabbing its contents and tossing it to various people. Jaythos's crossbow and quiver, Maeko's odd curved dagger, and a few other things no one had dared bring into Veka. Most had stuck to our easily hidden swords.

"We were also able to get supplies from the ship, as we hoped. Sven's illusion is holding strong." Sefen finally spoke. "Where to now, Tanner?"

I sighed, taking a deep breath and closing my eyes. I was fine. I could do this.

Keep it together.

I was sucked into Alenor's memories. Cities made of metal and lights that turned on themselves. An accident...fire. Searing pain up my body. Wait, these weren't the right memories...these were someone else.

What in the worlds was wrong with me?!

I tried to steer myself to The Living Stone, blocking out everything else that fought to get inside my stupid head. Instead, I thought of the voice that told me where to hide The Living Stone, and how to find it again. The journey...the pain. The knowledge that my own daughter had turned against us all.

I gasped as I just barely dragged myself out of the memories before I became sucked too far in.

"Are you alright?" Marion cocked her head and eyed me intently, looking almost...concerned.

Squinting incredulously, I nodded. "Yeah, of course. I do it all the time," I replied bitterly, before turning away to face Sefen.

"I know where to go." I hated how the memory had to be dug up over and over again, but it became clearer the deeper we went into Rugo. The closer we got, the more I could pinpoint the memory. It was like relearning an old habit, but instead of a habit, it was focusing in on a stranger's mind.

Jaythos voiced everyone's anticipation with a "Well?"

"Oh. Right." I gave a mischievous smirk—which was totally inappropriate for the urgency of this task—and continued, "It's in those mountains." I pointed to the direction of the mountains I'd seen earlier. "Just like I had thought. There's an old path that leads through them, and then a door to the key. It's going to be a bit of a journey, though. And there are a few twists and turns to make sure not just anyone stumbles upon the path."

"So where do we start, then?" Sefen asked.

"We could follow the main road for a while, but it's not like we can actually be on it..." I turned to Maeko now, trailing off meaningfully.

He only nodded in understanding, and I rolled my eyes, wishing for a more *vocal* affirmation. Huh. Big word. It sounded so strange even in my head. Was it a word I usually used? Affirmation...Affirma—

"We should probably get going, then?" Syvil asked, voice edgy as he looked at the skies. "We need to get into the rainforest. The trees here

340

are not good coverage…" His eyes continued to dart nervously along the sky. "…and we've already been spotted twice."

The reminder brought a solemnity to the group, one which even I felt. Until I realized I'd used the word *solemnity*. Whoever had the big vocabulary was really getting on my nerves. I wondered if it was Runin.

"Stupid head."

"What?" most everyone said in confusion.

Ugh. I hadn't meant to say that out loud. I could feel my face turning bright red. "Nothing. Are we leaving, or are we going to keep chattering like old maids?" I asked briskly.

Marion looked me up and down strangely once again but said, "I agree."

Just then, that trademark Drogan screech rent the air, echoing everywhere and shaking the very earth. Everyone ran for the nearest tree for support as well as cover, though no Drogan came to view—even after the roar finally ceased.

The minutes stretched into eternities as the sound echoed endlessly in everyone's mind—though in reality, it had gone long ago. Finally, I had the courage to loosen my grip from the trunk of my shelter, and slowly I emerged enough to see the others. Jaythos had his crossbow out, cocked and poised for anything that would dare to cross the sky as he knelt on the ground. He was the only one not hidden, and practically so, as no one else had a long-distance weapon.

Syvil was also crouching as if poised to fly off—though he was still in human form. However, his face was as pale as the snow from the Ice Lands to the north. I knew what he was wondering.

Wait, how did I know what the snow of the Ice Lands looked like?

341

"We need to get out of here…" Marion sounded just as shaken, and as I turned to look at her, I found she was as pale as Syvil.

No one argued…no one had to.

CHAPTER XXIII: Misery Likes Company

Jaythos:

All I could think of was Kearn and the Drogan's blood curdling roar—or scream. Kearn would be coming after us once they realized we were out of the city, if he hadn't paid with his life for letting us slip by, and honestly, I wasn't sure which was worse. Years of fighting my own people, even at times killing them in battle...and it never got easier. With my brother, it was certainly harder.

And seeing the hate in his eyes only made it worse. The hate I had put there when I'd left him behind. Broken the promise.

"What if they found Runin?" Marion's voice was low, but still shaken, as we made our way through the damp rainforest, the midday sun hidden behind the canopy of leaves rustling high above. But the humidity was enough to still make us miserable despite the shade that the trees provided.

"They didn't. It's the last place they would think of." Sefen's reassurance was pretty lacking in the actual assurance part.

"These bugs are worse than the dungeon," Tanner grumbled, slapping the side of his neck as one of the thousands of mosquitoes found its lunch as well as its grave.

"Not so loud," Syvil hissed, with a nervous glance upward. I saw the way he jumped at every sound, as well as the way Marion was seemingly trying to keep him calm; the subtle hand on his arm when he flinched at a bird cawing.

He needed to get himself together. We all did.

We moved on through the trees until they grew into the towering giants that reached to the sky. But with the shade and denser foliage came even more bugs.

"These bugs are going to *kill* me," Tanner again growled. "Aren't they dangerous? I read somewhere they cause diseases."

Wait, Tanner read?

In response to Tanner's complaining, Maeko stopped by a long, frilled plant, plucking a few of the leaves and handing them to Tanner.

Ah, yes, Greken ferns. I hadn't thought of those.

"For the bugs," Maeko said, when he received an incredulous look from the boy. "Rub it on your skin." He then turned to the rest of us. "You all should."

No one argued with him, finding some more ferns and doing as he said.

"We'll need to be keeping a watch for water, as well. You all are not used to the humidity," Maeko further ordered, taking the lead without contest.

I couldn't help but smile, glad to see my friend back in his natural environment. I could relate to the feeling of being away from home; neither he nor I had felt at home in Kaedovarna.

We didn't get much further when the sound of wings was suddenly heard overhead, and as much as I hated the climate of Rugo, I did appreciate the thick foliage and gigantic trees overshadowing our presence. They would need to go by foot into the forest if they wanted to find us. Hopefully we would be safe—for now, anyway.

That being said, we didn't want to push our luck, and so instead, pushed on with a quiet fervor. The nice, flat, more open forests of Kaedovarna had spoiled me, leaving the difficult maneuvering of the undergrowth just one more irritation to add to the stress. The running streams, while cool and pleasant, were a breeding ground for mosquitos, and then everything was just...so big. The trees, the trees' roots, the leaves, the bugs.... It was like wading through a world of giants, climbing over and under the trees like they were enormous and ancient ruins. Then on top of it, the forest was just...so...*loud.* Birds, frogs, and the howls of creatures we really didn't want to run into all added to the constant clamor. Granted, nothing seemed as daunting next to a Drogan, but I still didn't want to run into a panther.

And speaking of Drogans...the sounds of wings flapping in the humid air above the trees died away as the day wore on, but I knew that would mean nothing. It only meant those under Kearn's command would be coming after us on foot. Hopefully that didn't include Kearn himself.

"No, don't drink that!" Maeko came close to a shout as Sefen leaned down to take a palmful of water from one of the small creeks we were crossing. "We must boil the water to stop from getting fevers." Maeko turned to me, then. *"It is like overseeing a group of toddlers. Where's the common sense?"*

I rolled my eyes. *"You're asking this now? Kaedovarna spoiled them. Have patience. We don't need fighting."*

"I have no idea what you both are saying, but I'm assuming it's something pretty insulting." Sefen sounded just the slightest bit amused.

"Yes, pretty insulting," Marion piped up. "Now, let's boil the water and refill our canteens so we can keep going, and then you can all decide when the duel to defend your honor can take place."

Syvil snorted.

Maeko just chuckled, proceeding to take the flint from a bag of supplies even as I gathered some leaves and sticks for him to light.

"We'll have to be quick so as not to cause smoke. The trees should be thick enough, but best not press our luck," Maeko murmured to me, even as I took the small pan Marion handed to me.

"Agreed."

"Actually, we're fine, I brought this," Marion chimed in, as if it wasn't awkward to join the conversation…that we'd been trying to have by ourselves. Hence the switch of language. But without any sort of hesitation, she pulled something out of the small pack she carried. *"It's one of the filters invented by Alenor and Henry. We can just filter the water through here. It'll take time still, but no smoke."*

"Can you guys please stop talking in Rugonian, it hurts my head," Tanner groaned in…a perfect Rugonian accent.

Sefen threw up his hands. "Am I the *only* one being left out of this?"

With a sigh, I returned to Varnian. "Fine. Let's just get the water filtered and move on."

It didn't take too long for the filter to work its magic, and after stopping two more times that day, we finally stopped for the night, finding a shelter underneath the giant rootlike offshoots of a *ky'Ki* tree.

Though we stopped, no one slept, and instead we found ourselves sitting in a small circle, Maeko and I the ones 'on watch.'

"Are they gone?" Tanner dared to whisper, referring to the Drogans that had been hunting the air about two hours ago.

"Yes." It was Marion who replied, which was all the better, since she was a Drogan. It was nice to have some on our side.

Tanner sighed, leaning back against the hilly mound we were mostly using for cover. "Good." He breathed in, the breath shaky as he slowly closed his eyes. As if afraid to fall asleep. But it wasn't long until he had clearly done just that.

"I'll take watch," Sefen offered.

Though the last thing I was going to do was sleep right now, I nodded, sitting back down and allowing him to get up and take post at the edge of our natural shelter.

It seemed like the only one able to sleep at the moment was Tanner, and I rolled my eyes as the boy murmured softly in his sleep, turning over restlessly and mumbling something about not wanting to leave.

"So, do you make him take memories often?" Marion asked, her eyes also trained on the boy.

I shrugged. "Hard to tell. He likes snooping around." I'd given up vocalizing my disapproval of Sefen and others' methods. Instead, I'd learned to try not to think too much about it. Nothing I'd ever objected to had ever really been heard back at Valdon, and the excuse had always been that it was the end of the world. I seemed to have a habit of just giving up and taking the easiest route, didn't I? What a good little mindless soldier I was.

"His Gift is rare here on Baeno, and I have read much about it." Marion huffed and readjusted her position.

Turning to her, I hid my confused expression and simply asked, "Read?"

"Of course. I've been stuck here for over a decade. I had to make myself busy, somehow. And since all my friends have been kept prisoner from a Gift similar to the child's, I did as much research on the subject as possible."

That was...fair.

"I see," was all I managed. "Well, did you ever find anything interesting?"

"That it's easy for them to break their own minds." The reply was hardly warm. "And you seem to handle them very carelessly. No wonder Skayla is how she is."

I took to cleaning my crossbow in an attempt to keep myself occupied. Or to try and give myself time to reply. "Baeno is full of people who think they know best. I knew it was only a matter of time before we got ourselves into this kind of trouble one way or the other."

Syvil scoffed, apparently having been listening to the conversation. "Yeah, that is certainly true. I have not been impressed with what I have seen."

"Let's remember whose leader helped take over the world and murdered your own friend?" I regretted the words even as I gestured to Marion, and yet I had a lifetime of words I regretted. And actions. I'd add them to the list.

"I would be careful before you say that again. I can still eat you," Syvil growled through gritted teeth. It was a ridiculous threat coming from him, but I still regretted my words.

Maeko shifted in his position, but I gave a subtle gesture for him to relax. I was not helping; I was being the problem. As usual.

Marion's reply split through the tension, quiet and worried. "I would prefer you not let the Dragon come out like that, Syvil. Please."

Syvil's entire body stiffened, expression breaking into something akin to horror as he stared at Marion. "I...I wasn't serious."

"I know." Her tone was gentle, and yet something unsaid passed between the two.

Silence reigned again, and I even dozed off for a small period of time as the noise of the night echoed in the background.

And then Tanner started screaming. "Stop! Please! Shut up!"

Tanner:

"Come on, you two, the court won't wait forever!" Moira's voice rang clear through the house, peppy and authoritative as always. It's what we liked most about her. "Oh please, don't tell me you're going to show up to the Gaevnian Treaty Signing like that, are you?" She looked me up and down as I walked down the stairs, in my usual attire.

I rolled my eyes, sighing and flicking my hand—for dramatic effect— to creating what everyone would assume was simply an illusion of fancier, more 'proper' clothes.

"Show-off." Moira's smile was sly but small, and like a mother, she checked over my now-acceptable attire, then turned from me to Skayla, who was emerging from a nearby hallway, her stiff collar nothing compared to her rigid body.

"Oh come, crack a smile before someone thinks we're attending a funeral." Moira waved her hand at Skayla and then turned to the door. "Now if we don't get going, we're going to be attending a war council instead of a peace meeting." I turned to Skayla, raising an eyebrow and cracking a smirk even as I again fought the guilt of hiding my true Gift from my sisters. Why was I so hesitant?

Skayla rolled her eyes, but before we could think of stepping forward to follow Moira, our eldest sister called out, "If you rascals aren't behind me in two minutes, you're going to bed without supper."

There was a second of silence, and then all three of us had a good laugh.

If only this sort of comradery wasn't such a rare occurrence, these days.

And then, darkness. An incoherent mess. Echoes of memories and a sense of suffocation.

"It's taking too long to break him. It's too risky, Skayla." I heard the voices between my half-conscious state and the door that separated us. "If he doesn't know where it is, then it's best to kill him and find someone who does."

Skayla's laugh. "He'll cave. He's close, the fool. I'll get in his mind and he'll tell us what we need. And I'll use him to get it."

"You know what I've sacrificed for this. If he doesn't...."

"We'll have the world, silly!" Skayla laughed again. "With the world, where can they possibly hide it?"

"Henry, please—" My lungs seemed to freeze in the face of the horrible reality crumbling around us. Why had the Drogans turned so violent? It didn't make sense. What was Skayla thinking?

"You know where the key is, and I know where the rest is. Meet at Rugo and we'll try and send word to Sven and Moira. They can't find this, Aly."

I gripped his hand. "And I can't lose you."

I couldn't lose him...and yet I had. I was alone. Completely alone. Alone in the dark with the screams of failures and the ghosts of mistakes. Ones I couldn't distinguish. My mind crumbled beneath the laughter and tears that pummeled my mind like an unforgiving windstorm. So many images vying for the attention of my mind's eye. So many identities claiming to be mine. I wanted them to shut up—to leave me alone. I kept hearing Skayla's mad laugh roaring among them; a mad laugh that felt like it was becoming my own, echoing everywhere.

I wanted them all to stop. To go away and leave me alone. Whatever was left of my own head.

I was being shaken, darkness all around save a pale light—from the moons, stars, or a lantern I couldn't distinguish. My eyes widened as a hand was cupped over my mouth, and my struggling increased.

"Shh!" The whisper was barely audible and yet harsh. I recognized the voice but grappled a moment longer before being still. It was Jaythos, but he and another person were holding me down. "Tanner, what in Baeno—are you alright?"

I gasped and struggled away as he took his hand from my mouth and let me go. My back bumped against one of the large tree roots, and I struggled to catch my breath.

"Leave me alone," I growled in a hoarse whisper.

"Well, unfortunately, we can't. Your screaming could have alerted any nearby scouts to our position, so we need to get moving." Sefen's voice sounded from my left, and I flinched.

But also…. "My what?"

"You must have had a bad dream." I didn't immediately recognize the woman's voice, and it took a moment to remember that we'd picked up yet another misfit on our suicide mission. Marion. That was her name. She was Syvil's friend. Instantly, as it clicked, my brain tried to overload me with information, memories of flights and conversations over the last hundred or so years. I shook my head. *Focus, Syv—no Tanner. Focus, Tanner.*

My head hurt.

"We must leave." Maeko's deep tone was hard to hear above the noise of the rainforest. Or were they all in my head? Everything was so loud. So, *so* loud.

"Just shut up, please?" I rasped as I winced, hauling myself to my feet. Oh wait, I'd said that out loud?

I really wasn't sure until Syvil asked, "Tanner...are you alright?"

"I'm fine, leave me alone." I didn't have the patience to deal with pretended worry. I didn't have time to not be alright. I didn't have time— wait, this didn't sound like me. This sounded like someone else. Was it someone else? How did I know what my thoughts even sounded like?!

"Maeko's right," Sefen stepped in, offering me a hand. "We need to go."

I swatted it away and shoved down the memories that convulsed in the back of my mind. "Fine. Let's go," I grumbled.

"Are you going to be able to pull it together?" he whispered, concern etched in his brow. I could see it even in the dimness of twilight.

"Yes, just fine, as always."

I was given a look, but nothing else was said as the rest made swift work of packing up our pathetic camp. In a few more minutes, we were struggling through the undergrowth of the forest again, ears peeled for any sound that was out of place; any hint that we'd been discovered.

But I couldn't seem to pay attention. Every sound seemed to remind me of something that wasn't mine. Or was it?

"Tanner?"

I jumped as Marion's whisper came, paired with a light touch on my elbow.

"Apologies. You are out of sorts. Syvil and I are concerned." She matched my pace as I weaved around the giant roots and plants that stood ever in our way. "How long have you been made to take on others' memories?"

"I can handle it, don't worry," I straight-up lied. It was becoming clear that I could not handle it. Was it Sven's memories? Or Syvil's? Or was I just finally too weak to fight the incessant feeling of drowning in them all?

"You can certainly handle lying, that is for sure." Marion's comment would have been irritating if not for the twinge of concern in her voice—genuine concern I'd not heard often from anyone.

"I just...it's been a long few weeks." I wasn't used to having anyone press besides Baey, and Baey wasn't here. "Sleep will probably help." Anxiety spiked, and I found myself running my hand through my hair, taking in deep breaths through the nose and out through the mouth in an attempt to reorient myself. I wondered where in the worlds I'd learned that?

Worlds? Wait, no, I hadn't traveled off world, had I?

"I am not so sure about that. I know we don't know each other, but perhaps you should reach out to..." She looked forward to where Maeko and Sefen were leading the group. "Your friends."

Yeah. Her hesitance said it all. They weren't my friends. I was their ally. I was their tool; the easy way to cheat trust. I'd known that the day they'd shown up and taken me away from the closest thing to a home I had and the only person besides Baey who'd ever cared for me, and now I could hardly remember the woman's face, let alone her name. Everything else seemed to crowd it out, and now I desperately tried to remember. Desperately and in vain.

"Tanner?"

I snapped my head up just in time to hit it on an overhanging branch, barely stopping myself from crying out in exasperation rather than the pain of it. Great, now I had a headache, too.

"I am beginning to think you didn't hear what I said." Marion wasn't bothering to hide her concern anymore. I heard it in every syllable she spoke.

And it only made my own panic feel more real. I didn't want to think about it. I didn't want to worry about losing my mind, because there wasn't anything I could really do to stop it, and apparently the person that cared the most was a complete stranger. *And* a Drogan. Two of them.

Oh dear, was I really turning into Skayla?

"How long has it been this bad, Tanner?"

The persistence paired with my anxiety was unbearable. Well, my anxiety or Baey's—I didn't care to stop and dissect which was which. "I think after me screaming into the night, it's best to limit conversation and listen for an ambush, ah?"

Marion had adjusted her position to walking right behind me, and I was glad I couldn't see her reaction. I didn't want the silent lecture. I wanted to be left alone. I wanted this all to go away and for people to just leave me alone.

Or maybe I didn't. My brain went unwillingly to the way Marion had called me a child the other day, and in that moment, I just wanted to cry. I wanted to cry and just have someone care, and it took all my discipline to stop from breaking down there in the middle of the night.

There was no Baey for me to pretend for now, and I was too tired to pretend for myself.

I was really beginning to see how Skayla had turned so...demented.

THE LIVING STONE

CHAPTER XXIV: Climbing and Falling

<u>Jaythos:</u>

We traveled through the night, exhaustion tugging its ever-trailing leash behind us. Sefen was quieter than ever, but then again, no one really talked much these days. And that was making Tanner pay the price, it seemed. I thought of his eyes when we'd tried to wake him up, unnaturally open though he was still asleep. His begging for someone to shut up. Someone? Or everyone?

I felt a twinge of guilt for every time I'd ever suggested the boy take a memory. We had all always been so busy surviving, and I'd grown so tired of voicing my disagreements to Sefen when even his own wife would get nowhere. But now I wondered again at my decision to remain quiet. Quiet as Baey grew up with no training. Quiet as Tanner was forced to take memory after memory with no thought to the consequences. Why was I always so willing to play the good silent soldier? Why was I never willing to take the risk? Had I not learned my lesson with Kearn?

I was still yet to pay the full price for that mistake, and now I was already seeing what my silence had cost others.

"You are choosing to kill your countrymen just to protect a few strangers? Do you understand what kind of a lunatic you sound like, Jaythos?"

357

The words from the last letter I'd received all those years ago in Rugo still haunted me. When Bethyn had joined Skayla and I'd defected, I'd written for him to come after I'd abandoned him. That had been the reply.

"Shut up," I ordered.

"What? Not you too..." Marion's voice came from behind.

I had not realized that I'd said the words aloud. "I let my mind wander to worst-case scenarios," was all I offered as an explanation. Hopefully it would be enough.

Syvil—who had dared one last pre-dawn flight above to check for any pursuers—flew back down, shaking the moisture of Rugonian morning from his feathers.

Turning back into his human form, Syvil came to me and reported, "Nothing yet. But I guarantee they have reported back by now, and we'll be in for the race of our lives."

I noticed with rising displeasure the way Syvil had come to me.

Joy. I pretended not to notice Sefen's eye contact. How did they think I was a better idea than him? Didn't they see the way I just...let things happen?

"Go and tell the others," I requested simply.

Syvil raised an eyebrow, looked as if he wanted to protest, but obeyed. I busied myself with looking around and checking for any hidden scouts or any sign that someone might have heard Tanner's scream last night.

The sun rose and the heat with it, leaving little room for anything but sweating and panting. It was so insufferable one could barely think, let alone speak. I had grown accustomed to the weather of Rugo, long ago, but it had been years since I'd been here, and with the absence, I had forgotten the warmth. In fact, even Maeko appeared a little uncomfortable, the beads of sweat glittering on his bald head. Poor Syvil seemed especially displeased, constantly mumbling under his breath about our stupid world and flesh-eating bugs.

We trekked on against the heat and the threat of being found, wishing the mountains would be merciful and come closer into view, but also knowing Syvil could not even so much as check our progress until night. And then there was, of course, the constant threat of running out of water and the fear of dehydration. As much as we couldn't afford to stop, every time we found a decent spring or creek we would be forced to pause, filter the water, and restock.

Night fell again but still we trudged on, Sefen daring to light a small lantern-like flame to help light the way. Syvil, meanwhile, flew up for a few surveillance flights, but with little else to go on besides his coming and going, I could only guess it was about midnight when we found a thick patch of leafy bushes to settle down in for some rest.

"I'll take the first watch." Syvil—who had once again rejoined us in human form—was the first to speak, taking out his blade and inspecting it briefly before standing in the shade of a tree, his form melting away in the dark.

"And I'll take the second half," Sefen added simply.

No one argued, and it was probably more the fact that we were so spent and just glad we didn't have to stay up. Funny how I trusted the Drogan to keep a watchful eye more than the rest of us.

Settling down under one of the giant elephant ear leaf plants, I drifted in and out of sleep. The third time I awoke was just before dawn, and I stiffened for a moment at the sound of low voices. It was Marion and Syvil talking, and it took great effort to allow my muscles to relax.

"Is Fryn the only one you've had to fight besides Ovok?" Marion asked.

"So far, yes. I...wish there had been another way." Syvil's reply was soft. "Perhaps there was," he added. "Perhaps there was and the Dragon is just taking over."

"Syv...I didn't mean that. You're still just as much you as ever. This whole situation has turned us upside down."

The silence was long, and I found my eyes falling against my will. When I awoke again, it was from being gently shaken. I sat bolt upright, hand on my crossbow for a moment before realizing it was only Sefen, looking unamused.

"It's time to get a move on," he said simply before going to wake others.

Yes. We must. I got up without another moment of hesitation, helping Sefen in waking the others. And so began another day of the same drudgery. The same tense silence. The same dread and unanswerable questions hanging in the air.

By evening, a steady rain had begun, pattering above us and splashing mostly against the broad leaves of the trees. Of course, while it definitely lessened the storm, it did not completely protect us, and it was an unpleasant continuing. With all the rain, there wasn't much point in stopping, and so we were left in the misery of walking in the awful weather, at least glad for the progress.

That's when I realized we had begun to start a more uphill ascent. This was a good sign. Syvil had reported earlier in the morning that we'd been gaining on the mountains, but with that rain, he had not been able to check tonight. Now, the beginning of a climb was encouraging, though the knowledge of the easy trek being behind us soon was not so much.

"So, who is Captain Kearn to you?" It was Marion, coming up beside me as she and Sefen switched off hiding any sign of us the weather might not mask.

I tensed both at the name of my brother and the question it was included in. "Why does it matter?" I asked.

"Because he's been stationed in Veka for two years, and the way you reacted to Tanner saying his name is very indicative."

"And why are you being so nosy? I heard you talking with Tanner the other night. Are you trying to test weaknesses?" I tried to stifle my own bristling attitude. But I didn't like being prodded.

Marion sighed. "Because you are all making it very difficult to function as a group, and I'm trying to learn about you so maybe we can work as one. You are welcome to ask me questions. Tanner has my memories. I have nothing to hide."

Yeah. Tanner had mine, too. I shuddered, then realized there was no use in secrets. Not anymore. Not when almost everyone knew already, and those who didn't were the most competent of the group.

"He's my younger brother. I don't wish to discuss it, but I suppose you should know in case we end up meeting him in more...extreme circumstances."

"I see." Marion waited a while before saying, "I suppose that makes sense why you were one of the first ones to trust Syvil, then."

I turned and gave her a quizzical look, which earned me an eyeroll in return.

"Syvil told me about how you all met, you know. We did a lot of catching up in Veka."

Right. I supposed this was a perfect opportunity to at least turn the questions back on her and test her willingness to talk. "So, how do you know Syvil so well? It seems there are quite a few Drogans for you to know all of them." I put the question as matter-of-factly as possible.

"We are around the same age. Drogan children have been rare for centuries, and so whenever there is one, the whole community helps in raising them. Syvil and I were two out of ten children born between two and three centuries ago," she explained, not looking anywhere except forward now.

I swallowed my pride at the reminder of how infantile we must all seem next to them. "I see. How long *do* Drogans live?" I tried not to sound so unsettled by the sudden fact that both she and Syvil were at least three hundred years old.

"Well, first, we actually call ourselves Myrandi, but we've given up on that. Second...the oldest living I think is Ovok. He's two or three thousand years old. No one really knows for sure, because he's outlived everyone else." Her reply was followed by a shudder.

"And Ovok...you said he'd been the protector of your kind?" I felt intrusive, understanding how tangled one's origins and people could be. Or being afraid of those who were supposed to keep you safe. That's all Bethyn had ever been.

"Yes. He kept the Hunters out for the most part, and our society safe. But then...his daughter Rhioa died, and he went rather off the deep end. Said we had to get out before we were all destroyed. But Cyl wouldn't let us." Marion seemed to wander further and further away from the here

362

and now as she relived the beginning of what would turn into just as much a nightmare for her people as it was for all of us. I was beginning to realize this, at last.

"Cyl?" I dared ask. "You'd mentioned his name before."

"He was a Drogan in charge of guarding the Doorway to The Maze—and other worlds. He refused to let us through, and we had to fight." Marion's tone turned even more solemn. "He and Ovok had been friends once. But things change with time...and fear makes enemies of us all, I suppose."

"Hopefully not of all of us," I murmured, her remark hitting hard. Again, I thought of Kearn. He could never be my enemy. But I knew in my heart I was exactly that to him.

Tanner:

The further into Rugo we went, the more I hated it. The bugs, the heat, the constant and frantic search for water, the sticky humidity that came after rain; it was all enough to make you wish for a good snowstorm. Even when it *had* been raining, it had been unpleasant and lukewarm. How had Maeko or anyone else ever suffered through this for more than a week?

"We should stop and rest," Sefen suggested well into the night, and no one argued. I plopped down, resting my back against a tree and closing my eyes. It was so miserable.

There was only one thing I was thankful for in this forsaken country, and that was for the lack of need for a fire. It was warm enough without, and so we could hide our presence without freezing to death. Of course, right now freezing to death sounded pretty nice, comparatively.

I hated Rugo. Not even the part of Maeko in me with all the nostalgia and longing for home could change my mind. Maybe that made me a little happy, at least. Perhaps it really was me hating Rugo, not someone else. I clung to the little bit of emotion I could call my own.

As everyone settled down, the meager rations were distributed, and I found myself wandering off in thought. I wondered where the other Myrandi were—Lyri, Phaela, Tres. They were the others from my age that had come with us. And yet Sven had saved me. The most useless. The one that was too afraid. Not a fighter—

I startled, sitting up stiff as the tree I'd been resting my back against. So much for keeping a shred of my identity. I shook my head in an attempt to clear it, looking around and reminding myself that I was *not* a Drogan. I was losing it. I was *so* losing it.

Marion was looking at me again, and I wondered what physical reaction I'd let slip. Well, besides shaking my head. At least I hadn't screamed this time…joy.

That's when Marion got up and came over to me, sitting down and asking, "Still getting worse?"

"I'm sorry?" I didn't bother to hide the edge to my tone.

"I have read of those with the Gift of Mind. They are a rare breed here on Baeno," she continued as if nothing were amiss.

I just rolled my eyes. "Oh, have you? How nice." I really was being rude…. I blamed my stupid head.

"Do you know how to transfer memories, yet?" This next question blew away my annoyance, now curious instead. And perhaps embarrassment...did she really know more about my Gift than I did?

"Of course," I lied, trying to figure out what she meant.

She gave an amused snort. "You're not as good a liar as you think, you know."

I gave up. What was the point of hiding anything, anyway. "Fine, so what do you mean, transfer memories?"

The Drogan gave a sad sort of smile. "Memory Keepers are a subset of Mind Gifts, and get very easily overwhelmed and lost if they keep taking without getting rid of anything."

Yeah. That was a bit of an understatement.

"So, they would find ways to endow items with memories, to help get rid of them. It wouldn't completely do it, but it would stop them from returning, say, in a dream." The last part was said way too pointedly.

"Well, I'll figure it out then, thank you," I answered gruffly, leaning back against my tree and snapping my eyes shut.

"Hm," I heard her muse aloud, staying a moment longer before getting up and leaving.

I almost begged for her to stay, but then I saw everyone else watching us. I just...couldn't even think straight anymore. I was tired and confused, and I wanted to be myself and just go to sleep. But every time I closed my eyes, I would become someone else, or see someone else. Who even was I anymore?

My dreams were more memory than anything else, as usual. Perhaps not terrible like the other night, but still not exactly restful. Whether it was Jaythos sparring with Kearn—laughing and actually acting like a human being—or Maeko helping to school a young Queen Serafina, it was always laced with the bitterness of knowing it was gone. I should at least have been thankful that for the first night in ages, I didn't get Sven's memories, but I knew that wouldn't last forever.

That being said, I was greatly relieved as I awoke with at least some amount of decorum, screaming or struggling not a factor this night. Oh. Morning.

Everyone else was also getting up, and without a word, we once more set out. By afternoon, the gentle incline had become more rock-ridden than earth, and the forest slowly began to dwindle until, quite suddenly, the mountains were there, right in front of us. There was no clearing, no sign to announce we were there. Just rock…and a steep journey ahead of us.

The path I had seen in the memories was not in this mountain, but in one further into the mountain range, meaning this was about to get a lot more uncomfortable. We couldn't risk going on the main path, as Jaythos and Sefen had explained, so we would be going into the raw untraveled parts of the mountain and hoping it wasn't too impassable.

The first two hours were full of steep inclines and difficult terrain, but not unsurpassable, and though our progress was painfully slow, it was progress. As we hiked higher and higher, we were able to see the area around us, especially the blurs in the sky, flying about as they searched for us.

Maeko was leading as usual, being familiar with rock climbing from his youth. I told him as best I could where we were heading, and he was able to guide us better than I would have through this rough terrain. But with each step further into the mountains, I found myself more afraid of missing my step.

The sun was beginning to set when I realized the problem with that. We couldn't climb in the dark. What if we all fell to our deaths? We didn't escape being trapped in a city and then ambushed by kin just to fall in the dark! Whether it was the sudden fear of falling or exhaustion, I began inwardly panicking, and was just about to call up to Maeko about this problem when he disappeared from sight.

A moment later, so did Sefen, and as I grew closer to where they had been, I realized there was a small cave in the steep rock, offering shelter. Oh. Silly me. I scrambled up, Sefen helping me up onto the little ledge that lay before the natural shelter, and together we waited for the three remaining. Syvil, Jaythos, and then Marion taking the rear.

We were just helping Syvil up when I heard Marion scream.

Jaythos:

I didn't think, only reached out and grabbed Marion's hand as her foot slipped. For one, dreadful moment I felt her hand slipping through mine, sweat creating a slick and difficult surface, and even my quick reflexes were almost not enough. But then she managed to grab hold of it, hoisting her other hand up so that she grasped my arm with both her hands.

THE LIVING STONE

As I desperately tried to hang onto the ledge with my other hand, my shoulders threatened to separate from the rest of me with the strain they were under.

"Hang on!" Syvil shouted even as he morphed into his Dragon form.

But it was too late. My hand gave out, and both Marion and I started plummeting through thin air.

Joy.

Something inside me refused to let this be how I died, and even as I kept a firm hold on Marion, I somehow took out my knife with my free hand and dug it into the rock face. We thudded to a stop again, and the scream that wrenched itself from my lips did little justice to the agony that raced up and down my shoulders at the jolt. My hand was about to let go again when Syvil swooped down, grabbing Marion and sweeping up to the now distant ledge. I tried to get my now free hand up to help keep hold, but my whole arm was numb—or rather, I wished it was numb, with the way lightning was running up and down it. My fingers were slipping, and just as I was about to debate letting go, Syvil once more dove for me, grabbing me just as my grip failed. Seconds later, I was on the ledge, shoulders screaming louder than either Marion or I had.

"Are you both alright?" Sefen was beside us, eyes wide.

I tried to move my right arm to test it, but that's when I realized the real problem wasn't my shoulder but my elbow. I barely kept in another scream. "Just...fine," I grunted, closing my eyes and forcing myself to remain composed. Stupid elbow. This was going to be a blast.

"Marion? Mar, you alright?" Syvil's concerned whispers dragged me out of my own self-pity to turn my attention to my partner in misery.

Marion was huddled in the far corner, knees up to her chin as she rocked back and forth.

"I...I...." She squeezed her eyes shut. Syvil knelt down by her, speaking in a low voice.

"What's wrong with her?" I heard Tanner ask. The spots forming in my vision were making it tricky to see where everyone was.

I turned back to where I remembered Sefen being and sighed to hide the pain, asking as calmly as I could, "Do you know how to reset a dislocated elbow?" I figured if anyone would know, Namaya's husband would be the most likely, and I certainly didn't want to trust Tanner to do it unless there was no other option.

Fortunately for me, Sefen nodded and came down to my side. "Which one?" he asked.

I closed my eyes, already imagining the coming unpleasantness. "At least the right one...my shoulders hurt more than a griffon's mauling, so they might need...adjusting as well." My bigger fear was a torn muscle, as that wouldn't heal for a very long time. A dislocation was bad enough.

I was barely able to register that Sefen had grabbed hold of my arm before he reset it with a sickening click. A groan escaped me, and I nearly doubled over. "Thank you." I barely found the breath to say the words, let alone make them sound grateful. I tested my shoulders, and nausea swept over me as my left one was pierced with pain. I sighed. "...and my left shoulder...."

"Are you going to be alright?" Sefen asked, not yet moving for my shoulder.

The smile I gave was as brittle as my reply. "Chipper."

And with that, he set my shoulder…which was much more painful than the elbow. I could feel everyone's eyes on me as I cried out, and no matter how quickly I recovered myself, the lapse in my self-control was too late to take back. I took several deep breaths to try and calm myself and began getting up…but there were two problems with that: my left shoulder and right elbow. If I tried to use my left hand to help myself up, my shoulder would protest, but if I used my right hand, my elbow would do the same. I stayed seated for now, ignoring the now dramatic wish to sleep.

"You both need rest," Sefen all but ordered. "We can't travel until you're both well enough to climb again. This little cave is hidden enough that I think if we can get further in, we'll be safe until then—and don't even think of arguing, Jaythos."

He cut me off even before I'd opened my mouth. He was right, for once, but it could take a few days to be properly able again. I looked to where Marion was sitting down, still in shock, and decided it really was for the best. Even besides the shock, she looked about as bad as I did. And then we'd both be unforgivably sore in the morning.

"Let's move a little further inside to prevent any Drogan eyes from finding us," Sefen said as he got up and moved away, going over to the Drogans and Tanner and lending a hand to Marion. I knew what Sefen was trying to say: apologize. It was the closest he got to admitting he was wrong. He was trying to apologize for doubting Marion.

Marion's terror broke at last and she stared intently at my friend, slowly grabbing his hand and allowing both him and Syvil to hoist her up. I noted how she favored her leg. Hopefully no fractures. She'd hit it against the rock face a few times in our ungraceful descent.

"Please be more careful?" Maeko asked as he came over and offered me a hand, bringing my observations to an end as I had to once more think about how I was going to get up. "You have come too far to die."

I rolled my eyes. "I'll try and remember that." My reply was hoarse, and I realized my throat was dry from screaming. "But seeing as my arms will most definitely pop off if they are tugged any further, I think I would best use you as support under my arms rather than pulling them." The sarcasm was to mask the pain, but it was clear there wasn't a point. Maeko's concerned expression showed he knew. Well, I supposed everyone knew...it wasn't like they hadn't seen us all fall....

Without a word, my friend knelt down and hooked a hand under my right arm, allowing me something to lean into as I tested my legs to push off the ground. Barely, I remembered not to use my other hand to help me up, and so with minimal discomfort, I was able to stand, teetering only a moment before finding my balance. At least my legs still worked. Those were important.

"How do you feel?" Maeko asked, again using those penetrating eyes.

I immediately regretted my shrug. "Not bad, all things considered," I replied, interrupted in the middle as I tried to clear my throat.

Everyone now up, we limped further to the back of the little alcove, and soon, shadows surrounded us as Sefen allowed a small flame to dance in his palm, giving enough light to at least see where we were going.

"This looks...man-made." Marion spoke a coherent sentence for the first time since her fall. I looked over to find her tracing her hand against the wall. That's when I saw what she did: chisel marks.

"Yeah, it's very old, though. The memories are faint," Tanner mumbled. He sounded displeased.

Marion turned and gave Tanner a curious look but said no more, and soon all of us had sat down on the blankets that Sefen and Tanner had set out as some pathetic camp.

Giving Maeko a quiet thank you for helping me back down, I set my head against the wall and closed my eyes. It was cold now that we were away from the sun, and yet a fire would be suicide. Anyone would see the side of the mountain lit up.

Someone sat beside me and I opened my eyes, expecting it to be Sefen checking in on me.

I quickly swallowed my surprise as I found myself facing Syvil, exhaustion and worry rippling through his body. There was something...almost refreshing about the way he so openly showed his fear.

"Thank you for saving her," he said with an open relief. As someone from Bethyn, it had been drilled into my head from a young age that showing weakness was a death sentence, and when the war with Skayla had begun, people had rather started to think the same way—whether or not they realized it. Especially those at Valdon. And yet, somehow...somehow, Syvil's openness was not from a place of weakness but of honesty. It reminded me of Baey. It never stopped them from doing anything, and yet they didn't hide it like others.

It was odd how I missed the little girl now, when I'd tried so hard never to attach myself to her or anyone else.

Then I remembered I hadn't replied to the Drogan. "We're all working together. Everyone is worth saving," I said rather bluntly. Everything came out of my mouth that way, whether I intended it or not. Again, I blamed Bethyn.

But I blamed Bethyn for a lot of things.

"She is...she is all I have right now. I don't know what will happen to the rest of my people, and if she dies, there will be no one left." I couldn't tell if Syvil was even talking to me or himself at this point.

I was uncomfortable either way, but I could understand the sentiment. All my people were on the wrong side, too.

"She should have been the one in my place. She's the fighter and the flier. I...I am not good at any of this."

I sighed, wishing that giving reassurance was my thing. And yet, something inside of me stirred. Something that understood him. He was all alone, in a world where everyone thought he was an enemy. I knew how that felt. I still remembered the glares I'd gotten when I first defected. I remembered Maeko being the only one that saw me as anything except some disease, and I understood leaving people behind.

"You have saved our lives too many times to count, Syvil. I think you were just who we needed." I remembered when he'd killed his own friend for us. Fryn, he'd called them.

Syvil turned and blinked at me, perhaps having forgotten I was there. Maybe he really *had* been talking to himself. "Thank you." The words were sincere. "I'm sorry. I suppose I'm tired. I shall leave you." He went to get up.

"Syvil—" I called after him, keeping my voice low enough to not draw attention from the others.

The Drogan stopped halfway to his feet, turning and waiting.

"I suppose...none of us had ever thanked *you* for helping a bunch of dysfunctional strangers. So...thank you." Oh joy, my exhaustion and aching body were making my discipline lapse. But I somehow didn't regret saying the words. The hardened determination in the Drogan's eyes only furthered my own resolve.

A sad, small smile crossed Syvil's expression briefly before he nodded, a silent and deep gratitude passing between us as he got up and returned to his friend.

CHAPTER XXV: Well, That Was Close

Tanner:

I had never heard Jaythos scream before. It wasn't something I ever wanted to hear again, and the sound was still ringing in my ears for a good few minutes after we'd all gotten inside the cave. Or maybe it was someone else's scream from some stupid memory that wasn't mine.

Once Sefen had declared our fate, he and I made quick work of setting things up inside the cave for everyone and then helped both Marion and Jaythos further inside, and by the end of the hour, they were both passed out from the strain of what they had endured.

I tried to ignore the whispers of the little alcove. I didn't want to know. I didn't care who had made this stupid place or how old it was.

Just leave me alone, I pleaded to the walls.

Syvil sighed, glancing over at Marion a moment before murmuring, "I cannot imagine falling…and not having the reassurance of wings. Especially when one has always had them."

The comment was enough to drive me away from the memories that weren't mine, and I swallowed hard as Syvil's words hit deep. Falling was one thing…but falling and suddenly remembering you could no longer fly was another. I hated how easily I could relate to the feeling, and it took me only a few seconds to realize it was because of Marion's own memories. It had been a fear she'd carried with her since dying the first time.

No, no, stay away from that. I don't want to relive it, please. I begged my own head.

"So how far into the mountain range do we need to go?" It was Sefen.

For once, I was happy for the excuse to dig around in my head, only because it would bring me in the opposite direction of Marion's...experiences. But it was becoming increasingly difficult to wade through the mire of my befuddled brain. I latched onto the clocktower back in Veka, and slowly my mind found the bit of Alenor inside.

I inhaled sharply, replying, "It took me—uh—Alenor about five days, but I—she took a path. So it will probably be slower for us?"

"Hm." Maeko's brow furrowed in thought. "That means we are going to Mount *Vet De Lona*."

"Yes. That's it. That's the name," I replied eagerly, sitting up straight. *Vet De Lona*. It clicked into place.

"The mountain is impossible to scale. There are no paths there." Maeko's expression was dark. Well, darker than usual. He hadn't been himself since Sven had shown up, and even less so since the art gallery.

The memory stung, and I tried to move on quickly for both of our sakes. "There is a path, but it's hidden. Impossible to find if you don't know what you're looking for. It goes through the mountain in some sections."

"Should I scan the skies?" Syvil spoke up now, already staring back towards the mouth of our little cave.

"No. We don't need to risk losing anyone else tonight," said Sefen, who had been staring out to the distant opening of the little cave. I could practically feel the paranoia radiating off of him. I didn't have to guess what he was thinking about. He'd lost so much already, and today, he'd almost lost one of the only friends he had left. To say he hadn't been the same since Namaya's betrayal and death would be an understatement. She'd been the only thing keeping him together since the loss of their children, and I still felt the pain of loss as acutely as if they were my own. Every action he had made since then had been from the same fear. Baey's seclusion. His refusal to retreat from Valdon...it all revolved around that fear of loss. But somehow, it hurt. Hurt to know that I was apparently the most dispensable of everyone. Otherwise, Baey would have had a lot more company barred up in Valdon.

Maybe I'd still have half a brain.

"Tanner?" Speaking of...Sefen came over and sat down beside me.

I didn't bother to acknowledge him, staring instead at where Marion was sitting, still breathing heavily even in her sleep.

"Are you...holding up alright?" The question was awkward, and yet it at least sounded like he was genuinely concerned.

"Why? Need me to take another memory?" I turned and stared at the man, only to find a flash of hurt wash briefly over his expression.

"No, you just seem to be...I'm sorry I haven't asked sooner. I've been—"

"Preoccupied. Got it." I didn't have the discipline to keep my tongue back. "It's a little late to be asking now, Sefen. I'll get ahold of myself. I always do." The words tasted bitter in my mouth.

Sefen was quiet for a long time. "Look...Tanner...I'm sorry. I didn't realize it was affecting you like this."

My throat felt thick as I croaked out, "You never asked."

Silence was our company for the remainder of the evening, and an hour or so after the sun had hidden its head, everyone except Maeko went to get some rest. I found myself dreading sleep, wishing these memories weren't so vivid. Why did I never dream of my own memories? Did I even have any? In an odd spree of panic, I forced myself to recount everything since we left Patelayna, fighting to keep the narrative in my view. But even then, everything was colored by influences and memories that weren't mine. The art gallery, the museum, the sense of familiarity that always followed me, no matter if I had been there before or not. Who even was I? Was there anything about me that I hadn't stolen from someone else?

The thought haunted me until sleep overcame my senses.

I had lost count of the number of social gatherings, balls, and other miscellaneous parties we had attended. I was not one for grandeur, but the people were another matter. I took any opportunity to get to know the people instead of their titles, and while I usually preferred methods outside of formal events, this would have to do.

"Well, if it isn't a scoundrel." Queen Serafina's voice came from behind me. I turned and raised an eyebrow before putting on an offended facade.

"Why, I never. Such language used against me should not be tolerated." I couldn't help but smile.

The queen rolled her eyes, "I'm so frightened." And turned to her bodyguard, "What do you think, Maeko? Should I be worried?"

Maeko cracked a rare smile, looking me up and down before replying, "Seeing as he is shorter than a footstool, I wouldn't be worried."

"Why, I never." I put a hand over my heart, but was unable to contain my grin, giving a laugh as I asked, "Well, Your Highness, care to dance with a footstool?"

"Sefen, get the children!" Namaya shouted frantically amid the crowd of fleeing people, and I ran even faster as I saw Daryn and Varina among the panicking mass, lost and searching for us. Then I saw the soldiers, grabbing those running and putting them in the carts—or if too unwilling…ending them.

Fury rose inside me and I ignited my hands so that the flames danced dangerously at my fingertips, calling out to Daryn and Varina and setting ablaze a soldier that stood in my way. I didn't care if they were under some sort of influence. Not while they were after my children.

Namaya was beside me, sword out, and soon we were by our children, and I extinguished my hands so that I could grab Varina by the shoulder just as Namaya seized Daryn's arm.

"We are leaving, now!" Namaya somehow got her voice to sound above the chaos.

She gave me a look that read 'and then you and I are coming back to help.' I nodded, and then we led our ten- and twelve-year-old through the rioting streets. Namaya and I never once loosened our grips on the children, lest they slip away in the hoard.

And that's when the sky went dark.

The screeching roar was enough to make your blood run cold, and the enormous shadow that crossed the sky froze even my strength.

"What...is...that?" Namaya and I both were unable to move for a moment as the thing flew over, eyeing the blazing mess with cruel blue eyes.

"Ovok." I barely was able to breathe the words.

Ovok.

"Ovok." I found my lips repeating the words as I startled awake, again. This was getting repetitive. I suddenly regretted pushing away Marion's attempt to help, and all I could do was hope she got better soon, because I needed help...fast.

Wow. That was a little selfish. I felt a twinge of guilt, but it was drowned by the growing panic that I was losing my mind.

With a stretch, I did my best to pretend I was fine and not stuck in a pit of identities that weren't mine. Just focus on the here and now; think about the things around you. Pale light of morning filtering in through the entrance of the cave, and for once, I found the sun was not unwelcome. It was refreshingly cool in here, and the sun actually held a pleasant warmth to it that I rather liked. But why did I feel like I would regret enjoying the cold? Ah yes, because it would only get colder. Was the weather never tolerable in this forsaken country? I turned my attention to where Syvil and Sefen were sitting and talking, Sefen fiddling with some flames dancing in his hands. He'd been careful to keep his Gift hidden in the recent weeks, and yet his old habit seemed to return in the face of our idleness.

I turned my attention to where Jaythos had been the night before and was surprised to see he was still asleep. He really must not feel good— he had always been an early riser. My next stop to observe was Marion, and she also was still asleep. I felt a twinge of disappointment—followed by guilt at the feeling. But I needed help *badly*. I realized that now, and it was getting bad enough that I might just be desperate enough to apologize to the woman for all of my bad manners.

Maybe I could just sift through the memories I had of her and see if I could find all the information she'd talked of knowing.

Then I remembered the searing pain as jaws closed around my neck, and I gasped, pulling out of my head as quickly as I could.

No. I didn't want to see any of her head again. I didn't want to die.

Get a grip, Tanner. Maybe if I told myself that enough, it would work. For now, I would focus on anything that required minimal thinking, and at the moment, that was my growling stomach. Trying to think only of that and nothing else, I wandered over to Syvil and Sefen.

Syvil gave a nod of greeting and guessed my need, pulling some rations from the leather bag beside him.

Stale biscuits and dried meat. Just what I'd always wanted.

"So, when are we leaving?" I asked, after taking a few chomps of the rubbery food.

Sefen shifted uncomfortably, looking to the back of the cave. "We are going to lose a day, at least. Jaythos especially is going to be unable to climb. Marion has use of her arms, but her legs are pretty beaten up. No broken bones, though."

That was a relief, at least.

"When we do get going, however, I think I should take the rear from now on—in case," Syvil added. "As we discussed, though, I cannot carry you all—there are too many patrols looking for us, and there is little cover on the mountainside. We're lucky no one saw us when I caught them."

I scuffed my feet and took another bite of my breakfast, realizing this was going to be a very long day if we were sitting in this cave. Then it hit me. "Wait. What about rations? How are we doing with those?"

"We would have been fine, but depending on how long we have to stay here...." Sefen trailed off meaningfully.

Great. With that information, I decided it best to really savor my food, even if it was disgusting and not fit for a man. Maybe an empty stomach would be just the trick to keep me out of my own mind.

Then Sefen got up. "Maeko is probably spent. I'll go relieve him so he can get some rest." His voice was quiet as he moved towards the cave entrance, and he put a brief hand on my shoulder. Just like he'd always done for his son. I again noticed the signs of fear among the fatigue. I shook the echoes of my dream from my head. I didn't want that.

Go away.

I agonized over the change. Of course, *now* he was realizing—now that it was probably too late and my stupid head was crumbling to ash, did he care. It was almost worse than if he'd never seen at all.

By noon, the other two had woken up, both in a sorry state. Jaythos could hardly move, and Marion refused to go to the mouth of the cave. As much as I was dying to go talk to her, somehow I got the drift that it was a bad time.

At least by evening, she was up and about, her face and arms looking sorely beaten up. Bruises had formed, and her right eye was swollen, but at least the shock appeared to have worn off—probably due to Syvil going and talking to her for hours.

The wind picked up after nightfall, and I already found myself pining for a little heat. I was a fickle thing, wasn't I? I didn't bother figuring out who was the impatient one. Maybe it really *was* me. Wouldn't that be nice?

"We need to leave tomorrow," Jaythos announced, interrupting the conversation the others had been having. I hadn't really been paying attention.

"Tomorrow will be the judge, Jaythos. You need to rest," Sefen countered.

Mouth drawn tight, Jaythos again rotated his shoulder, as if to prove it could function. His hidden grimace was not exactly convincing.

Then Maeko spoke. "Jaythos is correct. We cannot stay here or we will be with no food. And soon we will not have to climb?" He turned to me at this.

I gave a nervous smile, hoping I wouldn't let them all down and get us lost and starved to death. "Yeah. After this mountain, the path will be easier."

Right? Yeah. Yeah, everything would be fine…. The question was: Would I be?

Jaythos:

This was going to be very interesting. I had to admit, though everyone seemed worried that Marion would balk at the idea of climbing again, I wasn't too fond of the idea myself. The last two nights, I had actually had nightmares over the thought of falling again, and now there would be no buffer of sleep to keep the nightmares from reality.

But I also wasn't about to stay here.

The morning sun shone brightly as we stood at the mouth of the cave, Marion standing next to me and cleverly hiding the discomfort she felt at being so exposed. Because that's how we both felt: exposed.

Maeko led the climb, skillfully making his way up the steep rock face as if he had not even the faintest fear of falling. Sefen followed more cautiously behind, leaving only Tanner to go before Marion and I were to start. I was so thankful that Syvil would be taking the rear.

"Are you sure you're up to this?" Marion breathed as she stood next to me.

I gave a very uncharacteristically nervous laugh. "We'll find out."

"Yeah." Her voice was a whisper.

"I will be behind you both, you babies. Get going." Syvil's insult was said in clear jest, hiding the nervousness in his own voice.

What a group we were turning into.

"Oh please, you still have your wings. Get them taken and then see how you like it when you are on a cliff." Marion gave a snort, rolling her eyes at me before turning back to face the dreaded climb. "See you at the top…or bottom," she murmured to me before taking a deep breath. And with that, she started.

Joy. Now I had to go.

My hesitation was nearly involuntary, and I tried to cover it up with the pretense of checking my elbow and shoulder. We'd used some of our packed supplies to wrap my elbow and shoulder in an attempt to keep them from going out of joint again, but even if that worked, this wasn't going to be pleasant. Hopefully it would be more pleasant than starving to death in a cave or being dashed to pieces by the rocks below.

With *that* lovely thought at the forefront of my mind, I at last gathered my courage and climbed out onto the steep rock face.

Even with the expectation of pain, I was not prepared for the searing jolts that skittered up and down my arms. Besides the thousands of tiny needles pricking my elbow and shoulder, my muscles burned and strained under my own weight. But I had to continue, stifling grunts of pain with each inch upward. Every new grip or foothold felt as if it could be my last, but still I went on, encouraged by the fact that Marion was still going, and Maeko's promise that it would soon level out.

But at this rate, I was going to kill him for lying to me, because even after the sun was shining high in the sky, we were still climbing. I started, all too casually, wondering how long it would be until Syvil would be picking my corpse up from the rocks.

Just as I thought that, my left hand reached for a handhold and as I put my weight down, my elbow felt as if it began to separate, causing me to let go abruptly, and therefore, nearly fall. Again.

But my reflexes got the better of me, and I grabbed hold of the out-jutting rock with my right hand, crying out as my shoulder protested to the quick movement and weight that followed.

"Are you alright?" Marion dared look down at me, eyes settling on mine in worry.

"Just great," I grumbled, realizing I couldn't actually move. "Maybe."

"That's it. I'm flying you up quick before anyone sees." Even before Syvil finished his sentence I saw a shadow grow and he had his claws gently around me, catapulting us both the last little bit of distance to the ledge everyone else was resting on. Syvil quickly disappeared, only to return with Marion in his claws.

As he shifted back to his human form, I got a look at where we were, noting with relief that this ledge was not like the last, but instead went on into the mountain as some sort of natural path. The climbing, for now at least, was done. I breathed a sigh of relief, rubbing my shoulder with my other hand and ignoring the pain pulsing from my elbow.

"We should rest," Sefen suggested in a very *un*suggestive way.

For once, I really didn't mind. No one else seemed to either, and we all plopped down on the ground without a moment's hesitation.

"I never got a chance to thank you for catching me." Marion sat down next to me, hiding her stiffness and grimace well as she did so.

I continued to message my shoulder. "Not a problem."

"I find it fascinating how those with one life are often quicker to throw it away than those with two," she mused aloud, her confidence having apparently returned, and with it, her usual composed character. It seemed I was now the one struggling more to get over the fall.

I furrowed my brow. "How do you mean?" In my experience, Syvil had seemed more likely to throw away his life for us, even though we'd been all too willing to leave him behind at first.

She shrugged—winced with regret—and said, "Drogans are always so careful to keep themselves alive. We fear losing a part of us. And some never recover from losing a form." The comment was somber. "But then, you're not even a third of my age, and you risk your only life for me, though you barely know me."

"I don't know...your friend Syvil has thrown his life on the line for us multiple times, even in the short time I have known him," I answered simply, even as I recalled the conversation from the other night.

Marion gave a small laugh under her breath. "That is just how Syvil is." As she said the words, she turned and looked admiringly at her friend. "He always walked the line closer to Human than Dragon. Meanwhile, after losing a form, I simply hid and hoped something would happen." Her expression darkened.

Wow. How was I relating more to these Drogans than I ever had to another living soul? I was beginning to think all the stress was really getting to me. Or maybe it was because I kept filtering everything through Kearn lately. The way I'd left him in favor of saving myself.

"I think you did what you could," I replied at last.

She went to open her mouth, but with the worst timing possible, Tanner came over and interrupted.

"How are you two feeling?" he asked, clearly wanting something else.

"Mending." Marion was the one who replied, a knowing look in her eye as she addressed the boy.

Rocking on his heels, Tanner gave a simple, "Good to hear."

But he didn't move. I got the gist. He wanted to talk to Marion without me listening, but I was not about to move. That would require using my arms, and so whatever he wanted so badly to talk about, he would have to do with me here, or wait until later.

Tanner decided on the former, as it turned out.

"Would you be able to show me that trick?" He asked.

Marion raised an eyebrow, a vaguely triumphant look sparking within. "I am not a Memory Keeper, so I can't exactly show you, but with your ability and my knowledge, I'm sure we can come to an arrangement...even if you need to learn some manners," she added the last bit with an admonishing edge to her tone. Almost as a mother reprimanding her son.

It was most interesting how well she handled him. Like a child; the child I supposed he had been for a while. It was easy to forget that in the times we lived.

"Good." Tanner's response was nervous, and he added a hesitant, "Can we start...um...now?"

Marion winced. "Unfortunately, it would put you in a bit of a vulnerable state, and with the current situation..." She trailed off a moment. "I'm afraid we need somewhere safer to work. Somewhere we have time to go through things. But we will do it as soon as we are somewhere safer."

I'd never seen such open distress in Tanner's face before, nor such panic. But he hid it all quickly. "Alright. Yeah. That sounds like a good plan. Sure," he said, before eyeing me and slipping off to a corner.

"How old is he?" Marion's question surprised me.

I realized I didn't actually know off the top of my head. It took me a moment to reverse-engineer Baey's age against his. "I think, maybe, seventeen?"

The noise Marion made was one full of remorse. "He is an infant."

"More so to you, I suppose. Humans mature a little more quickly than several-hundred-year-old beings, I suspect." But even as I covered up our own faults, I again felt a prick of shame at the thought of how I had treated him. I didn't want to become attached—didn't want to get sentimental when we had so many sacrifices to make. More than that, I was afraid being so would cause me to rule solely from the heart, and I couldn't let another scenario like Kearn's happen. But I found myself wondering why Tanner was so afraid. Was something wrong with the memories? What trick was Marion going to show him?

"Jaythos?" Marion's voice told me I had missed a question.

I turned to her, covering up the thought and replying with a "Hm?"

Now, she appeared perplexed. "You weren't listening?"

No. No, I wasn't, but I wasn't going to just tell her that. So instead, I shrugged, winced, and laid my head back on the rock wall we were sitting up against. I closed my eyes, breathing in a moment of rest.

Marion did not repeat her question, or if she had I had dozed off, for the next words I heard were from Maeko.

"We should get going."

No sooner had he said the words than a shadow fell against the sky.

As if on cue, we plastered ourselves against the walls that hemmed us in, trying to make ourselves as small as possible. The Drogan was enormous, larger than any I had ever seen. Which could only mean one thing....

Ovok.

His dark feathery form completely blocked the sky, lending any shadows we could hide in useless. All we could hope was that he didn't look down and see us.

I knew better than to reach for my crossbow this time, and instead, sat there as still as possible until the shadow that had taken our world passed over and back out of sight. There were no words to describe the relief as he kept on his path, oblivious to our presence.

Tanner:

I was frozen. It was just like that time with Namaya, that night with the children, when everything had been so ruthlessly destroyed.

No! Stop!

I composed myself, reminding myself that I had never been there even as my mind begged to differ, conjuring up the fear and numbness that Sefen had felt.

When at last Ovok was again out of sight, I turned and looked to Sefen, who was pale as the stone around us. Unsure what to do, I looked around to see how the rest were faring, none much better. The only ones relatively unaffected were Jaythos and Maeko, but even they were shaken.

It had just been so unexpected. We'd gone days without seeing a Drogan so close, and to not only see one so close, but *Ovok*.... I shuddered.

"We need to move." Jaythos's announcement was as grave as it was true. Without a word, everyone hurried to get up and we set off again, walking with a careful step and wary eye through the precarious trail. Maeko was a worthy guide, and between that and the map Runin had provided, we made good progress now that we could better trust our feet.

At least the fear of Ovok finding us now drowned out the clamor of my fraying mind.

The next few days were riddled with rain, darkness, and the ever-present fear of being discovered. Ovok had not flown overhead again, but he *had* been heard screeching in the distance. Every time the frightful noise echoed through the mountain, my blood ran cold. And by the faces of the others, so did theirs.

It was three days before the downward descent began. It was not nearly as steep as the climb up, and we were still able to keep upright—though balance was tricky. The new array of trees now scattered about the mountain also helped with cover from peering eyes. These trees were quite different from the tropical-looking ones on the lower part of Rugo, tall and thick with spiny grey needles that pricked and got in your shirt. Not exactly a pleasant alternative, but was there anything on this island that was pleasant? No wonder Maeko was such a…charming person.

Whether hours or days, I could no longer say with certainty, but finally the ground leveled out again. However, this posed a different problem, as we found ourselves between the two mountains. Exposed.

We walked through the night, but no one complained, knowing how precarious it was to be where we were. I was in front with Maeko, helping him now that we were getting close to where my memories would come in handy. We needed to find that path, but the only way I would know how to find it was by going on the main road first. It was risky, but the only way.

And so, that's what we headed for.

The sun had just begun to peek its head above the mountain tops when we came into view of the road. My feet had long since lost feeling, and my boots that had once been a curse in the long-forgotten heat of the city were now battered and torn, hardly fit to be called boots at all. Rags were a better name.

Syvil had turned into a horse-sized Drogan, probably to shift weight and relieve some of his aching limbs. It was also probably because if we were spotted, being in human or Dragon form would not matter. There wasn't enough cover here in this ravine.

We were just about on the road when Maeko stopped, holding up a hand for everyone to do the same. Every hair on my neck stood on end, and I, too, felt the unnatural stillness. Something wasn't right.

"I do give you credit for catching the trap, but it is sprung nonetheless, I am afraid." The chilling voice came from behind us, and everyone turned around, weapons out and ready. Before us stood a man, tall and well-built, greying black hair smoothed back to show two hard, brown eyes.

Syvil and Marion feebly whispered one name, "Ovok."

"You'll all want to put down your weapons, I'm afraid. Sorry about this." He held a wicked looking blade, idly swinging it in his left hand. "But I need what you are looking for. It's not safe in your hands." His eyes settled on me with an icy glare. "Children are not trusted with anything but toys." He then turned and faced the rest. "And neither are fools."

Jaythos's crossbow clicked in warning, but it brought no reaction.

"Ovok. Please." There was a tremor in Marion's voice as she spoke. "You brought us here to avoid bloodshed, I thought."

"There's always more to the story, Marion. Trust me when I say I am trying to do what is best for everyone. Now, put down your weapons before someone gets hurt." He cocked his head, and turned to Syvil. "Isn't that right, Syvil?"

"Do what he says." Syvil's voice was hardly even a whisper of the wind.

Jaythos's bolt whistled past my ear, flying right for Ovok's head. His duck was unnaturally precise, and the projectile instead bounced off the mountain rocks beyond.

"How fun." The tone with which Ovok said the words was anything *but* amused. "Drop your weapons, *now*."

I might even have obeyed, had my grip not been due to fear.

"Do as he says, or we're all dead!" Marion almost shouted the words, fear writhing in and out of her voice like a dying serpent. "Now!"

I dropped my blade and I heard a few others drop theirs as well, but Jaythos and Sefen remained armed.

"Think about this." Ovok's voice cut the air like a scythe. He walked forward as he spoke, his sword dragging the ground and making a wretched grinding sound as it went. "If you don't drop them as well, then the ones who *are* unarmed get killed."

The urge to beg them to obey caught in my throat, the speck of pride I owned keeping them down. But terror was a great moving force as well. I had never been so afraid, nor felt so helpless.

"Tick tock."

CHAPTER XXVI: Disaster Follows Everything

<u>Jaythos:</u>

It took every fiber in my body to convince myself to drop my weapon. This couldn't be the end of the road, it just couldn't. But when I heard Sefen's sword clatter to the rock, I knew the answer. Somehow, my hands allowed me to follow suit, and the echo of my crossbow hitting the ground resounded and died away like the hope of success.

"See, Captain? I told you I could do it without the archers." The smile on Kovo's face was filled with a bitter humor. But it wasn't Kovo. It was Ovok—my brain still agonized over the reality, and the constant reminder was just another shot to the chest.

As if on cue, the two dozen or so men that had apparently been hiding in the rocky outcroppings stood up. I immediately picked out the tall figure of my younger brother. He looked tired.

My fists clenched.

"Of course, My Lord." Kearn jumped nimbly from his spot on a boulder, heading to where Ovok stood, though in clear submission. This was a very different Kearn from the cocky captain I'd seen in Veka. This one was worn and strained.

My fingernails were digging so hard into my palms I thought they might draw blood, the panic of being caught swelling deep in my gut. We'd failed. We were all going to die. At least, that would be the most merciful option. I chanced a look at poor, terrified Tanner.

Ovok waved his sword at us, calling to the other soldiers, "I would suggest tying them up before the stupid ones try something. They always do." He sighed and shook his head, as if recalling such an instance.

The men were quick to follow the order, and we all were given various forms of restraint, Sefen getting full cuffs that encased his hands. Ovok was quite prepared, wasn't he? I heard Marion hyperventilating as she was secured, and Syvil was struggling frantically as three men grabbed hold of him and fettered his hands, feet, and neck.

"No. No, no, no," I heard him mutter as he struggled. He didn't stop until one of the men punched him in the stomach, sufficiently disabling him. I wondered why he hadn't shifted to try and take on Ovok, but then I remembered Hytat. He had no Sven to help him.

Ovok just sighed and shook his head, coming closer to us and taking Syvil's face to make the breathless Drogan look him in the eyes. "I think you've done enough swimming upstream. Don't make me take your form." The menace turned from Syvil to Tanner—who was white as a sheet—and his smile turned sad.

"You are going to have to tell me where it is." The sudden change from cruel to burdened was jarring, and yet somehow equally as sincere.

One didn't have to look to see Tanner was shaking from head to toe. "N-no," he stuttered uncertainly.

Sheathing his sword, Ovok stared the boy right in the face, worried lines now etching the ancient Drogan's face. "Don't make me do something we'll both regret."

"I...I can't." Tanner's voice was barely a whisper.

I gritted my teeth, suddenly freed from my stupor enough to spit out, "Leave the boy alone."

396

A sigh escaped Ovok, but he showed no other reaction to my words. Instead, he made his way back to Sefen, taking the chains that held him, practically dragging Sefen forward despite his efforts to pull against him. "Are you ready to have his death on your hands?" Ovok's expression had changed yet again, emotionless as a rock.

"P-please, don't," Tanner begged.

"Tanner, don't listen to him," I heard Sefen whisper through gritted teeth.

Those were the last words Sefen uttered before Ovok ran him through.

Tanner's scream echoed across the entire ravine even as I stood there, shock almost causing my limbs to give out. Sefen's lifeless body slumped at Ovok's feet, and I couldn't bear to look at the sightless eyes. Sefen.... He wasn't dead. He couldn't be. Not after all we'd been through. I refused to believe it.

"I don't have time to mess around, *child*." Ovok's voice did little to break the shell of shock.

"Monster!" Maeko yelled, held back by no less than four Bethynese soldiers. "MONSTER!"

Ovok's head swiveled in his direction, and those burning brown eyes could have been as deadly as his blade. "Would you like to be next?" That comment only spurred him to look back at Tanner, who had been hoisted up from his knees by two soldiers. "This time it won't be as quick. So, I ask you again, where is it?"

"You *worm*." Every sinew in my body was tense to the breaking point, and I was surprised I could still speak.

With another sigh, Ovok turned to face me, disappointment written all over his face. "Now, that's just insulting. Do you have any idea what a worm does?" He came over to me, grabbing me by the collar and throwing me to the ground. "They crawl. And since you've volunteered to be the next example, I think we can see about making you do just that. You're not too attached to your leg, are you?"

"Stop!" Tanner cried out, voice cracking in agony.

My chest tightened, and I spat out a mouthful of dirt as I struggled to my knees.

"Stop? I really would like to, but you are not giving me an option." Ovok's quiet reply was somehow worse than Tanner's shouts.

His sword came up to my throat and I tried to pull back, nearly falling backward in the process. All I could think of is how much I hoped Tanner wouldn't give in, and the sinking feeling in my stomach as I knew he would.

"Fine! Fine, just stop, please don't!" The boy's cries were anguished, and I felt an urge to stop this nightmare like I never had before. I was helpless. Helpless as always. In one last-ditch effort, I found my gaze lurching to Kearn, who was staring back at me with an unreadable expression. Blank. Unfeeling.

The sigh Ovok now made was relieved, and he swiftly pulled his sword away from my neck. "Thank you, Tanner. Now, where is it?"

I had no one to look to, no one to stop this nightmare for the boy. I found myself still staring desperately at Kearn, looking for any sign of hope—but he had averted his gaze to Ovok.

"I...I can't tell you—exactly, I mean. The memories, they are scattered and hard to say—but I can show you. I *will* show you." Tanner's words sputtered out one after the other, so afraid he could hardly put any words together into a cohesive sentence.

Ovok listened patiently, eyes trained on the boy with a bottomless brown gaze. "Sounds fair to me."

We didn't march that day. Instead, we spent the remainder being more properly secured and separated. Ovok took Syvil, separating him from everyone else and claiming him as liable to suffer consequences should Tanner lie. He claimed Syvil would reappear beside Marion should he die, and thus not only die once, but return to face further punishment, should Tanner disobey.

I was also separated from the rest, though not personally kept an eye on by Ovok. Panic and adrenaline receded, leaving a heavy cloud of defeat and a frightening amount of resignation in its wake. I couldn't get Sefen's sightless eyes out of my head, and now I wondered how long it would be until another of us joined him.

"How long are you going to keep this up?" Kearn's voice was far from a welcomed sound as it sheared through my hopelessness.

I looked up, jaw set, and asked, "Come to gloat?"

In reply, Kearn waved away my guards and stood before me. I noted the hand resting nonchalantly on the hilt of his blade. "Perhaps." The word was simple, and the quietness of it caught me off guard. "Now answer me." His tone turned cold as ice.

"You've already killed my friend. Why don't you go ahead and just kill me, too, while you're at it." My voice never wavered, resolute as I was distraught.

Kearn winced. "I wasn't the one that killed him. Don't put this on me."

The slow grip of bitter anger folded around me, and I clenched my fettered fists. "I'm sorry, what? *Whose* men caught us? Who chained up my friend so he could be slaughtered? Don't forget, you picked your side and knew *exactly* who you were joining."

My brother's expression was hard to discern. Empty, perhaps. Honestly, I couldn't care less in the face of Sefen's death.

"It was *survival*, Jaythos. You may have had plenty of friends to go to, but what about me, hm? All my friends had joined the army, and you knew very well you left me with Mother and Father. What was I supposed to do? Don't forget who left who, Jay." The words were fierce, even if he kept his voice down. "I joined what I thought would bring peace. I didn't want to kill anyone, but I thought if Skayla was going to win anyway, might as well be *with* my country. Tell me, how's your conscience holding up with all the Bethynese soldiers you've murdered? You left me, do you hear me? You *abandoned* me and left me in Bethyn. What else was I supposed to do?"

"Murdered?" The word could barely escape my lips. "At least they had weapons. Sefen was unarmed."

I was satisfied to see Kearn's complexion pale a little bit. "The kid was told he had a choice. And your friend had one, too. And so do you." The statement was firm.

So was my response. "I. Would. Rather. Die."

Kearn's grip tightened on the pommel of his sword. "Fine. Have it your way. You were dead to me years ago, anyway. But don't look to me for help again."

With that, he turned around, flicking his hand to the soldiers who stood just out of hearing. They returned silently, taking their guard without hesitation, watching me with hard eyes. My own people. The pain of our failure mixed with the bitter taste of my brother's words. I sat there the remainder of the night, unwillingly mulling over old memories over and over again, Kearn never leaving them. And now Sefen's face to join.

Tanner:

I felt like I was dying. My chest was so tight I couldn't breathe; my palms were sweating like a soon to be slaughtered pig; and my vision was so blurred I was sure I was going blind. Sefen wouldn't leave my head. I wanted to scream—to get rid of the ghost now forever stuck in my head. All that was left of him now was inside me, and being stuck with it was almost worse than seeing the blade piercing through his chest. I'd gotten him killed; it was my fault.

These dreadful visions filled the darkness of my surroundings, and I was petrified of falling asleep, lying awake and fighting to stop the tears and the pain growing in my chest. But the darkness was just as bad as sleep, leaving reality to the imagination to fill in the shapeless night.

My mind continued to wander, desperate to escape Sefen's memories: his hopes, his fears, the smiling faces of his children. Namaya. An entire family destroyed by Skayla's villainy.

401

Family. The word echoed through my mind, and somehow I lost myself in someone else. Someone else and their family. Or was it me?

"Come on, Kearn, there's other things to life other than swordplay." I smiled, hoping Father's near-oppressive dream for us both to be officers on the Council of Generals wouldn't take too much of a hold. Kearn was bright, and I wished he would try his hand at other things. My hope was to get Father to let me bring him when I journeyed to Rugo to accompany the ambassador.

My brother was always one smirk away from a jokester and a frown away from a philosopher, leaving you to guess at what he was thinking. Sometimes, I thought he really did like the life of a soldier he was being trained for, but at other times, I would see the suppressed spirit within.

"But it's so fun." Kearn rolled his eyes at me, sheathing his practice blade all the same as I also put mine away. We had been sparring for at least an hour. It was my last week here, and I had only two days left before I would leave.

Kearn jogged up to me with his usual energy, and with an arm around him, I led us back to the house, both joking over nothing really. I still feared what would happen if I left, but the excitement at the prospect of getting away was near electric. Bethyn's sense of national pride and duty was unifying and gave a sense of brotherhood, but it was also stifling...like being slowly choked. I feared it would do the same to Kearn.

"So, what's the plan for tomorrow? Something dangerous, I hope?" he asked as we entered the house. The smell of Mother's fine cooking floated through from the kitchen to the hallway, and my brother and I paused to appreciate the sweet fragrance of spices it held.

"Not too dangerous. Jaythos needs to be in one piece to leave, and you need to be rested and able to continue your drills." Mother's voice rang from the kitchen, stoic as ever.

My sigh was genuine, but Kearn's was playful—that, or better hidden.

"But of course, Mother," Kearn cooed back.

"And wipe your feet!" It was as if she could see us as we left the shoe mat and were about to head into the drawing room, boots riddled with mud.

Like toddlers caught in the act of stealing sweets, both of us paused to obey her command. Yes. I had to bring Kearn with me—somehow, I would make my parents come around. Whatever would I do if not?

I hadn't meant to fall asleep, and didn't notice I had until I'd woken up. For a moment, I was in blissful obliviousness, waking to the sun just peeking its head above the mountains. Then, slowly, reality crept back. My swollen eyes, my half-closed throat. I sat up, looking over to see the half-asleep form of Maeko. But then, beyond him...I saw dozens of soldiers littering the ravine.

Oh.

I spotted Kearn almost instantly, walking with determination over to where Marion was being watched. Marion was wide awake, pale, and half-dazed. Kearn stopped by her guards, giving some brief orders and then kneeling down to ask Marion something. He looked perplexed, and was it me, or did I hear Ovok's name whispered? Then he stiffened at her reply, stood up, and ordered the guards to return before walking away. It was hard to associate this hardened captain with the boy I had just seen in Jaythos's memories. *This* man was frightening.

But at the moment, wasn't everything?

I watched stiffly as Kearn then turned and headed straight for us, expression still unreadable. Ever so subtly, I gently began nudging Maeko awake.

Not that he'd *really* been sleeping. The man was up and alert even before Kearn reached us, leaving me to feel even more weak at how I'd given into sleep.

"Get them up and ready to go. We leave in an hour." Kearn's orders were directed at our guards, even as his eyes were trained on Maeko. The hate was palpable.

"Bethynese scum," Maeko growled.

Kearn's gaze hardened even further—if that was possible—and he spat into the dirt at Maeko's feet. "You're just sore because your country gave up without a fight." With that, he pivoted on his heels and went in the direction of some tents that had been pitched last night. Ovok's was no doubt the one Kearn was heading for.

I thought again of Syvil, and how he had been taken by Ovok—taken for leverage in case I failed. His and Marion's terror had drained me of all hope. I knew if *they* were afraid, then Sefen's death was just the beginning. And if his death was the beginning, what came after would be even worse. Worse for us all.

It was a good ten minutes before anyone exited the tent, and when at last someone did, it was Ovok, dragging Syvil behind him. Kearn followed closely. Once out, Ovok handed Syvil's chains to Kearn, and—to my horror—headed straight for me and Maeko.

Bile rose in my throat.

He was in front of me in seconds.

"Alright, Tanner." Ovok's use of my name was so ordinary it sent chills down my spine. "It's time. Don't disappoint. I know the destination isn't more than a couple days away, judging by your rations, so if we don't reach it in a reasonable timeframe, I will have to resort to unpleasant business. You understand, don't you?" Every word was earnest and without falseness or falter, and all I wanted to do was curl up and die. He meant every word, and the fact that he appeared just as reluctant to do any further harm to Syvil was almost worse than if he had approached it with glee.

"But—we were delayed. Our rations aren't accurate—"

"Don't argue. I will know if you're leading me wrong."

My tongue felt swollen and heavy, sticking to my dry mouth like a fly to the glass of a lighted lantern.

Ovok cocked his head in the way Syvil had always done. The movement was so animalistic, so creature-like. "Come on then, up we go," he ordered, motioning for me to get up. Logic and reason were blotted out by the fact that I couldn't breathe. I was going to die. That's what my brain kept screaming over and over. It was what Marion had repeated as the life had bled from her.

Seconds passed before I found myself getting to my feet.

"You were heading for the road, so we take it somewhere. I assume *Vet De Lona*?" the ancient Drogan asked as he stood beside me.

Barely, I nodded. A moment of lucid thinking made me wonder at his familiarity with the landscape, but it was buried with the fact that he knew where we were going. How long had he known? Had it been when Syvil had saved Jaythos and Marion? Or had it been even before that?

"Excellent, then we should reach there by this evening. Horses are wonderful things, I must say, but not quite as nice as wings. Have you ever flown?" Ovok was so conversational, and yet every word he spoke was breathed with a silent death, and the glimmer in his eye proved he knew it.

I swallowed the unbidden memory of an afternoon ride with Namaya. Involuntarily, I brought my hands to my ears, trying to shut it out. Trying to ignore the memories of the man I'd killed.

Go away! Please. Please, just go.

"Tanner?" The voice sounded like Sefen's at first. My horror grew at realizing it was his killer's.

"No. Not flown."

Ovok sighed. "Just as well that you haven't. If you do...it won't be a good sign."

An involuntary shudder ran through my entire body as the fear of falling through the air rang all too clearly in my mind.

We traveled long and hard, but the passing of time had stopped for me as I led Ovok and his soldiers. Leading them astray was out of the question; it was clear Ovok was far too intuitive for such an amateur trick, and I knew what would happen if I did. Syvil's dead-eyed resignation was almost harder to bear than the fear. Once, when I'd stolen a look at him long enough to gain eye contact, he'd given a sad smile of reassurance...only it hadn't been reassuring.

I was weak. I knew—I *knew* The Living Stone was not a fair price. And yet, I had barely been able to watch Sefen die. I couldn't watch Ovok follow through with his threat on Syvil or any of the others. Screams echoed in my head and I knew Sven's nightmares had returned. Only they were becoming my nightmares, now. I was the one responsible for deaths this time.

"I am sorry it has to go this way, Tanner." Ovok's voice was an unwelcome break from the oppressive silence, and I shuddered.

"I'm sure you are," came my tense reply, trying to sound brave even as I continued on the cowardly act of defeat. It was all over, and I was driving the nail in the coffin.

Baey would be so disappointed in me.

Ovok's inhale was somehow an echo of my own torn-up self. "I warned you. No one else has to die. I take little pleasure in making others suffer, no matter how it seems."

"Oh, yeah. Well, I saw what you did to Sefen. What you did to Sven." My jaw clenched.

Ovok's shoulders tensed. "Sven had information I needed. Sefen was a self-righteous idiot."

"You tortured them. You *killed* Sefen!" I yelled, the shout falling away under the ancient anger of my captor.

"You've stolen enough memories, child. You're telling me I'm the only one who's resorted to such violence under extreme circumstances?"

"Don't twist this. You're a monster."

Ovok scoffed, something akin to sadness flashing briefly into view. "Don't label me, child. You don't know me. But remember this; we all become what we fear in the end. What do you fear?"

I forced myself to keep eye contact, shriveling under the hard gaze and the question. I knew what I feared most...but I took comfort instead in the fact I'd struck a nerve, and while I didn't dare test my luck and press the conversation, I couldn't help but wonder: Why *was* Ovok going after The Living Stone? What was the point? They already had the world.

The rest of the day consisted of trying to just...not think. Thinking meant Sefen, and Sefen just brought memories that weren't mine. Bitter memories of what was now lost forever. Dead.

By the time the sun set I could have screamed, wishing nothing more than to be left alone. Wishing nothing more than for Ovok to just leave but no. There was no hope, now, and no Baey to give it. As we stopped for the night, all I could do was look up at *Vet de Lona* as the grand mountain loomed overhead, its ancient stone face casting a shadow over the already darkening surroundings. Just what I wanted: more gloom and despair.

I jolted back to the here and now at the sound of an approaching horse, and soon found Kearn passing me and coming alongside Ovok.

"Make camp. We will begin climbing tomorrow. Keep as few as possible down here with the horses—the boy says the path is too narrow for anything but our feet," Ovok ordered, apparently guessing the captain's intent.

"Yes, My Lord." Kearn slowed his horse to drop back, and a moment later, I heard his voice as he called out to his men. "Prepare to set up camp and secure the prisoners! Yelsi, see to watering and securing the horses. Gvar, watch that the rations are properly distributed. We'll have no opportunity to resupply until we return. Berro, pick a handful of men to remain here with the horses while we are in the mountains." And so went the flurry of orders, my mind lost to the rest as echoes of familiarity rang sharply, reminding me of my own time in the Bethynese ranks. The organization. The respect. The discipline.

Wait, not me. Jaythos.

Remember; we all become what we fear in the end. Ovok's words rang in my head, drowning out the memories that weren't mine, but somehow giving me even less comfort. Was I becoming Skayla? Was I losing it?

I hardly registered being taken to Ovok's tent, away from where the others were being secured. Even as the soldiers drove a spike in the ground to tether me to, I gave no reaction. I felt cold all over, desperate to fight the inevitable and yet not even knowing where to start.

"I assume you will not be wanting your dinner?" Ovok's all *too* casual tone penetrated the dismal silence as he entered, two bowls of broth in his hands. He set one by his cot and came over to where I was forced to sit on the ground.

"You assume correctly, worm," I spat.

Ovok looked almost amused. "I see you have a little bit of Sven in you, as well. Where are *you*, I wonder?"

I froze. "Leave me alone."

"I'm pretty sure you are, Tanner." The Drogan sounded sad, and yet it only made me sick.

I decided the only retaliation I could give instead was to kick the broth over, watching its contents soak into the dirt.

Ovok sighed. "You starving yourself will do just as little to help Syvil as you lying to me." The threat was a dangerous one.

"How do I know you won't just kill them all anyway. You seem to enjoy pain and suffering," I croaked, voice as broken as my spirit.

His expression turned stricken, and the way his fists clenched and he looked almost...distressed was not something I'd expected.

"Do not mistake my desperation for pleasure. I had been trying to stop more bloodshed. If he and Sefen had told me where you all were to begin with, your friend Namaya would never have died. No one else would have had to die."

"She was a traitor, not a friend." The words didn't feel like my own, and guilt welled up in my chest. Perhaps not a friend to me, but a wife and a mother figure to Baey, nonetheless. I didn't have friends.

"So that justifies her death? She *understood* there was no battle left to fight, and she wanted to see her family again. I hope for your sake that is someone else talking and not your own sentiments, because you have just as narrow a mind as everyone else on this planet if that's not the case." He laughed, a cold, bitter laugh. "Your world was so *insufferably* selfish, and you know what? It still is. I think you know it, too. Everyone goes about as if they think they are the only one who has suffered, and the only one who has a right to kill me, or Skayla, or whatever enemy they've contrived. They have no understanding of anyone but themselves. I mean, look at you. Did anyone at Valdon even care about you, Tanner? I can't imagine those with the power of Mind were well received after Skayla's turn. So, how much do any of your so-called friends really care what happens to you beyond what information you give me?"

I said nothing, willing myself to shrivel up and disappear, but no such mercy came to me. Memories of being taken from Tali's house, of my Gift being exposed. Of Sefen deciding they could use me despite the reservations of others at Valdon. The sideway glances I used to get before Valdon's halls were emptier. For the first time in perhaps years, I had flashes of memories I knew were my own, and I hated it. I wanted to shove them back in the corner. I wanted to forget about the isolation and the all-too-clear message that I was a tool, a weapon. An advantage against Skayla that everyone was just using.

"Leave me alone. I'm giving you what you want. Why are you still talking like you have to convince me?" I growled, letting the rage from my childhood rise in my throat.

Ovok didn't turn to face me as he went over to a pile of maps, pretending to look them over a while before replying. "I am simply trying to understand you, Tanner. Because no one is as they seem in this forsaken world."

THE LIVING STONE

CHAPTER XXVII: Failure Is a Bitter Poison, Death a Worse One

<u>Jaythos:</u>

Another night passed in agonizing defeat, forced to watch my wayward brother from afar. I wondered what would have been different if I had defied Father and brought him with me, all those years ago. Or if I'd gone back to take him by force when the war had begun. Would Sefen still be alive? It was a small comfort that he hadn't been the one to drive the blade into my friend's chest, and yet I couldn't help but wonder how willing he would have been to do so, had Ovok asked. It hurt to wonder, and regret tugged at me even as I entered into dreamless sleep.

I woke early and as unrested as the night before. Besides my guards, the camp was completely quiet.

Well, except for Kearn.

And he was coming my way.

Joy.

As he had the other day, he waved the guards away, and I soon found myself alone with my brother as he sat down beside me, handing me a small piece of bread.

"I thought you had given up." I let a little contempt filter into my voice as I spoke. I didn't take the bread.

Kearn let out an exasperated sigh and plopped the meager ration on the ground next to me. When I still gave no reaction, he took out the curved knife that hung by his belt—the one I had given him long ago—

idly cleaning it as if I couldn't just reach over and grab it. Whether meant as a taunt or not, frustration mixed with the longstanding guilt at the reminder that escape was futile. Even if I were to take the weapon, by the time I reached any of the others, I would be caught again, and Syvil would be left to pay the price. Syvil and Tanner, and I was unable to bring myself to add to their suffering in any way.

"Well? Why did you leave?" The question was short and terse, but that's all it needed to be. "I feel I deserve *some* form of explanation."

I didn't reply for a long time. Why did he ask this so bluntly? The only thought that came to my mind was that maybe he wanted closure before…before I was killed. "I had to get out…and I accepted the position because I thought maybe I could bring you with me."

Kearn's work on the dagger came to a halt. "But you didn't, did you?" The reply was sharper than the weapon in his hands, and pierced deeper than it ever could.

"I tried, Kearn." I was defensive now, apprehensive of the way it all fell apart when I explained it out loud. Years of justification melted away under the scrutiny of my younger brother.

Kearn's head snapped to the side and he faced me fiercely. "You *tried*? Does it look like you tried hard enough? It must have been an awfully good effort for me to not even know you wanted to bring me in the first place." He kept his voice low but only barely.

He was right. He was right, and I knew it. "I didn't want to get your hopes up." My excuses grew weaker by the moment. Why was I even bothering? I'd created this mess, created the killer my brother had turned into.

The sound of metal against metal cut sharply through the air as Kearn thrust the dagger back into its small sheath. "Well, you definitely succeeded in *that*."

"And what about my letter?" I shot back.

Kearn just rolled his eyes, getting to his feet and brushing himself off in disdain. "Oh, please. And if I had written you a letter asking for you to return and join me, would you have gone?"

Kearn's look of pain and betrayal brought everything to a head. He was right; I had left him…left him to Father's influence and the army's pressure to stay loyal.

"I'm sorry." The words somehow escaped from the walls of my mind and slipped out my mouth, barely breaking through the tense quiet. The words I should have said long ago instead of fighting my conscience.

Kearn's entire body froze, his intense blue eyes searching me in a mixture of disbelief and desperation. For a while, there was no reply, only searching, and when he finally did speak, his voice was quiet. "What?"

The years of anger towards him continued to melt within me, revealing the hate had never been pointed at him but myself. "I never should have left you," I replied. It was too late, and I knew it. But still I said it.

Kearn's hand came to rest on his dagger, fingers idly massaging the sapphire stone set in the pommel. "Well, you're here now, Jay. Don't you see? Kovo—Ovok—" I caught a briefly perplexed look, as if he was as confused by this revelation as we all had been. As if he still wasn't sure about it. But then he went on. "He's granted hundreds a second chance—with no MindHold. If you come with me, he'll do the same for you. Please, come back. Make this right." The plea broke me, bringing me back to the tearful goodbye when I'd been posted to Rugo. The last time I'd seen Kearn. But I had seen firsthand the horrors Skayla and Ovok had made reality, and the reminder of what Skayla had done to Sven was enough by itself to jolt me into the here and now.

Why was family always so complicated?

But the desperation on my brother's face remained, and as I spoke, I felt I was betraying him all over again.

"I can't. Kearn, I'm sorry. But I can't."

The change in my brother's expression was like an ocean tide. Slow and excruciating, but in time, covering every other emotion that had been there before. When he spoke at last, his tone was harsh and back to the distant, cold captain. "Then you aren't really sorry." His nails dug into the dagger hilt, as if desiring to crumble the sapphire stone to dust. Before I could even formulate a response, he left.

Once more alone, I watched as the camp slowly woke with the sun, wondering how long it would be until Kearn would be ordered to kill the rest of my friends. If he would have to choose between me and loyalty.

At this rate, he might even enjoy ending me. I'd hurt him enough.

"On your feet," Kearn spat in my direction as he passed by, and soon, I was hauled up by the guards. It was only a few more minutes before I saw Ovok lead Tanner out of the tent, the boy pale and weary-looking. But then again, all my companions seemed that way. Marion, Maeko, Syvil...the last of whom was chained more heavily than the rest. To stop him from shifting and flying away, no doubt.

I didn't like the look in his eyes. The resignation. But then...maybe it was the same look in my own. Because what exactly could we do?

It didn't take long for the group to organize. With a portion of the Bethynese soldiers left behind to guard the camp and horses, we set out, Tanner leading the way with Ovok. Kearn took a position behind me, and each of the prisoners were further separated by a soldier, with three or four soldiers up in front to guard Syvil. All of our chains had been exchanged for rope, a choice I imagined was made with the impending climb in mind.

The first leg of the journey started with a tunnel, hidden in the rockface. I was too far back to see exactly how they opened it, but probably some trick of The Crafters. We spent about an hour in the humid, cold tunnel, darkness surrounding us as the way grew steeper and steeper. Then, eventually, we came suddenly back into the light, the midday sun shining unforgivably into our eyes. What laid before us was a path, and looking to my right, I found myself staring down into the emptiness of a cliffside. The only way was forward or back.

The path was just as Tanner had said: narrow and precarious. This was going to be…fun. I wondered which would be better: for us to plummet to our deaths by accident here, or live long enough to see what Ovok would do to us.

Without a word, we continued on.

Slipping was an ever-present threat in everyone's mind, and the constant sound of feet against stone was often accompanied by the echo of some small misstep.

The day was long, and the night brought little comfort. *Vet de Lona* was known as unclimbable for many reasons, and not only would it be a multi-day journey, but resting near impossible.

And indeed, sleeping was as difficult as it was disconcerting. With the only way to rest being to sit on the ledge-like pathway, we were forced to do so, our legs often dangling off the cliffside and into the steep drop-off below. Fortunately, no one rolled off in their sleep...so far. I wondered if Marion had slept at all because of this. I knew I hadn't.

It had been two days into the journey up Mount *Vet de Lona*, and Kearn had not spoken one word. I could feel the hostility seething through him, and every time I heard his footsteps fall on the path, I thought of our conversation and how I had failed him. I looked up at the clouds gathering above us, apprehensive at what that would mean for us. I hated Rugonian downpours enough *without* the added threat of a slick pathway.

As if things couldn't get any worse, it didn't start to rain until the sun had set. So not only could we not see the path very clearly, but the path was also extremely *slippery*. Not to mention the usual torches could not be lit to help us see the way.

And yet, we didn't stop. My guess was the path was almost too narrow, and therefore impossible to rest even if we wanted to. Besides, with all of the rain, it was possible one could slip merely by trying to sit down.

The rain fell in torrents, and any thought other than that entailing my next step was drowned out, leaving me straining in the dark to wonder if every step would be my last. I felt Kearn holding onto the back of my shirt, and wondered if he was doing it to keep his own balance, or to steady me.

And that was when a scream pierced the air.

Marion.

I couldn't see, but without thought or consideration I lurched forward, desperately trying to get to her.

She was falling. She was falling again.

The soldier blocking my path nearly fell off the edge as I tried to make my way up to the front, and I was forced back by Kearn.

"Jaythos, stop it, you'll kill us all!" Kearn's shout was lost on me as I struggled; for now I could just make out the scene ahead.

Marion was barely holding on by the fingertips of her left hand as she dangled from the edge of the path, the terror in her eyes somehow visible through the condemning gloom.

I struggled harder, feeling both Kearn and myself begin to lose balance. "Let me go! She's going to—"

Before I could even get the words out—before anyone else could try and give her a hand—she let out one more scream and fell.

"Marion!" My scream pierced the callous night, echoing against the rain and darkness.

<u>Tanner:</u>

"Marion!" I cried out as I saw her and the soldier behind her slip. There was only a little space between us, and I turned completely around and tried to backtrack to her, but just as I was close enough and reaching out a hand to offer to Marion, she gave a shriek and fell. In a last-ditch effort, I lunged for her hand—though it disappeared only a moment after leaving the ledge—and felt myself falling after her as I did so. That's when I felt someone grab me by my waist arm, pulling me back onto the ledge after getting a firmer grip on both arms.

It was Ovok.

Shock overwhelmed me, but somehow, nearly unconsciously, I knew this would be my only chance. Something in that twisted head of his had to be of use, and this would be the only chance at getting it. Marion was dead, and he would pay. I allowed the memories to flow through him and into me, gasping at the sure weight and not fighting it anymore.

The last thought I knew for sure belonged to me left an aching hole inside.

Marion was dead.

I stood there in the dark room, the door shut behind me. No one knew I was here—no one even knew that I was aware of what had happened. I'd flown here expecting to discover why exactly a person as good as Tyron was participating in experiments with the world's essence in a way even I was loath to try. Instead, I had arrived just in time for my daughter's funeral.

Oh, Rhioa.

From where I stood, I could see nothing but the shadow of the bed in the center of the room, the body shielded from light by the drapes around the bed as well as the curtains over the windows.

I breathed out, not having felt this distraught since I had seen what Dyress had done to Kassander. But even that was nothing compared to this pain.

With one more breath, I walked forward, my footsteps echoing hollowly around the room like the sorrow banging against the walls of my heart. I could see her now, my Little Rhy. She was so still, her hair tucked neatly behind her as she lay on the bed, awaiting her final resting place.

"Oh, Rhy," I breathed, wishing this once I could stoop low enough for tears—but those had not come for centuries. Instead, just the emptiness would suffice.

I took her hand, the limb cold with death. She had been so happy—happier than I had allowed her to ever be—and so I had let her go with Tyron. Against my better judgement, I had let her go. And now? Now she was dead. Not just her Dragon form, but this one also.

Releasing her hand, I caressed her forehead, pushing back a stray hair that had fallen in her eyes. Bending down, I kissed her gently on the head, wishing she would come back to me. Wishing I had been better. Then I felt it.

The pulse.

Surely, the essence of this world would not stay in something that was dead, so why did I feel its presence here? Suddenly feverish, I searched out her hand and pressed to find her pulse. She was dead—she had died days ago! Why was I allowing my grief to delude me?

*I stood there in agonizing silence, waiting for something—anything—
to happen. Nothing. In a pathetic, last-ditch effort, I laid my ear to where
her heart was, just in case. Moments passed, but just as I was about to
give up and finally resign myself to reality, I heard it. I waited longer, sure
I had imagined something, but sure enough, the sound repeated itself. It
was far away and terribly slow, but it was there. Somehow, it was there.*

Rhioa wasn't dead.

I gasped, bolting upright and trembling. Sweat poured down my face,
and at first, all I saw was darkness. Then, slowly, my vision cleared, and
I found that, in fact, it wasn't the middle of the night but instead afternoon,
the sun shining right in my eyes. Where was I? What was happening? I
felt numb all over, and for a moment, I forgot that what I had just
experienced was not my own memory.

Then, like a good Rugonian downpour, it all came crashing down.

Marion.

Grief overwhelmed me, but before I could properly process anything,
I heard a nearby voice break the silence.

"Finally, you're awake. Did you find what you were looking for?" The
voice was cold and dangerous, clearly knowing what I had done.

Ovok.

CHAPTER XXVIII: Can a Ghost Be Alive?

<u>Jaythos:</u>

Marion. The look on her face before she had fallen was imprinted in my mind, melding with the time we had fallen together. But this time...this time, no one was able to save her. I'd begged to try and strain for a glimpse to see if she had fallen on some out-jutting ledge, but the rain had clouded any hope of searching, and Ovok had ordered us to hurry on, several of the other soldiers having barely avoided Marion's fate.

The path at last widened out not far ahead, and we found some shelter under a rock formation and stopped for the night. But Marion's terror was all I saw.

Even into a nightmare she followed me, her eyes wide with terror as I reached for her, just out of grasp to save her as she flailed into oblivion. And then she turned into Kearn, my sins and failures coming back to haunt me.

I was startled awake by another cry, this one real and tangible. Tanner. Seeing the panic-stricken boy, I scrambled up in some stupid desire to help, but was immediately yanked back down by Kearn, who sat beside me as guard while his men slept.

I turned and frantically looked for Maeko, suddenly wondering if I would wake to find yet another friend dead. But I couldn't really feel any relief as I laid eyes on him a little ways off, clearly deep in his own grief as he stared into empty space, oblivious to anything around him. I wondered if he was preparing himself for whichever of us was next to join Marion.

"Finally. You are awake. Did you find what you were looking for?" Barely, I heard Ovok's words filter down from where he and Tanner sat.

Tanner. He'd passed out after Marion's fall. What did Ovok mean, find what he was looking for?

Suddenly, I realized what had happened to Tanner. He had gotten ahold of Ovok's memories and must have passed out from the effort.

I was impressed, but any of that emotion quickly died away and left fear in its wake. Was Ovok going to punish Tanner for such a bold move? I didn't think I would live with myself if I had to watch…. I strained to hear the rest of the conversation, unsure how I would even stop Ovok if he *did* try something. Something inside me tore as I wondered if I would need to watch every single person here suffer—if Kearn would fight to keep me alive and I would be the only one to survive. Or the last to die.

"I suppose Marion's death is enough penance for now. But try that again, and…well, you've been in my head. You know quite well what I'm willing to do." A chill ran through my body at Ovok's words. I just wanted him to leave Tanner alone. And now that was even more impossible than ever. If Tanner really had taken his memories, I couldn't even imagine what Tanner must now have living in his head. Again, I thought of just how easily I'd brushed him aside—how easily we all had. Now the only person who hadn't was dead.

And yet I saw the way Tanner's eyes moved to Syvil, who was just beyond them, propped up against the stone wall and paler than a corpse. He had hardly reacted at all since…since Marion had…I tore my eyes from the Drogan, trying not to think how Syvil had just lost the only friend he had left who wasn't in a MindHold.

"Now, rest up, Tanner. Let's try and avoid anyone else being tired enough to trip, shall we?" Ovok remarked casually, getting up and walking over to check on Syvil's restraints.

Rations were soon given out, and then we resumed the march up the mountain, the path now safer between the fact that the path had dried out after the rain and that the sun was now out to illuminate the way. Some of the soldiers picked up small talk among themselves to pass the time, and everyone acted as if Marion hadn't just fallen to her death. As if so much blood hadn't already been spilt. As if they weren't letting Ovok torment a child.

Another day, more endless, mind-numbing travel. By evening, we reached an even wider path, and so we camped there for the night.

"How many more have to die before you'll listen to me?" Kearn's question came from next to me.

"For once in your life, Kearn, be quiet." I would have regretted the words sooner if I was not so clouded with grief and his lack of sympathy.

"You're *my* prisoner, Jay. Don't forget that." His words were brittle and sobering.

I gritted my teeth. "How could I?" The earlier guilt in regards to my harsh words melted away as he so eloquently reminded me that he was, after all, on the wrong side. For all I knew, he could be enjoying the grief we all were trying to stifle.

I continued to wrestle with myself, reliving Marion's final moments over and over in my head as I tried to come to grips with reality, bringing me back to the feeling I had carried when this all began so many years ago. The feeling of a bad dream that one could never wake up from.

"How long did you know her?" Kearn sat down beside me, tone breaking from the callous to at least pretending to care. I didn't know if he actually did, and I wasn't really sure it mattered to me anymore.

"I am sorry, Jaythos. But it isn't like any of us pushed her off the cliff. Perhaps if you had—"

"Don't even try to justify it," I growled. "She's *dead*. Right alongside Sefen. One of many casualties because of *you* and who you follow."

"And so are hundreds that your friends have forced me to bury." Kearn was equally vehement.

I said not another word, only staring out into the darkness.

We were almost there...I knew it. The path had grown less steep and was wider, for one. But it was that feeling of defeat that truly told me. The closer we got, the worse it became, and now it was an ever-present thunder in my ears.

By noon, we had arrived at the stone Tanner had described. It was a strange thing, carved with some form of family crest: a castle, crossed with a feather and a dagger. Above the castle was a tree, alive and blooming at the top and withering away at the bottom.

"This is it." I could just hear Tanner's voice from where he stood by Ovok. He sounded so frail...so lost. My heart sank lower into despair. The poor kid.

"Where is it, then?" Ovok's question was not challenging but calm.

We were all crowded around the rock with the crest, and I spared a look at the rest of our tattered and weary group. They all looked...equally horrible. Maeko was as a stone, cold and lifeless, his fists clenched at his side. Meanwhile, Syvil never raised his eyes from the ground, and his shoulders were hunched in something worse than despair.

"Could I have the key?" Tanner looked pale and small, hands fiddling with the secure ropes that held him.

Ovok didn't hesitate, pulling the thing from his coat pocket and handing it to the boy.

Tanner's eyes clouded over for a moment. When he returned, his eyes looked just as far away, and without a word he knelt in front of the rock with the crest. Holding the key in front of him, he traced the carving with his free hand, slowly stopping on the feather's point. He pushed the edge, and it sunk in ever so slightly, groaning as it heeded Tanner's touch. At the same time, it sank, the blossoming tree above it emitted a cracking sound as some dust flew from it, revealing a keyhole.

With a sigh, Tanner slowly placed the key in the hole, turning it in a full circle. The rock wall to our left in turn cracked and scraped as it dislodged, pulling behind itself to reveal a door about three or four times the size of a man. The door was very clearly The Crafters' work, riddled with gears and cogs that shone in the noon sun.

Tanner removed the key, walking over to the door and turning to the rock wall still intact just to its left. He pressed something I couldn't quite

427

see, and another keyhole appeared. He placed the key in this one, and once again turned the key full circle. As he did so, the gears in the door began to turn, creaking with the years of disuse. Then, for all of that effort, a small door opened from within the larger doors—this one an ordinary size.

"Complex little toy, isn't it?" Ovok mused aloud as he stepped forward. "Better come, we don't have all day." And with that, he led us all into the mountain.

Our failure was nearly complete.

Tanner:

We walked into the long dark hall, the door remaining open behind us.

"Keep two of your men at the door," Ovok ordered Kearn. "If you and I aren't the ones to return, order them to kill on sight."

My fingers tapped restlessly against my leg, but I was tired of trying to wonder whose habit that was. I knew I wasn't me. I knew I wouldn't be me. I doubted there was even much of me left, and clearly the part of me that was left only got everyone else killed.

I had walked only about two more steps after this before I felt the tile I had just put my foot on sink. Before I had time to speculate and panic, there was a click, and the hall was suddenly drowned in light as lanterns that had apparently been lining the wall lit themselves.

Oh. That was nice. I should have known better than to think Henry or Alenor would have placed boobytraps.

"Interesting." Ovok's voice echoed down the seemingly endless hall, bouncing off the tall arched ceiling until it made everything feel as vast and empty as the feeling inside me.

We walked down the hall, the warmth of light from the lanterns falling short of making the mountain feel anything other than a cold tomb. What was this place? The further along we went, the larger it became, and soon doors and side corridors began popping up on either side of us. Memories pulsed all around me, each footstep begging me to give in and absorb the long-forgotten tales in this ancient mountain. But too many other memories were tugging in my mind, constantly wrenching me in all directions and wrestling for control. I couldn't afford any other memories...I was getting worse—less focused and less able to keep on task. Acquiring Ovok's memories had been a terrible idea. I had never taken on three thousand years' worth of memories—not from a person, anyway. It was hard to remain in the here and now.

Keep it together, Tanner. I realized that I'd lost hold of the memory I needed. I stopped, the rest following suit, trying to breathe and calm myself—and not think about Syvil, who stood there, tied like some animal. All he had ever wanted was to be free. I had seen the memories...he and his other Drogan friends talking late into the night in the old days, where ancient and modern forces alike were on their side, sharing knowledge and not hunting them down to destroy their race.

"What is he doing?" Kearn was barely keeping his patience. I realized I had allowed myself to drift again. Just what we needed.

Ovok put a hand on my shoulder, even as he answered the captain. "Breathe, Kearn. If there is something I have learned in all my years, it is the art of patience." His grip tightened ever so slightly, and my breath caught with the tension. "And resolve."

I wasted no more time in getting the pair of spectacles out of my pocket and using it to aid in retrieving the more exact memory of direction.

"This way." I continued straight again, the way now clear once more. We traveled only a few more steps before turning left into another corridor. This one's arched ceiling was not quite as high, but neither was it small or unlit, and we continued down much the way we had in the main hall. Then we came to a door, clearly from a time before The Crafters or any of their fine inventions. *This* door was wooden, carved with strange and wonderful depictions of light and it being given to a people—most likely the people who had made this place. I grabbed hold of the metal latch and tried to open the door, the hinges clinging stubbornly to each other like the rusted companions they were. I pulled harder, but to no avail, and eventually Ovok had to help me. Together, we got it, and with a sickening squeal the door flew open, nearly knocking me off my feet and right into Ovok. Fortunately, my feet were just steady enough to keep from such a terrible fate.

"Shall we?" Ovok's smile was small, but against the lantern light, it appeared huge and savage, something desperate in his eyes. I thought again of the memory of Rhioa. And then of Ovok. Such a monster should not be allowed to love. Funny thing was, that thought didn't seem mine...but...maybe Ovok's?

I shook my head, desperately trying to stay focused. I had to. For Syvil.

And so I did.

We passed through the door, and what greeted us on the other side was not exactly what I had expected. And yet...at the same time...familiar.

It was *huge*. We had entered into some sort of cavern, the ceiling rising indefinitely and the space even wider. I gawked, trying to figure out how something of this size could fit inside the mountain, even as my mind made calculations as if I actually knew what I was doing. We hadn't even been near the bottom, and I hadn't *felt* a downward slope anyway.

But those technical thoughts were drowned out by the ones full of wonder as I stared at this underground abandoned city. There were houses everywhere, carved into the walls as well as lining carved-out streets. The houses themselves were elaborate, with pillars and grand windows—void of glass panes—gracing each dwelling. What stunned me further was how nothing appeared to decay. There were some wooden bits for houses or booths, but nothing was rotting or crumbling. It was as if it had been built yesterday.

Of course, wonder soon turned to reality as I remembered who I was here with, and so I took a deep breath and began navigating us through the vast city, wishing I wasn't leading Ovok to the heart of our world.... This was the end. Perhaps Namaya had been right.

We wove through the streets, the memories so thick I could practically see them. It was frightening at first—something I had never experienced before—but truly, as we went further in, I could see silhouettes of people walking up and down the streets, talking to neighbors or buying fruit in the marketplace. There was a power here I had never felt before, and I knew we were getting close to The Living Stone.

"Wait, Castyle! Please, come back!" The shadow of a girl ran after a boy, passing through us as we walked. I jumped nearly a foot in the air, eyes wide.

"What is it?" Ovok's voice had a filter of concern, though I knew it wasn't for me.

I took a deep breath. "Sorry. Memories here are very vivid," I murmured, keeping myself from following the forms of the two as they faded into fog the further away they went. It was as if this mountain was a living history book one could just sit and watch.

But I couldn't.

I tried to ignore everything going on around me, to ignore the nagging and prodding to allow myself to be carried away to the past. When the here and now was such a nightmare, I longed to just give up and go. Perhaps I would become so engulfed in the memories that I would never return—and Ovok could never reach me. But even if I was able to, I couldn't just give in. Not with my friends left behind.

"This way. We have a bit to go, yet." I returned to the task at hand as quickly as I could, reminding myself over and over why I was here. Memories brushed past me on every side, but at last, I was focused enough to stop any further faltering in my mental step. But the shadows were all around me, running back and forth, talking with one another, and startlingly, even running in panic, as time held no bounds on the memories.

We made our way through all of this to a large, majestic-looking building carved from the mountain wall. The pillars lining either side of the carefully chiseled doorway were elegant, looking like marble. Baey would have been lost for words at how expansive all this was, but instead

I was here, wondering how she'd take our failure. Sefen's death. Would anyone be able to tell her? Were we all about to die?

There was an acute humming that drove through every vein of my body as I crossed the threshold, but the feeling wasn't exactly unpleasant.

"Aha. We are close." Ovok's tone was satisfied as he no doubt felt the pulse of power.

Yes, yes, we were, and it terrified me. This power I felt coursing through me was about to fall into the hands of the most frightening being on Baeno. A little cliché-sounding, but true nonetheless. I thought again of Baey and all the others. What were we doing to them? What would happen once Ovok got the stone? As I took each step forward along the long and arching hallway, my dread and guilt grew until it was almost overwhelming. The shadows around me acted more like the haunting ghosts of those I would doom by what I was doing. And yet still, I led on.

Which is why it startled me so much when my feet suddenly came to a halt, almost causing Ovok to run right into me.

"What is it?" he asked simply. Dangerously.

I saw the shadow vanish from behind the giant pillars that lined either side of the hallway, and for a moment, I could hardly breathe. But then I snapped my eyes away and realized my gaze would only draw Ovok's to where they led. "Nothing. Another memory." I mumbled the lie seamlessly—at least, hopefully seamlessly—knowing any chance of getting out of this depended on me not giving away the shadow that was now following us.

Marion.

Jaythos:

The stupid kid. I knew he couldn't help it, and I knew I would do the same, but that didn't mean he wasn't stupid for doing it. We were now about to hand over the most powerful thing on our planet to a monster psycho. My mind reeled with a thousand different ways to create a last-ditch escape effort, but every single one fell short. There would be no escape this time, and we all knew it.

When Tanner stopped, however, some gut feeling tugged at me. Like the others, I followed his eyes, but just as before, there was nothing there. At least, that's what I thought.

"No more stopping. Unfortunately, we do not have the time, and we don't need you getting lost in the ancient memories of this place." Ovok sounded neither patient nor impatient, but still, the point was made.

We moved on, and that's when my keen eyes finally caught a glimpse of what Tanner had seen. I forced any trace of alarm or shock out of my expression, as hiding in the mountain's shadow stood Marion, looking fiercely determined. Determined, but most importantly...alive. Well, alive but motionless as she sat in the shadows. Hope pulsed stronger than The Living Stone's presence, and yet the feeling was almost more painful than the defeat it had chased away.

At last, we crossed the entirety of the hall and came to a much larger doorway. Intricate markings were carved along its border, but none of them were in a language that was familiar to me. Ovok stepped in front of Tanner now, going up to the entrance and tracing the strange language.

"Kearn. You and your men stay and watch your brother and the others. I will take the Drogan and the boy."

Syvil flinched.

Kearn didn't appear pleased with this arrangement. "Is that wise, sir?" He asked with a respectful nod. As if doubting Ovok was fine as long as he did it respectfully.

I could have snorted in contempt—but perhaps I was just sore at him to begin with.

Ovok, in the meantime, arched his eyebrow in interest, but replied patiently, "Yes, thank you for your concern."

And so, while Maeko and I were secured, Ovok disappeared with Syvil and Tanner. I dreaded to think what Ovok might do.

"Did you hear that?" One of the soldiers nearly jumped three feet as something echoed down the halls. It was faint—almost a whisper.

I turned to Kearn and smiled coyly. "Perhaps it's your guilt come to haunt you."

Of course, he just bit back with, "Are you sure it's *mine?*" Though he was quickly distracted as the distant sound became a rising moaning.

"Iarin, take five men and scan the area." Kearn's tone betrayed his own unease, and I couldn't help but smile a little at it.

Iarin didn't appear pleased, and yet knew better than to argue an order. Interesting that Kearn allowed his soldiers to even show something like displeasure. No shouting, no punishment. Just brief eye contact and then eventual obedience.

The echoing whisper turned into a moaning, bouncing off the halls endlessly until it was overwhelming. Marion made quite the wailing banshee, I had to say. It didn't help that shortly after the small search party departed, a piercing scream interrupted the moans, causing even me to jump and wish I could cover my ears. A shiver ran down my spine.

"What in Baeno?" Even Kearn looked scared half out of his wits as he muttered the words, hesitantly taking his hands from his own ears.

I did the same just in time to hear a different cry—this one different. This one from a man.

"Varn, Yelsi, Gvar, and Beyn, stay with the prisoners. The rest of you, come with me." Kearn's expression was perplexed as he gave the orders, hand on the hilt of his sword as he and the others headed warily down the hall.

Silence.

Maeko and I just looked at one another.

"What do you think it is?" Varn, probably the youngest of the four men left behind, asked shakily.

Gvar replied almost too quickly, "Nothing but the wind and our imaginations," and then proceeded to rub his neck like it was home to a noose.

Meanwhile, Yelsi rubbed his arm with an open nervousness. "If you believe that, then there's something wrong with your ears. You saw how the boy kept stopping before. It was like he was seeing ghosts...."

That's when my eye caught sight of Marion, her eyes almost glowing in the dim light of the strange lanterns that illuminated the city and its halls.

"Where are they? They should be back by now—why aren't they back?" Yelsi shifted his weight from one leg to the other like a fidgety mare, fingers tapping feverishly quick.

That's when the fire started.

All around us in a perfect circle, flames burst from the ground, causing all of the guards to jump three feet at least. Marion must have grabbed some of the lanterns.

"You will pay. You all will pay." The voice was eerily calm and infantile. Even I had shivers running down my spine.

Then, with ghostly grace, Marion appeared, walking through the flames calmly and entering the small circle. The four men all had their swords out and at the ready, but at the sight of her, they almost all began to shake. In fact, Yelsi dropped his altogether and ran in a panic.

And, to be honest, Marion was such a ghastly sight I didn't blame them. She was covered head to toe with mud—every inch of her so that she looked ghoulish. Her eyes reflected every ray of light with vengeful glee, and as she pointed a single finger at the remaining three, she whispered, "You will pay. All of you."

That was enough for Beyn, who promptly fled after Yelsi, shouting for Kearn. With him gone, Marion made a sudden lunge at Varn, and the other two of us jumped up to help her.

There was a brief struggle, but Marion had so beautifully painted the mood that the remaining two men were almost too overcome by shock to fight back. Marion disarmed Varn and knocked him senseless while Maeko had a firm grip around Gvar's neck and was mercilessly choking him.

"Stop!" I didn't know what was coming out of my mouth, but it got Maeko's attention enough to loosen his grip, just in time for Gvar's eyes to roll back in his head as he passed out on the cold stone floor.

Maeko cocked his head at me, but I only thrusted my bound hands out to Marion. "Who knows when Ovok will return, let alone what he might be doing to Syvil and Tanner."

Marion wasted no time in cutting the bonds with a knife she'd gotten from one of the soldiers, and I had only just time to whisper, "It's good to see you alive."

She only scoffed and ran over to Maeko to help him. But I could see her shaking hands. "Yeah, don't make me do that *ever* again," she growled.

Taking up Yelsi's abandoned sword, I made for the doorway Ovok and our other friends had disappeared through.

"We need a plan," Maeko whispered harshly, barely loud enough for me to understand from where I was.

"Too late. We need to get out of here before the others come back," was all I could think to reply.

"Yes. Free Syvil and we have a chance." Marion hurried after me, followed by Maeko.

We would need a Drogan if we wanted to go up against Ovok, and the shaking Syvil appeared to be the best we had.

The doorway apparently led into a long—albeit much smaller—hall, the orbs lighting our way as we ran down it. No wonder Ovok had not heard the commotion—this place was endless.

"Tricks won't work on Ovok," Marion murmured from behind me.

I was fully aware, as was everyone else, and yet, we had to do something.

"We *need* a plan," Maeko insisted. My adrenaline was pumping, and in that moment, I just wanted to run as fast as I could to stop Ovok.

Breathing hard, I muttered, "Fine. But it needs to be quick. He could be about to kill them for all we know." I didn't bother to hide my tension; everyone felt it.

CHAPTER XXIX: The Living Stone

<u>Tanner:</u>

We stood there a long while, just staring at it as it sat there on its crystal pedestal, basking in its own emerald light. I remembered it; remembered holding it and its glow in my hands. Of taking it like a thief in the night. Of hiding it away where my Skayla couldn't find it.

"Fascinating," Ovok mused aloud, deepening the mesmerizing spell.

It was a thousand shades of green light, bound together inside a stone that was littered with bronze and gold gears, each turning at different rates and yet still somehow working together in unison. It was as if it were a heart, pulsing with each mechanical beat.

And then Ovok reached for it, and the spell was broken.

"What are you going to do with it?" My voice was hoarse as I watched his wicked hands wrap around either side of the melon-sized stone.

Ovok scoffed. "You've been inside my head. You know very well why I need it." The green light illuminated his face as he turned to look at Syvil and me, smiling slightly. The lack of the menacing grin one would expect only made the smile seem more unnerving. "Are you just afraid of what the answer would make you think?"

He wasn't wrong. But neither was he completely right. "If she needed it so badly, why didn't you just show up and ask? Maybe we would have been able to help." My voice gave way to frustration and desperation.

Ovok shook his head, seeming to grow in the power he held. "Come on, Tanner. The people in your world have never looked beyond themselves to help another. Not even *you* trust them—and you're supposed to be on their side."

A lump formed in my throat.

"Stop! Ovok, please!" The voice sounded absolutely terrified as it rang through the tall oval chamber. All three of us turned to the entrance just in time to see...to see....

"Oh, Marion." Ovok shook his head in disappointment. "If I were you, I would have just stayed dead."

There was an unearthly roar, and suddenly Ovok began to swiftly grow and change: hair becoming deadly black feathers with silver-white tips; hands becoming claws; teeth becoming fangs; and the sword in his hand becoming one with his claws. I had seen Syvil change, but something about Ovok's was different—spellbinding and yet terrifying. I stumbled back as I realized he would soon engulf me with his monstrous size, and the room that had seemed so expansive before was suddenly much smaller as Ovok took up more and more of the space. Still, there was enough room for him to fly, and already he crouched, one scaly claw clutching The Living Stone as he looked about to take off. Then I realized he was also about to scorch Marion out of existence, and in that moment, I found myself yelling her name. I hadn't even wrapped my head around the fact she was alive, and now she was the idiot who was just standing there, about ready to be burned dead.

And that's when Syvil, in Drogan form, lunged at Ovok, small as he was. A hand grabbed my shoulder as the two beasts began flailing about, and I was yanked out of their way just in time. Confusion, shock, and...well...confusion...stopped me from processing anything but the

Drogans locked in combat, one clearly outmatched by the other. But Syvil had one advantage: free hands.

I realized the person who had grabbed me was undoing my bonds, and the person who had pulled me back was none other than Maeko. My eyes would have fallen out of my head had I opened them any wider.

"Jaythos! Your brother's coming!" Marion called over from…somewhere.

"How—how did—"

"No time. Survive first. Is there any other way out?" Maeko kept a hand on my shoulder as he spoke. I glanced around, noticing Jaythos nearby with Bethynese weapons. But I forced myself to focus on the memories of this powerful place—beyond the chaos and imminent danger of the dueling Drogans.

"Yes. But it's all the way across the ro—"

That was about when Kearn and his men burst into the room, seething with rage and panic. Meanwhile, Ovok and Syvil threw themselves at each other, hovering yards above the ground now as they fought over the stone. The screeches from Syvil each time Ovok landed a blow or bite were ear-splitting.

"Lead the way, Tanner." Jaythos twirled his sword with deadly skill as Kearn and his group ran for us. I didn't hesitate, running as fast as I could in the opposite direction, trying to find a way to stay out of the Drogans' path of chaos.

"We can't leave Syvil!" Marion shouted as they all followed.

I heard something along the lines of "And we won't, but we have to get to an escape route first—" right before an arrow whizzed by my ear. I may or may not have screamed…a little. I was very done with stress, and yet I knew nothing was going to change. We were all probably going to die, and it was about time I sucked it up and stopped acting like a selfish little toddler.

"Keep going!" Jaythos shouted as we dove for the cover of a rock. He remained in the open, and soon, the sound of metal against metal echoed about the chamber, mingling with the screeches and growls of the warring Drogans above.

"Take this." Marion shoved the hilt of a short sword in my hand after only a moment of crouching behind the sanctuary of stone.

I looked at the sword only a moment before my grip tightened with determination. We weren't surrendering this time. No. It was escape or death, and looking in Marion's and Maeko's eyes, I could see they were thinking the same thing.

"Ready?" Marion looked at both of us, eyes piercing in a fierce desperation.

And with that, we burst from cover, a few crossbow bolts barely missing us as we ran into the fray. Both Maeko and Jaythos were barely holding ground, but with our reappearance, Kearn and his men—who had apparently been slightly thinned since only half an hour ago—lost their clearer advantage. But still they had someone using Jaythos's crossbow, and as I battled for my life, I saw Maeko narrowly avoid a bolt to the shoulder, losing his balance and falling forward in the process. Barely did I regain focus in time to dodge my opponent's blade, and I almost fell over from the abrupt move I had to make.

I somehow dug up the strength within and escaped the sword again coming towards me—making a sprint right for Maeko and barely in time to block the blow that was meant for his head.

But I was outmatched, and I was fortunate Maeko recovered himself in time to save *me* from the Bethynese soldier's deadly strokes.

Then a blood-chilling screech nearly ruptured our eardrums as Syvil screamed, and for a moment, the entire fray stopped right in the middle as we looked up to see Syvil clinging stubbornly to Ovok as the bigger dragon bit at his neck with his savage teeth. I watch in horror, wishing to scream out for them to stop. Then, somehow, Syvil dug his claws deep into Ovok, and the latter let out a roar more akin to annoyance as he released his prey for the moment.

Moments before the terror was broken and we resumed fighting, however, I caught a glimpse of something falling from Ovok's grip in his shock, and Syvil—bleeding and failing as he was—dove for The Living Stone as it plummeted downwards.

Jaythos:

It was a good thing the coward who had stolen my crossbow couldn't shoot to save his life, and it was a good thing for him I decided to spare it, for in the seconds of distraction from the Drogans, I made a run for him. The look in his eyes was priceless as he realized, too late, I was not bound in the same spell as everyone else, and I leaped upon him before he could even get halfway to loading the thing.

We grappled desperately on the ground as he tried to choke me, both equally unwilling to die. I didn't want to kill *him* either, though, and so was frantically trying to come up with some sort of way around it. As my breath escaped me, I somehow got a hold of a knife in his belt, and forcing hesitation from my mind, drove it into his arm. He screamed, fortunately at the same time as Ovok. I had gotten the upper hand, and before he could even block out the shock of pain, I had him in a hold that was much stronger than his. He was passed out in seconds, and by that time the battle on the ground had recommenced, I was now the one with the crossbow; and nobody knew it. I started picking people off quickly—trying for nonlethal spots as best as I could, but each bolt I loosed was painful for me.

There were only a few bolts left, and before I knew it, I only had two—forcing me to return to combat. As I ran to rejoin the fray, however, I spotted Maeko and Kearn, both mercilessly locked in combat. Maeko was a ruthless fighter, only making the panic in my blood boil as I realized what was about to happen. The only way one of them would win would be killing the other. The only way Maeko might lose is if he held back for my sake.... If only I could incapacitate Kearn...but Kearn was blocked except for his head, and the only way to take out Kearn would be to shoot to kill. Just then, there was a rumbling, and some debris from the cave wall came crashing down from the Drogans fighting above us.

Maeko and Kearn narrowly avoided it, but the former was hit in the hand, causing his sword to go flying as Maeko struggled to keep oriented. The look of hate in Kearn's eyes told me what was about to happen next. Maeko was going to die. My brother was going to kill him.

Without thinking, I ran for it, shoving Maeko away just as the sword blow meant for him came down. I tried to bring my sword up in time to block it but I was too slow, and the sickening feeling of metal passing through my chest erupted in a flurry of pain as darkness and light flashed before my eyes.

Barely, I registered the sword being abruptly pulled out, and only barely did I see Kearn's look of horror before my vision began to blur. Someone shouted my name as I gasped for breath and fell, but I couldn't distinguish voices. Everything was leaving so quickly, and I thought of how terrible a brother I had to have been to force Kearn to live with this. It would have been more merciful to shoot him, after all. But perhaps he was right. I was the coward.

Kearn:

"Jay! What have you done?!" My voice was a curdling scream as I stared at the collapsing form of my gasping brother. In that moment, all the talk and betrayal and heat of battle left me, and not caring if the other man slew me where I stood, I jumped, panicked, to my brother's side, barely catching him before his head would have thudded to the cavern floor. It was as if reality itself had stopped, and I realized suddenly the fighting around us—except for the Drogans—had.

"Jay. Jay, come on, don't you test me." I had only cried once in my life, and it appeared the second time would be for the same reason. He was leaving me again...but this time, it was my fault. All my fault.

"I'm sorry, I'm sorry. Please. Jay. I didn't mean to." It was as if I was a child all over again but so much worse.

His eyes opened a crack, but they were foggy and sightless as he tried to focus on my voice.

"I'm sorry." The whisper from his lips was almost inaudible. What had I done? What had I *done?!*

"Idiot!" The man I had meant to kill was kneeling on the other side of him, giving me a vengeful stare I deserved. If he had killed me, I wouldn't even have flinched. But he didn't. He and I just sat there with Jaythos as he slowly slipped away. No one was fighting.

But that's when the cave started shaking. I grabbed Jaythos's clammy hand and looked up, just in time to see the smaller Drogan flying right for the ceiling. Ovok was furiously close behind, and I barely registered that the small one now had the stone. They were about to break the ceiling.

"Cover!" I shouted as loud as I could, already taking Jaythos by the shoulders to move him. The Rugonian and several others helped as the rest ran for cover or others who needed help to do so, and together we ran as close to the wall as we could just as the whole room shook.

Rocks flew everywhere as the two beasts broke through, and I closed my eyes, leaning over Jaythos so he would not be hit.

Finally, the rocks settled, and we sat there, a big gaping hole now filtering in the mountain sunshine. But I didn't gawk, only turned directly back to Jaythos. He would be gone soon.

Again, I grasped his hand. "Jay. Please. You can't go. Not like this."

He just stared out at nothing, struggling to breathe as he lost blood. The rest of his companions bounded over, and soon the lady, Marion, was on the other side of his head, wiping away the hair from his eyes.

"You fool, what were you thinking!" She choked a little as she spoke. The young boy sat down next to her, distraught.

"Is he going to be alright?" His question held the answer.

Only vaguely did I see the small shard of green he held, but at that moment, I didn't care or register it. Only the dying breaths of my brother.

What had I done?

THE LIVING STONE

THE END

...FOR NOW

THE EXILED: BATTLE FOR THE BLACK QUEEN

Astra is safe in Litash....

Or is she? After her presence is revealed to the Court of Litash, she is put on trial for breaking the terms of her exile. But things in Litash are much worse than Astra realized and she soon finds that Tyron's obsession with her has spread chaos across the continent.

When Astra finally stumbles upon the true goal behind Tyron's twisted Game, she's faced with a choice that leaves worlds hanging in the balance. Can she risk the ones she loves to finish The Game? What will happen when Tyron decides to raise the stakes?

About the *A Daughter's Ransom* series:

The TetraWorlds live in ignorance of each other's existence....

One fallen behind in a Medieval time of fantastic and dangerous creatures, another fallen asleep in the comfort of their Victorian age, and the last torn apart by its own Modern innovation. When a dark threat rises up against them—one so quiet that none know to stop it, a Guard from each world must be called to protect their planet's source. But what will happen when these worlds entwine?

About the author:

NIAMH SCHMID:

Born in Clifton Park, New York, Niamh is (unfortunately) a human being. She would much rather be off in some pretend world battling an ogre or taming a rabid pegasus, but instead is currently engaging in being an adult. Niamh has a B. A. in Piano Performance and enjoys teaching through her private piano studio, where she offers both piano and violin lessons. In her spare time, she cares for her two mini ponies (or monsters), Freddie and Taffie, as well as her Dorkie (dachshund/yorkie mix,) Tobie. She also loves to compose, collect stamps, and dabble in being a very mediocre artist.

www.ingramcontent.com/pod-product-compliance
Lightning Source LLC
Chambersburg PA
CBHW070829260626
47170CB00007B/2315